The
Celestial
Steam
Locomotive

The
Celestial
Steam
Locomotive

VOLUME I OF
THE SONG OF EARTH

Michael Coney

HOUGHTON MIFFLIN COMPANY
BOSTON
1983

Library of Congress Cataloging in Publication Data

Coney, Michael.
   The celestial steam locomotive.

   I. Title.
PR6053.0453C4 1983   823'.914   83-8567
ISBN 0-395-34395-X

Printed in the United States of America

S 10 9 8 7 6 5 4 3 2 1

For Sally Coney
with love

CONTENTS

They ride the sky-train SHENSHI from Azul to Santa Beth.
The driver's name is Silver and the fireman's name is Death.
                    — The Song of Earth

The
Celestial
Steam
Locomotive

PROLOGUE: A PLACE CALLED EARTH

They call me Alan-Blue-Cloud.

That is what they call me when they gather to hear my stories, when the Dedos (Daughters of Starquin), the Dream-Essences and the ex-Keepers come together in form or in spirit on the barren hillside that I inhabit. Sometimes manlike creatures come, too, and sit beside the stream that skirts the hill, clasping their arms about their knees and gazing up toward me. I don't know what they think of while they listen. They sit and they watch, sometimes as many as fifty of them, chunky and hairy, while the aesthetic forms of the higher beings flit among them or hover over them, or just *are*.

I tell them tales of Old Earth.

Time has lost its meaning now. Nothing much has happened on Earth since the Departure, and many of the higher beings have forgotten what happened before that. Me? I can't forget. I remember everything except how I came into being and how I came to live on this hillside among the rocks and loose scree. Everything else I remember, and many things that happened before I existed — these memories I have gleaned from legends and stories and books and computers of man. I am memory.

Memory is unnecessary on Earth. Out *there*, in the Great-away and on the other worlds, things are happening all the time. So memory is important, out there. Occasionally They come too, and ask me things.

It is difficult to distinguish fact from legend, and after much consideration I have decided it doesn't matter. I have spoken with men, with Dream People and Dedos, with Specialists and *Cuidadors* and psycaptains, and I have found no consensus on what is *fact*; it depends on the viewpoint. Interestingly enough, *legend* — which is by definition distorted — gives a far more acceptable view of events. Everyone agrees on legend, but nobody agrees on fact. So I simply repeat what I hear, with no embellishments, but with due warnings.

The story I am about to tell is substantially true.

It concerns three people of differing backgrounds who came together and tried hard to accomplish something that was important to them — and although they didn't know it at the time, it was important to a Supreme Being too. They succeeded in what they attempted, which gives the story a ring of triumph and glory. The three people became, in fact, legendary figures . . .

My story takes place during the year 143,624 Cyclic, and it is about three humans of varying species who became known as the Triad. There are other stories, too. These stories relate to events that took place at different times during Earth's history, but they are all essential to the central theme of the Triad, and of Humanity.

Humanity . . . I see thirty-two humans listening to me now, and it is satisfying to see children among them. Other living things are in the valley, sensed in the infrared or in a nearby happentrack or visible as light sources or as dancing souls. An Almighty Being is also with us this evening, passing through our speck in the Greataway, pausing, maybe out of gratitude for a favor of long ago. He listens.

You are listening, too.

HERE BEGINS THAT PART OF
THE SONG OF EARTH KNOWN TO MEN AS
THE CREATION OF THE TRIAD

where three humans come together
after their several adventures,
having been chosen by Starquin the Five-in-One
for the purpose
of fulfilling his mighty Intent

Manuel

Manuel sniffed the air.

The eastern sky was dark, blending with the greyness of the sea. Manuel — a Wild Human who was superstitious, like all of his kind — wondered if God had thrown up a veil there, to hide some terrible mischief he was perpetrating out in the South Atlantic.

Maybe he would ask God about that, later.

The strengthening wind brought the tang of ozone. Manuel sniffed again and felt momentarily light-headed. There was a storm coming and tomorrow there would be driftwood on the beach, and perhaps pieces of fascinating wreckage. The oxygen-rich air lifted the boy's spirits. He gave a shout of joy and ran across the sand, paralleling the waves, kicking them as they swirled around his ankles and were spent and easily defeated.

Giving the ocean one last kick, laughing, he turned and ran toward the shack that sat huddled under the low cliff. He opened the door and entered — and stopped dead.

Somebody was there. He smelled a presence, and as his eyes became accustomed to the gloom, he could see a figure sitting in his only chair. He froze, fearing that it was the strange old woman who had been seen around these parts lately.

But the voice was low and soft, with a Pu'este intonation. "Hello, Manuel."

He exhaled, his gaze straying to the place where his Simulator was hidden, but the carefully placed heap of brush was undisturbed.

"Hello, Ellie," he said casually, wondering.

Ellie was safe as a tame guanaco. She was the niece of old Jinny in the village of Pu'este — and, some said, a daughter of one of old chief Chine's more human moments. The chair in which she sat had been fashioned by Manuel from a driftwood tree stump, and her form was soft and sweet against the wizened timber. So far as Manuel could tell in the half-light, she wore very little.

"Manuel . . . ?"

"Yes? What do you want, Ellie?"

She hesitated. Manuel was strange, that much was acknowledged in the village. But for two weeks, now, his body had tormented her with unconscious challenges and she'd felt herself wriggling, her breath coming faster when he was near. That morning he'd passed her on the road, and she thought she'd seen something in his eyes when his gaze met hers for an instant. So here she was. But he was known to be strange.

"I was waiting for you," she said.

Manuel likewise was on his guard. He had his desires too, and a while ago they'd centered on another village girl, a darkly pretty thing called Rhea, after a ridiculous local bird. Recently Rhea had asked, "Why do you keep looking at me like that, Manuel? You want sex — Right, let's get going. I don't have all day." And afterward, when he'd clung to her in affection and gratitude, she'd said, "Get away. You're making me sweaty. Don't you have anything to do . . . ?"

Innocently, Manuel said to Ellie, "What were you waiting for?"

She didn't answer. Instead she asked, "Why do you live here all alone?"

"It's peaceful. I like the sound of the sea."

"You like the sound of the sea." She repeated it carefully, as though it were a foreign language.

"You haven't told me why you're here, Ellie."

"I was curious. You're a strange one, Manuel, you know that? What do you do in church? I saw you coming back. You spoke to Dad Ose up there, but you did something else. You went inside by yourself. You've got a girl in there?"

"I spoke to God. Why did you come here?"

"I saw the clouds and I said to myself, 'I'll see Manuel.'"

"Don't lie to me, Ellie."

"I wanted sex," she muttered. She'd never been ashamed of it before, but now, with this odd youth standing above her, it seemed an inadequate reason for having come. Her body began to cool down. Fleetingly she wished she were back in the village helping fat Chine fight off the encroaching guanacos.

"Is that all?" Manuel seemed disappointed.

"Well . . . It's good enough, isn't it? You do find it good, don't you, Manuel?" She was out of the chair, reaching for him.

"I can't describe how I find it." Millennia ago Wild Humans might have had a word for it, but not now. "I just feel that sex isn't good enough by itself. Just touching for a few seconds and then walking away, like animals do. It's not enough."

"I'll stay the night if you want me to, Manuel."

"That's not what I mean." His gaze moved toward the hidden Simulator again and he found himself thinking of his latest composition. He called it *The Storm*. It was the best mindpainting he'd ever done, but he still wasn't satisfied with it. "There's something inside my mind that I want to use . . . that I want to *give*, Ellie. I don't know if I can give it to you. I don't think you'd understand what it was, if you had it."

"Try me. I'm a very understanding person, Manuel. Joao, Pietro, the others, they all say how understanding I am." She was standing very close, so that her hard little nipples touched his chest with their fire, and her lips turned up to his. "Sex is the most wonderful thing there is. It's the best thing we do, better than eating roast peccary, and it makes you feel so good. What's the matter with you, Manuel? I'm prettier than Rhea, surely. You didn't mind sex with her." She pouted. "Aren't I good enough for you?"

"There has to be something more."

"What more can there be?"

"You don't feel anything more?" He took her hands, and now he was the desperate one, trying to see into her eyes in the dim, storm-laden light.

"I feel enough, Manuel. Don't worry." She spoke softly, mimicking his way. If this was how the strange boy wanted it, why not? There were worse ways.

"And what do you feel, Ellie?"

"I need a man, of course. You *know*."

"Ellie . . . Please go away. Go back to the village. There are plenty of men there." Still holding her hands, he led her outside, where the wetness swept in from the sea, a blend of rain and salt spray, and the horizon was very black. And the air was like whiskey.

Ellie sniffed it and, suddenly exhilarated, tossed her head, so that her hair flew like blackbirds, and laughed. "You're crazy!" she shouted into the wind. "A crazy boy!" Something flashed by; it might have been a Quickly. "And I'm crazy too, coming here. Goodnight, Manuel! Sleep well, and dream of what you might have had!" She made a playful snatch at him but he swung away, smiling too.

He watched her go and wondered at the thing she was lacking, and — of course — regretted not having had her anyway. But he had more important things to do.

THE QUICKLIES

*M*anuel had built the shack when he was fourteen years old. That was five years ago. Pu'este had endured for untold centuries and the people lived in stone houses, rethatching the roofs every fifty years or so. But Manuel's shack, like Manuel, was different, fashioned with painstaking care from driftwood and whalebone, mud and dried kelp and vine, a cohesive mass of matted material hard against the low cliff of brown sandstone at the north end of the bay.

Manuel was proud of it and didn't mind people visiting; naively, he thought they came to admire. He became mildly annoyed when the Quicklies ran by, though — fighting and snarling and bumping into things and frightening the vicunas. In the early days he'd made a few abortive attempts to befriend the Quicklies and had even persuaded a gentler female to snatch food from his hand. But the thing that always puzzled Wild Humans had soon happened, and the female Quickly had been moving much more slowly the following morning — and then she had died, attacked by her own kind and mortally wounded.

Manuel piled more driftwood on his fire, then pacified his vicunas, which had become alarmed at the sudden sparks and crackling and were stamping and tossing their heads. He looked eastward, where the horizon was now massed with huge black clouds. He walked to the water's edge and turned. From here he could see over the top of the low cliff to the distant hills. Tiny forms were moving. The guanacos were still converging on the valley. Dust clouds rose as the wind brushed the village fields. Wise Ana — the plump, cheerful woman who lived alone in a sandstone cave beside the road to the village — was gathering in her wares, closing down her store for the night. Sapa cloth fluttered. Thoughtfully, Manuel returned to the shack and brought out his meal, a reef fish wrapped in leaves and clay. He laid it in the fire.

He was sucking his fingers clean when he heard the twittering clamor from farther up the beach. The Quicklies were coming, probably hunting for food. He stepped into the hut and brought out the rest of his catch, three parrot fish that he'd been saving for his evening meal. He laid them on the beach; then, on an impulse, returned to the shack and brought out his most prized possession — the Simulator. He sat down before it and turned it on.

Manuel often found himself doing things for which there could be no explanation under the code of human behavior existing in the year 143,624 Cyclic. Wild Humans ran for shelter when they heard the Quicklies coming. As they ran, they caught up sticks, rocks, anything they could lay their hands on to defend themselves. The Quicklies were the ultimate in abominations and, so it was rumored, could strip a man to the bone in fifteen seconds flat. The rumor lacked concrete evidence, since nobody had ever lived to tell the tale, but it served to explain the curious disappearances that had bothered the fat chief Chine for many years.

"Elacio's gone," Chine had said one day. "The Quicklies got him. I saw his bones washing out on the tide."

Manuel, who happened to be near, broke into the chorus of superstitious groans from the villagers. "Elacio fell into the Bowl," he said, referring to a peculiar local landmark. "I saw him down there yesterday. His neck was broken. The sirens had already started to eat him, but you could still tell who it was."

"Get back to the beach where you belong," snapped Chine. "It would be better for us all if the Quicklies took you, one day."

"May God go with you, you young sinner," said the priest, Dad Ose, unctuously.

Chine had shot the priest a look of piggy ferocity, suspecting him of enlisting divine protection for Manuel in the youth's encounters with the rapacious Quicklies.

And this stormy evening Manuel was once again risking his life — or at least chancing the destruction of the Simulator, the most wonderful object he'd ever possessed.

Misty clouds swirled before the machine, a three-dimensional image thrown by a battery of projectors on the front of the cabinet. The clouds took on form, substance and pattern. This was Manuel's favorite image: *The Storm*. He'd created it himself, out of his own mind, with the aid of a helmet that fed his thoughts into the cabinet.

"Ya-heeeee!"

The yell meant the Quicklies had sighted Manuel. They'd been racing about the beach randomly, like speeding electrons, so fast that the eye could hardly follow them, kicking up sand, splashing through the shallows, actually running across the surface of the water like basilisks and vaulting the waves. They yelled and leaped, and occasionally fell to fierce quarreling. As Manuel watched, one of them, a little smaller than the rest, slowed down, aged and died. It fell to the sand, revealing itself as a chimpanzee-sized humanoid with a large head, hairless, very thin.

"Ya-heeeee!"

The Quicklies arrived. Manuel felt the usual nervous tightening of the throat. He gulped and with his foot pushed the parrot fish toward an area of blurred disturbance in the sand. Then he snatched his foot away. You couldn't be too careful, and despite his scepticism about Chine's theories, he couldn't suppress the vision of his foot becoming instantly skeletal, gleaming white.

In fact the fish became skeletal. He never saw the Quicklies eat them: One second the iridescent scales were glowing in the moist air, the next second the bones lay dispersed in little heaps, the flesh absorbed into the Quicklies' phenomenal metabolism.

Then, as happened sometimes, some of the creatures began to stand comparatively still, watching him, blinking with unbelievable rapidity, so that their big eyes appeared out of focus. The outline of their bodies was blurred too, since it is not possible for Quicklies to stand completely motionless.

They babbled at him in the thin rattle of sound that he'd never been able to understand. It seemed to him that they talked faster every time he met them, and he had a scary thought: Maybe they were in fact speeding up toward the point where they simply became invisible and were able to do completely as they pleased.

They were sitting down! This was something new. One by one each upright form disappeared, to be instantly replaced by a sitting one. They sat in a circle, watching the Simulator with wide eyes. One keeled over and died, its outline firming up. It was an old, old man, tiny and pathetic, not in the least threatening. The body remained for a moment, then disappeared. Manuel refused to consider what had happened to it. The other Quicklies continued to watch the Simulator.

The colors of Manuel's mind-painting played. They swirled in a curious helical pattern like smoke or clouds. They were turquoise and grey, joyful and sad, and they were reflected at the lower part of the painting in a way that suggested wet sand and sea and things found and lost. They were wonderful and unique in each moment, and they represented the perfect amalgam of art and technology — the strange mind of a young dreaming Wild Human named Manuel and the invention of some long-forgotten scientist who had found how to give substance to those dreams.

And the Quicklies were crying.

They sat blinking and blurred, and it was odd to see the tears running down those joggling faces just like normal tears, just as slow and trickling. The Quicklies sat there aging, using up the few precious hours of their lives in contemplation of Manuel's masterpiece, while they cried at the beauty of it. And yet — so it always is with art — they were not satisfied. One of them was trying to communicate with Manuel. She raised her hand. She was a middle-aged female and she spoke with excruciating care — and each syllable took her a subjective month to say. But her meaning reached the boy. For the first time ever, a Quickly had spoken to him. She spoke, and she died, carried away in late middle age by some undiagnosed disease that ran its course in two seconds.

She had said: *It needs more love.*

The Rainbow — Earth's great computer that sees everything and knows everything and still has not run down — recorded that scene. And over the millennia to come, historians would puzzle over that moment and speculate on the identity of that determined little Quickly who devoted her last years to one purpose, to one sentence that was to plant a seed of knowledge in the mind of young Manuel, later to become celebrated as the Artist in the Song of Earth.

Manuel regarded the mind-painting, and he thought about the word *love* and the emotion it might describe. He'd put into that painting something that embarrassed him, something that had caused him to keep the machine and its projections away from other people, to hide it from those prying fingers that delved through his possessions whenever he was not at home.

He didn't know the thing was called "love." But the word sounded right. And he was not alone.

Somewhere, other people knew of love. It just so happened that up to now he'd never met anyone else who possessed it. Wild Humans have basic needs, such as staying alive and breeding, and love was a luxury they had lost a long time ago. Nobody in the village possessed it.

He'd hidden his love because others might laugh at it — as Ellie had laughed at it — but he'd shown it privately to the machine. And now the Quickly woman said he hadn't shown enough. What else did the mind-painting need? Helplessly, he looked back at the Quicklies.

Two more lay dead, disappearing even as he watched. Others looked terribly old. He was wasting their time. Hastily he switched off the machine, ignoring their twitters of despair, and carried it back to its hiding place. When he returned, the Quicklies were gone. They must have been starving. Some distance out to sea the water was in a turmoil. The Quicklies were probably fishing, knifing through the water with a speed no fish could match.

For a while he sat and watched the storm clouds gathering, big merino clouds just as Insel had forecast yesterday, sending a gusting wind as a storm messenger. Then he stood, glanced around and found everything in order, murmured a word of encouragement to his vicunas and entered his shack.

THE STORM

*H*e sat in his chair, dismissed an intrusive image of Ellie's warm body, put on the helmet and relaxed, watching the projection area. He began systematically to discipline his thoughts, concentrating on the storm.

Manuel's images swirled. The walls of his shack trembled to the wind. Something pattered on the roof and rolled off. The sounds did not distract him; they were essential to his mood. He thought loneliness, he thought the wind, the broad beach, the creatures that burrowed into the wetness. The sea. He was painting another storm — and this time he was trying to put more *love* into it.

The images firmed but they were not right, not what he wanted. The shapes suggested womens' bodies — breasts and buttocks. The gale took on an appearance of long tawny hair, swirling. He forced his thoughts toward the elements themselves, rather than the images they dragged from his subconscious. The breasts became sails, full and straining, the lithe limbs formed the geometry of a ship. He thought of Man and the ocean, of death and power. The projection area showed shapes without form but with infinite strength — almost terrifying. Manuel shivered and took the helmet off. He was beginning to get a feedback effect from his own projected thoughts. And he hadn't got the love in there, even now.

*

He remembered the day he'd been given the machine. A nothing day, when he'd tired of the beach, tired even of the ocean, and walked into the hills until even the great Dome was a small bubble behind him and his breath came quickly from oxygen starvation. A day of strange unrest when he wondered at everything: the Dome, the sky, the village, the purpose. A day of changes.

As he lay on his back catching his breath and watching alpaca clouds, he heard a voice.

"Manuel."

A tall woman stood there, dressed in a black cloak. Her face was pale and her eyes regarded him dispassionately. Some versions of the legend relate that she then cried, in a ringing voice, "Arise, Manuel, and fulfill your destiny!" And she may have, but the Rainbow says not. Reality is never quite so dramatic as legend, although it can be interesting enough.

The woman stood, and Manuel lay looking at her — rather sulkily, resenting her air of authority. She carried a smooth-sided box. Finally, Manuel climbed to his feet and leaned against a stunted tree.

"I must talk to you, Manuel. You are young and naturally rebellious, but I am hoping you will have the sense to listen to what I say and not treat it as the ravings of an old woman. And I am old, older than you could ever guess." She watched him calmly and coldly, and there was something unearthly about her that cowed Manuel and made him bite back the sharp reply that rose readily to his lips. It seemed the wind had stopped blowing now and the horse clouds hung motionless, as though pinned to the backdrop of the sky.

Manuel swallowed and said, "I'll listen."

"You are going to be a famous man, Manuel. In the distant Ifalong minstrels will sing of your exploits — and of your companions. You will have adventures such as men have never dreamed of."

"The Ifalong?" The word was unfamiliar.

"You probably think of Time as a single thread extending into the future and never ending. That is the general view in your village. But you must think of Time as a tree, Manuel. A tree that grows forever, always creating new branches."

"That would be a big tree," said Manuel, thinking literally.

"Out in the Greataway there is a tree called the 'beacon hydra.' It extends a thousand kilometers into space and is so huge that its very bulk will affect the orbit of its planet. I want you to think of Time as bigger even than the beacon hydra. Each branch and each twig represents a possibility where your future life might take one course or another, depending on what you do. Or what others do. The possibilities are infinite, and each possibility is called a 'happentrack.'

"The Ifalong is the total of all these happentracks in the future, when there are a billion different ways things might have happened."

"Oh." He thought about that for a while and it seemed to make sense. "And how about the Greataway? What's that?"

"The Greataway is just about everything, Manuel. In the old days, when your race used to travel in three-dimensional ships, they called it 'High Space.' But Space is all bound up with Time too, and could consist of an infinite number of happentracks. The 'Greataway' is the name for all of that."

"Who are you?" asked Manuel. "How do you know all these things?"

"I am a Dedo," said Shenshi, for it was she. Then she laid the box on the ground beside Manuel. "This is for you."

"What is it?"

"It's an old machine. They were popular many years ago. You are an unusual boy for your time, Manuel, and I think you will find this machine interesting."

"What does it do?"

"Nothing that does not come from yourself. It will help you develop your talents, ready for that day when the Triad is formed and Starquin is released from the Ten Thousand Years' Incarceration. Then your purpose will be fulfilled, and mine, too." Her voice was utterly without emotion, as flat as if produced by a machine.

There was something about Manuel's purpose being fulfilled

that struck a sinister note with the boy. He gulped and looked into the hooded eyes of the woman, but could read nothing there.

He blinked, and she was gone.

He carried the Simulator home. He was an inquisitive boy, as well as an intelligent one, and he soon found out how to put the helmet on his head and arrange his thoughts and produce his mind-paintings. Others tried, people who spied on him and wondered at his machine. They sneaked into his shack and donned the helmet, and some of them produced representational images: a particular hill, a jaguar, the Dome.

Only Manuel could coax *feeling* out of the Simulator, however.

*

The door burst open and the gale swirled around the room, bringing sand and weed, knocking things over. A man stood there, peering into the gloom. "Manuel?"

"Yes?"

It was Hasqual. Although a villager, Hasqual was a wanderer at heart and only the thin air kept him in the vicinity of Pu'este. On occasions when the winds shifted, he'd been gone for months, returning with tales nobody believed, disturbing yarns that frightened the kids.

"This is going to be a bad storm, Manuel."

"I know." The youth's face was somber in the diffused light from the Simulator.

Hasqual watched the images abstractedly. "You'd better come up to the church for the night — most of the village is there. Some of the roofs have gone already. A heavy sea could sweep right over this place of yours, and the tide's coming in fast."

"I'll stay here."

"You're a damned fool, you know that?"

"It's not your problem."

"Suit yourself." Hasqual was gone and the shack was empty again.

Manuel went to the window and looked at the storm. Rain

was drilling against the crystal. Some trick current of the wind made it stream upward and sideways, rather than down. Now the clouds became patchy, the rain intermittent. The wind was rising still, driving salt puddles across the beach, whining about the woodwork of the shack. Manuel wanted to shout, to sing. It grew darker, and the storm became a secret monster, tromping around out there, occasionally bellowing.

He went outside and secured the crude storm shutters against the windows. He dragged his boat farther from the water, finally tucking the craft right under the cliff near the shack. His vicunas were gone, probably sharing with Hasqual a presentiment of giant waves. Manuel returned to the shack and stood dripping in the middle of the floor in the darkness, feeling drunk, feeling omnipotent with the richness of the air.

The colors played before the Simulator. Manuel wondered about kindling a lamp, but decided against it. He stood watching the tiny shifting clouds; then he sat down and put the helmet on again. Carefully suppressing the elation that threatened to exclude everything else from his mind, he thought of the hurricane. He allowed the tumultuous sounds from outside to soak into his brain. The twisting clouds in the mind-painting ordered themselves; the foreground became a realistic contrast to the fantasy of weather. He thought *a crab* — and a crab appeared in the picture: not factual, just a suggestion sidling across wet sand.

Something pounded on the door.

The painting was beautiful, yet it still lacked that indefinable element. Manuel tried a few thought-images; ships, fish, storm-tossed trees. They didn't work. He erased them hastily before they intruded upon the colors of the storm itself.

Outside, the wind rose to a sudden crescendo. The pounding on the door intensified.

Manuel tried people in his picture, slipping in girls, forgetting them as quickly. They didn't fit, either. They were too . . . earthy.

He became aware of the door. He removed his helmet and listened. He heard a voice, a cry of desolation, of distress, of loss. It struck something deep inside Manuel — not simply because he was a compassionate person, but more because he felt a strange and wild recognition, as though the cry had come from within his own soul.

So now he wondered if he'd imagined it. He listened, breathless. He heard it again: a sobbing. A cry for help.

Now he thought he'd be too late. He ran to the door and fumbled with the heavy bar, releasing it and throwing it aside. The wind snatched the door out of his hand and crashed it against the wall. Something fell to the floor and smashed. Manuel stood in the open doorway, staring . . .

That moment is caught forever in a million minds. It will never be forgotten so long as there is a memory in the Rainbow, so long as Man walks or crawls or oozes.

THE STORM-GIRL

She stood in a deep drift of coarse weed, and tiny crabs crawled around her legs. More clumps of weed flew past, wind-borne. One wrapped around her shoulder and she flinched, shaking it off. She stood blinking at the diffused light of the Simulator with blue eyes, watching the miniature storm with wonder and a little fear, her long fair hair plastered wetly around her neck and trailing away like the tatters of a flag in a battle. She wore a ragged loinskin and not much else; just the remains of a fine skin shirt clinging to one breast, leaving the other bare. She was a picture, a storm-painting of beauty and perfection distilled from a thousand myths.

"Come in!" shouted Manuel as a wall-hanging flew past him, sucked out into the wild night. He saw the tide, only meters away.

The girl entered and he forced the door shut, barring it again. She stood in the center of the room, water flowing from her body, eyes downcast, her clothes stuck to her. She said nothing. Her stance was oddly submissive; possibly she was in shock. She was different from any girl, from any human Manuel had known. She was incredibly slim, with none of the heavy-chestedness of the village girls, yet a quiet strength flowed from her.

"What were you doing out there?" Helplessly, Manuel regarded her. "Maybe you'd like a hot drink." He forced himself to stop staring and busied himself about the shack, puffing the dull embers of his hearth into life, throwing on dry brushwood, so that it crackled and blazed and the girl looked like a goddess of fire. He poured milk into a pot and stirred in a pinch of peyote, then hung the pot from a hook among the flames. He looked around, wondering what else he ought to do. He wasn't used to company. "Here, dry yourself," he said, hating himself for his thoughtlessness and handing her a fur. "And here's a dry robe."

She took off the remains of her clothes, watching him with blue eyes set in a grave, oval face with a small nose and round chin, saying nothing. The mouth was sad, but he felt it would smile nicely, given something to smile at. The impossibly slender body was strong, with neat pink-tipped breasts and solid thighs. Manuel was staring again. She was the most beautiful thing he'd ever seen in his life. She dried herself and drew the robe around her body.

Manuel pulled himself together and poured her a drink. It was barely warm, but the peyote would do her good. He guided her to his chair and she sat down. She sipped at the drink, her gaze wandering around the room, pausing here and there before returning to Manuel. She still hadn't spoken.

Soon the mug was empty, and he took it from her, placing it on a shelf. When he turned back, she was asleep. He sat on the floor and watched her for a long time, saw her lashes lying against her cheek, watched the slow rise and fall of her breasts where the robe had fallen open, admired her hair, her nose, her toes. She slept on. He wanted to awaken her, to talk to her. He hadn't heard her voice yet. It occurred to him that she might not speak his language.

As he sat irresolute, his gaze fell upon the Simulator, still projecting its storm-image, recalling his mind to the hurricane that buffeted the shack.

He placed the helmet on his head, keeping his eyes on the images.

He thought.

A paleness appeared among the wild eddying of clouds, at first formless but becoming clearer by the second. It was a face, a girl's face, melancholy and oval, with a round chin, blue eyes and a cloud of fair hair flying in the wind. The hut shook to a fresh blast. For a long time Manuel sat there, taking the helmet off in case the girl-image became too definite, watching the shift and play of color while the wind howled in from the sea and the girl lay asleep. It was not perfect. It needed days of work, yet. Other moods must be captured within the complex patterns of the Simulator, other images to lend the creation depth. It was not perfect, but the basic elements were there. The storm, and the girl.

It was a beginning . . .

*

By morning the main force of the storm had moved inland, ploughing a furrow of destruction fifty kilometers wide across the villages of the coastal strip before disappearing into the interior and spending itself among the mountains and ruined cities. The villagers of Pu'este returned to their huts — or what remained of them — and began resignedly to reroof while the strength of the rich air remained in the valley. The guanacos remained, too. They had been converging on the village for days, and now they formed a vast carpet of life that had to be shoved aside before repairs could commence.

Insel cocked an eye at the tattered sky. "Snake clouds," he murmured, but Chine told him to shut up and help with the roofs.

Down on the beach, Manuel's shack was virtually untouched. Snug under the overhanging cliff, it had sheltered him and the girl while the storm passed overhead and the surging tide spent itself just short of his door. Now he went outside to inspect the damage.

There were a few shingles missing from the roof, but he could fix that soon enough. And it didn't matter that the entire building had shifted slightly on its base. His boat was still intact, lashed securely to the exposed roots of a cliffside vine. He untied it and dragged it to its accustomed mooring beside a rocky shelf that had once projected a few meters into the sea but was now part of a sandy peninsula. The forces of the storm had changed the geography of the beach, and the pattern of rivulets and lakes in the flat sand was altered, too.

After a storm the beach was usually strewn with weed: kelp and wrack scoured from the deeper reaches of the continental shelf. The weed today, however, was like nothing Manuel had ever seen. It was scattered over the sand in vast blanketlike areas, and it had drifted against the cliff base in layers like emerald felt, each layer a meter thick. It rose against the corner of the shack too, green and fibrous, like ripped pieces of some giant mat, and its scent was powerful and heady. Manuel identified it as the source of the strong ozonic smell that he'd associated with his burst of creative energy the previous night.

He returned thoughtfully to the shack.

The girl was up, walking about with a dancing, light-footed motion as though she could not trust the solidity of the floor. She wore the robe he'd given her, but it hung open, showing breast and thigh. She seemed heedless of the chill the wind had left behind. She watched his approach gravely. Manuel, struck speechless by her beauty once more, uttered a croak, cleared his throat and finally said, "How do you feel?"

"I feel so heavy that my ankles might break. And the ground is so hard, here." Having made this unusual pronouncement, she regarded him with interest. "You look very strong." With her dancing, gliding step she came to the door and looked around at the beach, the sandstone cliff and the storm debris. Finally, she looked at the sea for a long time.

A tear started at the corner of one slanting eye.

"Who is your king?" she asked, as he kicked weed from the doorway.

"What do you mean?"

"Who is in charge of you? Who do you work for?"

"I work for myself. I'm Manuel. I fish and hunt . . . And I do mind-paintings," he added, indicating the equipment. The box was switched off. Inside, the memory of his recent painting was stored with many others, awaiting recall at the touch of a button.

Wrapped loosely in the robe, the girl toured the room, picking up ornaments, artifacts, pieces of rusted, ancient machinery and examining each with absorbed attention. She particularly liked a bright stone on a silver necklace and held it up to the light exclaiming at its brilliance.

Manuel watched her, wondering.

"You have beautiful things here," she said. "You must be a very wealthy man."

"Not really. Here ... Here's something you'll like." He switched on the Simulator. The colors began to play.

"What is it?" She stared at the images, then smiled for the first time. "It reminds me of home. That's a storm, is it? Oh ... And is that me? It's beautiful, Manuel."

"It's not finished. There's a lot more I want to do."

"You mean ... *you* did it? You made it yourself?" She frowned. "I don't see how you managed to get my picture into that box."

"While you were asleep." He explained the workings of the machine to the best of his scanty knowledge, and she seemed to understand.

Her name was Belinda, and she spent most of that morning in fascinated exploration of his possessions. Later he got her to sit for him and he captured her image on another channel. Then he went back to his first painting, *The Storm*. She sat smiling faintly at him while he watched her and allowed his impressions of her personality to fill out and lend depth to the images.

Without his conscious volition, ragged blocks of the fibrous weed intruded themselves into the bottom foreground of the picture ...

Belinda cooked the evening meal. She prepared a kedgeree of clams, kelp and other things that she'd gathered from the tidal flats, together with herbs from the low-lying meadows to the north. She'd been searching the salt grass for some time that afternoon, and Manuel had kept his eye on her, climbing to the top of the cliff in order to follow her movements and make sure she didn't wander away altogether. Behind him the guanacos were stirring, clambering to their feet, so that the lowlands rippled with brown and grey. The leading animals were picking their way delicately up the rocky hillside and disappearing over the crest, their instincts telling them that the time of rich air was over for a while and that they should head off northwest to the grazing lands, following a pattern established over a thousand generations.

Manuel had watched them go, and there was the beginning of a terrible regret in him. When Belinda had finally returned from her wandering, she was oddly breathless and pale . . .

The meal was delicious. Manuel couldn't remember when he'd last eaten so well. But when he complimented Belinda she said, "I could have done better with a sun oven."

She never volunteered any information about herself; neither did Manuel ask. It was enough that she was there, sharing the shack with him. After supper they sat in comfortable silence while the tail end of the gale blew itself out and the sea birds returned to scavenge the shore for leavings. Later Manuel took her hand and, finding no resistance — why had he expected any? — led her to bed. There was almost a desperation in the way she responded to his lovemaking. And afterward she clung to him, and he marveled at it. For the first time in years he didn't feel alone in his emotions. But much later he awakened and heard her crying, a quiet breathless sobbing. He didn't dare to ask what the matter was.

They slept late. When they finally arose, the tide was in. Chunks of matted weed floated high on the water.

"I wish I could live here forever," she said that evening, as they sat in the doorway and watched the wheeling gulls and the sun turned the mountains crimson and the smell of oyster stew pervaded the shack.

There was a thumping in his chest. "Why can't you?"

She said nothing, but an expression came over her face that he'd seen on the night she came to him: a forlorn look, a kind of resigned sadness. Then the artist in him responded and he put the helmet on and captured the essence of her mood — without knowing the reason for that mood, but maybe guessing it. They ate, and now he was sad, too. When they made love that night it was Manuel who was the desperate one, who lay awake for hours listening to her shallow, too fast breathing, who in the end had to awaken her and say, "Don't ever leave me, Belinda . . ."

She said nothing. She hugged him, her heart racing against his chest, then she just lay there. He couldn't tell whether she was asleep or not.

The next day the village was empty of guanacos and the mood of elation was a memory. The villagers pottered about in desultory fashion and Insel watched the clouds. Over the next two days, the restlessness grew in Belinda. Manuel was forced to abandon his mind-paintings while she moved about the shack, tidying the already tidy shelves, frequently sitting down to recover her breath. Once she cut herself and lay in a half-faint, the blood oozing slowly, dark and strange, from a small wound in her finger. Manuel bandaged her and kissed her, then sat regarding her helplessly. He didn't know what to do, and at the back of his mind was the terrifying knowledge that he was losing her. He put the silver pendant around her neck, partly as a sign of love, partly, perhaps, as a mark of possession . . .

That morning he went out into the rain and dug the beach for clams. He found himself throwing the mats of weed against the walls of the hut, as though to enclose Belinda in a blanket of life. But the weed itself was dying now and the ozone tang changing to the stink of putrefaction. He found himself thinking of the Life Caves in the hillside a kilometer away: Belinda's symptoms were very similar to those of the Chokes. But the beach and the ocean were important to her, and maybe she couldn't have withstood even that short journey. In any case, could he condemn her to a cave for the rest of her life?

Then one morning he awakened with a feeling of aloneness. He stretched out an arm. The bed was empty. Hoping still, he ran across the room and threw open the door — maybe she was digging clams. The tide was in, buoying up the rotting weed and other storm debris. The beach was empty. The water heaved tiredly and quietly. She was gone — as he had known she must go in the end — and now his life was as empty as the grey horizon.

SHANTUN THE ACCURSED

*T*he Song of Earth is the name given to that great spoken-and-sung history of Mankind that arose at the beginning of the Dying Years and that spans the period from the arrival of Starquin to the present day, when various creatures gather in lonely places for storytellings.

The most important characters in the Song of Earth are *not* the Triad — that is, the Oldster and the Artist and the Girl-with-no-Name — of which Manuel was a member. Because those three are human, however, the human minstrels understandably gave them the leading role in the great events leading up to the Battle with the Bale Wolves, the removal of the Hate Bombs and the release of Starquin from his Ten Thousand Years' Incarceration. But the Triad lived and died over a short period of time around the 143rd millennium, a microscopic speck of time when considered against the sweep of the Ifalong. Although the minstrels do not admit it, the Triad was just a means to an end.

Infinitely more important among Earth residents are the Dedos, those creatures of mystery who shaped the course of terrestrial events from beginning to end, by a word here, a suggestion there and the gift of a machine to a young man named Manuel . . .

The Dedos have their own legends, cold, emotionless tales of Purpose. One such tale is that of Shantun the Accursed, who brought shame on the Rock Women for all time. It is a cautionary tale, told to emphasize the importance of the Duty, told to the Dedos' daughters over the long millennia of their childhood, told again and again so that its impact will constantly be refreshed in those memories that must of necessity be ancient — yet never told to humans until now.

*

In the beginning, Starquin the Five-in-One created the Rock Women, and he called them Dedos, meaning "fingers" in an ancient Earth tongue. He created them from his own essence and from material plentiful on Earth and suitable to the characteristics of that planet. Already the Greataway was seeded with his Rocks, which acted as relay stations for his Traveling. Now he set the many-faceted Rocks at certain points on the continent of Pangaea — and he set the Rock Women down with them, and charged them with a Duty.

The Duty is so strong that no Dedo can help but obey it, because it is carried within the fabric of her flesh in the form of a gene. To fulfill the Duty is the sole purpose of the Dedo, the sole reason for her creation. Or it was, until the infamous deed of Shantun the Accursed.

The Duty is to the Rock and to those who travel by means of the Rock. When a Traveler in the Greataway approaches, the Rock will glow on one or more of its facets. It may also utter a high-pitched hum. The Dedo, on seeing the glow, will place her palm on the lighted facet. Then the essence of the Traveler will combine with her own — but briefly, just long enough for her to divine his intentions. Whereupon she touches another facet that speeds the Traveler to the next Rock on his route, which might be kilometers or light-years away. The Traveler will only occasionally appear physically at the site of the Rock — indeed, in most cases the Traveler is not of a species that has physical form. But the Dedo, absorbing his essence, will inevitably learn a little of his psyche.

In the year 92,640 Cyclic, the human race discovered that

the Greataway consists of infinite dimensions in space/time spanning the routes between Rocks. It was illogical, it was impossible — yet humans discovered how to travel through it and arrive intact at their destination without ever discovering the existence of the Rocks or, indeed, of the Dedos. The Rocks flickered weakly as the humans passed through, but these new Travelers needed no assistance from the Rock Women.

Starquin pondered.

Then, a few centuries later, he charged each Dedo with a new Duty: Whenever the Rock should give that characteristically weak flicker that signified that a human was taking a free ride, she should put her hand to the facets to absorb the human's psyche and intent. And if the Dedo absorbed the intent, then so did Starquin, because he was in constant psychic contact with her. He was a part of her and she of him, in simple human language.

Starquin charged the Dedos with this new Duty because he did not trust the humans, who were savage and immature compared to other users of the Greataway.

But it was too late to embody this new Duty in the Earth Dedos' genes.

*

Wuhan had felt the first sign of failing powers over 30,000 Earth-years ago, so she had given birth to a child who had bred true, becoming a girl. She named the child Shantun and taught her everything about the Duty, the ways of living and humans. They lived through difficult times when the humans were numerous, but they concealed themselves well, and the Rock, too. During certain ages when human technology bloomed and it seemed they would fill every corner of the Earth with themselves and their machines, they even lived among humans as part of their society, using their cunning to conceal the Rock from them. Then humans would die back again and the machines would rust, and life would become simpler.

Shantun grew slowly by human standards, but in 30,000 years she had attained the stature of a human child of eight, and her mental powers were well beyond that. However, because she was immature, her emotions still existed and were childish. By now the humans had moved away, and Wuhan and Shantun lived in the purple pavilion, which is the Dedos' tradition. The climate was going through a temperate period and living was easy.

"Mother, now that the humans are gone, doesn't time seem to pass more slowly?" Shantun sat at the entrance to the pavilion in the afternoon sun, watching the animals gathering at the waterhole, lion and wildebeests in temporary truce.

Wuhan glanced at her, not with love, but with that indescribable together-emotion that a Dedo alone feels for her parthenogenic child, who is essentially the same person as herself.

"It's just that human lives are so short that they live them as busily as they can. So we tend to hurry, too. Now they're not common in our area and we can live at our own pace."

"Do you like the humans?"

"Like?" Wuhan affected not to understand — a mere pretense.

"Well, you know . . . Do you ever feel any other duty, besides the *Duty?*" This was a clumsy way of putting it, so Shantun indicated the injured dik-dik she was ministering.

"Would I feel obliged to tend a sick human, and would I feel fulfilled after doing it?" Wuhan thought. "Probably not. The whole thing is too irrational. It could never be compared to the satisfaction of answering a Call. That is joy. Sometimes when a Traveler's essence enters me and I feel the warmth of his psyche, I get so weak I could faint. I break out in a sweat, and there's a sensation that grows inside my body until my skin wants to explode with the pain and joy of it. You wouldn't know, Shantun — but your time will come when I'm gone. To you right now, it is just the Duty. But when you are mature — when you become a Dedo — it is the Joy." And she looked sternly at her child, to impress her with the awe of it all.

"Humans are animals. I like this animal." Shantun patted the dik-dik, which was struggling to its feet, the Healing Stone having done its work.

"The Duty is paramount. Do not waste the Healing Stone, and set that creature free, Shantun!" The older woman was conscious that the conversation had gone too far — that her daughter might dare to question the Unity of Purpose, next. "A Dedo must have bonds with none but Starquin himself. That is the Logic. You are behaving like a human."

"I'll tie him up for the night." Shantun attached a thong to one of the pavilion poles, then tied it lightly around the dik-dik. The tiny antelope pushed her arm with its nose and the girl was oddly moved. There *must* be something more than the joy of Duty. There had to be. "He can't go out in this dark," she explained lamely.

"You have time." Wuhan's voice was resigned. "You have aeons to get this foolishness out of your head, fortunately." So saying, she composed herself for sleep and Shantun departed into her half of the pavilion. Outside, in a charmed circle, gnus and zebras grazed, alert to give warning of the approach of any night predator. The Dedo had some power over them, too.

So night came to the veldt, and with it came the night prowlers — the big cats, leopard and lion. Another cat was abroad that night too, one that did not need to rely on stealth, so swift was he. He walked slowly on long legs, his long tail held low but ready for use as a counterbalance when he went into his bounding, swerving run. He walked quietly and the gnus and zebras ignored his coming because he was not a hunter of such large game. Although his pace was swift, his jaws were small. In all, he was a curiously built animal, and the Song of Earth tells a strange tale of his ancestry.

And now he heard something, and his instinct told him the prey was small and suited to his talents. He uttered a low cough and went into his run, because now he could see it, tiny in the starlight, and helpless.

Wuhan awoke to a snuffling noise. She swung her feet out of the bed and parted the entrance flaps of the pavilion, and saw what she saw. And something irrational happened inside her, something her ability to see into the Ifalong had not allowed for. She moved to protect a creature that was not of her own species. She tried to snatch the kicking dik-dik from the cheetah's jaws.

Shantun heard the noise too, and rushed from her bed. But now the cheetah was gone. Her mother lay on the dusty ground. The dik-dik stood nearby, trembling, wounded. Wuhan had suffered the worst wound, however. Small and elderly, she had fought the cat off, only to suffer a dreadful gash across the throat. Already she had lost much blood, and she was soon to die.

Shantun dropped on her knees beside her. "What happened?" In the dark she couldn't see the worst of it.

Wuhan tried to speak, but failed.

"I'll get you into the pavilion. You're hurt." Shantun was strong. She began to pick her mother up.

Wuhan tried to struggle, to say something, but her speech was gone.

And nearby, the Rock flickered . . .

Just the faintest flicker, but Wuhan knew. And she knew she must get to the Rock and gain contact with the human Traveler, for Starquin's sake. She tried to shake off Shantun, and when she realized the girl was too strong for her, she tried to shout, to point. The Rock! The ROCK!

Shantun was crying, "Oh, Mother, you do feel it. You do know what I mean — this liking for other creatures. You protected the dik-dik, and the cat hurt you for it. Oh, Mother, I like you so much!" Only then did she feel the blood, and a chance shaft of moonlight showed the well of her mother's throat. "Mother!"

THE ROCK!

"Oh, Mother . . ." Shantun laid the small form on the ground again, gently, and the tears fell from her face onto her mother's. "This is my fault. I should never have brought the dik-dik home. It was injured and I should have left it out there to die, because that's the way of life on Earth, and there's nothing wrong with that." She ran for the Healing Stone, but returned too late.

Wuhan twitched once, appeared to be trying to move her left hand, then sighed and was still forever.

And something entered Shantun, possessing her, firming her resolve. "A Dedo must have bonds with none but Starquin himself, and my mother has paid for her transgression — and mine, too, perhaps. Now I see the Logic and I will transgress no more." She untied the dik-dik and it limped away. She walked over to the Rock and touched it experimentally for the very first time.

The Rock was cold and dark and quiet.

"I dedicate the rest of my life to this Rock and to you, Starquin," said Shantun formally.

*

That is the story of Shantun the Accursed, she who brought shame on the Rock Women for all time, for she was an evil woman, and a wretched one, because she paid heed to human ways. She neglected the Duty, questioned the Unity of Purpose and denied the Logic — and she was responsible for the death of a Dedo, her mother. As a result, her name is held in everlasting contempt by the Rock Women, for she failed to heed the calling of the Rock.

The Rock had flickered and humans had traveled the Greataway without the knowledge of Starquin. It could have been anyone, any insignificant trader with a cargo of harmless goods, stealing a ride.

But it was not just anyone. . .

It was the Three Madmen of Munich.

When humans discovered the Greataway, they traveled it by means of a process they called the Outer Think, which was distinct from the Inner Think, a longevity process. They had begun to spread, and other peoples had begun to take notice. One such people — who have never been seen with human eyes — lived on a world known simply as the Red Planet.

The progress of Mankind had annoyed the people of the Red Planet, who moved in with a frightful Weapon that capitalized on Mankind's greatest fear.

Earth threw up her defenses in the year 93,763 Cyclic, almost 50,000 years before Manuel met Belinda. Earth sent up the Hate Bombs.

The Hate Bombs were areas of insane psy that spanned the happentracks of each Greataway path. They were not tangible. They were essentially a bloated human emotion, the quintessence of murderous insanity, held in place and sustained by the mysterious force lines of the Greataway.

They were planted by three devils specially cloned from ancient genetic material. The virulence of the Hate Bombs made it impossible for any living being to traverse that area of the Greataway. It effectively sealed off Earth from the attacks of the Red Planet. It also sealed her off from her own colonies.

More disastrously, the Hate Bombs trapped Starquin in a terribly small area just a few light years across, in the vicinity of the Solar System.

Starquin raged.

It became the Purpose of the Dedos to influence events on Earth toward the eventual removal of the Hate Bombs and the release of Starquin, the great Five-in-One.

Scanning the Ifalong, the Dedos saw a way to accomplish this. It was a tenuous thread of events stretching into the distant future that depended on the coming together of three people, who would thereafter be celebrated in the Song of Earth as the Triad.

One of those people was Manuel.

Another was an old Cuidador named Zozula.

And the third was a girl with many names, and no name.

THE COMING OF THE MOLE

He cannot hear, he cannot see, he cannot speak his name.
His mind is filled with greatness but his heart is filled with pain.

— Song of Earth

Zozula didn't know that he was destined to become a household name in millennia to come. Although he'd never heard of the Girl-with-no-Name, he would shortly see her — but without realizing her significance. And he would have been horrified to think that his name would become linked with one Manuel, a barrel-chested young Wild Human who was at that moment walking along the beach ten kilometers away, lamenting the loss of his love.

Because Zozula esteemed himself a True Human, one of the last survivors of the First Variety of the Second Species.

He stood on his lofty viewpoint on the catwalk that girdled the lower part of the Dome. The upper part was curved into the clouds like the arch of the sky itself. From here he could see Pu'este in the distance, an untidy clutter of huts with a pathetic little church standing on top of a knoll.

It was no better than one would expect from Wild Humans, who worshiped strange gods. Zozula smiled to himself. He liked to step outside the Dome occasionally and look down and see the curious insanitary way in which the rest of the world lived. There had been a storm, and the villagers would be repairing their roofs. Nearby, a figure trudged toward the Dome, wheeling something in a barrow.

They were so vulnerable down there, the Wild Humans. So much at the mercy of the sun, the wind, the atmosphere, predators, disease . . .

"Hello! You up there!" The man with the wheelbarrow had halted at the base of the ladder and was staring up at him. He was a Wild Human, of course, but dressed in a colorful robe unlike the rags that his kind usually affected.

Zozula was about to ask him sharply what his business was, when something familiar about the newcomer made him pause. "Haven't I seen you before?" he called down.

"My name is Lord Shout," said the man simply.

And with a certain pride, which made Zozula smile to himself. How could a Wild Human rise to this kind of eminence? By ruling other Wild Humans, presumably. He noticed the heavy body of the other, the telltale undershot jaw, the abundant facial hair.

And twenty years rolled back . . .

*

Lord Shout had arrived one day on some kind of quest or mission — one of those peculiar rites with which Wild Human culture was infested — and had climbed to the catwalk around the Dome. In the course of this, he had come across a transparent area in the Dome's surface and had looked in.

He would never forget what he saw.

It was terrible in its unexpectedness. He saw thousands upon thousands of humans lying unconscious on white benches, tiered above each other and below. He could not see the bottom tier or the top; they stretched farther than the eye could discern, all bathed in a blue light, all the bodies tapped with pale tubing. It was eerie, it was unearthly, it was immense. But one thing made it more macabre, more pitiful.

All the people were big babies.

Not small, normal babies, such as the mothers in Lord Shout's tribe might coo over, but big babies, the size of men and women. Chubby and naked and *huge*, plump-cheeked and round-eyed and button-nosed — but as tall as Lord Shout and probably heavier. They lay pink and quiet on their benches, and

Lord Shout groaned to himself as though he felt some comment was needed. He'd known the Dome from a distance all his life. It had been part of his existence, towering from the plain, solid and permanent. And now it suddenly revealed that — all this time — it had been harboring something coldly terrifying.

Zozula had found Lord Shout crying.

"How did it happen?" Lord Shout had asked. "In God's name, how did they get like that?"

Zozula had been touched by the sight of this strong, hirsute creature so shocked, and had explained to him in some detail the tragedy of the Dome, as told to him by the Rainbow.

"It all started a long time ago, in the fifty-fourth century Cyclic, as I understand it . . ."

That was almost 90,000 years ago. The Consumer Wars were over and Anticonsumerism had won. Shortage of fossil fuels and the high cost of travel resulted in increased use of self-contained recreational centers. At the same time there was a growing demand for visual rather than physical entertainment, accelerated by the decreased oxygen content of Earth's atmosphere as the oceans' oxygen-producing creatures dwindled. The first Domes were built in the mid 56s, the later, solar-powered models in the late 57s.

During the Great Retreat and the subsequent Nine Thousand Years' Ice Age, the Domes were probably responsible for the survival of the human race.

But then came the creeping onset of neoteny, the failure of the breeding programs and the vicarious consolation of Dream Earth, where the neotenites lived imaginary lives in a corner of the Rainbow.

"Can't you do anything about it?" Lord Shout had asked.

"We're trying, believe me," said Zozula. "We have a full-scale research program on another planet. The only trouble is that the neoteny factor, which is responsible for their appearance, can't be eliminated. It seems to be a dominant gene present in all samples in our tissue bank — even in my own tissues, we've found. I'm lucky to be built the way I am. My own body is the last of its line. And like all the other Keepers in there, I'm dying slowly. We practice our Inner Think, of course. But we can't live forever. And when we've gone — the present generation of Keepers, that is — there will be nobody else. No True Humans to take our place. I don't know what we'll do. I suppose we'll have to recruit the neotenites, but they're terribly weak and susceptible to disease."

A lot of this had gone over Lord Shout's head. "Why not let all those poor monsters die? What's the point of it all? What's so important about the Dome, and True Humans? It's only *you* that call yourselves True Humans. Personally, I'm quite happy with my own body. At least I can withstand the climate without getting out of breath. Shouldn't that be the measure of a True Human?" His shock and sorrow were turning slowly to outrage.

"We have a duty to those creatures in there. We've failed them often enough already. Now we must keep them alive until we can breed True Human hosts for their minds. There are ten thousand of them in there, all living their thinking lives in the Rainbow, waiting for us to find them bodies. Would you want to be responsible for wiping out all those minds?"

Lord Shout was becoming furious.

"God damn you," he said. "If there is a God — and I still believe there is, in spite of what I've just seen — may he twist *your* body into a monster and feed *your* brains into a computer." He spoke very formally, as though uttering a sacred curse.

Zozula couldn't remember his own reply. Whatever it was, it had been inadequate and hadn't satisfied Lord Shout or himself. As if offering some kind of excuse, he'd taken Lord Shout into the Dome and shown him Dream Earth, the imaginary world where the neotenites exercised their minds in environments of their own invention, among phantom forests and meadows, cities and seas. Lord Shout had remained unconvinced.

Zozula had been very thoughtful for many months after that meeting, and the other Keepers, or Cuidadors, had noticed and commented, but he'd kept his own counsel. He was the head Cuidador, hardly an appropriate person to start voicing doubts about their mission in life.

And now, twenty years later, here was Lord Shout again . . .

*

But changed. The pride was there and he tried to meet Zozula's gaze levelly, but his eyes were haunted.

"It's been a long time, Zozula," he said quietly.

"Time to think. Time to come to terms."

"For me or for you?"

"I've never forgotten what you said. And I've never been able to decide whether you were right or wrong."

And Lord Shout said, "I was wrong."

Zozula stared at him. "How can you say that? You believed what you said. Any Wild Human capable of thought would· have said what you did. I've spent nearly twenty years knowing you may well be right, and telling nobody. You spoke as you saw it, as an independent man — and I respected you for it."

"Please don't respect me any more, Zozula. All that was twenty years ago. I don't need respect, now. I need pity. Are you human enough to grant it to me?"

Zozula descended the ladder. The barrow stood there, crude and wooden, Wild Human–made. In the barrow lay a creature.

There was a long silence.

Eventually Lord Shout said, "My son, the Mole . . . You can see he's not normal. He's been deaf and blind since birth, and . . ."

"Even if we could treat his physical abnormalities," Zozula said gently, "our Cuidador code doesn't allow us to practice medicine on Wild Humans. We have a duty to the species as a whole, and we've already paid a price for interfering with the course of nature. You people out here — you represent a hope for Humanity. Natural selection must be allowed to take its course."

"I wasn't going to ask for treatment."

"What, then?"

"Mole, here . . . He's known *nothing*. Can you imagine what that's like? He's never seen a tree, or a wave on the beach. He's never heard the jaguar roar, and he's never seen its beauty. He's never even held a conversation with another human. He's fifteen years old, and he's never seen a woman . . ."

"I'm truly sorry, but I don't see what we can do."

"I want you to take him in. I want you to treat him like the rest of those . . . neotenites you have in there. Lay him down on a shelf and plug him in and let him dream real dreams in the computer. That's the only way he'll ever know what the world is like."

"The neotenites have been dreaming for thousands of years. The world they've created in Dream Earth is nothing like the world we know. The Mole would find it frightening and I'm afraid the images would drive him mad."

"I'll take that chance."

"I'm sorry. We're full to capacity, you understand? In order to accommodate the Mole, we'd have to eliminate a neotenite's body, which automatically means eliminating his mind. You must see why we couldn't do that."

"But you told me you have ten thousand bodies in there. What difference can one more make? You could make up a spare bed, surely?"

Zozula said, "We could if we knew how. But we don't. We simply don't have the knowledge to fabricate the bed, the life-support terminals and so on. I'm sorry." Then, seeing the expression on Lord Shout's face, Zozula took pity and said, "But we can do our best for him."

"Anything."

"Does he talk?"

"No, of course not."

"Well, what kind of things does he think about? He's deaf too, you said? What's happening in his mind?"

"I don't know! For God's sake, Zozula, I've no idea! I feed him and keep him clean, and sometimes he waves those . . . things. I've no idea what's going on in his mind, or even if he has a mind. He's my son, and I don't know anything about him!"

Zozula looked at the misshapen head, at the blank places where the eyes ought to be, and just for a moment imagined a whirling of thoughts in there, quick and brilliant, unable to find release, belying the terrible blankness of the exterior. Who could tell? He drew a parallel with the Rainbow — seemingly an immense bank of fog occupying one wall of a vast room, useless and mute unless you knew how to communicate with it.

And the tragedy was, that skill in communication was

virtually lost. There were programs of great value in there, knowledge and techniques that could probably solve all the world's problems. But they couldn't be drawn out, understood and learned from. Nevertheless they were *there*.

The Mole's thoughts were probably *there*. If the Cuidadors couldn't help the Mole, nobody could. For a moment Zozula thought about the Mole's thoughts and the form they might take — and the germ of an idea took shape in his mind.

He said, "Help me carry him up the ladder."

THE DYING GODDESS

After Zozula had settled Lord Shout and the Mole into their quarters, he made his way to the relaxation room. Three of the Cuidadors sat there, and the dead echo of long silence was in the air. Zozula sat down on a golden couch, not knowing what was going on.

Eulalie said finally, an edge of horror in her voice, "I'm dying. That's what you're afraid to tell me, isn't it?" She had risen. Now she walked to the window and looked down at the clouds, looked up at the brightness of the late afternoon sky, pale grey through the age-darkened glass. She couldn't look at Zozula.

Ebus, the Dome physician, said, "There are some more tests I could make."

"How long do I have?" She swung round.

Ebus hesitated, glanced at Zozula, who was still sitting and gazing at his wife and companion of many centuries, uncomprehending. How can you comprehend death, when you live that long? Ebus said, "Maybe a week."

"A week? There's been a mistake, Ebus." The horror had become desperation in her voice. "I've practiced my Inner Think religiously, every morning. I've never been so in tune with myself. I feel fine, except for . . . Look at me!"

They looked. It was not easy to believe Eulalie was dying. Tall and beautiful, she wore a long white dress of Grecian style;

her hair, likewise, was long. Over the millennia the Keepers had come to dress like the gods their charges considered them to be. There was scarcely a line on her face, her neck was pale and smooth, no veins marred the delicacy of her hands.

"We keep up appearances," murmured Ebus. Why should he remind her that the Inner Think was not perfect because humans were not perfect; that concentration lapsed, cells were missed; that the thinking areas of the brain were themselves the most difficult to revitalize? She knew all that.

An hour later they were able to face the situation more reasonably. Ebus now went to the heart of the matter. "This doesn't give us long to find a replacement," he said.

"Ebus!" Zozula was outraged. He glanced at Eulalie. She met his look with understanding and sympathy. He and she were different from the others. They were throwbacks. Like Manuel, they knew love.

And now, born of love, an idea slipped into Zozula's mind.

"There's one way out, if you can bring yourself to take it," he said quietly. "Those happenings in Dream Earth — who's to say they're less real than what happens out here? It's a logical little world in the computer — up to a point — with its own rules. If you could bear the change, it's possible that we could program your brain-patterns into the Rainbow and hook you up to a spare host."

So much for Zozula's high principles. An hour ago he'd spoken about the Cuidador's duty to the Dream People and the impossibility of finding room for the Mole because it would mean erasing a neotenite's mind. Now, in shock and grief, he was suggesting doing just that.

They watched Eulalie. She took a peach from a bowl and bit into it, savoringly, as though it were the last thing she would ever do.

"So I would live on as a Dream Person, with one of *those* bodies?" she asked calmly.

"I'd be able to visit you, of course," said Zozula quickly. "Maybe your real body wouldn't be very pleasant, but that's immaterial. You could Bigwish yourself into whatever Dream form you chose. Your present form, if you wanted."

And Eulalie was tempted, let there be no mistake about that. When a person has lived as long as she had, even the unthinkable can seem better than dying. She thought for a long time before replying. "Thank you, Zo. But that would only be dragging things out. My time's arrived, and I'll accept it. Ebus is right. Our first duty is to the Dream People, and the most important thing now is to find a replacement for me. As it happens, I do have a replacement in mind."

Juni, the dietician, spoke for the first time. "She'll be a . . ." She couldn't finish. Distaste wrinkled her perfect face.

"A blubber." Ebus used the unkind word for neotenite. "That's right — there are none of the old humans left."

"There are humans outside."

"Barrel-chested freaks," said Ebus. "Don't fool yourself, Juni — they're a completely different variety. They've evolved away from the true form just as radically as the neotenites have, only their adaptation is much more favorable. They're hardy, but you can't say much else in their favor. I'll support Eulalie's choice. A blubber it must be. And you never know — Selena might have a breakthrough in the breeding program before long. Only yesterday she said that gorilla-man of hers — what's his name . . . ?"

"Brutus," said Eulalie sharply. Ebus could grate on a person sometimes.

"Yes. Brutus has come up with a new approach that she has some hopes for. Funny, isn't it, to think of a Specialist leading the way in genetic research?"

Eulalie went to her room, took pills and slept, and dreamed of decay, and awakened with her throat hoarse. She guessed she'd been screaming. She caught sight of a little cleaning cavy slipping discreetly away and wondered if she'd also been incontinent. It seemed she'd been seeing that little rodent each morning for many years now, without giving it any thought.

*

It was an unhappy, silent dinner that night. Selena, the biologist and geneticist, arrived late and depressed. With her was her assistant. Although she didn't intend that Brutus should eat at the same table, she needed his moral support. He was a man of heavy build and gentle nature, and over the years Selena had learned to depend on him a lot. He stood a little behind her, hands making slight washing motions, smiling apologetically. There were gorilla genes in his make-up, a frequent characteristic in those skilled in medical science.

"What's the matter, Lena?" Zozula asked her.

Brutus was shaking his head in huge embarrassment.

Selena said miserably, "I'll have to deprocess this year's crop, every last one of them. They were telepaths again, too — wonderful minds. Do you know, Zo, it's been two hundred and eighteen years since we've successfully bred a True Human — and the same goes for all the other Domes on Earth. Why? What's gone wrong? How can we ever awaken the Dream People if we only have neotenite bodies to give them? What does that say for our duty? Sometimes I wonder why we're here at all!"

Meanwhile Brutus wrung his hands and agonized for these True Humans who were burdened with such great duties that their very souls seemed to shrink under the weight of them.

Eulalie was sitting there. She didn't know whether to put on a brave front, or to let herself go, break down and join Selena in tears. She decided the latter course would look like self-pity, so she set her face in an expressionless mask. It was the worst possible time for Selena's announcement . . .

After dinner Zozula, Juni, Eulalie and Ebus visited the Rainbow Room. Eulalie sat in her accustomed seat and placed her hands on the tactile surfaces of the console, tuning in. The room began to fill with images. She saw blue skies and a hot sun, so she formed clouds and dropped rain. She saw a storm at sea and a boatful of Burts and Bucks and Sophias and Gretas who were enjoying it too much and growing prideful in their immortality, so she turned down the wind and smoothed the ocean, and the Burts and Bucks and Sophias and Gretas grew bored and began to bitch and quarrel like normal people again. Eulalie scanned Dream Earth quickly, watching the Dream People playing while their bodies lay at rest elsewhere in the Dome. The 52nd millennium was a popular choice at the time.

Eulalie said, "Somewhere about here..."

They swung over mountains, green fields and a sparkling river. Snow and more meadows, brown timber chalets. Tiny yellow flowers and a fresh scent they couldn't smell. Eulalie locked in on a girl walking up a hill, following a rough path in the sunlight. She wore a white blouse embroidered in red and a short green skirt. Goats parted to let her by, watching with wise idiots' eyes, munching.

"We'll hold this image..." said Eulalie.

The girl had been singing, but now she stopped. Above the brow of the hill a chalet had come into her view, painted brown and yellow and red. People sat at tables on the balcony. Nearby a ski lift strode up a mountainside. The girl was not very pretty compared with the other people. She smiled.

She said, "I wish..."

"Oh, no!" whispered Eulalie. "She must *not* wish. We could lose track of her that way!"

THE GIRL WHO WAS HERSELF

*H*er heart felt so joyful that there was not room for it, no room in her small body for all this happiness. In any case she was breathless from the climb. She paused and, without realizing it, found herself saying, "I wish . . ."

And somewhere else, Eulalie said, "Oh, no! She must *not* wish!"

The girl — who in legend would ever afterward be known as the Girl — caught herself and laughed. The goats, the sheep, the mountain laughed with her as she reached the chalet and climbed the steps to the balcony. Here were wooden tables and chairs, with scarlet serviettes and bright silver cutlery, opalescent china. There was a smell of new cedar and grass, coffee and bacon. Most of the tables were occupied; people chatted and laughed and ate. The Girl sat down at a vacant table for two and indulged in a daydream: If she opened her eyes, Burt would be sitting opposite.

"Can I get you something?"

She opened her eyes and found a breasty waitress leaning over her, a relic of some forgotten smallwish that nobody had been dissatisfied enough to alter or abolish.

She smiled at the mirage. "Coffee, please. And bacon and scrambled eggs. Two. And apple juice first."

The waitress smiled back with inappropriate seductiveness and swayed off to the kitchen. The Girl sighed with satisfaction, relaxed and regarded the diners. The man at the next table had his back to her but looked familiar, and as he turned to address his companion, she saw that it was BURT! and her heart thumped and she was breathless. But then she saw his eyes. They dwelt on her for an expressionless instant, and he was not *her* Burt, he was just *a* Burt. She could tell. After all, if her Burt were not different from all the others, how could she love him the way she did?

Her coffee arrived and she drank thoughtfully. An Elizabeth I swept by, regal in flowing robes, a caveman grunting beside her and taking advantage of his present guise to behave like an animal. He caught the Girl's eye and, instantly forgetting the Elizabeth I, sat down heavily opposite the Girl. He seized a croissant in his hairy paw and munched, watching her unblinkingly.

"Go away, please," said the Girl.

"I stay." The caveman grinned with his mouth full. He was totally naked, although furry. Mercifully, the table hid him from the waist down.

"Move on, you bum." A quiet voice spoke. The caveman looked up; then his eyes widened and he scuttled off. The David, smiling pleasantly, sat in the vacant chair. "Do you mind?"

"No, I'm glad." The Girl smiled also. "I don't like cavemen. I can't understand why anyone should Bigwish themselves into one," she added in a burst of confidence. David seemed nice.

But then, they usually were . . .

"When you can't think of anything else, you revert to the animal," said David sadly. "It's a trend. I'm sure there are more cavemen about these days. Last week a pack of them stormed a casino at Monaco and smashed up the equipment. By the time we'd smallwished it all together, there wasn't an atom of psy left among us. By the Rainbow, was I ever exhausted . . ."

The Girl was about to say that Yourself was a very good person to be, when all other guises had become boring. She'd been Herself for some years now, and it wasn't always easy without a Dream persona to blanket the emotional shocks so frequent in Dream life. But she didn't say anything. Instead she listened to David and thought about her Burt. Her thoughts were real love thoughts, quite unlike the stylized, glamorous imaginings of most Dream People. Soon her meal was finished. But David showed no sign of leaving, so she made some excuse and stood. When Burt appeared, she didn't want him to see her talking to another man; she had a suspicion that he was inclined to jealousy. She descended the steps to the grassy meadow, looking around. People were emerging from cabins, carrying skis. She watched Burt's cabin, trying not to appear too obvious.

She saw a Jayne leaning against a tree, her face buried in her hands. Being Herself, the Girl was of a sympathetic nature, unlike normal Dream People who can only think of themselves. The Girl straightaway became sad. She approached the Jayne and put her hand on her shoulder.

"Can I help?"

She was too late. Jayne, in the grip of some unknown sorrow, had Bigwished her way out of it.

Impulses sped to the Rainbow's Composite Reality bank. An electron fled from the liver tissues of a sloth, and a memory stored itself in an impure quartz molecule. Minute electrical charges flickered to and fro, adjusting the Composite Reality, adjusting every Dream Person in the Dome.

The Girl watched Jayne with horror, as life and death and torture and Reality flashed through Jayne's mind — as she saw the Earth for what it really was. For just an instant, a lifetime's instant. Then Jayne's face shimmered and her body shifted, straightened.

Jackie smiled. Dark, wide of mouth, eyes wide-set, too.

"Hi there, friend," said Jackie. "What goes on here?" Her voice was musical, with a slight, indefinable accent. "A ski chalet, is it? Great!"

The Girl chased a memory of a sad blonde for a moment, then it was gone. She never gave the Jayne another thought, because the Rainbow thriftily deletes memories of nonexistent personae.

Burt appeared, carrying climbing gear. He closed the chalet door behind him and walked toward the Girl, smiling. He was tall and broad, dressed in heavy clothing that made him look like a huge bear, and the Girl loved him with all her heart. He wore ropes over his shoulder, and big boots with spikes, and a strong belt around his waist upon which bright climbing things glittered.

The Girl walked toward him. Little blue swallows swooped and turned around the yellow eaves of the chalet. The Dream People on the terrace were laughing.

Burt walked right on past the Girl as though she wasn't there and took the arm of the Jackie with the wide mouth. She laughed and hung onto him, and together they walked toward the mountain.

The Girl watched them go.

THE ORACLE IN THE FOUNTAIN

Within a crystal rising ninety meters high,
There lives a sad-eyed woman who can never tell a lie.
— Song of Earth

*T*he Girl just had to get away. She smallwished, a special smallwish that the Dream People use when things get on top of them and they need a few straight answers. She wished herself before the Oracle.

The misty clouds cleared and she was standing before the moat of a fairy castle with pink walls and a multitude of blue spires that towered into the clouds. The drawbridge was down and the portcullis was up. She walked hesitantly forward.

"Come in."

The voice came from all around her, or maybe from within her mind. She crossed the drawbridge, while tame unicorns watched and golden carp leaped from the blue waters of the moat, twisting to catch a glimpse of her. There was music in the air, tinkling and melodic. She walked on through the archway as tall men bowed, dark-haired and muscled. A courtyard occupied the middle of the fairy castle, and in the center of the courtyard a fountain played. People moved to and fro in stately fashion, left over from smallwishes — not real, but beautiful and dressed in diaphanous robes and adding to the atmosphere of the place.

The Girl stopped before the fountain. The waters rose before her, but never came down. They lifted into the clouds and became clouds themselves, tipping the castle spires like cotton wool, yet still letting the sunlight flood the courtyard. As the Girl watched, the rising waters formed a globe before her, playing over the surface in a thousand conflicting currents. A face appeared within the globe, the face of a beautiful woman, more beautiful than any man's smallwish, with hair of finest silver threads and eyes of a color beyond the spectrum.

"What's your name, child?"

"I have no name." The Girl regarded the face with awe and admiration. "I am Myself."

"When you have all of history to choose from, that is something to be admired. Place your hand in the waters."

The Girl did this.

"Now ask your question."

"My question is about the future. I simply want to know what is to become of me. Why am I here in this place, and why can't I join in the fun like everybody else? Why do I feel it is so important to be Myself, when it only causes me pain? Why can't I make friends and be loved? It seems to me there is something wrong with the world when the whole purpose of existence is to pleasure yourself until you're sick. Surely there's something else!"

"That's a lot of questions."

"Once I thought I'd found something else. . . I met some gloomy people in a small cottage. They weren't laughing or drinking, and just for a moment I thought they made sense. Then they began to do the most awful things to each other, and they wanted me to join in with the whipping and slashing and crying, and I knew they were just the same as the others, only the opposite, if you know what I mean."

"I'm sorry, I don't know what you mean. Define your question."

"Tell me my future." *And if it will be like my past,* thought the Girl, *I'll take a ride behind the Steam Locomotive, that's what I'll do!*

"You are aware that the Ifalong is not the same as the future. The future is a myth, because it is nothing until it happens, and then it is already the past. I cannot predict your future, but I can foretell your Ifalong. Will that suit you?"

"Yes, thank you." The Girl watched as the beautiful face

shimmered and the waters bathed its surface more frequently, little streams spinning in countless directions yet never clashing, never splashing.

At last the face cleared. "This is your Ifalong. The greatest probability is that you will find love, knowledge, fame, beauty and an identity."

"Is that all?" asked the Girl, after the Oracle had been silent for some moments. "I could have all that with a Bigwish."

"The Ifalong does not permit details. Only the general course of events can be foretold. That is all." The face was gone, and the fountain became once more a slender column ascending to the sky.

For a while the Girl watched it, disappointed. Then, as the attendants began to usher her back over the drawbridge, she said quietly to herself, *Maybe there is nothing more. Maybe this is it, this is what it's all about.* And she smallwished, and found herself standing outside the Love Palace. Sometimes the Love Palace was a catharsis even for her.

WHEN EULALIE CAME DOWN

As she entered, the Girl was wondering just how she could persuade Burt to become Himself. It would take a Bigwish, and Burt was a very active person, forever smallwishing himself here, there and everywhere. The Girl lived with the constant fear that one day she would lose touch with Burt altogether. It had almost happened once, when Burt had been John and had Bigwished without her knowledge. It had taken her months of searching in the Andes, the Pacific, Nairobi, Nice, Pompeii and sundry planets before she'd finally found him in a later sector of history sitting with the Three Madmen of Munich and flinging Hate Bombs into the Greataway. Fortunately, the acts of the Dream People, though extravagant, have little effect on the real world — otherwise the Song of Earth would have had a different ending. Somehow the Girl had recognized her man even then, and just for one night, they had loved.

"You are beautiful," said a golden-haired youth softly, taking her hand and leading her down by the pool where a seven-headed monster thrashed and spat fire and clouds of steam arose. It was frightening, and was intended to be so, because many Dream People found fear an appetizer — which is how the Locomotive came into being.

The golden youth whose name, he said, was Hermes, laid her down on a soft couch and made tender love. She found she was watching the mists swirling about the far-off ceiling, wondering how high it was and what kept it all from falling down, and what Burt was doing right now... She became aware that Hermes had finished. Although they were still coupled, he had rolled his chest away from her and lay with eyes closed, face set in a childish pout. She wondered how long the Pleasurers of the Love Palace lasted before they tired of the endless empty lovemaking and Bigwished themselves into Annes and Edwards. She wondered how long Hermes would last. She watched his dissatisfied face. It shimmered...

Horrified, she disengaged herself roughly and stood. Hermes — or whatever he was becoming — rolled off the couch with a thud, out of sight on the other side.

The Girl fled. She ran past satyrs and muses, naiads and graces. She ran past pools and fountains, stairways and doorways and finally collapsed before a great pit from which flames rose high, too breathless to run farther, lacking the psy to smallwish herself elsewhere.

She found a stone seat and dragged herself onto it, gasping for breath. She considered for a while Hermes' incredible rudeness in Bigwishing at such a time — then decided he wasn't worth the bother. Was this the love the Oracle had referred to? She watched the pit, wondering what its purpose could be. It was thirty meters in diameter, and the walls, wherever they were not hidden by flames, were smooth and glossy. The flames burst upward with a great roaring like the roar of a dragon, rising fifty meters or more to a place where they were cut off abruptly — as though, having reached this height, they were no longer needed. There was no smoke. As the Girl watched the flames, drawing strength from their fearsome energy, a face appeared before her.

The goddess Eulalie had come.

Afterward the Girl was never able to say exactly whether Eulalie had appeared out of the flames or materialized before them. Whichever it was, the Girl immediately knew Eulalie for a goddess. She just *appeared*, the way a person would expect a goddess to appear.

"What can I do for you, my dear?" asked the beautiful woman.

The Dream Girl's mouth was still hanging open. She closed it and gulped. "What do you mean?"

"You can have anything you want."

Now, the gossip of the Dream People abounds with the sightings of gods. And almost inevitably, the gods of this gossip come making big promises; just as inevitably, there is a catch.

"What's the catch?" asked the Girl suspiciously.

Eulalie smiled. Only a Girl-who-was-Herself would ask such a question. "Don't be alarmed. I'd like you to wear this cap, that's all. For a week you must put it on every night before you go to sleep. At the end of the week I'll grant you a wish. Whatever wish you like, Big or small, without loss of psy. Does that seem fair?"

On almost any other day the Girl might have had second thoughts, but this day she said, "Yes."

"Perhaps you'll tell me what that wish will be, so that I can make the arrangements."

The Girl smiled like the morning. "I'll wish for Burt to love me."

"Which Burt?"

"You know, *my* Burt. If you're a goddess you must know the Burt I love. Please make him love me back."

Eulalie nodded and vanished, leaving behind a machine.

*

In the transient way of Dream Earth, the Girl became momentarily famous. Only one person other than herself had seen the goddess in the Love Palace, and that person was one Richard, a notorious liar. But there was no gainsaying the Cap of Knowledge. The Dream People gathered around and examined it, marveling at it. They placed it on their heads, but here they were disappointed because it did nothing for them. One strange power the Cap had that made it unlike any other thing on Dream Earth: It could not be wished away.

It continued to exist regardless of the psy exercised against it: a cabinet with a helmet attached, almost identical in outward appearance to Manuel's Simulator because both had been manufactured in an age of standardized packaging, millennia ago. The jealous ones hated the Cap because it belonged to the

Girl and not them, and they wished so hard for it to go away that they exhausted their psy and had to stay in the Love Palace for weeks.

The Girl wore it every night, as the goddess had bade her. The Dream People gathered around to watch her sleeping — Johns and Abrahams, Runas and Raccoonas. The playboys and playgirls lost interest by the second day, but the good folks stayed, as did Those-who-were-Themselves.

Then, six days later, the goddess Eulalie appeared again.

Legend says she came riding a dolphin, but legend lies. In point of fact she materialized in the bow of a Spanish galleon that was rounding Cape Horn in exceptionally fine weather, which Eulalie herself had arranged. The crew were bored. Someone had just suggested smallwishing to the Arctic, but nobody was about to summon up the psy; it was too much effort.

When Burt saw the beautiful creature in the bow he nearly dropped his drink. She sat on the bowsprit, naked and golden in the sunlight, more lovely than any Dream Person on Dream Earth, because she willed it that way. She smiled at Burt and the smile seemed to spread itself around his body in electrical charges. He glanced around. The other Dream People were drinking in the cabins. He moved closer, smiling easily.

"Hey there, beautiful. I reckon you're worth any man's smallwish."

And inside him the shy, real man cringed. Why was his Dream persona so damned *obvious?* The real man trapped inside was quite nice — which the Girl had sensed, of course. Which was why she loved him.

But nobody on Dream Earth can fully control his Dream persona; the personality comes with the body. So Eulalie went to work on him. She was feeling faint and the motion of the boat didn't help, so she had to move fast.

"Maybe a real man's smallwish," she said. "I have no time for fakes. Bigwish yourself into something authentic."

"Aw, come on, baby." Burt sidled closer with a smile like greasepaint. "They don't come any more real than me."

"If you come any closer, I'll wish myself away."

"Hey, you wouldn't do that now, would you?" He reached out to touch her.

She shimmered.

"Hold it!" Burt was alarmed. Eulalie steadied up. Burt considered. He didn't stand a chance, of course. His very make-up was geared to find an image like Eulalie irresistible. He argued, but quietly, so as not to bring the others out of the cabin. He pleaded . . .

He surrendered. For her sake, he would become Himself.

Eulalie hung on, feeling sick and tired but looking wonderful. Burt closed his eyes, concentrated all his psy, tensed his huge muscles and Bigwished. Eulalie saw his outline become blurred and quickly recalled herself to Reality through the Do-Portal.

There was only one way to make this vapid Burt truly love the Girl, she'd decided, and that was to trick him into becoming Himself. Then he might have the sense to recognize her qualities. People-who-are-Themselves scream a lot, but some say it is worth it to be able to feel real emotions.

Back in the Rainbow Room, Eulalie walked to the console, leaning heavily on a valet. Her heart was fluttering painfully and the floor heaved like an ocean.

Now she had to introduce Burt and the Girl to each other, because otherwise the Girl would not recognize him . . .

That was Eulalie's last thought, as the agony exploded in her chest. The valet caught her, held her and gave the alarm.

WHEN THE DREAM GIRL BIGWISHED

On the ninth day the Girl awoke, threw the Cap of Knowledge across the room and burst into tears. Eulalie had failed her. The Oracle had lied. Burt had not come. And her mind was filled with strange words without a key to their meaning: Cirrus, Hate Bombs, Anticonsumerism, Gulf Stream, Inversion Layer. They kept interfering with her normal thoughts. They meant nothing to her. They were facts without a reason.

She sat on the side of the bed with her head in her hands, staring at the pattern on the carpet, which made no more sense than her thoughts. Burt had not come.

Ergo, Burt did not want to come. So all the powers of the goddess Eulalie had not prevailed upon Burt, because the hold that that soulless Dream Jackie had on him was too tenacious. And because the Girl herself was not pretty enough . . .

She had waited two days beyond the appointed time. She had given the goddess a fair chance. Her throat was choked up with misery, her head ached, she was alone in a world of indifference, of empty heads, blank faces, hearty laughter and pointless adventure. So the thought came again into her head, as it came into every Dream Person's head from time to time: There must be something better than this. Love, knowledge, fame, beauty, identity — where were they? Was even the Oracle phony? And the gods — were they Dreamers too?

She took her hands away from her face. She walked over to the mirror and looked at herself. Her face was red and puffed from crying. In addition, her nose was too big and her eyes too small. Her hair was a mess, her ears stuck out, her chest was flat. Small wonder, she decided, that Burt couldn't stand the sight of her. So she closed her eyes and concentrated. She'd almost forgotten how. She settled on the image she wanted, held her breath and thought: *I wish* . . .

Back in the Rainbow Room, Cytherea saw a red star flash but thought nothing of it. It happened all the time. She didn't really understand the Rainbow, and was just filling in until Zozula had recovered enough from the death of Eulalie to take over again.

The Girl hung in limbo as Composite Reality adjusted. She saw ships and stars and yellow mists. She saw bleak devastated landscapes, puny attempts at cultivation, twisted plants. She saw the Dome without knowing what it was. She saw endless shelves filled with endless empty big children and a tired woman who spent forever trying to get those children to look right and breed right.

In that instant when the Girl was Nowhere, she saw Everywhere and Everwhen. She saw the Planet-with-no-Name, which was destined to bear her name. She saw terrible sick areas of the Greataway, and caught a glimpse of a trapped Thing greater than anything imaginable. She saw Keepers tending stored minds. She saw the Invisible Spaceships and knew something of the creatures of the Red Planet, intelligent and cruel. She even flicked through the Greataway behind the Celestial Steam Locomotive . . .

She saw millions of years in one instant. She saw what every Dream Person sees when they Bigwish. And like any other Bigwisher, she forgot it all, instantly . . .

*

So Marilyn stood in the floodlights outside the huge, bright building, remembering nothing of the past, thinking only of the present. Lights burned in all the windows and couples

could be seen on balconies, romancing. Music came from
within, and the sound of laughter. All around were lawns and
shrubs, dark pools, and illuminated fountains, rose-pink and
sky-blue. People sat on the benches, talking quietly, kissing,
drinking. Beautiful people, dressed in ermine and silk, sapphires and rubies.

Marilyn wore a simple white dress with an ordinary pearl
necklace, a plain diamond tiara in her blonde hair. She was
as beautiful as any woman there. Aglow with happiness, she
climbed the white marble steps, and the scarlet-uniformed
doorman threw the door open with a flourish.

"Marilyn!" he announced to the crowded ballroom.

The music paused, people clapped; then the dance resumed.
A dark man, tall and broad, stepped up to Marilyn. "Would you
like to dance?" he asked. He was a Burt. He was wonderful,
thought Marilyn. They danced, and it couldn't have been better, not even if she'd smallwished the whole thing herself.

A tiny voice said within her: *He isn't the one.*

But he is, he is, thought Marilyn.

The music ceased. Burt wanted to take her out on the terrace, but she demurred and made for the ladies' room. She had a
suspicion that her lipstick might be slightly smudged. And she
wanted to look at herself again. The ladies' room was crowded,
but she managed to find a place in front of a long mirror. She
dabbed at her lips while others jostled about.

The image in the mirror applied mascara.

Startled, she looked around, then laughed. She had mistaken
her neighbor's reflection for her own. She tended to her appearance, then went back to the ballroom. Another Burt asked her
to dance. She noticed that Burts and Marilyns were very popular this season, which was comforting. It was good to be among
her own kind of people. She half-remembered being lonely,
once.

The tiny voice whispered: *He's not the one, either!*

Burt swirled her about the floor and it was marvelous. Everything was marvelous. The music paused and the doorman
bawled "Marilyn!" and that was marvelous too — the more the
merrier, birds of a feather. The domed ceiling was decorated

like a birthday cake, hung with glittering revolving spheres. Every so often a shower of vivid balloons descended and Marilyn used her sharp heel to pop them.

She danced all night.

The next day she lay about on the grounds in the sun with Burt and danced all the next night. It was difficult to imagine anything better than this. The band was perfect, indefatigable, all dressed in crimson and gold, blowing gold trumpets, silver saxophones. Then the band paused . . .

It was the funniest thing; people often laughed about it afterward. There was silence while this comic little man came in among the dancers. He was bald and short and fat, and his clothes hung about him like broken wings. He walked around peering into peoples' faces, moving on, peering. He looked dirty, he stank and he was totally incongruous in this company. That was what was so funny, the incongruity. Everybody laughed and laughed.

The little man peered into Marilyn's face, and she recoiled a little because there was something desperate in his eyes that wasn't funny at all. She laughed loudly to make him go away and to drown out that irritating small voice inside, which was spoiling her fun. He performed for a little while longer, making them all laugh, then he made for the door and they never saw him again. The band struck up and Burt whirled Marilyn along in his strong arms, smiling at her with even white teeth.

"Oooooh, look!" somebody cried.

Blue rain was falling through the ceiling, slanting among the dancers in a sparkling azure mist. The Dream People exclaimed in delight. It was so pretty, and nobody was getting wet.

REINCORPORATION

The Rainbow was malfunctioning in other ways, too. Recently the images had been sporadically washed over with an unpleasant green color, and the movements of the Dream People had become jerky, occasionally freezing for a few seconds.

"Somewhere in there," said Juni grimly, "is a girl who knows how to operate the special effects. You'd better find her soon, Zozula. It'll take ages to train someone else, and heaven knows what damage will have been done by then. We must keep Reality within reasonable bounds, otherwise the Dream People will begin to believe a spiral moon is the norm. And how does that fit them for normal life Outside?"

The other Cuidadors had retired for the night, all except Zozula, haggard and grief-stricken, sitting at the console and searching endlessly, filling the Rainbow Room with battling dragons, hurricanes, floating islands, Bale Wolves, convivial scenes in spacebars, lovemaking in zero gravity. Everything became green again, quite suddenly, as though the sight of all this artificial pleasure made the organic constituents of the Rainbow feel nauseated.

And every so often the images shifted, showing quick flashes of Reality: the interior of the Dome, the jungle, the ocean. Bits of the past were plucked from real history: a primitive execution. Happentracks of the Ifalong were displayed in a frightening nova. As though the Rainbow — that Earth-girdling, linked, organic-mechanical-electronic repository of human knowledge and intelligence — were going crazy.

"I have to find her," whispered Zozula to himself. "Eulalie said . . . Eulalie . . ." He pressed his lips together.

Juni's voice came from behind, startling him. "Much more of this and the mind of every blubber will be wiped clean. And then where would we be?"

"Somebody will have to go in through the Do-Portal," said Zozula.

"Go in and do what?"

"There are . . . creatures in there. Half-human, half-Rainbow. They may know what the trouble is. We can ask them, at least. I'm not getting anywhere with this console."

"Well, *I'm* not going in there."

A door opened and Brutus appeared, effortlessly wheeling a big metal container hung about with life-support systems. As if this were a signal, a huge replica of him appeared in the middle of the Rainbow Room, peering this way and that from under heavy brows while he worked with strong and nimble fingers, whittling a stick. An angry red wash swilled over this scene from another happentrack. The real Brutus stopped in his tracks, watching the scene with alarm.

"Maybe we should send Brutus in there," said Zozula. "The Rainbow seems to have some kind of empathy with him."

"Not Brutus. Not a Specialist," said Juni.

"Why not?" He looked at her in surprise.

"It's not . . . appropriate."

"Well, he's Selena's assistant, after all. She says he has an amazing ability with programs that she herself had found unintelligible."

The Rainbow suddenly tolled, a deep bell-like reverberation. There was a gibber of accelerated sound. The Brutus-image was dancing about like a performing animal. "Who else can we send in?" shouted Zozula above the din. "Do you want us to call a meeting of Cuidadors and discuss it? You know what *that* means."

"Zo — I don't care what else you do, but you can't use a

Specialist for this job. Not this particular job, you understand me?"

"No, I don't."

Juni made a small gesture of impatience, glancing at Brutus, who had drawn closer, mesmerized by his own image. She said quietly, "The blubbers are True Humans, Zo. Or they will be, once we get the genetic program sorted out. Their minds, their thoughts in the Rainbow — they're True Human minds."

"I know that, for God's sake."

"Well, do I have to spell it out for you? I'm not letting any Specialist get in behind there and have the chance to meddle around with the lives and minds of ten thousand True Humans!"

"But Brutus? He's just a gorilla-man."

"Exactly!"

"You're talking nonsense, Juni."

"No. You're living in a world just as unreal as the blubbers' dreams, that's the truth of it! Listen to me, Zo. The Specialists envy us and resent us. We clothe them, we feed them, we command them — at one time we *made* them. They may seem subservient, they may obey us, but always remember that some of them were bred with qualities that made them almost . . . superhuman. Remember Captain Spring!"

Zozula laughed outright. "Captain Spring is just a legend!"

"She was real, and in many ways she was better than True Humans. The resentment of the Specialists has been building for millennia, Zo. Don't you understand, they hate us! And you want to turn Brutus loose among thousands of helpless True Humans? He'd wipe out the whole lot! He'd erase them!"

She stormed out and Zozula stared after her in dismay. She was quite capable of routing the Cuidadors out of bed and calling for a vote of no confidence. He turned to Brutus.

"I'm sorry," he said. "Her tongue runs away with her sometimes."

Brutus's deep eyes were unfathomable. In his low, slow voice he said, "Just tell me to go through the Do-Portal and I'll do it."

Zozula was silent.

The Brutus-image disappeared, to be replaced by something

equally strange. The red wash had faded and the distant ceiling of the room had become a pale blue.

There was a city of tall pink buildings with lofty walkways between and wheeled vehicles below. People of True Human appearance walked about. There was a spaceport, and a broad river that looked familiar . . .

Zozula sighed. This was not Dream Earth, but it was no more real. It was a historical scene, probably. He guessed it to have been around the Age of Resurgence — the 80th millenium. Checking his guess, he requested a date. The Rainbow told him: 143,624 Cyclic.

That was the present day!

The angle of vision changed as though the observer had stepped back, and now the surrounding landscape could be seen. Zozula grunted. He had recognized the delta north of the Dome — in fact, as he watched, the Dome itself came into view, along with the village of Pu'este, looking as it did now.

Was this real, or was the Rainbow creating anachronisms? Storing the information away in his mind, Zozula requested Dream Earth.

*

A clear image appeared. In a ballroom there was a party, people laughing, dancing and drinking, and blue rain falling.

Zozula passed a hand over his brow and attributed a momentary dizziness to simple exhaustion. It had been a long time since he'd slept, and the memory of Eulalie was still strong, so that in his tiredness he kept getting little hallucinations, seeing her face suddenly or hearing her speak a fragment of a sentence. So when he heard the soft voice behind him — "Zozula" — he swung round with a sudden wild, irrational hope.

But it was an old woman dressed in a black cloak.

"How did you get in here?"

"It's of no importance." Her eyes were pitiless and Zozula suddenly shivered. There was total calculation and knowledge in the way she looked at him — and there was no sympathy. "I believe you seek a girl who is lost in your machine."

"How do you know that?"

"I know everything, Zozula." She stepped forward and stood beside him, and it seemed as if she brought a cold wind with her. She placed a hand on the console and the colors of the Rainbow faded. One face appeared: that of a young blonde woman, smiling, looking up. Then the background filled in: a shower of balloons, a crowd of people jumping up and down, batting the balloons to one another and spilling drinks. Now sounds of laughter came, and delighted screams and sharp reports as the balloons burst.

"She," said Shenshi. "She is the one."

"No," said Zozula. "That's a Marilyn. The girl we're looking for is Herself. And I'd be glad if you didn't interfere with —"

"She is the one. You may reincorporate her. She is the girl who will be called Elizabeth in time to come. She has been chosen by a chance of happentracks, as have you. You, she and a young man named Manuel will form the Triad. You will remove the Hate Bombs and free Starquin from his Ten Thousand Years' Incarceration."

Gazing into her face, hypnotized, Zozula said, "I . . . don't know . . ."

"Follow your happentrack, Zozula." The dark eyes seemed to contain Universal knowledge. Shenshi looked at him steadily for a moment, then left.

Zozula blinked. Something momentous had just happened, but for the life of him he couldn't remember quite what it was. There was an image of a girl in the Rainbow Room, a beautiful girl with fair hair. Obviously she was the girl Eulalie had trained. Leaning forward, he stroked the tactile surfaces in an ancient pattern, his fingers fumbling because he'd never issued this particular instruction before. Like a child learning to write, he murmured to himself:

Reincorporate . . .

*

Zozula opened an ancient panel stiff with dust and noted the position of a winking blue light. Then he took an elevator to the appropriate level. His heart was pounding. He summoned two Specialists to his side — raccoon-women, dedicated nurses — and asked them to make up a stretcher. They followed him as the walkway bore them past endless shelves of barely living beings. The smell was indescribable: a sweet, deathly stink of antiseptic and human wastes. Here and there nurses scurried, watching viewscreens, making minute adjustments to valves and drips, sponging down their fleshy patients.

I wonder what the nurses think of them, Zozula speculated. He stole a glance at the raccoon-girls riding the walkway with him, neat and pretty with bright eyes, ready smiles, trim figures . . . And he thought of Brutus, tirelessly working to reproduce the True Human form, without success. *We count them as our inferiors,* thought Zozula, *yet they spend their lives working to preserve the helpless and mindless remains of the True Human race. Can't Juni see that counts for something?*

And one of the nurses grinned at him and gave him a wink of joyful sexuality.

Maybe I've lived too long, thought Zozula, smiling back despite himself. *As time goes by I seem to accumulate dilemmas like warts.*

They arrived at their destination, which was indicated by a blinking blue light and a crowd of excited nurses. A small man — indistinguishable from a True Human except for a dark nevus covering the upper part of his face — was obviously relieved to see him.

"Thank Whirst you've come, Zozula. I've never seen anything like this before. This patient suddenly began to show the most peculiar symptoms . . . We had to restrain her — I'm sorry. And the blue light keeps flashing. Why does it flash?" He asked in bewilderment. He'd never seen this happen before, neither had his ancestors ever described it. It simply never happened.

"I've reincorporated this patient," Zozula explained.

There was a murmur of excitement. "Has a True Human been bred?" somebody asked.

They were pleased at the possibility. They wanted it to happen.

"I'm afraid not. We have no replacement for Eulalie except . . ." He regarded the neotenite, which was now twitching, its eyelids flickering.

"Poor girl," said a nurse.

"Wake her very slowly," said Zozula.

*

In the morning Zozula called on Lord Shout, whose quarters were situated in a remote area of the Dome and at a great height. As he entered, he was alarmed at the strange quality of the light: yellowish, with hard shadows. Then he became aware of the vast panorama spread before him, a dizzying view of mountains, valleys, tiny villages and, blue and hazy, the ocean.

"What . . . ?" He sat down quickly and closed his eyes.

"I sent two of my tribesmen up the ladders and they cleaned off the crystal," Lord Shout explained. "I hope you don't mind. They didn't like the job much, I can tell you. It's almost two kilometers up, and the winds are strong out there, so they tell me."

"It certainly looks . . . different."

"It was always meant to be that way, you know. It's just like an ordinary window that got dirty over the years."

Zozula opened his eyes carefully. "It's the height. There's so . . . so much out there. I've only seen Outside from ground level before. Did you have to open up all that?"

"It's the way I think," said Lord Shout simply. "I think Outside, you think Inside." He glanced at the creature in the corner. "I wonder how the Mole thinks."

Zozula said carefully, "I don't want to get your hopes up too high, but we have a vacant bed coming up. I've reincorporated a neotenite. I'd like the Mole to take her place."

"But you said Dream Earth might drive him mad!"

"The decision is yours, of course. It's a chance you'll have to take. But ask yourself — what's the alternative?" He nodded toward the Mole, who was unusually active today. Grimaces furrowed his face and then were gone. Odd croaks and hoots escaped him. His appendages pattered against the floor.

The decision was quickly made. "It's very kind of you to go to all this trouble," said Lord Shout.

"I have other motives. I think the Mole may have developed in an unusual way. With only logic to guide him, his mind could be a thing of purity and perfection, which would help us tone down some of those ridiculous excesses of Dream Earth. And there's another thing . . ."

He paused so long that Lord Shout said, "Yes?"

"He might be able to help us to a better understanding of how the Rainbow works and find us some of those old genetic research programs . . . Somewhere in there is the answer to the neoteny problem. Somewhere, the Rainbow is storing the recipe for True Humans."

"Aren't you placing too much emphasis on physical appearance?"

"Yes, I am. I've often thought about that. But it's my duty, after all. It's why I'm a Cuidador. It's part of my job to preserve the True Human form, so what else can I do?"

There was a faint buzz at the door and a nurse came in, bright and pretty. She gave Lord Shout a special smile, then went to attend to the Mole's needs.

After she'd gone, Lord Shout said, "She's a Specialist, that nurse. A raccoon-girl. Her name is Felicia, and I slept with her last night. She's loving and intelligent." He awaited Zozula's comment.

After a while, the Keeper said quietly, "But she won't bear your child. Whatever you say, however you feel about her, however often you do it, she's a different species. And that's our tragedy."

THE MARTYRDOM OF
RACCOONA THREE

*P*olysitians, Paragons, Wild Humans, True Humans, neotenites, Dream People ... It is difficult to conceive the sheer diversity of human species and varieties developed over the course of history — particularly in such a time as now, when so many of those varieties have become extinct.

There was the First Species: the union of ape and Paragon known as Original Man.

Then there was the Second Species, in three varieties:
True Humans,
Wild Humans, adapted to oxygen-deficient air,
Polysitians, adapted to oxygen-rich air.
And the Third Species, the Specialists, in countless varieties.
Next there was the Fourth Species, in two varieties, the first of which was the neotenites. This is neither the time nor place to discuss the second of those varieties, for the Song of Earth must retain some mystery.

And finally there was the Fifth Species, which Manuel and Zozula knew as the Quicklies.

These were the forms of Man.

*

Of all these forms, the most diverse was the Specialists. There is a famous story that tells of their beginnings, during the period known as the Renaissance Years. The events told in the story took place in the year 91,137 Cyclic, when Space exploration was in a temporary eclipse. Mankind, for a while, and not for the first time, had turned in on himself. The Renaissance Years were the years of artistic experimentation, of the great playwrights and poets, actors and moodmen. The theaters and opera houses were full again, the city streets sprouted statues, and living murals decorated the walls. New programs were fed into the Rainbow, and the Dream People dreamed fresh and beautiful dreams before they returned to their bodies, because neoteny had not claimed them yet. Composers and emotes gathered in asqui rooms and talked and sang while day and night went by unnoticed. It is said that the roots of the Song of Earth sprang from this age. It was a good era to live in, an age of wealth and idleness, of freedom from danger. High Space was dead, but there was plenty happening on Earth.

Into this age the Specialists were born . . .

They were hardly noticed at first. Men quoted verse, and women fashioned pottery glazed with timeslip, giving a magical luster. And the darling of the footlights was La Rialta of the thunderous voice and incredible range. La Rialta . . . The name stirs a million memories in the Rainbow. La Rialta . . . The ultimate in womanhood, a great, lovely, sexual creature who sang like an angel — or like the Devil, if the role demanded. La Rialta, who in her later years ran to fat, so that she dominated the stage like a mountain, mocking her suitors, who scurried around her like rodents with their tiny voices and puny frames. La Rialta, symbol of an age of opulence and art.

But somebody had to do the work behind the scenes.

Around this time Mankind was in the midst of its love affair with the kikihuahuas, those space-going genetic engineers who had progressed far beyond the use of machinery. And there was a lesson to be learned from the kikihuahuas.

The lesson was put to practical use by one Mordecai N. Whirst, a dour and seemingly emotionless individual from Scotia. Using principles known for millennia, coupled with no small measure of courage, he proceeded to alter the make-up of human cells, replacing certain genes with genes selected from animal stock. There is no way of making that statement without being aware that it would have shocked and horrified almost every human born before that date, and quite a number thereafter.

But people soon got used to the datachimps, who pounded untiringly at computer keyboards with nimble fingers, great accuracy and little imagination.

Physical courage, patience, quick reactions and many other qualities became available in the laboratories. The kikihuahuas had used the techniques for thousands of years, so why shouldn't humans? The newcomers were called Specialists, in recognition of their special abilities and the special tasks they were expected to perform. They took over quite a lot of work from the aging machines. Specialists prepared food, piloted solar shuttles, stood guard outside restricted areas. A Specialist was appointed file clerk to the world premier.

And a Specialist murdered La Rialta.

*

Raccoona Three did not have the looks that humans of her era could sympathize with. Humans — although they did not know it — were beginning to evolve from the Second to the Fourth Species. Their cheeks were plump, their faces broad, their heads relatively big, and they liked it that way.

Raccoona, as she took her place in court, was ugly.

In an earlier age she would have been considered cute and pretty, with short dark hair and bright brown eyes, a tip-tilted nose and a neat, very feminine figure. But in the year of her trial she was considered sharp-featured and thin. Public sentiment was strongly against her, and the trial was only a formality.

"You are accused of the murder of the singer La Rialta," said the judge. "Let the trial begin." Below the dais, a datachimp tapped mindlessly at his keyboard, feeding details of the trial into the corner of the Rainbow that served as jury. Behind the judge, a mighty screen played awesome colors.

Raccoona trembled, and her gaze sought out the elderly man

who sat with counsel for the defense. "Oh, Daddy," she whispered, a plea which he could not hear. "Help me to be strong."

Soon the prosecution said, "I call Professor Mordecai Whirst."

The elderly man, avoiding Raccoona's eyes, stepped up to the stand and sat down. He, too, was thin by the standards of the day, somberly dressed and dominated by a sadness that everybody could feel.

"You are Professor Mordecai N. Whirst?"

"I am."

"What does the *N* stand for?" asked the judge curiously.

"Nothing."

The judge showed a flash of irritation, wondering if he was being made a fool of. "You mean *Nothing,* with a capital *N?* Or just *nothing?*"

"Nothing. It's just a letter. I don't know how in hell it got on my I.D. It's always been there. Computer error, I suppose." His voice was flat and despondent. He wanted to get it over with. "I got tired of correcting it, so in the end I let it stand."

"So Raccoona Three is a Specialist," said the prosecution in due course. "You created her in the laboratory, is that right?"

"No. She is third generation," said Whirst.

"What is she for?"

"For?"

"What is her purpose?" The prosecution indicated the datachimp. "There is an example of a useful Specialist. I am sure that this court, despite its prime objective today, would be the first to admit that a limited selection of Specialists can take much of the drudgery out of life, despite the misgivings we may have concerning the circumstances of their creation. However, the court is a little puzzled as to the usefulness of the accused. You are not in the habit of creating young women whose only qualities are their femininity and animal nature, are you, Professor?"

"Objection!"

"I will rephrase that. What is the accused's occupation?"

"She is the daughter of my personal secretary. She lives at the institute. Damn it, she's only a kid!"

"And you are . . ." the prosecutor consulted his notes, "two

hundred and three years old. Well, well . . . Tell me, Professor
— why a raccoon?"

"There's more to the creation of Specialists than the simple
permutation of human and animal genes," said Whirst irritably. "There has to be a degree of compatibility — a consideration that must outweigh the usefulness factor in the early
stages. A number of different combinations were tried out before we came up with the datachimp, for instance. As I recall it,
we had a gibbon-man, a baboon-rhesus-man, a lemur-man —
all of which could have done the job, but none of which possessed the necessary physical stamina and resistance to
disease."

"So what happened to these . . . failures?" The prosecution's
tone was deliberately ominous.

"They were allowed to live out a natural life span. We are not
barbarians. And as for raccoons . . . Fifty years ago we were
experimenting with a number of different species, of which
raccoons were one. Generally they were a great success. They
were hardy, intelligent, friendly . . ." The last word was out
before he could stop it. "We are allowing them to run through a
planned series of generations. At this stage it's too early to talk
about their use."

"Do you ever get weighed down by the responsibility of playing God, Professor?"

"Objection!"

And so it went on. In the end Whirst was allowed to resume
his place. An expert took the stand and was quizzed on the
animal psychology of Specialists.

*

The defense counsel's name was Abel Schot. He was a dull,
good man, and Mordecai Whirst had hired him for that reason
— because he would lose the case.

Whirst wanted Raccoona to die. He actually wanted his creation, whom he loved like a daughter, to be found guilty of the
murder that she had undoubtedly committed, to be taken from
this place and executed in accordance with Universal Law.

The strain was almost unbearable.

"They were rough on you today," said Schot. The bar was

full. The courtroom was just across the way and the case had attracted great attention. It was the trial of the year, of the decade. Hate groups with placards sat at tables. They were all against Raccoona. The placards read PUT THE ANIMAL DOWN and similar legends. Music played: an aria sung by La Rialta.

"They can have their fun," said Whirst.

"Listen to me, Mordecai. The opposition have no case, don't you realize that? Murder can only be committed by a *human*. It's defined in the Earth Branch of Universal Law like this: 'The unlawful, malicious and intentional killing of one human being by another.' That's clear enough, isn't it? And Raccoona isn't human. She has animal genes in her make-up — you could testify to that yourself. She's a Specialist, Mordecai, so she must be innocent!" Schot was desperate. He couldn't afford to lose a case this big.

"I wouldn't try that line if I were you." Counsel for the prosecution, arriving, had overheard and now sat down at their table. "This trial is taking place because the people want it. A beloved public figure has been murdered — brutally murdered — by your client. If you make so much as one attempt to get it dismissed on a technicality, then I'll tramp all over you. And so will the judge, and so will the public. Remember that, Schot."

"But the computer . . ."

"The Rainbow decides on the rights and wrongs of the case put before it. If Mankind wants a trial, then by God the Rainbow won't stand in its way. The Rainbow is our servant, Schot. It is the jury, not the judge."

Mordecai Whirst said flatly, "The trial will go through to the bitter end. I'll see to that."

Abel Schot groaned.

"I believe you mean it," said the prosecutor. "You're a strange man, Whirst." A nearby placard read: WE DEMAND THE WORST FOR WHIRST. "You realize you're on trial too — and every one of your creations?"

"I know that," said Whirst.

*

Cities had come and gone, nature had come and gone and come again. The Mordecai N. Whirst Institute stood alone on the clifftop with a view of wind-sculpted trees, grey waves, spray-drenched rock. It covered five hectares and contained laboratories, living accommodations and paddocks . . . •

Whirst was home. Raccoona Two passed him in the corridor and they exchanged a glance of mutual commiseration, but neither spoke. He went to his study. After a decent interval, Vixena came in and kissed his forehead as he sat in his favorite chair.

"Bad day, Dads?" She sat opposite him in her accustomed place, crossing her legs and flashing him a mischievous grin. She was a beautiful woman, all quick movement and tossing russet hair. The prosecution would enjoy getting her on the stand.

"We're throwing Raccoona to the wolves, aren't we? Isn't that bad enough?" For once, her brazen sexuality grated on Whirst.

"I'm sorry. I feel the same as you, Dads, but I'm not good at showing it. You have nobody to blame but yourself."

He regarded her, remembering a remark of the prosecutor's. *Am I playing at God?* he wondered. *But that's ridiculous. Those are only words designed to appeal to the simple masses. Human beings have been evolving for millennia. One of the results of this evolution is me, a person with the capability to accelerate that evolution. It's no different from using a computer to design a computer. There is no God; there never was. I must try to bring that out in court. Why do I have to go through this nonsense? In the end the facts will win, because we have the Rainbow. Public sentiment is powerless if it is wrong-headed. What I'm doing at the institute is neither right nor wrong, neither good nor evil. It is expedient. And if in the process it results in a little more excitement and beauty around this dull old Earth, what's wrong with that?*

"I couldn't do without you, Vix," he said.

"I wouldn't be here without you. And I'd like you to know just how much we all appreciate what you and Raccoona are doing, Dads. If it gets too much, you can stop it at any time. Nobody will blame you."

"We're going through with it. Even if I wanted to stop now, Raccoona wouldn't agree. You've no idea how determined she is." There was a touch of pride in his voice. They were all his children. "She's going to be a heroine, in years to come. It's . . . it's unfair that she won't be alive to enjoy it."

*

Raccoona was frightened. Anyone would be frightened, sitting there unable to run while the hunters closed in. In time the Specialists would speak of her bravery, of how she sat there proudly staring her captors in the eye — and of how the prosecutor was unable to meet her gaze. And of her steady hands and calm voice. And even, in the end, of the way she walked steadily to her death, scorning the sedative. Raccoona the Martyr was the stuff of which such legends are built.

But Raccoona the girl was terrified as she sat there and shook and cried and lied, and her gaze darted this way and that as though seeking escape, and she had to be escorted to the toilet frequently. Such details as these do not find their way into legends. Raccoona the girl became a trapped animal and looked like one — a fact the media were quick to point out.

"So after all this," said the prosecutor, "after all these lies and evasions and histrionics, we are left with the following inescapable facts: The victim, the opera singer known as La Rialta, visited the Whirst Institute on the evening of February ninth. She was admitted by Raccoona Two, the accused's mother, and shown to the study of Professor Whirst for the purpose of a business discussion, so we are told. She may or may not have been seen in there by one Vixena — but that creature's evidence cannot, I think, be relied upon. La Rialta was certainly seen ten minutes later by her chauffeur, running from the building — insofar as a woman of her build could run — pursued by the accused. She never made it to the vehicle. She was attacked by the accused and most foully done to death with a knife. The police were radioed instantly by the chauffeur, who also apprehended the accused. When the police arrived, the accused was found to be drenched in blood and her prints were on the knife. It is an open-and-shut case." The prosecutor gazed around the court. "I have nothing more to say."

"Let's stop this farce, right now," whispered Schot to Whirst.

"Only if you can disprove their case," said Whirst. "I will not have it dismissed on a technicality."

"There's something else — new evidence. I found out last night." He regarded Whirst expressionlessly. "You knew all the time, of course. You must have known."

"Known what?" Was there a trace of alarm in Whirst's voice?

Abel Schot leaned across and whispered something in Whirst's ear. Video recordings showed him doing this, and attempts were made to lipread the words, but unsuccessfully. It remained one of the big mysteries of a somewhat mystifying trial. At a later date, in possession of all the evidence, the Rainbow was able to piece together a probable approximation of the eight syllables recorded on video, but they were never made public.

Meanwhile, Mordecai N. Whirst was known to reply, "I can only instruct you to keep your mouth shut — and I am Raccoona's legal guardian and therefore your legal client."

It was at that moment that the Great Datachimp Scandal blew up.

*

A satisfactory scandal must have an image on which the public can hang its imagination. The trial was being watched in every barroom on Earth, so the suitable and spectacular image that was provided was seen by a large proportion of the population and discussed knowledgeably for years afterward. It didn't do the Specialists any good at all.

Because suddenly the Rainbow scowled.

Thunderclouds passed across the huge screen behind the judge. Counsel for the prosecution stopped in mid-sentence. The judge swung round, following everybody's gaze. The Rainbow rumbled. The screen flickered. The onlookers were puzzled and not a little alarmed. Then the Rainbow spoke. Words flashed across the screen.

It appeared that a discrepancy lay between the audio pickup and the keyboard input. The audio pickup was only a safeguard, a rough check on input data, but inaccurate because of the difficulty of translating all types of speech precisely into computer language. So the audio was only an approximation of what was said, but enough to alert the Rainbow.

The keyboard input was being faked.

It took only a moment to establish that. Guards descended, wielding weapons. A growing roar of outrage shook the Earth.

And a sniveling, gibbering datachimp was led away. This was the image that was burned into the public mind, this small animal-man who had betrayed his trust to try to save one of his own kind. A tiny, strange, dangerous thing between two huge human guards with ordinary flat faces and disgusted expressions. A little creature with a wise old-man's face who had the temerity to show *imagination* and to try to cheat human law. Like Raccoona, he had lost some of his humanness, and the ape in him was very pronounced as he struggled and yelped and darted trapped little glances around him from under heavy brows.

It was a telling image.

Years afterward, Vixena's daughter asked the aging, ailing Whirst about the Great Datachimp Scandal.

"It nearly lost us everything," he said. "The datachimp thought he was doing the right thing in trying to protect Raccoona. He didn't know she was already doomed — somehow or other he had failed to grasp the implications of the trial. He saw it in simple terms. A Specialist's life was at stake and he had the power, by subtly altering the evidence fed into the Rainbow, to save her. But the Rainbow was too clever for him."

"What happened to him?" asked the little girl.

"Funny ... that's a thing not many people ask. The datachimp had proved to the satisfaction of the public that Specialists are not to be trusted. It was what the public wanted to hear, and the public was duly outraged. But Raccoona was the scapegoat — somehow this new crime got transferred to her. The datachimp became immaterial."

"So?" said the child, impatient, just like any other human child. "You still haven't told me what happened to the datachimp."

"He was put down."

"Found guilty and executed?"

"No. He was put down. Painlessly destroyed, like an animal."

"But that's murder!"

"Exactly. That's what the whole thing was about." He smiled at her outrage. It was all a long time ago, and it didn't excite him anymore.

*

Tradition dies hard. Humans love a show. When the Rainbow gave its verdict, it didn't flash it on the screen. It spat out a little plastic card, which the judge picked up. He paused while the suspense grew.

Whirst said unsteadily, "Raccoona, my darling. Please be strong." He stood beside her now. After all, hadn't they said he was on trial as well? But his role was easy. He was not going to die.

"Oh, Daddy, I'm so frightened."

And Whirst said, "If you want, I'll stop it right now. I still can." This is no myth. Whirst actually said that; the words are on record, and the video caught the tears.

Raccoona said, "No."

The judge said, "Raccoona Three. The Rainbow, representing the total of human knowledge and being completely impartial, finds you guilty as charged. Do you have anything to say before I pass sentence?

Raccoona said, "No," very quickly, very quietly.

"Then I must sentence you to death in accordance with human law."

Whirst whispered, "Thank you, Raccoona darling. The Specialists will never forget you. Neither will I."

And the judge was saying, "I would be failing my duty if I did not express my concern — and the concern of all Mankind — at the implications of this case. Raccoona Three has been found guilty, and deservedly so, and she will die. This is her punishment for the brutal slaying of a beloved public figure. But she is not the real villain of the trial. She is simply a tool, a creation of a man who must be feeling just as guilty as she, if he possesses any humanity at all. Mordecai Whirst — do you know what you are doing? When I see you standing there with your creation I am reminded irresistibly of the legendary Frankenstein. He failed to control his monster, just as you have failed. It is an apt comparison, don't you think?"

Quickly Whirst began to answer. The fool had to be stopped. The case was over and the datachimp was dead, and Raccoona would soon die too — but that should be the end of it. The world was listening to these words. The situation was in balance. No human judge, secure in his office and loving the sound of his own sanctimonious words, should be allowed to prejudice the great issue.

"Blame me if you like," Whirst said, and the world heard, "but don't blame the Specialists, and don't ever call them monsters. They have served Mankind for over a hundred years now and they have served us well, while our machines broke down around us and we slowly lost the ability to repair them. The Specialists do all the things we lack the ability or the inclination to do, and they do them without complaint. Don't blame them because of one crime.

"And as for me, you asked if I know what I'm doing. Perhaps I can answer that question best by telling you what I believe — what makes me tick and why I have devoted my life to the creation of the Specialists.

"I believe that we have wasted our abilities and the resources of Earth for forty thousand years. Has nobody ever heard of the Consumer Wars of the fifty-fourth millennium? Won't we ever learn that minerals are finite, whereas life is infinite?

"I believe that when we evolved on this planet we inherited a trust. The trust was not Earth itself, with the riches that lay underground and in the oceans. Neither was the trust the stars that we plundered for their wealth after we had emptied Earth. No — the trust was Life. The cells, the chromosomes, the genes. They were given to us to use wisely. And did we do this?" He paused, and the world waited. "No, we did not. In our conceit we arbitrarily stuck our finger into the stream of history and said: *That* is what a man is. *That* is the supreme life form, *that*, and no other. Even though the Second Species of Mankind was already beginning to evolve into something else!

Even though the idiocy of what we said was right there in our mirrors! We had the vanity to consider ourselves perfect.

"Life is ours to use, and use it we must, because it is our only resource that is not in short supply. So let's drop this pride, this worship of a form that is changing with every generation, this nonsense about the sanctity of human life. Let's realize that we are one animal among many, and they are all changing, and we can make a better life for everbody if we help them change.

"There is an intelligent life-form out in space that is infinitely more advanced than ourselves and that gave up the use of machinery aeons ago. I'm sure we've all heard of the kiki-huahuas. Once they were like us. Now they have progressed. They are humble and kind and clever and infinitely good — and they are genetic engineers. One day, we shall be like them.

"Let's make it soon, shall we?"

*

When the minstrels tell the story of the Martyrdom of Raccoona Three, it's easy to think that it all happened quickly, that the animal-girl was executed and suddenly the lot of the Specialists improved. It didn't happen that way, though.

It was a gradual thing. Mordecai Whirst didn't live to see the end of it, neither did Vixena Ten (who was actually called Vixena Rhodez, since proper names were one of the earlier changes). The vixenas stayed with him to the end, because they were his favorites. And his favorite of all was the first Vixena's granddaughter who, before his death, got the truth from him.

"They say Raccoona could have saved herself," she said one day. Specialist history was her best subject.

"She could have, but she didn't," he said. Enough time had gone by now. Changes were happening. A True Human had been convicted of assault upon a coati-girl. A dog-man had been allowed to enter law school. It was time to tell the truth — so it is probably from that day that the simple record of trial and execution became the Martyrdom. "It was her idea and I went along with it, although I could have saved her too."

"Did she kill La Rialta?"

"She did."

"Why?" asked Vixena, a little disappointed. "How could she do a thing like that?"

"A group of people — mostly True Humans, I'm pleased to say — were planning a general strike by all Specialists. It would have paralyzed Earth, and it would have brought people to their senses and made them realize just how much they depended on you people." He sighed. "We were hasty in those days. Hasty and just a little too idealistic. Looking back on it, perhaps it's as well it came to nothing. But we'd been planning it for years while we moved Specialists into key positions.

"La Rialta and I would have been the chief spokesmen. Two public figures fighting for the underdog, if you'll excuse the expression. And La Rialta had the world at her feet. Everybody adored her.

"But then, little by little, she began to get nervous. She realized the strike would set True Humans against her — and she couldn't bear to lose all that adulation. She began to set little conditions on her involvement and to engineer small delays to our plans. In the end there was a hell of a row and she left, threatening to expose us. Raccoona overheard all this. She saw that it could be the end of all our hopes.

"You know what she did. She was very loyal. She proved that again, in court."

The voice was fainter now; he was tiring. "After the deed, Raccoona suddenly saw that we didn't need the strike. Murder is defined as 'the unlawful, malicious and intentional killing of one human being by another.' She had killed a person humans loved, and they wanted her blood. They wanted her tried out there in public, and found guilty, and executed with due ceremony.

"They ignored the fact that by trying Raccoona for murder, they were admitting she was human.

"In the heat of the moment it seemed unimportant. The trial was the thing. They wanted to crucify her with due regard for the law. She mustn't be permitted a simple animal escape like the datachimp. They didn't want her quietly put down. That fact was registered in the Rainbow the moment sentence was passed. Mankind decrees that murder was committed, there-fore Specialists are human. Now the Rainbow applies that rule to every decision it makes.

"The Third Species of Man has arrived."

Vixena sighed. It all seemed so long ago, and tomorrow she was running in the council elections. "Poor, fated Raccoona. Brave Raccoona. That story that she could have saved herself in spite of public opinion, it's probably a myth. A flourish to make a better yarn. Whether she was a Specialist or not, the humans wanted a show."

"I told you, she only had to reveal one little fact."

"What was that?"

"That La Rialta was a Specialist too."

"What!"

"Yes. If she'd revealed that to the court, public interest would have died of embarrassment and the judge would have declared 'no trial.' One animal kills another. So what's new?" Even now, there was bitterness in his voice. "La Rialta was the result of a unique experiment we've never repeated. But she wanted to be human. She left the institute at an early age and assumed a new identity with the aid of a datachimp who loved her."

The evening was calm and rosy, and gulls swept across the clifftops, rising on the faint breeze. Somewhere within the in-stitute the sound of laughter could be heard. The evening meal was cooking, roast pheasant. Vixena could smell it faintly and her mouth watered. The sun sank into the crimson pillow of the ocean, and blue nightfall climbed the sky from the east. Vixena said, "Tell me, Pops."

"You know it all."

"I don't know that one little thing you never told anyone. What did counsel for the defense whisper to you? You know, those famous words they speculate about in all the history tapes, when you lost your temper and told him to keep his mouth shut?"

Mordecai Whirst chuckled. "That? It was sad, really. He'd just found out La Rialta was a Specialist and he'd been trying to persuade me to have the trial declared void on that basis. He wasn't aware of our plan, of course. And he wasn't aware that public ridicule was the last thing the Specialists wanted to suffer, at that time.

"What he said was: 'La Rialta was a hippo.'"

MANUEL TALKS WITH GOD

*A*nd so the Specialists took their place in human society. In time the Whirst Institute fell into disuse, and by the 106th millennium, around the Age of Regression, creation of new Specialist varieties had ceased. As humans retreated into the Domes and neoteny began to claim them, the Specialists went with them, to serve them again.

Outside, the Wild Humans evolved. They became primitive, almost savage in their struggle against their environment. In a few of them, however, the old humanity lived on.

One such Wild Human lived on a beach near the village of Pu'este . . .

*

Manuel mourned. Unaware of the momentous happenings in the nearby Dome, he had spent the days in remembrance of Belinda — of her slim beauty, of the inspiration she had given him and the love she had brought him. Stumping around his shack dressed in his trailing pacarana skins, he lost track of the days. He took fish from the waters of the bay, he milked his vicunas and combed them for wool and made butter and cheese. He did this to stay alive, but the fun had gone out of his life, and the passing villagers, calling down to him as he dug for clams, received only a curt nod. They went on their way shaking their heads. The young man was unhappy. It was a pity. But whatever the misery, no doubt it would pass.

"The guanacos will return," said Insel, meaning that things run in cycles.

Insel was right. For a man as young as Manuel, despair cannot be sustained. One fine morning of horse clouds, as he sat at the door of his shack watching the sea and dreaming of the reappearance of Belinda, he surprised himself by throwing his head back and giving vent to a roar that sent the gulls winging from his roof and caused a pair of capybaras to run for shelter under the brow of the low cliff.

It was a roar signifying frustration, bitterness and, above all, annoyance with himself. The time had come to pull himself together. "I've been behaving like a fool," he told the vicunas. Standing, he caught up a rock and hurled it out to sea. "Lying around like a sick sheep. Now I'm going to do something. Dooooo something!" he shouted in the undisciplined way of one who spends too much time alone and does not have to consider the ridicule of human listeners.

He climbed the track to the clifftop. Before him the old road wound its potholed way to the village, where people were already moving, hoeing and weeding their crops in the dusty fields behind the houses. Old Insel, who was cloud-struck, lay on his back nearby, watching the sky. He murmured ancient saws, reassuring himself and anyone who happened to be near, "Horses high, good days nigh." Nearby, Prior carved a totem, while Jinny spun a cloud of flossy cottonweed to decorate its tip and appease the gods. Dad Ose, the priest, who disapproved of such nonsense, was nowhere to be seen.

Manuel called to the villagers as he passed and they waved back, glad to see him out and about again. Whatever had been his problem, it was over now. Insel had been right.

Manuel climbed steadily toward the church. He admired its lines and, as usual, wondered at the ancient workmen who had fitted those smooth rectangular rocks so neatly together, all those thousands of years ago. In its way, the church was as wonderful as the Dome.

Within his huge chest Manuel's lungs worked easily in the thin air. Scarcely out of breath, he paused at the church entrance and smiled at the priest, who sat with closed eyes against the wall.

Dad Ose was enjoying the sun, dozing, knowing it was time to practice his daily Inner Think but letting the midsummer warmth leach the discipline from him. By the standards of the village people he looked fifty years old, but diligent application of the Inner Think had already afforded him a life of 496 years. This extreme age, and his consequent encyclopedic knowledge of village history, had earned him the respect of the people. He wanted little more, having realized long ago that his invisible God lacked the dramatic impact of the clouds that the village people preferred to worship.

Hearing Manuel's step, he opened an eye. "Can I help you, young man?" he asked.

"No, thanks," said Manuel politely, walking past him into the church.

"Wait! Where do you think you're going?"

"I'd rather be alone, thank you, Dad Ose." Manuel turned to face the priest, who was now silhouetted in the doorway, rigid with indignation. "I wish to talk privately with God."

"You what!"

"I said I wish to talk with God. That's what your church is for, isn't it?"

"I . . . Get out of here, right now!"

"Why?"

Dad Ose stared at the young man. Manuel was taller than he and several hundred years younger. He couldn't throw Manuel out physically. Besides . . . Applying a small measure of Inner Think, the priest calmed himself. Incredible as it might seem, Manuel could be sincere — in which case, he was in for a sad disappointment: God had never spoken to Dad Ose yet, so it was hardly likely he would stoop to granting a young fisherman audience. On the other hand (on a more mundane level) Dad Ose didn't think Manuel intended to carve sexual graffiti on the altar. There was no harm in humoring the boy.

"I apologize, Manuel," he said sincerely. "You may meditate all you wish."

"Oh, I don't think I'll be very long," said Manuel.

*

Manuel walked confidently to the end of the church, ignored the altar, with its selection of idols ancient and modern, and paused outside the vestry door.

"God?"

Dad Ose arrived at an open side window, leaned against the warm stone and looked in. Crickets chirped and the long grass tickled his bare legs. Manuel was standing in a shaft of sunlight and his head was cocked as though he were listening.

Then the boy said, "You remember the storm, God — when all the lifeweed came onto the beach?" He smiled at his own silliness. "Of course you remember — you sent it. Well, there was a girl . . ."

And he told the story of Belinda.

Now Dad Ose wanted to creep away. This was a private thing, and he had no right to listen even if it was his church. But he couldn't leave, now. Manuel would hear any movement. Dad Ose listened in sadness and sympathy, unable to escape.

What disturbed him, though, was the way Manuel would stop talking every so often and appear to be listening. It was just a little eerie.

"So what shall I do, God?" Manuel asked eventually. "I've just got to see her again. Where is she? Where do I find her?"

And he listened.

And — Dad Ose stiffened with a thrill of horror — *was that a voice?*

No, of course not. It was the wind in the bell tower, the distant sigh of a llama, it was the sea. It was not a voice.

Manuel nodded. "If you say so." His voice was unhappy. He turned away. He said quietly, "Thank you, God."

In the warmth outside, Dad Ose shivered. He swung away from the window and returned to the entrance in time to meet

Manuel coming out. Manuel nodded and smiled and was about to pass on, when the priest spoke.

"What were you doing in there, Manuel?"

The youth looked slightly puzzled. "Talking to God, of course."

"Of course. That's what you said before. But . . ." The priest struggled for the right words. "You can't really expect me to believe that, can you?" He smiled with an effort.

"It doesn't matter." Manuel was clearly depressed.

"No — I want to know. What's it like, talking to God? How does he sound?"

"Well, you know that, Dad," said Manuel in surprise.

"Of course I do — I was expressing myself badly. I'd just like to know what he said. You understand, I must know what goes on in my own church."

"Oh . . ." Manuel flushed. "I have a . . . problem, over a girl. And so I asked God's advice."

"Isn't that rather a small thing to bother him with?"

"Not to me, it isn't. And anyway, he seemed quite happy to talk about it."

"He is very understanding, Manuel. And what advice did he give you?"

"He told me that what I asked was not simple. He talked about strange things — happentracks, I think he said. And he said that in the Ifalong — I think he meant in the future — I would meet Belinda again, but then I'd lose her forever. And he said that I must go to the Dome very soon, maybe tomorrow, and speak to the man there, which would set everything on the right happentrack. He didn't tell me what to say to him, though."

They turned and regarded the Dome, which dwarfed the hills a few kilometers away. As they watched, the thing happened that never ceased to puzzle the Wild Humans. Near the curving top of the Dome, where the horse clouds passed close overhead and the grey opalescence of the massive hemisphere changed subtly to aquamarine, there was a flash of light.

In truth it was more like a *puff* of light. The flash was brief and diffused and seemed to have no source, and within it something solid and glittering was half seen, traveling outward with incredible speed, disappearing instantly as though it had accelerated past the speed of light and disappeared into some undimensional limbo.

"He wanted me to try to make friends with the man at the Dome," said Manuel. "And he doesn't really call himself God, by the way. That's what you call him."

Dad Ose regarded the youth helplessly. After 496 years, he could accept the inexplicable flashes from the Dome; the terrifying snake clouds that made people choke and die; the Quicklies, with their bewildering life-style; the fleet guanacos, with their uncanny sense for approaching disaster — he could accept all this. It was part of life.

But he would never accept the notion that Manuel talked with God.

It was humiliating and unthinkable that this youth with the strange emotions should be able to communicate with a being in which Dad Ose himself only half-believed. And Dad Ose was supposed to be the expert. Not for the first time, he wondered if he was being made fun of. He flushed. He tried to remain calm.

"Are you sure you don't hear the voice in your own head?"

"Of course I do. You know what it's like." Manuel smiled.

This was too much. "Why do you lie to me, Manuel?"

"Lie? Why should I lie?"

"Trying to make a fool of me. Of me, Dad Ose, old enough to be your father many times over. The voice of God, eh? Why should God want to talk to you — a nobody? I tell you this, Manuel — in future you'll put your questions to me, and I'll speak to God for you. It's an impertinence for a young man to address him directly!"

"If that were so, God would have told me."

The priest gazed skyward as if seeking guidance. The fleecy horse clouds had given way to high wispy guanaco clouds, moving fast. There was dirty weather brewing again. The wind brought a whiff of kelp. Dad Ose inhaled and felt the lift that oxygen-rich air brings. He was silent for a while, thinking.

Then he said, mildly, "Tell me what God's voice sounds like."

Although the Rainbow monitored all activity on the Earth's

land surface during those years, it could not look inside people's heads. Only the Dedos could do that. So it is not recorded when Manuel first became aware of the real difference between himself and other people. Here the minstrels must needs use poetic license, and they did:

> Dad Ose asked the Boy about the prophesy he heard,
> And Manuel knew that he alone could listen to
> God's word.

Manuel looked at him with his brown eyes and brushed aside the forelock of black hair. "It's big," he said, watching the priest with sudden compassion. "It's big and you hear it not in just your ears, or even your head — you hear it in all your body, and in all that your body has been and ever will be. It's an everything thing. It takes you. It fills you. You understand it better than men's words, better than anything you've ever seen or wondered about, better even than your own thoughts. And you believe what it says."

Half-convinced despite himself, the priest asked, "Does it scare you?"

"Not really. But one does what it says."

"Otherwise . . . ?"

"I think God might stomp on the whole world."

"Just because *you* disobeyed him? You, Manuel?"

"Yes," said the boy simply, and the priest found himself shivering as the wind gusted cooler and he caught a glimpse of a future in which he was no longer immortal, about which he could do nothing, from which neither he nor the human race could escape.

"God be with you, my son," he muttered as Manuel left.

It was time for his Inner Think, but he was too upset to concentrate properly. He tried, however. He sat cross-legged on the stone floor, the sunlight blinding on his white robe, twisted his hands into the traditional position and thought: *I live, and I will always live. Every cell of my body is regenerating at this very moment and will always do so . . .* And he tried to thrust his consciousness down into those cells to encourage them and lend their physicality to the strength of his mind. *Dying is meaningless. There is no reason for it. I will eliminate the Clock that tells my body to age. I will eliminate, eliminate the Clock.*

His concentration was gone. He couldn't speak to his body. He was watching a beetle crawl from sunlight into shadow while half his mind thought of Manuel.

How dare that kid say he'd spoken to God!

Dad Ose stood, dusting his robes off. Maybe a day without the Inner Think wouldn't matter. Maybe he'd try again in the evening. And then again, maybe Manuel's presumptuous sacrilege had cost him, Dad Ose, fifty years of his life. He flexed his muscles experimentally, and it seemed to him they felt older and feebler. Fear touched him, turning to anger. Manuel was trying to make a laughing stock of him, and Manuel ought to be dealt with severely.

But meanwhile, the sun was hot.

LEGEND OF THE AXOLOTL

The place where the Triad would meet was waiting for them, and those three people's happentracks were converging on this spot. The spot is now marked with a monument that may or may not be in the right place, because landscapes change. Legends change, too, over the aeons, and one particular legend is of interest because it is an analogy, telling how the Girl and her fellow neotenites came to be. It is a little more dramatic than the slow march of countless generations through which the neotenites evolved, and it goes like this:

There is a pool of water in a dusty place and animals come to slake their thirst there. Anteaters and ouakaris, cavies and capybaras drink together with none of that uneasy watchfulness that you see when carnivores are about, for there are no carnivores in this region. The animals drink long and leisurely, and the pool reflects their faces and the blue sky above them.

Axolotls live in the pool. They spend most of their time on the bottom, their small feet resting lightly on the pebbles and mud, stirring with the light currents when one of the larger animals comes wading nearby, but otherwise not moving much. They are silvery white and translucent, with pink frilly gills rising from beside their heads like soft horns. The humans of these parts call them water dolls, and accept them and their strange secret as a part of nature and therefore natural, without thinking too much about it.

What is the secret of the axolotls?

They are child salamanders, trapped forever in immaturity and forced to live and breed that way.

How did they get like that?

We must go back to young Earth, when Pangaea was one huge continent and the Dedos were lately come . . .

*

There was a Dedo named Kweilin who lived alone in her pavilion somewhere near the center of Pangaea. The area abounded in large animals, and some presentiment had caused Kweilin to decide to have a child. It is often said of the Dedos that they have the ability to foresee the Ifalong as accurately as the Oracle of the later Dream People; and Kweilin, ages earlier, had that power. She foresaw a happentrack in which she was surprised and mortally wounded by a thylacosmilus, a marsupial tiger of her time. It happened away from the pavilion and her Rock, and she was unable to get back for her Healing Stone, so she died.

If Kweilin was indeed on that happentrack, she would be needing a daughter.

She composed herself and allowed her psy to penetrate deep within her body until she became aware of her womb, and the egg waiting there. Carefully, she activated it. For a few days she watched over it. Then, satisfied that all was well, she withdrew her essence and resumed a normal life. The Rock was busy, winter was coming and the crops had to be stored. She had plenty to do, so it was several weeks before she discovered that all was not well within her womb.

She found out one day in midwinter when her work for the day was done, the fire built and crackling in the stone hearth of the pavilion, the life on Earth slow and herself with time to spare. She looked within her body, inspecting the growing child.

It was a mutant. She was not going to have a daughter, after all. By that one-in-seventeen chance, something different had happened, and the thing in her womb was one of those odd creatures who are no use to Starquin or themselves, being without the inborn Duty, without even the capacity to reproduce themselves. Such creatures, when they occur, are simply turned loose to fend for themselves after the minimum of mothering.

Oddly enough, they do quite well in the wild. They are strong and crafty and seem to have an affinity for animals. And, the Dedos sensed, Starquin seemed to have some feeling for them, useless though they are. Some Dedos called them "eremitas," although in legends they received a different name: Paragons.

Kweilin at first was mortified. She felt she had failed in some aspect of the Duty — or worse, that there might be something wrong in the make-up of her body. But this was nonsense, of course. The Dedos are pure; they can be no other way. Eventually she came to realize, as had many Dedos before her, that the birth of an eremita was perfectly normal, but rare. Therefore eremitas had their place in the scheme of things. Within a short while Kweilin had accepted this, and she settled down to her long pregnancy, concerned only to get it over with, to raise and release the eremita and to commence a true child before the thylacosmilus got her — if indeed it ever did.

She was four years pregnant and approaching the end of her time when the dreadful thing happened.

It was midwinter again and the snow lay lightly on the ground and the cold wind crackled among the yuccas. The nearby waterhole was frozen over and Kweilin had to smash the ice with a stone in order to fill her clay pot. The mature salamanders had long since left the waterhole and lay comatose under stones, half-buried in loose soil, hibernating. The many-faceted Rock, a little warmer than the surrounding earth, stood free of snow, a glittering black diamond as tall as the Dedo herself.

Kweilin had gathered sticks and built a fire in the pavilion, in a cloth-walled area open to the sky between the two chambers. The fire had been burning for two days, and the salamanders, sensing warmth, had drawn near. It was evening, the sky cloud-

less and the stars hard and brilliant, and Kweilin sat on a has-
sock filled with vicuna wool. Her mind traveled among the
stars as she thought and speculated; yet she was ever alert for
some sign from the Rock. Her face was hot with the flames.
A salamander dashed forward and seized a blazing brand.
Kweilin leaped up.

The creature had slipped under the loose foot of the cloth
wall, and now it tried to retreat that way, dragging the fire
behind it. Other salamanders appeared, taking their cue from
their leader, pulling and worrying at the fire, scattering the
glowing sticks. A fountain of sparks rose into the night air. The
sinuous bodies of the salamanders glistened and writhed as
they tugged the blazing sticks loose, oblivious of the heat, even
enjoying it. Kweilin ran around the fire and tried to kick the
salamanders away. Some of them were bigger than her foot and
merely rolled with her kicks and returned.

A thread of flame ran up the pavilion wall.

Kweilin screamed. She began to beat at the flames with her
hands, but the wall blazed on, billowing in with her blows.
Other fires started as the salamanders escaped with their
sticks, dragging them under the fabric. As she beat at the walls,
a flame trickled up her robe. She felt it, saw it, tripped and fell.
The flames were all around her, leaping against the black sky,
consuming the dry fabric, while the salamanders darted here
and there, running unharmed through the flames . . .

Later Kweilin found herself lying on the hard ground some
distance away from the smoldering skeleton of the pavilion.
She wanted to get back to her possessions, to use the Healing
Stone there, but she felt too weak, and the dusting of snow was
cool against her wounds. She lay and watched. The fabric had
dropped from the frame of the pavilion like cooked skin and lay
in a glowing heap.

It seemed to Kweilin that a huge salamander straddled the
ruins, the dying flames licking his belly while he watched her
with glowing, knowing eyes. Then he nodded his head a few
times, in that mechanical way peculiar to cold-blooded creatures, and was gone.

Kweilin crawled back to the wreckage . . .

In later years Kweilin often wondered if the terror of the fire and the pain afterwards had caused that strange quirk that set her child apart from all other eremitas, who were perfect beings, if useless. She had reared the child to the best of her ability and, after a couple of centuries, she set him free to fend for himself. His name was Siang and he was to become a legend because of the Thing-he-did, later. Whether the Thing-he-did was a good thing or a bad thing will be forever debated among Dedos.

Starquin had no doubts. The Thing-that-Siang-did was to Starquin's perfect mind so wrong, so contrary to the rules of interspecies contact, that he did something totally illogical, something that had never happened before.

Starquin lost his temper.

Somewhere up there, out there and everywhere, there was a flash of quick, hard psy that passed through every sentient creature in the Solar System, and many creatures beyond that system, too. They felt it as pain, as heat, as sorrow. They felt it for an instant; then it was gone. The more intelligent ones wondered for a moment, then shrugged in their animal way and carried on. The lower animals paused momentarily in their eating. Ten billion gossamer gadflies died.

The Thing-that-Siang-did is another story.

The thing that Starquin did may just possibly be true. It is said that he raged for a microsecond, then found an outlet. He vented his rage on the creature that had caused all the trouble: a small salamander that lived in a particular region of Pangaea, an amphibian that mated in warm ponds and gave birth to its young there — young that metamorphosed after a while, turning from a swimming water doll to a crawling land salamander.

To the salamander Starquin said: *"You will live in water all of your life. You will always be a white newt. Never again will you play with the fire you love so much. You will be born in water, you will live and die in water, and you will never, never feel the warmth of flames upon your flesh again."*

Starquin knew that was the worst punishment of all, for a salamander.

BY THE AXOLOTL POOL

*T*he Dome had become hostile. The food chutes were delivering only sporadically and the food itself tasted unpleasant. The various robots still obeyed orders, but in a curiously sullen manner. The Rainbow thundered from time to time and the vibrations could be felt in distant regions of the Dome. The Cuidadors felt beleaguered. Only the Specialists seemed unperturbed, going about their duties cheerfully — with the exception of Brutus, who was morose and withdrawn.

"Still brooding about what I said," concluded Juni irritably, not being a person to feel remorse. "As if we don't have enough to worry about. And that Mole of yours doesn't seem to have done much good, either, Zo."

The disincorporation of the Mole had been an anticlimax. He had been prepared and bedded down by the raccoon-nurses, and the various electrodes and tubes had been attached. Zozula had thrown the switch personally, dispatching the brain-patterns of the Mole into the computer.

The Rainbow had displayed opaque clouds, as if considering the matter. Then there had been a brief growl that shook the room. Then nothing. The Mole had presumably been absorbed. Zozula had tuned into Dream Earth.

Nothing was changed. The parties went on; the adventurers fought wild beasts; the Love Palace was doing a roaring trade. This was unexpected, since ancient records indicated that the introduction of a new mind always resulted in a pause in events while Composite Reality adjusted. It was as though the Rainbow had simply rejected the Mole's mind.

Unable to face the hostility of the Dome and the complaints of Juni, Zozula had gathered up the Girl and gone Outside.

*

The axolotls drowsed in a pool of warm water. They moved slowly under their shimmering ceiling, isolated from the world their ancestors had known. They were trapped in eternal childhood, but they didn't know it. They felt like adults, and only Starquin knew what they had lost.

One of them began to eat in slow, huge gulps, consuming the larva of some insect before relapsing into its accustomed torpor. "Just a little, not a lot'll satisfy an axolotl," runs a local saying. They were undemanding creatures.

A shadow fell over the pool. Human voices spoke.

"I feel . . . strange. Maybe I should lie down for a while. I don't seem to have any strength. My limbs feel so heavy."

"It'll take a while for your body to adjust." Zozula regarded the Girl. He hadn't been able to find clothes big enough for her, so he'd wrapped her in a blanket and half-carried her out of the Dome, past the Bowl, to this quiet place. He needed to adjust, too. The last few days had passed in a dream that was part nightmare.

"Why did you bring me here?" The Girl watched his face with baby-blue eyes. Her speech was slurred and awkward.

"You must become one of us — a Keeper. A Keeper has died, we need a replacement, and you have all the relevant data in your mind. So you must take her place. You must supervise the natural effects and live with us."

"No!" The Girl made a sudden small gesture of impatience. "I'm bored with this game. This landscape — it's dull. And you're dull, too. Forgive me for mentioning it, but maybe you should change your type. I think I'll smallwish away. I need to look at myself. I don't feel right at all."

In her drugged state, she still thought she was a Marilyn.

"Listen to me . . ."

"I wish . . ." Her plump face was set. "I wish I was back in the Pyrenees, fifty-two six hundred, or thereabouts." She clenched her fists.

Nothing happened.

She opened her eyes, saw Zozula and the pool and, looming over everything, the giant Dome. "I must be out of psy," she said miserably.

"You're not out of psy. You're in the real world."

"I know that."

"No, you don't. You have no idea. What's happened to you is stranger than you've ever dreamed of — and you've been dreaming all your life. Now, just sit still and listen . . ." And Zozula went on to tell the Girl everything: the Dream People and their lives of pretense in the Rainbow, the Do-Portal through which he'd brought her into the real world, the continents and the oceans and the Wild Humans living in their primitive villages along the coast, the horse clouds and the snake clouds — and the Chokes, which could kill you. He told her all this and more, while the sun dropped behind the hills and the shadows reached toward them. He told her about the other things — the legends and the half-truths, and his feeling that there was Something Else, a great Existence beyond the physical evidence of the real world.

And the Girl didn't believe a word of it.

So Zozula resorted to the final proof.

He took a small knife from his pocket, drew her arm toward him and nicked the flesh, just below the elbow. Blood flowed.

"What did you do that for?" The Girl snatched her arm away, staring incredulously at the blood. "What have you done to me? How *could* you do this to me? Was that a smallwish? If it was, it was the cruelest one I've ever known."

"It's no smallwish, my dear. That cut is real. It's the most real thing that ever happened to you." Zozula's heart bled, too.

"I feel so strange . . ." Her eyes were tightly closed against the pain. She'd never known pain before. "My arm, it . . ." She wanted to say "It *hurts,*" but she could not voice the concept. "I've never felt so unhappy in my life. Go away! Leave me alone!" Tears trickled from beneath her lids and, after a while, she opened her eyes to see if he was gone.

He still sat there, watching her. She smallwished again, and nothing happened. She opened her eyes. The pain was subsiding but the outrage remained. She looked at her arm, really seeing it for the first time. She stared. The drug was wearing off.

"Yes, it's your arm," said Zozula.

"But . . ." The cut forgotten, she prodded the plump flesh, kneaded it and noticed that her fingers were short and podgy. "What's happened to me?" she whispered, and she crawled to the edge of the pool.

And looked down at her reflection.

TRIAD!

••••••••••••••••••••••••••

Come! Hear about the Trinity of legendary fame,
The Oldster and the Artist and the Girl-with-no-Name!
 — Song of Earth

The Song of Earth tells many versions of that meeting between the Oldster and the Artist and the Girl-with-no-Name,
each version reflecting the culture, the hopes and prejudices of
the minstrel. One thing all versions have in common is the
axolotl. The symbolism of that tiny creature has appealed to
countless generations. It was the original neotenite. And in all
those versions, the axolotl pool is just about the only thing that
is correct.

In the Rainbow, however, reposes the truth of one particular
happentrack. And on this happentrack there was no joyous
clasping of hands, no sense of the fulfillment to come, no pre-
monitions of glory.

What really happened was that Manuel arrived in the middle
of an argument. The other two were hardly aware of his presence. Zozula looked a little sheepish and the Girl looked —
well . . . grotesque. The sight of her caused Manuel to hesitate
and to swallow unexpectedly, so that he almost retched.

She was sitting beside the pool like a sun-softened sack of
lard, weeping.

"What kind of monster have you turned me into? I was beautiful, and it cost me a whole Bigwish. I was a Marilyn! And now
you've spoiled it all. I'll be stuck with this body for years,
now!"

Manuel looked around, seeking something to divert her, but the evening landscape was bleak, the scanty wind-blown scrub like drowning fingers in a dusty sea, the wind suddenly chill, the axolotl pool dark and foreboding and the little creatures themselves moving below the surface like pale shadows of corruption.

He placed the Simulator on the ground. "I have something to show you," he said tentatively. "This is going to make you feel better. It's called 'love.'"

Zozula gave him an impatient glance, then turned to the Girl again. "You remember Eulalie, the goddess who contacted you? She was my wife. She was dying, and we needed you to take her place. She put all the knowledge of the Dream Earth technology into your head."

But the Girl wasn't interested in that. "How can you say this is my real body? I know what I really look like. I spent years as Myself. I wasn't all that pretty, but I liked Myself. That was the real me. But this body is some kind of a freak. In all the Big-wishes people have ever had, I'm sure they never thought up anything so repulsive as this. You must be sick, really sick."

Zozula tried to explain. "Yourself isn't really *yourself*, if you know what I mean. Yourself is what you might have looked like on a different happentrack, where neoteny hadn't happened to people. Yourself is a white lie the Rainbow tells, to make everything seem a little more real. Living there in the Rainbow, able to do whatever they like, people can lose all pride. So the Rainbow tells them this one little lie: That people — real people — still look the way they used to millennia ago."

"Well, what about him?" The Girl pointed at Manuel. "He doesn't look so bad to me!"

"He's just a Wild Human."

"Well, make me into a Wild Human, then, if you've run out of your own type of body."

"Wild Humans are not suitable hosts." As Zozula spoke to the Girl he gave Manuel a furious look and jerked his head in a gesture of dismissal. Matters were difficult enough without this youth hanging around. "You wouldn't understand the details."

"Try us," said Manuel.

Now Zozula gave the boy his full attention. "Just who in hell are you?"

"Manuel," said Manuel. There was little else he could say. But the effect of the name on Zozula was surprising. His anger faded, as a curious recollection touched his mind for a moment and was gone. Manuel? "It's a common enough name," he said. Then it came to him: a recent dream, and a woman in black saying, *"Zozula, you have been chosen. You, she, and a young man named Manuel will form the Triad. Look after the others, and always remember Shenshi, for I have some vanity, too."*

He regarded the boy in sudden interest. "Why did you come here?"

"Perhaps to learn," said Manuel. "Look!" He pointed suddenly upward, so imperiously that they followed his gaze . . .

The slow curvature of the Dome was visible as a black mass against the deepening gloom of the coming night, and the stars were appearing around its rim. The Dome was huge, pressing down on them, with no clouds to conceal its immensity. No lights showed; the dust of aeons had blanketed the ports. Yet something was happening up there, far away in the sky near the horizon of the black arc. Just for an instant a faint halo glowed. Then there was a flash that was more than simple light . . .

And the three of them, down beside the axolotl pool, saw in their minds something that their eyes couldn't possibly have registered. The Girl gasped and Manuel smiled, and Zozula grappled to retain the image of flashing steel and whirling wheels with heavy spokes, pumping rods and a core of great heat, and two men . . . Then it was gone, and they were left with only the power of it.

"The worst thing . . ." the Girl said softly, "the thing you do when there is nothing else to keep your humanity alive. Some of us call it the Celestial Steam Locomotive. You ride it when you've tried everything else."

"Will you explain it, please?" Manuel asked Zozula.

Zozula looked at him for a long time, and in the end saw

something that satisfied him. Slowly, knowing very well he was offering an excuse and not an explanation, he spoke.

"A long time ago Mankind reached the stage where only a select few people could understand enough to keep up with technological advances. And as time went by, fewer still built upon the work of those few, and then just a handful, the most brilliant minds on Earth. Then maybe a couple, dreaming incredible dreams, directing work that only the Rainbow could understand. They built on the work of generations of others, and they died. That was the end of it. Humanity was surrounded by machines that ran themselves — though *how*, and what some of them *did*, nobody knows. Other machines helped them. Maybe the Rainbow knows all the answers. But we don't even know what questions to ask, or how to ask them. So I'm not ashamed of admitting that I can't explain the existence of the Celestial Steam Locomotive. I have to put up a front, though. It can be terrifying for the Keepers when their own leader admits he doesn't know what's going on . . ."

The Girl said, "I've always known exactly what was going on, because I made it happen, more or less. So this is the real world? Well, I don't like it. Take me back to my own world, please."

"Let me show you something," said Manuel once again, and he activated the Simulator.

"Just another machine." Zozula watched the lights begin to glow. "I've seen these before."

The images began to form before the Simulator, brighter than usual, because of the darkness around. A pale mist, glowing on the faces of the watchers and plating the axolotl pool with silver. The little water dolls, disturbed, rose to the surface and watched, too.

"The storm, you see . . ." The clouds were there, building up, and below them the tossing waves; and below that again, huge and graceful shapes that puzzled Manuel because he hadn't put them in the picture himself. Were these shapes some residue of Belinda herself? Something from her mind that had slipped into the picture while he was composing it? They swam in formation, the whales, and there was something organized and purposeful about their movements. Then they were gone and the clouds were suggesting the flying hair of a girl swimming, dancing underwater. Manuel had composed all this. He remembered. He was trembling and his palms were moist.

"Remarkable . . ." Zozula was leaning forward.

The Girl was silent. She'd never seen anything like this before. She'd never imagined such a thing as abstract art could exist. Where she came from, people were practical. They wanted something? They got it. They were bored with something? They threw it away. Art? It had no place in the relentless pursuit of pleasure. It was too slow, too introspective, too passive. Yet this performance by the barrel-shaped boy's machine was oddly fascinating. In some way it made her think of a childhood she'd never had.

Manuel said apologetically, "I was told it didn't have enough love. But I think it has more, now."

Zozula said quietly, "It has love." It seemed Eulalie was very close to him again.

And now Belinda was there, dancing before the little group, dancing in the dark like a glowing naiad — not like a girl would dance in the flesh, so you could see her elbows and her knees and her pores, but dancing in the minds of the watchers. An axolotl would not have recognized any human figure in those images, but the humans did. For them, the clouds spelled *love*.

The Girl was crying, sobbing quietly as she watched, blinking because she didn't want to miss anything.

The mists, deepening their rainbow colors, gave one final message of hope and courage and loss, and faded away. Manuel switched the machine off.

Zozula was talking softly, almost to himself. ". . . but there is no hope, is there? The Dome is dying. Everything's dying, slowly. What's the use of love, now? Love died early in the game." His gaze was turned inward and he'd forgotten he was a Cuidador in the presence of two lesser mortals. Then he blinked and looked at Manuel — and now he saw him. Something passed between them. He said, "Forgive me, boy. My wife just died."

Manuel said, "I'm sorry. I just lost somebody too."

After a pause, Zozula asked, "The storm-girl?"

"Yes."

And because Zozula and the Girl seemed receptive, Manuel told them the story of Belinda.

Afterward Zozula said, "I kept almost seeing her in your mind-painting, and then she was gone again. Why couldn't you have made her a little more clear?"

"I know how she looks. I'll never forget that. I wanted to show how she made me feel."

"Was she a Wild Human?"

"She was not from the village. Neither was she from the Dome. She never told me where she came from. I was afraid to ask too many questions, because . . ." He hesitated. "I don't like being laughed at."

"We won't laugh. Go on."

"I didn't want to pin her down. She never seemed quite real. I think I was frightened that if I really tried to identify her, I'd find she didn't exist. She was full of life at first, and she made me laugh a lot. She only had a few rags of clothes, and they were mostly skins. Later she became quiet and she seemed to get very weak. She was very thin and breathless . . ."

"Thin? Like me, you mean?"

Manuel laughed. "She was much prettier than you, Zozula."

For a while now, an excitement had been growing in Zozula that he could barely suppress. Now he speculated aloud. "A slim human, breathless in an atmosphere that a Wild Human can easily withstand . . . Where could she come from? Is there really some kind of city in the delta jungle? She could have drifted down the coast from there, in a boat. They're out there somewhere, the True Humans. They must be."

"I'm tired," the Girl said suddenly. "Can we go back now?"

Zozula said, "We're not going back to the way we were. Not yet. There are more important things on Earth than creating special effects for a lot of selfish zombies. I've lived all my life in and around this Dome, did you know that? And suddenly I'm beginning to realize I haven't been doing my job properly. I've visited the village twice and communicated with people in other Domes. But I have to admit that I know nothing about the world. That's a sobering admission for a man who's been top god for longer than I care to remember. So now, I'd like to find out what's going on out here. I'm going to ask some very small questions. Ones that I'll understand the answers to. Then maybe I'll be worthy of my job and able to solve some of the problems we have in there."

"Take me back first," said the Girl anxiously.

"No. You're coming along. There's hope for you, Girl — you were crying at Manuel's pictures. You come with me, and perhaps we'll find you a proper body."

Manuel picked up the Simulator.

"And you too, Manuel. The three of us — we each have something I haven't seen in anyone for a long time, except for my wife — she had it. But maybe we're the only three left. Let's stick together for a while."

So that was it. Nothing dramatic, no thunderbolts from Starquin, no sudden materialization of Dedos, no mysterious writings on rocks. This account of the formation of the Triad may not be as dramatic, as flamboyant as some, but it has the ring of truth. *Let's stick together for a while.* Very probable words, when spoken by a man who needs company and love, when spoken to two young people who have demonstrated that they can help fill his need.

HERE ENDS THAT PART OF
THE SONG OF EARTH KNOWN TO MEN AS
THE CREATION OF THE TRIAD

OUR TALE CONTINUES WITH THE GROUP
OF STORIES AND LEGENDS KNOWN AS
IN THE LAND OF LOST DREAMS

where the Triad meets many strange creatures
and, in so doing,
learn their own faults,
return to the real world
and prepare to meet their destiny

THE ASTRAL BUILDERS

*T*here was a river that flowed from the mountains behind Pu'este to the cool waters of the old South Atlantic. It is gone now. The jungle has turned to desert and the drifting sand has obliterated the watercourse, but in the 143rd millennium it carried green glacial run-off through the hills, passing several kilometers north of the stupendous structure of Dome Azul, through the coastal rain forest to a flat delta.

Here in this delta lived the greatest and smallest civilization that Earth has ever known.

Their minarets rose from the ground into the clouds. Their machines hummed quietly in vast underground chambers. Their vehicles glided without wheels, without sound, along broad avenues lined with trees that grew nowhere else on Earth — indeed, nowhere else in the whole of the Greataway. They sent their ships around the Galaxy and they saw creatures that no man or alien had ever seen before.

They were sterile.

Consequently, they poured into their art everything that another race might have poured into procreation. Their paintings were breathtaking, their songs would make people weep. Their statuary was dancing stone, and their poems spoke of emotions that ordinary humans had never known but that to these people were as real as the trees and the crocodiles.

And all this within a delta island no more than a kilometer across. No human outside the delta ever saw this wonderful civilization, except for a brief glimpse afforded to a Cuidador named Zozula, by way of the Rainbow. And when it died, it left no remains other than a whisper that became a legend.

The river flowed swiftly on two sides of the triangular island; on the third side lay the ocean. The river water was cold. This, and the crocodiles, discouraged the people from leaving the island, where they grew a few simple crops and fished when the mood took them, meanwhile creating, creating. The river flowed brown for most of the year, having picked up silt and broken vegetation during its journey through the rain forest.

But once a year it flowed clear and green, and carried to the delta a flotilla of tiny boats carved from balsa: model galleons, frigates and dhows.

And in each boat lay a human baby, crying and waving tiny fists at the sky.

*

Hopho soared in the clouds. He had linked the minds of Antilla and Buth, Lergs and Stril, and added a couple of ideas from Sintel, and fashioned the whole into an intricate composite that would solve all the mysteries of the world — once he had found the means to turn that last key . . .

"Hopho!"

The cry cut through his dreaming. In his agitation he lost control of a billion carefully constructed memory banks, which promptly dissolved back into the aether.

"Hopho!"

It was a real cry, a shout made by physical waves, and it shocked him. He slammed the door on his vast imaginary computer, commanding it to stay intact until he got back. He ran down the marble staircase, dreamed up by Fabel, into Eloise's time-city, leaped into a transporter imagined by Awa, flitted through Trippata's hyperspace to the terminal of Su.

He dismounted. An invisible hand was shaking his shoulder. He went through the ritual of decuerping. This was his own invention — a rapid way to return to the physical world.

"Hopho!"

The sense of touch returned and he felt a coolness against his back. He felt the hand as well as the shaking; it was warm. He heard the voice again: "Hopho, decuerp!" and he smelled the stink of the jungle. His mouth tasted sour. He opened his eyes. He was back in the physical world. The jungle cried. He heard it, tasted it, smelled it, saw it, felt it with the five senses of discomfort. He wished he were back in the plenum. Physically, he rose to his feet and, physically, slopped through the mud to the riverbank.

He saw the little boats. He lumbered down onto the beach, kicking at the dreamers recumbent on the mud, yelling, shaking them awake. Their eyes cleared and they began to climb to their feet. The shout was taken up by twenty voices.

"Decuerp! Decuerp!" They moved slowly and painfully, handicapped by a genetic defect.

The tiny boats drifted round the river bend in twos and threes — coracles, clinker dinghies, pinnaces. The thin cries of the babies came clearly across the water.

The crocodiles came too. They rose from the banks and glided into the water. They closed on the small craft and crunched them in long jaws. They tossed the babies into the air and swallowed them whole. The tribe screamed in despair.

Some of them struggled up the bank to outflank the brutes. Others waded out to create a diversion. The crocodiles cruised the deeper water, picking off the tiny boats as they rounded the bend, gobbling the living cargoes. The people wept and splashed. The boats were coming thick and fast now, twenty or more spread out across the river's width. Some of them hit whirlpools and spun. Others, with tiny sails, reaped the wind and made sudden aimless darts to and fro. These were the ones that stood the best chance of survival.

Hopho waded out to intercept a schooner. On a broad reach it sailed directly toward him, pursued by a crocodile with a fast rippling wake. Hopho could see the occupant: a plump baby wrapped in a scrap of cloth, face scarlet and puckered with crying. It lay with its head against the transom, legs on either side of the mainmast. It squealed and kicked, and its foot became entangled in the threads of the self-steering gear. The sails luffed. The little schooner came up into the wind and stopped.

Hopho shouted and scooped at the water with cupped hands, trying to draw the boat nearer.

The crocodile nipped the transom, teeth like pincers, nostrils cavernous behind the baby's head. Hopho dredged a rock from under the water and threw it. He was unused to physical coordination and the rock hit the surface an arm's length before him, splashing water into his face.

When he opened his eyes, boat and baby were gone . . .

Scenes like this happened annually between the years 143,306 and 143,624 Cyclic, throughout the short life of this great and imaginary civilization. It is of little importance in the sweep of history, although it remains forever the guilty secret of many generations of Cuidadors in Dome Azul.

Because the Cuidadors destroyed the civilization of the delta, unwittingly.

*

When the delta civilization is mentioned in present-day singings — which is not often — its people are referred to in the masculine gender. This is for convenience only, because in fact they had no sex. They did not carry the seeds of the Inner Think, either. And they were sickly; they lived, on average, a mere forty years.

The very existence of the tribe depended on their rescuing from the crocodiles each year a number of babies greater than the number of people who had died. Some years they succeeded; other years they failed. Sometimes older people had to sacrifice their own lives for the sake of a baby.

Sometimes the baby was not worth it.

Hopho was thirty years old and brilliant beyond measure. When he saw a baby approaching in a kayak he knew it was probably destined to be less intelligent than he. However, he also knew that he probably had only ten years left to contribute to the imaginative gestalt of the civilization.

He ran awkwardly upriver. Lergs was also wading toward the

kayak, and Hopho sensed that Lergs's chances of survival were poor. Lergs reached for the little boat with a fat arm. The water swirled nearby.

"Lergs!"

Hopho dragged the kayak ashore. The baby looked up at him with clear blue eyes and smiled. Hopho seized Lergs's arm and felt the whole body jerk spasmodically as the crocodile tore at some underwater part. Hopho pulled, feet sinking into the ooze, and suddenly Lergs slid free. Hopho dragged him into the shallows.

Lergs was terribly light, and he trailed a cloud of red.

"Let me go, Hopho."

"We'll fix you up. Eloise is good with wounds."

"No. Push me out. It's better."

"I need you for the gestalt, Lergs!"

Lergs smiled, a quick baring of teeth. "That's the first time I've heard you lie, Hopho. Face the truth, friend, you'd do much better with someone young. Someone like Trevis. I'm just a muddled philosopher, but Trevis has a clear mind. He can trace the movement of galaxies for a million years into the Ifalong. With his talent, you'll have what you want. You already have all the reasoning power in the rest of the team, and all the knowledge. Trevis has an instinctive grip of the Ifalong. With him in your team, there's nothing you can't do!"

Now Hopho spoke aloud, using a brief sentence culled from the grunts of the Wild Humans.

"I love you, Lergs, my friend," he said.

It was a primitive statement, like death, and when the crocodile pushed its snout out of the water and took what was left of Lergs, Hopho did not object.

The little boats came on, borne on the snaking currents of the big river that in the Ifalong would be dead and dry and blowing sand. Only the crocodiles would survive, moving on elsewhere — timeless, perfect creatures.

*

The little boats were fewer now, and more crudely constructed. Only the occasional one rounded the bend. Upstream, the great river was smooth, its waters almost empty of human life. Some boats had floated out to sea and their occupants would soon die. Most had been destroyed by the crocodiles, and the green waters were strewn with wreckage. A few had been gathered in by the people of the delta and the babies were being fussed over and wrapped in coarse cloth. Traditional food was being prepared from the pounded root of the *hierba lechera*.

In the year 143,299 Cyclic, a Wild Human named Dolores had made the mistake of thinking such a baby was one of her own species. She'd taken it from the water, wondering, and carried it to her village. It had been seven years before she realized her mistake, and her tribe had forced her to take the child back to the riverbank and leave it there. The child had been the first member of the delta civilization and, the following year, had retrieved two little boats from the crocodiles . . .

Now the delta people prepared for the year to come.

They caught and dried fish and they sowed seed. They rigged primitive shelters for the babies and the people who were going to look after them. They discussed their projects and decided on the most suitable gestalt teams.

They decided Hopho's project held the most promise for new discoveries. Antilla, Buth and Stril were going to join him again. Trevis volunteered to replace Lergs.

"No!" said Yato, who worked alone.

"Why not?" Hopho respected Yato. They all did. He was a brilliant abstract historian. In the course of his lifetime, and without building on the work of any predecessor, he had traced the flow of human existence up to the present day. Working by intellect alone, he had seen the Beginning, visualized the emergence of life on Earth, evolution, diverging happentracks, wars, ice ages, everything . . .

For instance, Yato had informed the tribe that the Dome, a great mound in the distance, was probably full of sleeping humans living vicarious lives in the circuits of a giant computer.

"Technology would always outpace the ability of the mass of people to adapt to it," he explained. "And at the same time, increased leisure would encourage the development of sedentary pursuits. Finally, people wouldn't be able to face the real world — the crowding, the pressures, the foul atmosphere, the hopelessness and pointlessness of death — so they would build a safe place where they could dream forever. And to help them dream, they would build a vast storehouse of knowledge with almost infinite reasoning capacity, a composite of all the smaller computers they'd built over the ages."

Now Trevis picked up the thread of that explanation — and Trevis was a futurian. He began to project Yato's theories and to evaluate all the happentracks of the nearby Ifalong.

"If I join your group, Hopho, the tribe is doomed. We will have the capacity to gain total knowledge of the Galaxy from the beginning to the end of Time. So we will be destroyed, because someone more powerful than us will want it that way."

"What could be more powerful than us, if we have total knowledge?"

"Brute force will always defeat knowledge, Hopho."

"With what motive?"

And now Trevis smiled. "It's a very old motive and it has no meaning to us. But for what it's worth, I'll vocalize the way the Wild Humans say it: *jealousy.*"

"We cannot stem the flood tide," Hopho quoted an old tribal saying to hide his unease, "but at least we can move into another dimension."

"Not this time. We're going to be hit in our most vulnerable spot. Shall we cuerp?"

So they lay down together: Hopho, Trevis, Antilla, Buth and Stril, and they allowed their minds to wash over one another. Together they climbed out of their earthly environment, using Moloquit's simple astral escalator. Moloquit had died a long time previously, but they had retained his most powerful images. Soon they arrived at a stage that Hopho could only describe as the *right place*, although it was not a place in any normal meaning of the word. They picked up the threads of their last great works, and their thoughts were like an infinite spider's web glittering with the dew of ideas. Knowledge flowed like electricity; theories were formed, accepted, proved, built upon. It was an ecstasy of learning and there was no limit to it. There was nothing they could not know. Yato's seeds bloomed and all the past was catalogued. Finally, Trevis's new images began to flow into the gestalt. It was as though he were saying:

"We know the rules and we know how it was. Now let's discover how it will be."

And another year went by.

THE FIRST QUEST OF THE TRIAD

Through swamp and steaming jungle to the delta in the north,
Three people reached the Astral Builders, where they found a fourth.
— Song of Earth

Zozula said, "I thought the Mole might help us put the Rainbow right, but it didn't work out. Now, the other day I saw something strange in the Rainbow: a city inhabited by True Humans, in the delta. At first I thought I was scanning an ancient memory bank, but the Rainbow said it was the present day. There were land vehicles and starships and pink towers — all kinds of wonderful things. It was a very advanced technology. We must visit those people and enlist their help in putting the Rainbow right, before the whole Dome is destroyed."

"There's no city in the delta," said Manuel.

"Have you ever been to the delta?"

"Well, no. But Hasqual has. He's traveled all over the world. If there were a city in the delta, he'd have told us. All there is, is swamp and jungle and crocodiles, and a few tribes of hunting people. Life is hard in the jungle." He regarded Zozula critically. "I can't imagine True Humans wanting to live there."

The Girl said, "You never know. I've known jungles to cover whole worlds. It's easy to miss something."

"Quite right, Girl. It's worth investigating, anyway. Your Belinda had the appearance of a True Human, Manuel. She had to come from somewhere. We must explore every possibility," said Zozula cunningly.

It was morning and they sat in the ground-level of the Dome.

These were the Transitional Quarters that millennia ago were used to house visitors from Outside whom the Dome inhabitants did not quite trust because of their unpredictable nature or their unusual diseases. In these cases, communication between the inhabitants and the newcomers was by visiphone and all elevator shafts were sealed off. Whole communities had grown up in the Transitional Quarters from time to time, had endured for a century or so and then died out or moved on. And the robots, cleaning cavies and washdogs had been sent in to remove the traces of their existence.

For the last couple of hundred years Zozula had maintained a stable of shrugleggers and vampiros in the quarters for use on his occasional forays Outside.

Manuel bit into a slab of food, which, if he had known its constituents, he would never have allowed near his mouth. But the principles of the Dome's recycling system were mercifully unknown to him. The sticky confection tasted good and the prospect of action began to appeal. "All right," he said. "We have to start looking somewhere."

The Girl said uneasily, "It's not far, is it?"

"We will ride shrugleggers," said Zozula and left them for a moment, to return with three shambling beasts the like of which Manuel had never seen and the Girl had certainly never dreamed of.

"What are they?" she asked. "They don't . . . bite, do they?" She was learning to anticipate pain.

"They're harmless animals, bred many years ago in much the same way as the Specialists were bred. I believe there are bear genes in their make-up."

Zozula was wrong, of course. The shrugleggers were discovered on Ilos III in the year 83,426 Cyclic. Armless bipeds with gigantic thighs, they foraged in the ooze of swamps and were brought back to Earth for use as beasts of burden in remote areas during a period when human philosophy was influenced by the Kikihuahua Examples.

Zozula strapped harnesses onto the creatures, providing seats high on their backs. "Come on, Girl. Manuel and I will help you up."

A short while later they rode out into the morning sun, the

shrugleggers striding steadily north, following the course of the stream that carried away the run-off from the Dome. Behind Zozula, jerking irritably at the rope fastened around its neck, a vampiro hopped and scuttled, trying to keep up.

No humans saw the departure of the Triad on their first quest. Only a scattering of guanacos, munching thoughtfully, raised their heads and watched them go by with expressions of supercilious disinterest. It was a quiet, warm morning and the delta forest could be seen as a smudge of green beyond the broad brown plain. Behind them, trails of smoke from the cooking fires of Pu'este rose vertically in the still air.

Above, wispy elongated clouds moved slowly eastward, out to sea. Manuel glanced at them unhappily, but said nothing. Presumably Zozula knew what he was doing.

*

By late afternoon Manuel was not so sure. The arid grassland was behind them and they were entering a transitional region of fleshy scrub and a few tall trees, and it was clear that their present rate of progress would bring them to the forest proper by nightfall. The sun hung low over the mountains to the west.

Finally Manuel called, "We have to stop!"

Zozula glanced around irritably but made no attempt to check the stride of his shruglegger.

Losing patience, Manuel shouted, "If you want to die, I don't!" and brought his shruglegger to a choking halt by throwing his forearm around its neck and pulling back. He slid to the ground.

Stopping his beast, too, Zozula looked down at Manuel. "What do you mean, die? Are you suggesting there's danger ahead?"

"There's always danger in the dark. We have to camp here and now, because if we go any farther it'll be too late to light a fire. And I'm not going to be caught in the open without one." As he spoke he was tugging up clumps of dry grass and piling them in a heap. Then he squatted down and, cocking an eye at the sun, began to focus the rays of his hemitrex — the hard shell of a jellyfish evolved to deflect harmful rays — and direct a cone of light onto the tinder. A wisp of smoke rose.

Zozula conceded defeat, scrambled from his shruglegger and helped the Girl down. Manuel began to cook strips of dried iguana on sticks that he pushed into the ground and set at an angle, while the Girl watched this demonstration of competence with some awe.

"I wouldn't know how to do it," she said. Even the wind on her face felt strange.

"You'll learn," said Manuel. Seeing Zozula was out of earshot, untying the vampiro, he added quietly, "I hope Zozula learns, too. All this is about as queer to him as it is to you, but he won't admit it. There *is* danger, you know. Real danger. We have to take precautions."

She said, "Just tell me what to do."

"Here, take these sticks and cook yourself something to eat."

Zozula arrived, leading the vampiro, which was blinking at the fire unhappily. "Now, then," he said briskly, "we'll just set up the vampiro and we'll be all ready for the night. Oh — and you don't have to eat that stuff, Girl. I have plenty of real food here." He reached into a bag under the vampiro's chin and produced squares of confectionery. The Girl, who had already gagged over a shred of half-raw iguana, took a piece gratefully.

"I'll get used to your kind of food before long, Manuel," she said. "I really will."

Manuel grunted, munching with noisy appreciation at his meat. Then he stood in some alarm as Zozula clapped his hands with a sharp report.

"Stand back," said the Keeper imperiously, "while I set up the vampiro." He gestured to the animal, which didn't move. Shouting an unintelligible command, he clapped his hands again.

Slowly, reluctantly, the vampiro began to open its huge, membranous wings.

The vampiro had been created at the Mordecai N. Whirst Institute many thousands of years ago as a traveling companion for members of various cults who, partly under the influence of the kikihuahua teachings, preferred an open-air life. The vampiros were basically huge bats that provided shelter and could be used as a light pack animal. When given the appropriate command, the vampiro would spread its huge wings, curving them around its body to form a tent that could sleep four humans.

If this operation is to be performed successfully, it is important that the vampiro's wings should not touch the blazing sticks of a roaring fire.

Screeching and trailing smoke, the vampiro reared up and began to flap wildly, fanning sparks and embers into the faces of the Triad. With an oath, Zozula threw himself at the beast. "Help me, Manuel!" he shouted. "The bastard's trying to take off!"

Before the youth could move, however, the vampiro wrapped its wings protectively around itself, nursing its pain — and incidentally nursing Zozula, who found himself smothered in a leathery embrace. Manuel hesitated, torn between the need to help the Cuidador, whose face was turning purple, and the need to laugh. The Girl had no such dilemma. With no real appreciation of danger, she was almost crying with delight. This was much better than Dream Earth. The vampiro stood rigidly erect, clutching Zozula to its breast, so that only his long nose and furious eyes could be seen above the cloak of the creature's wings. His muffled shouting ceased and his eyes began to bulge as the vampiro's fingerbones tightened like steel bands across his chest.

Manuel seized a brand from the fire and waved it in front of the vampiro's eyes. It stumbled backward, releasing Zozula, who fell to the ground, coughing weakly.

"The vampiro is not accustomed to fires," he muttered. "You should have realized that. He's spent most of his life in the Dome. You scared him out of his wits."

Manuel hung his head. "We need the fire," he said.

Zozula, recovering, began to bustle about, shepherding the vampiro to a safe distance from the flames, tethering the shrug-leggers, who had been watching events with some alarm, taking an inventory of their meager food supply, and all the while stumbling over roots and bushes and cursing, being unused to walking on anything other than a smooth floor.

They spent the early hours of the night under the tent of the vampiro's wings, but shortly after midnight the fire collapsed and the wind carried a drift of sparks toward the creature. Panic-stricken, it folded its wings about itself and shuffled rapidly away into the bush.

In the morning they awoke stiff with cold. A dank mist was rising from the river, and the sun, low in the east, was obscured by high, trailing cloud. Manuel shivered. Beside him the Girl stirred, wheezing. The fire had burned out and they couldn't light another until the sun emerged. Manuel sat up. A half-memory came to him and he looked at the river thoughtfully.

"Did you hear anything during the night?" he asked the Girl. "Anything strange?"

"I heard a terrific screaming once. Then it stopped."

"No — you always hear screaming at night. It's animals getting killed. This was something different . . ." He heard it again in his mind — not a screaming, more like a keening. Voices raised in thin cries of sorrow.

"Where in hell is that vampiro?" grumbled Zozula, roused by their conversation. He scanned the scrub, staring at the wall of the nearby forest. "And what's happened to our food?" he said suddenly.

Containers lay scattered and empty. The Triad regarded this mess in dismay. "We'll have to go back," said the Girl.

"We can catch our own food," said Manuel.

"That stuff?" The memory of the dried iguana was vivid.

"There'll be fruit in the forest. You don't have to eat meat. We can catch fish and steal a few eggs. You'll like it, Girl." Manuel was disappointed at the prospect of returning to the Dome.

She looked at him. "All right, then."

Zozula untied the shrugleggers and they mounted. "This is not a good start," he said sternly. "I daresay we can find food, but unless we can track down the vampiro we'll have no shelter at night. If the creature's gone into the forest, we'll never find him."

"He wouldn't go in there," said Manuel.

"Why not?"

"His wings are too big for him to be able to fly in there. The trees are close together, you know? He'd never go anywhere he couldn't escape from." Manuel had an instinctive understanding of animals.

"Well, where is he, then?" asked Zozula irritably.

They found the vampiro less than a hundred meters away. The lead shruglegger, forging through the long grass, suddenly shied and almost threw Zozula from its back. Sliding to the ground, the Keeper regarded the remains of the vampiro's carcass in some fear.

"There's . . . there's hardly anything left of him. What on Earth could have done that? Vampiros are vicious brutes in a fight. Whatever killed this one must have been very strong . . ." The thigh bones were cracked open, splintered by powerful jaws. Ants swarmed over the remains, picking the bones clean. The only recognizable parts of the giant bat were the wings, twisted backwards at an angle and draped over the grass, out of the way, so that the killer could get at the soft parts of the body.

"Jaguar," said Manuel. "If we hadn't lit a fire, we'd have gone the same way."

"Dead, do you mean?" The Girl clung to her shruglegger's neck, learning the ruthlessness of the real world and finding it frightening. "Totally Dead? Just like that, with no choice, no chance, or nothing?"

"You have to be careful Outside," said Manuel gently.

They rode on into the forest. Now the shruggleggers began to prove their worth, forcing their way through the undergrowth with scarcely a pause, vines and creepers snapping like spiders' webs before the thrust of their powerful thighs. The forest canopy closed overhead and they were enveloped in the warm, fetid smell of the place. Howler monkeys announced their presence with whooping yells and the cries were taken up elsewhere, echoing into the depths of the jungle.

Around noon Manuel raised his head, sniffing, then directed his mount down a barely visible trail through dense brush. The giant strides of the shruglegger carried it at a deceptive speed while Manuel leaned out, peering down. Suddenly he threw himself to the ground and, after a brief struggle, emerged from the undergrowth with a small squealing peccary, just as Zozula and the Girl came hurrying into view.

"What do you mean by going off like that and leaving us?" Zozula asked. "What's that you've got there?" He looked flustered, glaring down at Manuel, breathless, as though he'd been running himself.

"It's a peccary."

"I can see that. What's it for?"

"To eat, of course." The little creature kicked and screamed.

"Eat? But it's *alive!*"

Manuel pulled out his knife and expertly drew it across the throat of the animal. Blood sprayed. The peccary stopped kicking. Manuel held it upside down, allowing the blood to drain warmly to the ground. The Girl watched with open-mouthed interest. Zozula, turning away, was violently sick into the bush.

They cooked the peccary in the next clearing they came to, for as Manuel pointed out, in the forest you could only cook around the middle of the day when the sun shone directly down, affording occasional shafts of light where the hemitrex could be used. It was just another piece of Outside lore that convinced Zozula of the boy's value to the expedition — and of the shortcomings in his own knowledge. He was beginning to realize how lucky he'd been to survive his own previous short trips Outside.

So they ate the peccary — Manuel with relish, Zozula cautiously at first, but with increasing enthusiasm, the Girl with difficulty and at the cost of one small, almost rootless tooth. "Suck the meat as we go along," Manuel suggested. "There's no need to hurry it." And he found some fruit too, ripe, dark globes of sweet pulp that she was able to take quite easily.

They reached the big river shortly after they'd eaten, although they didn't see it at first. The stream they'd been following widened and the ground became swamplike, so they turned east, toward the sea. Before long they caught glimpses of an immense spread of brown water through the trees, flowing sluggishly east. The shrugleggers splashed on. The air became uncomfortably humid and thousands of tiny, biting flies joined them.

"This is awful," said the Girl. The others silently agreed and even the shrugleggers seemed dispirited, their stride flagging, their hairy bodies soaked with rank sweat and swamp water.

By late afternoon Zozula had had enough and asked Manuel with unusual deference, "Shall we stop for the night, now?"

"If you like."

"How do we light a fire?" They'd turned away from the river and halted on a knoll that appeared a little drier than the surrounding forest.

"We can't." Manuel glanced up. The sun was too low now, striking the forest at an angle and totally absorbed by the canopy.

"So how do we keep the . . . animals away from us?"

"We climb a tree," said Manuel. "The shrugleggers can look after themselves."

At the Delta

···

So it was that two days later three exhausted explorers reached the lazy, branching waters of the delta. They found a small tribe of Wild Humans living in a clearing who were able to direct them toward the Island of Lazy Children, as they called it. The Triad crossed deep arms of the river on the shrugleggers' backs. The creatures were excellent swimmers, moving fast, with powerful froglike sweeps of their legs, and easily outpacing the crocodiles. The sun was at its height when they reached a sandy bank free of vegetation.

"This is the place," said Zozula. "According to those people, it's the only inhabited island in the area." He would have seen the buildings by now, if there had been any. He remembered the tall minarets, the vehicles, the people of True Human form, and he compared that vision with this: a muddy beach, a tangle of scrub beyond. An enormous disappointment was mounting in him, and yet his disappointment was not unexpected. He sighed. "The Rainbow's been acting so strangely, lately. It got the timeframe wrong."

"I don't even see any ruins," said Manuel. He kicked at the sand as though hoping to uncover a midden. "I told you there was no city."

"The Rainbow can project into the Ifalong," said Zozula dully. "The city might not have happened yet."

"You mean we've come all this way for nothing?" asked the Girl.

"No," said Manuel. "There are people here — the villagers said so. We only have to find them. Perhaps they can tell us something."

"I think we've found them." The Girl pointed down the beach. One of the recumbent forms that at first glance they had taken for land manatees had raised itself up on one elbow and was looking their way. It lifted a hand and waved feebly.

And so the Triad met the Lazy Children.

Zozula regarded the row of dirty, seminaked people lying in the mud. Was this what they'd come to see? These people were no more True Human than the Girl. They were fat and weak — in fact, they bore a clear physical likeness to her. There were eight of them, a group of five and a group of three. Only one of them seemed to be awake, and now he smiled pleasantly, indicated himself and said: "Trevis."

Then he shouted, a series of fluid sounds. The first word was undoubtedly "Eloise," as though it were a summons.

"Manuel," whispered the Girl, "are these men or women?" She'd seen weird things in Dream Earth, but at least people were divided into two more-or-less distinct categories. She found these almost hairless humans with vestigial genitals slightly unnerving.

"I'm not sure. A bit of both, I think." Manuel also felt some distaste. Then a movement caught their attention.

A figure walked toward them from the forest, carrying a small baby about one year old. It was the baby that made the Triad decide that this particular Lazy Child was female, which later proved to be an accurate assessment.

"I am Eloise," said the girl. "And you must be from the Dome." She regarded them in turn, nodding as she examined the Girl. "You're exactly as we thought you'd be. I'm afraid we may seem a bit strange to you, though." She glanced downstream. "And we're nervous too. Some of us may be hiding within ourselves."

"You've nothing to be frightened of," said Zozula gruffly.

"We have everything to be frightened of," said Eloise. "You are going to destroy us."

She overrode their protestations.

"Yes, you are," she said. "Even though you don't know it. Even though you may never know it. Trevis says so, and Trevis is almost always right, particularly when he projects from the theories of Yato. There are some queer things happening in the Greataway these days, and some beings are moving to protect themselves and their territory. Recently I caught a glimpse of a great knowledge out there — it just touched me for a moment as it traveled in that weird vehicle we see in the Greataway sometimes."

"The Celestial Steam Locomotive," Zozula guessed. "I'd heard it could transcend the Dome. That proves it — it's in the Greataway."

"The Skytrain isn't the kind of place where you'd expect to find much intelligence," the Girl objected. "From what I hear, it's full of a bunch of idiots from Dream Earth who have nothing better to do than to gamble with the only lives they have."

"Anyway," said Zozula to Eloise, "what do you people know about the Greataway?"

Eloise ignored his question. "The intelligence was there," she said, "and it was traveling. It was very clever in its limited field, and its math was almost as advanced as ours. That's how I came to notice it — the math. We named it the math creature, but it seems to have dropped out of sight, now. Probably your Rainbow killed it out of jealousy."

"How do you know —"

She glanced at Zozula thoughtfully. "I'm sorry we're not True Humans and that we have no city. But you see, we build these things in our minds, so it's natural for us to imagine our bodies in a perfect form, just like our machines and buildings and mathematical formulae. It's just as easy as building ugly."

"How do you know all this about us?" asked Zozula harshly.

"I'm telepathic, of course. Now, as to what you want from us — "

"What I want," said Zozula, "is to *talk*. I don't like having questions lifted from my mind. I'd rather put them myself, if it's all the same to you."

Eloise grinned suddenly, like a child. "You should see what Trevis can do!"

"Tell him not to, please."

"Now you're the frightened one!" Eloise sat on the sand, feeding the baby from a pale gourd because she had no proper breasts. The infant coughed and spluttered but seemed to be getting the pale liquid down. Apart from a hint of hydrocephalus, it looked a normal, if fat, infant. "I didn't bear this baby myself," she said in answer to the Girl's unspoken question. "That wouldn't be possible, I'm afraid. It . . . came from another tribe."

"But you are female?" the Girl couldn't help but ask.

"I feel female. That's enough for our purpose. And now — although Trevis is telling me it's inevitable that you will destroy us — I think it's dangerous to discuss our tribe any further . . ." Her eyes were inward-looking. "We have theorized that Space and Time can be infinitely divided into . . . 'happentracks,' you would call them. Since the number of happentracks arising from any moment are infinite, there must exist in the . . ." she glanced at Zozula, ". . . the *Ifalong,* many happentracks on which you do not destroy our civilization. In spite of what Trevis says."

"Civilization?" Zozula found the word presumptuous.

"You must have seen our work, otherwise you wouldn't have come here. Our art, our science . . . everything. I think civilization is the right word in your language — it's a little bigger than a culture. Don't be put off by our bodies. That's a very unimportant plane of our existence."

Eventually the strain went out of the atmosphere as they lit a fire, aroused the sleeping figures, cooked Manuel's meat and talked. The Lazy Children were particularly interested in the Girl, covertly inspecting her as they ate, nodding to one another as though telepathic points were being made.

"Where are the rest of your tribe?" asked the Girl at one point.

"In the forest," said a Lazy Child named Hopho. "We raise crops in there, after a fashion. We're not very practical people."

The Girl began to climb to her feet. "I'd like to see."

"No!" Eloise pulled her down again, adding apologetically, "The less you see, the better. These people here are our leaders. They can tell you anything you want to know."

"I want to know how the Rainbow picked up your . . . your imaginings," said Zozula. "The Rainbow only monitors physical events, so far as I know. How can it possibly record thoughts?"

Hopho said, "We do more than think. Our work is very factual and logical, and our latest gestalt — that's Trevis, Antilla, Buth, Stril and I — is the most powerful we've ever had. We've transcended the limitations of our own craniums and tapped into the Greataway. Somewhere out there our city exists — maybe on just a single happentrack — and our starships, our art and our mathematics. Your Rainbow is aware of this. It didn't find us on Earth with its scanners. It detected us in the Greataway . . ."

Later, Zozula asked, "Why are you so sure we're going to destroy you? You don't interfere with us in any way. I'm in charge of Dome Azul, and I certainly don't bear you any ill will."

Gently, Trevis spoke. "Thank you, my friend. But you are not in charge of Dome Azul. The Rainbow is."

"Nonsense! We can ignore the Rainbow anytime we like! And anyway, why would the Rainbow want to destroy you?"

"Because we are a tiny nuisance to it, a cinder in its eye that affects the clarity of its logic and vision. And the Rainbow senses our potential for greatness, our huge knowledge that expands much more quickly than its own — because the Rainbow was designed only by ordinary human minds and by itself. We sit in the Greataway now, and the Rainbow sees us like a small, deadly snake; dangerous but vulnerable. The original purpose of the Rainbow was to serve and protect humanity. Now, it feels it has to protect itself. It is very simple to stamp on us . . .

"When your Rainbow issues our death sentence," Trevis continued, "you will not recognize it as such. So you will not be able to help us. It was preordained, ever since Mankind first gained his thirst for knowledge . . ."

By evening the conversation had turned to the problems of the Dome and the growing unpredictability of the Rainbow and the machines it controlled: the robots, the kitchen, the recycling unit. "That's why we came, mainly," said Zozula. "We thought you'd be able to help us. Unless we get the Rainbow repaired quickly, it will destroy the Dome. There are other Domes too, all over Earth. I called one of them, and its terminal of the Rainbow is acting strangely too. We can't identify the problem."

"I'm sorry," said Trevis.

"I took a chance the other day," said Zozula. He told them about the Mole. "I'd hoped to send him into the Rainbow as a kind of interpreter, because in some ways he's like you — he's grown up without outside influences and he might have brought a pure kind of logic with him. But the Rainbow rejected him. It pushed his mind straight back into his own head. Now I simply don't know what to do. The Mole was our last hope, but he just sits there and we don't know what he's thinking, or if he's capable of thought at all."

"Perhaps Eloise could help you."

"Eloise?" He regarded the female thing.

"She's probably our most intuitive telepath. She could tell you what's going on in the Mole's mind. Perhaps she could prepare him, too; make him a bit more compatible with the Rainbow."

Eloise said quickly, "I'd be happy to come back to the Dome with you."

"Why?" Zozula was suspicious.

"I work alone here, building a time-city. I'm not a member of any gestalt, since my partner was taken by crocodiles two years ago. So nobody will miss me for a while. If you will bring me back when I'm through, I'd like to go with you. It would be a new experience, and I'll be able to use it in my time-city."

"Eloise has traveled before," said Trevis.

Zozula was still uncertain. "How do I know you won't wreck the Rainbow? You say it intends to eliminate you."

Trevis said, "You have to understand the Ifalong. Certainly there may be happentracks where Eloise destroys the Rainbow. But I can visualize a million times more happentracks where Eloise's help is instrumental in your success."

"Is that the best chance you can give us?"

"There's no such thing as certainty," said Trevis with a smile. "That's one of the drawbacks of the Greataway we live in."

And speaking soundlessly to Eloise, mind to mind, he asked, *"Why did you tell them about the math creature?"*

"Our tribe is doomed anyway. If they seek the math creature – as they will – our fate will take a less direct route. That will result in our surviving on just a few more happentracks. By helping them, I'm increasing our chances of survival."

"I'm sorry, Eloise."

"And besides," she admitted, *"I want to meet the math creature."*

THE AQUALILY GROTTO

Zozula led, the Girl followed and Manuel brought up the rear, with Eloise riding beside him. The extra load did not seem to bother the shruglegger, who strode powerfully on.

There was an air of disappointment about the Triad on the first day of their return journey. Privately, Zozula doubted whether Eloise was going to be much help to the Mole. From the glimpse he'd had of the Lazy Children's incredible imaginings in the Greataway, she could make matters worse. But at least she was telepathic . . . He swung round in his saddle suddenly, wondering if she was reading his mind at that moment.

She smiled at him innocently. She had been describing her previous travels to Manuel. It seemed that she'd spent several weeks with a Polysitian island chief before being taken back to her tribe in some disgrace, which she did not specify. Manuel asked her what the Polysitian girls looked like . . .

A slim girl walked through his mind.

"What was that!" He almost fell from the saddle in surprise.

"That was a Polysitian girl. That's what you wanted to see, wasn't it?"

"But . . . I expected you to describe her, in words. Instead I *saw* her. Did you do that?"

"Of course."

"But I thought you only read minds."

She laughed. "If I can build a city in the Greataway, it's not difficult to build a girl in your mind, Manuel."

"I . . . suppose not." He regarded her in awe and fell silent, savoring the remains of the vision she had given him.

In midafternoon they camped in a clearing and Manuel built a fire. The sun was high and hot, the clouds wispy as though shredded by their passage over the eastern mountains. Zozula, blundering about the camp, was ill-tempered and short of breath. The Girl and Eloise lay against a grassy bank panting as though they, and not the shrugleggers, had been doing the carrying. The beasts themselves huddled under a tree in the shade, hanging their heads and sweating.

Only Manuel seemed unaffected, gathering wood, whistling, picturing the girl Eloise had drawn for him. Belinda *had* looked a little like that . . .

"There's no damned air in this jungle." Zozula collapsed in the shade, gasping.

"Snake clouds," explained Manuel.

"Snake clouds?" Zozula exclaimed. "Aren't those the clouds that tell you the Chokes are coming?"

"That's right, but we have plenty of time. The Chokes won't be here for two days at least."

Zozula climbed to his feet, eyes widening in alarm. "*You* may have plenty of time. You people have adapted to this. But what about us? Have you thought of that?"

Manuel hadn't. He regarded them in dismay. Zozula was right. "Well, you didn't say anything," he said defensively. "The snake clouds started on the day we left the Dome. I assumed you knew all about them."

"We don't all live Outside in this poisonous air, Manuel. Things are a little more civilized in the Dome."

"I can't breathe properly right now," said the Girl anxiously. "What do your people do when the Chokes get bad, Manuel?"

"They go to Life Caves," Manuel muttered.

"Well, let's go to one, then."

"I don't know where there are any, except near the village."

"Oh." She subsided, gasping.

"What does your tribe do, Eloise?" asked Manuel.

To save time, she built them a picture of a delta backwater with the tree branches woven to form a vaulting canopy, leaves threaded into the holes and bamboo walls between the trunks. The water was covered with a solid mat of oxygen-producing lifeweed — the same stuff that had littered the beach when Belinda came to Manuel. On the shore around the backwater lay the Lazy Children. At first there were a number of babies in the picture, but Eloise hastily removed them.

"We're too far away from the delta now," said Zozula. "There's only one thing to do. We'll have to travel all night and all day tomorrow and hope we reach the Dome before we run out of air."

Even as he said it, he knew it was hopeless. They didn't have time.

By late afternoon they were moving again, urging the shrug-leggers to greater efforts. The beasts were clearly faltering, their chests heaving, their fur soaked with sweat. They moved through the forest in a solid phalanx, drawing strength from one another, sometimes even leaning against one another.

Suddenly Eloise said, "What do the animals do in the Chokes?"

Manuel explained. "They've adapted. The guanacos and such like migrate to the best places nearest the ocean. Then they just stand and wait it out. They do the same thing when the air is rich, too. In normal times they wander about in the foothills."

"Those are open-ground animals. What about the solitary ones that live in the jungle? They can't migrate."

"I don't know. I know nothing about the jungle."

"I think the animals have their own places here," said Eloise.

"Maybe, but I don't know where they are." Manuel's mount was stumbling, threatening to dump him and Eloise onto the swampy ground.

"I do," said Eloise. "There's one near us now. I can feel the animals."

"What's that?" Zozula aroused himself from his torpor. "Animals? My God, haven't we got enough problems without animals?"

"I think these animals are harmless," Eloise said, guiding Manuel's shruglegger northward . . .

*

It was a vaulting grotto of muted green, here and there starred with crimson where the last rays of the sun reflected from a leaf or touched a lofty branch. Neatly circular in the center of the clearing lay a large pool, the surface almost completely blanketed by aqualilies. Stimulated by the devitalized air, the aqualilies throbbed with delayed photosynthesis, pouring a heady brew of life into the grotto. With it came an elusive, almost soporific fragrance from a multitude of pink waxen flower cups. The forest creatures lay around breathing quietly.

The nostrils of crocodiles snuffled between the lily pads and bright frogs squatted on the pads themselves, ignored by their sometime hunters. Capybaras gathered on the shore, resting on their sides like fat mother pigs, while peccaries wallowed quietly in the shallows, also ignored by the crocodiles — and by the jaguars too, three of them, sprawled in forked branches. The smaller animals moved among all this, the cavies and pacaranas and the little rodents and snakes, and the birds perched almost motionlessly, just occasionally preening themselves before settling once more into sleep. It was a gathering place of the common and rare. A thylacosmilus lay beside a tree, flanks heaving gently, a marsupial remnant of some forgotten zoological re-creation thousands of years ago, doomed to extinction for the second time in Earth's history. And on the opposite side of the grotto, hidden and sensed only as a presence, lay an unimaginable creature: the familiar of a Dedo, which she had created for protection — huge and savage, the master of plains and jungle from whom the jaguars fled. Yet the creatures near this thing showed no fear. Nothing showed fear; nothing showed hunger.

The flowers poured out their perfume.

Eloise and the Triad found room for themselves among a group of flightless forest condors and lay down. Nobody spoke. Zozula's testiness waned, and with it the Girl's fear and Manuel's guilt. Eloise, her unusual mind attuned to the peace in the minds all around her, went to sleep first, and the others soon followed.

They awakened occasionally during the next two days, looked around lazily, felt no hunger, thirst or fear, paid no heed to the threadlike shiftings in the soil beneath them and went back to sleep. It was three days before the flowers faded, and Zozula, awakening in shafts of noon sun, saw menace in the closeness of jaguars and anacondas and roused the others.

"We'd better get out of here fast," he said. "We could get ourselves killed . . ."

All around them animals were moving, stretching, stumbling half-drugged into the forest, where the air was fresh and new. Overhead, a horse cloud momentarily obscured the sun. The humans left on the backs of their mounts; the thylacosmilus, old and emaciated, wandered away to die later; the jaguars yawned in their trees and felt the pangs of hunger, unsheathing their claws.

Not all the animals left. A multitude of small rodents remained, their legs trapped in the aqualily roots that now emerged from the top dusting of soil like worms, and, tightening, began to draw their prey toward the waters.

The little animals barely struggled, as though knowing that nothing is free and that the life-giving lilies had just as much right to the tribute of the forest as did the jaguar, if not more so.

ELOISE AND THE MOLE

••

Will this room suit you?" Zozula asked. It was close by Lord Shout's chambers and the view was similar.

Eloise blinked at the height and said, "I've lived in some odd places. Did you know, I lived on the Polysitian islands for a while, working for Or Wai'ki?"

"I didn't know you people ever left your home."

"How do you suppose we learned your language?"

"Oh, I see." Annoyed at himself, Zozula asked, "What were you doing for this Or Wai'ki?"

"He wanted dreams. I gave them to him: warm sands, tall palms, the smell of roasting pork after the fun of the hunt. But he would always twist the dreams around to suit his own . . . peculiarities. He was disgusting . . . In the end I got the better of him." She grinned briefly at the memory.

"Could I find those islands?" asked Manuel, thinking of the slim girl.

Eloise smiled. "Only the Polysitians can find their islands."

"There will be a record of them in the Rainbow, Manuel," said Zozula confidently. "Once we can train the Mole to interpret the data, we'll have the answer to that mystery."

Manuel was unconvinced. Belinda seemed to be moving farther away from him. Only a few days ago Zozula had been positive her tribe lived in the delta. Now she was on some mysterious Polysitian island. He looked at the Girl, who shrugged.

They went into the next room. The Mole had been disconnected from the Dream Earth terminals and brought back to his accustomed corner.

Eloise blinked — a habit of hers when surprised or shocked — and leaned suddenly against the wall. "Poor thing," she whispered. Her own tribe contained some oddities, but this was beyond her experience.

"You'll be well rewarded," said Lord Shout hastily. "And Zozula will make sure you get everything you want during your stay here."

"How . . . how long will you need me here?"

"As long as it takes," said Lord Shout.

There was a silence while the Mole made paddling motions with his appendages.

Then: "I'll help you look after him as well, if you like," said Eloise. "You won't need the nurse. And . . ." She pointed to the robot that had been standing against the wall, refusing all commands.

"You don't have to." Lord Shout looked at her wonderingly. "It wasn't part of the deal." *Surely she can't want to,* he thought. The Mole sat quietly in his corner, making meaningless gestures.

Zozula, Manuel and the Girl left, sensing that this had become a private matter.

"How does he make his needs known?" asked Eloise once they were alone.

It was embarrassing to explain the croaks, grunts and limbwaving with which the Mole expressed himself, but Lord Shout explained nevertheless. As Eloise had correctly divined, it was a relief for him to share the burden.

"How do you know what he's thinking?" asked Eloise.

"I don't. I never have." *For all I know, he hates me.* Not for the first time, the figure of the Mole appeared malignant as he squatted there.

"Haven't you wondered?"

"All the time. But ... I don't really believe he does think. How can he? He has nothing to relate his thoughts to."

"But his ... his face keeps changing all the time. There's something going on in there." There was suppressed excitement in Eloise's voice. "I'll be able to tell you what it is."

Suddenly Lord Shout was scared. "About Or Wai'ki," he said, "you said you got the better of him. What exactly did you do?"

She smiled at the memory. "I dreamed him a man-eating ichthyosaur and had it go for him."

"But couldn't he have simply woken up?"

"It was a very strong dream," she said, and her eyes were like diamonds. "By the time I let him awaken, he was ... different."

The Mole looked terribly vulnerable. "Suppose you don't like *him?*"

"*I* don't know." Suddenly she was younger, an impatient child. "It's a chance you must take."

"Go ahead," he said eventually.

Eloise sat beside the Mole and put her arm around him. She showed no evidence of revulsion. The Mole did not react. There was a silence. She laid her head against his. She closed her eyes.

As Lord Shout watched, Eloise's expression gradually changed from puzzlement to astonishment. She said nothing for a long time.

"Well?" asked Lord Shout at last.

"I ... I don't know how to tell you this, Lord Shout. There's ... there's nothing in there. His mind is blank. There's nothing happening."

"But he's moving!"

"They're just reflex movements," she said gently. "There's no intelligence in his mind at all. It's completely empty. I'm so sorry."

"Oh, my God," said Lord Shout, gazing helplessly at his son.

∗

"Nothing?" repeated Zozula heavily when Eloise reported to him. "You mean he's just not thinking at all?"

"It can happen, Zo," said Selena. "It sometimes happens to our specimens on the People Planet. The human element simply isn't there, and we're left with instincts only, like one of the lower animals."

"I really thought he'd be able to help," said Zozula. "I thought he'd have developed all of his own ideas without being distracted by the real world, so they would be based on pure logic. I suppose I really thought his mind would be like a computer. No wonder the Rainbow didn't accept him into Dream Earth. There was nothing to accept."

Selena's gaze traveled around the Rainbow Room. The Rainbow was indulging in one of its ever more frequent tantrums, and jagged flashes of color sparked across the room, hurting the eyes. "What do we do now, Zo?"

"I don't know." The head Cuidador sat in an attitude of defeat. Beside him stood a waiter who had ignored his request for a drink and was, apparently, on strike. One by one the machines were breaking down, either because their programming had been scrambled by the Rainbow or, quite possibly, because the Maintenance Bay was malfunctioning.

Eloise said tentatively, "Can I make a suggestion?"

"Of course. Anything."

"Perhaps you should find the math creature and get it out of the Rainbow. I had the impression that the Rainbow didn't like it — that it was being sent into exile. Maybe it's irritating the Rainbow, like a bad tooth. And if you get it out of there, maybe it could help you. It might provide the logical mind you're after, to help you identify some of the programs."

Zozula said slowly, "That sounds like sense. We'll have to go through the Do-Portal and locate the Celestial Steam Locomotive. Then we should be able to reconstruct the math creature's journey. Will you come, Eloise?"

"No, thank you. I'd rather travel in the Greataway with my own tribe. Trusting my existence to a crowd of smallwishers doesn't appeal to me." The Girl had explained the Locomotive to her.

"Manuel and I will go, then. The Girl can track us at the console."

"I'm coming with you," the Girl snapped. "You need me. I know more about Dream Earth and the Locomotive than either of you. One of your Keepers can track us."

And so the Triad set out on their second quest.

THE CELESTIAL STEAM
LOCOMOTIVE

Zozula led them across the kilometer-long Rainbow Room to a place where pink fog hung thickly. "This is the Do-Portal," he explained. "It's the gateway to Dream Earth and the rest of the Rainbow. I should warn you: There's a creature on the other side who will ask questions. Leave the answering to me."

"What kind of a creature?" asked Manuel.

"Just a computer thing called the Reasoner. A kind of guard." He took hold of the Girl's arm and led her through the fog. Manuel followed.

The fog took on shape and substance. Around them lights darted and flashed like tiny comets. Soon Manuel could make out a sad, grey face, hanging there unsupported.

"What is your purpose?" asked the Reasoner in a slow voice.

"We wish to enter the Rainbow," said Zozula.

"Why?"

"We seek a being of a special kind known as the math creature, and we wish freedom of travel in order to do this."

"I don't understand how the Rainbow can help you travel," said the Reasoner. "How will you proceed once you're inside?"

Zozula was on uncertain ground and the Reasoner knew it.

"I suspect that the Dream People accidentally hit on a dimension of the Greataway a long time ago. They use it as a plaything, but my observations have led me to believe that it involves genuine teleportation, similar to the Outer Think that humans used to practice."

"You refer, of course, to the Celestial Steam Locomotive."

"That's right."

"Transportation in the manner you suggest is dangerous and unreliable and has been proved addictive. It's safer to walk." The lugubrious eyes searched their faces.

"The possibility of success outweighs the danger." Zozula had been through this before, many times. Cuidadors are valuable and so is the Rainbow, and the purpose of the Reasoner was to ensure that they considered all the consequences before passing on.

The eyes had swiveled to the Girl. "You have a neotenite with you. Her body is unsuited to traveling."

"We know that. We will help her."

"The young man is a Wild Human. He is nervous and bewildered. Traveling in the Greataway involves an element of Belief. He looks like a sceptic who might panic."

"On the contrary, I've been amazed at his adaptability to unusual situations."

"Has any of you traveled in this way before?"

"No."

"Are you proposing to disincorporate?" The Reasoner had become interested. After countless millennia of asking standard questions and probing similar replies, he had at last been presented with a new concept.

"Probably not. I'd like to try as we are. If we disincorporate we become similar to the Dream People in status, which means that we couldn't reincorporate at our destination. We want to *get off* the Train."

"Has anyone ever done that?"

"I really have no idea." Zozula made his voice offhand, confident. "I'd be glad if you'd let us pass, now. We've considered the matter thoroughly and, right or wrong, we are determined in our purpose." This was the standard Statement of Absolution, which let the Reasoner off the hook.

"Pass," replied the creature automatically and relapsed into its normal amorphous state, many of its cells expanding to gaseous matter and merging with the vast body of the Rainbow. A large proportion of the Rainbow is composed of tissues from terrestrial and alien creatures, organic matter being far more effective in the resolution of complex problems than the original and cumbersome conglomerations of chips and circuits — although these are in the Rainbow, too. A small part of the Reasoner remained coherent, wrestling with the implications of the recent conversation, devising an endless series of questions with probable answers for use if a similar situation developed.

The three humans moved on into a world of half-seen shapes, strange smells and odd sensations.

Zozula, in touch with his surroundings and experienced in the workings of the Rainbow, said, "Here." A small globe of light swam toward him and he cupped it in the palm of his hands.

He concentrated . . .

*

First they heard the sounds, a distant rumble rising to a roar as the mists fell aside and revealed a vast, star-roofed chamber whose pellucid walls were lined with insubstantial gothic columns. It was a pounding roar with a four-beat rhythm, accompanied by a surging hiss. Manuel flinched as the others walked forward, and he held back, watching with scared eyes.

The Locomotive thundered in the center of the chamber.

The flimsy walls of the chamber vibrated. The carriages trailed behind the Locomotive endlessly, disappearing into the void. The squat chimney hurled smoke into space, and the wheels whirled in a flashing blur.

Yet the train remained stationary.

"What is it?" asked Manuel, still hanging back.

"The Celestial Steam Locomotive." Zozula was not so confident as he sounded. "It'll take us where we want to go."

"It's scary." Manuel was a brave youth, but this was the first time he'd seen a large and complex piece of machinery in action. He could imagine only too well the result of falling into that churning steel. A thrill of primeval fear tingled down his spine. "Let's get away from it, shall we? We could ride mules instead."

"The Locomotive was made by men, so it's much safer than mules, Manuel."

"But . . . how does it work?" The boy watched a glittering piston shuttling to and fro.

"Some of the principles are lost in antiquity." Zozula watched the valve gear too, but with awe and fascination. "I became interested in the Locomotive some time ago, so I did some research, with the aid of the Rainbow. It seems the machine is driven by heating water until it becomes steam, using a coal fire. The steam tries to occupy a greater space than before and pushes against a piston. The piston is joined to the middle wheels by a connecting rod, and the driving wheels are coupled together with another rod."

The Girl fidgeted. Manuel asked, "What's that big metal box, there?"

"The cylinder. This type of locomotive has four of them, one on either side and two more inside. That's where the steam goes before it pushes the piston, see?"

"I see that. But what I don't see is — what's it all *for?*"

"For?"

"All this noise. All this effort. What does it do?"

"Well, I . . . Once there were locomotives all over Earth and they pulled trainloads of people along steel rails . . ." Zozula went on to describe a period in Earth's history that he only half understood.

Manuel's mind began to wander and his gaze slid across the platform, which looked as though it was paved with a white quilt, to the faint columns against the wall. It seemed he saw a figure standing there. Zozula droned on. His words meant little to Manuel, who couldn't understand *why* vast numbers of people should want to move from place to place. The story lacked credibility, and he suspected Zozula had made it up to cover his lack of knowledge.

The Locomotive began to lose its terrible aspect and Manuel edged toward it while Zozula talked. The Girl stumped for-

ward until she stood beside the great machine itself. The
wheels whirled within a meter of her body and sparks and
smoke erupted in a fountain from the chimney above. Steam
hissed from the glands where the piston entered the cylinder
and the din of exhaust was a throbbing roar. Zozula talked on,
shouting to make himself heard.

Suddenly the Girl shouted, too. "No!"

"What?"

"You make the Locomotive sound fusty and ordinary and
dull, no better than a mechanical llama." The wheels had no
rails beneath them. They spun above a bottomless void that
dropped sheer from the platform edge. "The Locomotive is the
most beautiful thing in the world, and at first it was the best
thing Mankind had ever done. Everything about it is perfect
and has its purpose, and the decorations add to the beauty of its
shape, instead of hiding it." Her fingers traced the brass bead-
ing around one curved splasher. The warm metal was vibrant
and alive. "This Locomotive is the distillation of everyone's
idea of what a machine should look like. It's composed of a
million smallwishes, a million dreams of beauty." Above her
the huge boiler throbbed, tapering from the square-topped
firebox to the black cylindrical smokebox. The boiler, like the
cab and tender, was a warm green lined out in gold and black.
Above the buffers sat a large brass bell.

"And the worst thing is," said the Girl, "that this lovely
machine is used to provide pleasure for idiots."

Zozula looked a shade annoyed at having his discourse interrupted. Manuel's curiosity had been aroused, however. "How
did it happen, Girl? How was the machine built?" Daring, he
reached out and touched the hot metal, which throbbed with a
thrilling kind of life he'd never encountered in the village.

"It's a legend of the Dream People," said the Girl. "Zozula
will probably say it's all a load of nonsense. I thought it was
real at the time, and I think I met a man who was actually
involved in building it. Although Bigwishes make you forget
most things, you know. Maybe it *is* nonsense."

"Don't bother about Zozula," said Manuel. "Tell us how it
came about."

And so, standing in that phantom railway station in Dream Earth, the Girl told the Artist and the Oldster the story of the Celestial Steam Locomotive. And she told it accurately and well, and the Rainbow recalls that all this *did* happen, even though it happened in Dream Earth.

This is the story she told . . .

*

Once there was a man who had tried everything Dream Earth could offer and had eventually Bigwished himself into the form of a small child, in the hope that a new innocence would give meaning to his life, and in the hope that he could somehow build a solid background of facts and memories and events for himself and thereby gain a true identity. He intended to grow up slowly, the way children used to — to experience puberty, adulthood and middle and old age. And in the end, he determined, he would experience death. He would snuff himself out, Totally. In the space of a mere seventy years, he reasoned, he would gather a rich and complete viewpoint on life, far more than he'd ever achieved in his previous shallow persona, in thousands of years of cheap fun.

It was a brave and commendable program.

One day the Truthful-Woman-who-dwelt-in-a-Fountain had a visitor. It was a small boy, about eleven years old. He was crying. He'd been in his present form long enough to have relearned what Dream Earth — life, in fact — is all about. He was scared.

"They tell me you can see into the Ifalong." He wore a lustrex shap from a forgotten era and he was twisting the fabric nervously between his fingers.

"That is sometimes true. What is the matter, boy?" There was no real sympathy in the Oracle's voice. People had forgotten how to be moved by childhood's woes.

"I want to know what will happen to me."

"Whatever you want will happen. Surely you know that."

"I may have made a mistake. I think I've done something stupid."

"Everybody does. It doesn't matter."

"I think I've killed myself."

Now the Oracle's curiosity was aroused. "Tell me."

"I Bigwished myself into this form five years ago. Life hasn't been easy since. You've no idea how cruel people can be to a kid — all those psycaptains and Romans and Goths, they don't give a damn. Being a kid is worse than being Yourself."

And the Oracle delved into her memory and saw a face, smooth and beautiful, and a legend of horror that might have been more than a legend. It was a legend that, thousands of years later, she was destined to repeat to a fat and ungainly girl who could barely walk. Quickly dropping the train of thought, the Oracle said, "Perhaps you should have thought of that before you Bigwished."

"I wanted to live life like a person of Old Earth. You know — grow up, grow old and die. I wanted to know what life was really like."

"If you're telling me you've changed your mind, fine. In fifty years or so, when you've built up the psy, Bigwish into something else, why don't you?"

Now the boy's voice broke. His Bigwish had been very comprehensive. "I won't be able to build up the psy fast enough. It seems I'm slow to recover. Even if I never smallwish again it'll take me at least eighty years to accumulate a Bigwish. I'll probably be dead before then."

The Oracle was silent for a long time. Her mind flicked through the Ifalong and she could see no way out. "You will die," she said at last.

"You mean I won't be able to Bigwish in time?"

"You won't."

"So what shall I do?" The voice was a wail of despair.

Maybe it was at that moment that the Oracle felt an awareness of what was in store for Mankind in the Ifalong. If so, it is paradoxical that the medium should have been a scared Dreamer who had bitten off too much. The Oracle didn't answer for a long time. As she searched the happentracks, adding a human touch to the mechanical deliberations of the Rainbow, a panorama began to unfold that made her feel faint with its sheer immensity. She saw a coming-together and a branching apart, a discovery and a great Rebirth. Possibilities flooded through the synapses, data clicked in from all Earth and the far reaches of the Greataway. Rainbows from other Domes lent their input, and the Oracle let it all come, let it all come, sifted it. At last, very conscious that she was sitting right at the conjunction of radiating happentracks of enormous import, she said very slowly, having analyzed the probable effects of different word-patterns:

"Perhaps you should make the most of what time is left to you."

"What do you suggest?"

"Man used to be creative. Perhaps too creative. But in recent millennia he found things too easy and Art disappeared. It's easy to smallwish up a Picasso, but it's a different matter to paint *Guernica*. I think perhaps you should create something."

"Create what?"

"If I told you that, I'd be doing your work for you. I suggest you study Man's early history, before he became absorbed in passive pursuits. Smallwish yourself a history terminal, let the data flow over you and immerse yourself in the thinking and emotions of the time. Then, when you're ready, create something big. The ultimate work of art, based on an era before Art became a meaningless concept."

The boy thought deeply. Tiny images went through his mind, traces of a wasted life that each Bigwish was supposed to erase but never quite did. Psycaptains and Romans and Goths, and women of all times. When at last he looked at the Oracle, his eyes were shining.

"I'll do it," he said.

*

The boy studied history, as the Oracle had suggested, and, as time went by, he tried everything. He painted abysmal pictures, he wrote verse that no minstrel has repeated since. He chopped chunky nudes from rock, he built a minareted temple that kindly Dream People quickly smallwished into nothingness. He was labeled a madman. He sang songs without melody in a tuneless voice, and people avoided him. And in no time at all, so it seemed, he was fourteen years old and passionately interested in the bodies of women. Fortunately for history, the fear of ultimate death was even stronger than this interest, and he channeled his burgeoning drives into his quest. It is fair to say that by now he probably had more drive than anybody in Dream Earth. So he continued to study with a growing frenzy while he wove monstrous tapestries, created and destroyed perfect football teams, designed dancing dinosaurs and spread across the countryside a sinuous and psychic River of Knowledge up which people swam, growing ever more learned as the strange water penetrated their pores, until, addicted, they could not rest until they reached the source. As their knowledge increased, so did their awareness of what they did *not* know — and so did their fear of what awesome Consciousness the source might be. In their minds the source gained a capital S, and the seeking of it lent a new meaning to life and the purpose of Mankind. It is perhaps significant that nobody ever reached the Source; their minds exploded with accumulated trivia long before that point. In their zeal they had forgotten that knowledge, to be useful, should have a directed purpose.

And if they had discovered the Source, they would have been disappointed. No august Being sat there on a throne waiting to welcome them into an unimaginable Kingdom. Instead there was a little black box and a multicolored cable leading to a concealed terminal of the Rainbow. It was nevertheless an incredible achievement on the boy's part. He had succeeded in creating real objects on Dream Earth — the box and the cable — a feat that could normally only be matched by the Keepers. It didn't happen again, not for millennia, not until the Cap of Knowledge appeared. The boy was unique. He was ready.

He was sensitive, at the most sensitive age. He had redirected urges. He dreamed of power, of might and thrust. Things from the past moved in majesty through his mind. He was still a child, and he thought as children always had — and the images began to clarify, began to take shape from a particular period of Earth's history, from a fleeting instant in Time when Mankind had grown a million years in one century, a time of quick changes and therefore of haunting nostalgia. That was what art and beauty were all about: nostalgia. He woke one morning trembling at the discovery, knowing where art had gone. If nothing changes, then there can be no nostalgia for things past and lost. And without that beautiful sadness, art withers.

He sat on a grassy slope overlooking a valley, and another child's mind sat in his mind, guiding him. There was a stream in the valley and he smallwished and threw a bridge across it, an old brick arch, moss-dappled and sturdy. Then he leveled the ground and laid a path of crushed rock. He placed balks of timber crosswise on the path and gave them a tar scent of their own. He placed two cast-iron chairs on each balk, then he laid twin gleaming rails in the chairs and pinned them in place with wooden blocks, so that they were exactly four feet, eight and one-half inches apart, an ancient measurement that the child's mind within his mind had taught him. For a long time he sat there regarding the track through the valley and the little bridge.

Then, all psy'd out, he rested for nine years.

They came to him slowly, the Dream People. Over the years they dropped by, the mandarins and the troglodytes, Java Man and Miss Orange Blossom and the Travelers, and they admired his panorama. They were tempted to spoil it, to send a golden projectile rocketing along those rails, but they didn't. Instead, forgetting for a moment their relentless quest for pleasure, they gave a little of their psy and helped him.

A Captain Sylvia laid a frame. She laid it carefully, to the boy's instructions, not sure what she was creating but wanting to help. She created a strangely wrought, roughly rectangular thing of steel, and placed it between the tracks. Then, wondering what had possessed her, she jetted to Jamaica. Everybody jetted to Jamaica, that era.

Now they came more often, partly out of a most unusual pity for this person who was destined to die, and partly from curiosity. At this stage, the boy could have become a cult figure and his work ruined by overenthusiastic helpers, but it didn't happen. History does not relate why. A Shut-Out created the driving wheels, a bogus Thing-from-the-Nameless-Planet forgot to be fierce long enough to couple them and a sad Girl-who-was Herself spent a long time on the intricate axleboxes, finally threading the axles, pressing on the wheels and mounting them on the frames. For a few months — an incredibly short time in history — people rode the frame up and down the track, marveling at its mysterious ingenuity and the mind of the boy who had created it. For them it was enough, and for a while the boy had no more visitors.

Nine years and two months from the beginning, the boy had gained enough psy to build cylinders, pistons, connecting rods and valve gear. He was now a man, had patience and had come to terms with his existence. He knew he would complete the work in the end, and he therefore built carefully and well, expending a wealth of psy on detail, so that it became doubly difficult for any vandal to smallwish the thing away. Some of the Dream People even became interested enough to dig into the history of the period themselves and began to arrive with their own ideas. There was little confusion. They were all working toward a common goal, and that goal was beauty. They built a boiler of riveted copper and filled it with copper tubes, and each joint was perfect. They built the tender to match the engine, slab-sided and six-wheeled. They put on boiler fittings of the finest workmanship, and the chimney was a thing of love. Next came the painting and the embellishments: the gauges, the handrails, the whistle and the bell.

Finally they lit the fire and watched the boiler pressure rise, and stood around as the boy (who was now an old man) hauled on the regulator. Steam hissed into the cylinders, the piston rods slid smoothly and, with not so much as a smallwish from anybody there, the Locomotive moved forward with a sound and a smell that touched every Dream Person with magic.

History records that the old man died two days later, his life's work complete. He was sure that he had created the ultimate work of art, and there was not a Dream Person present at that inaugural run who would not have agreed with him.

In one respect alone he failed. He had been unable to give the Locomotive a name. No mere word seemed adequate to express the feelings that the Locomotive aroused in its admirers.

In due course the Locomotive did acquire a name — one that

was totally suitable — but nobody ever knew quite how or when it happened . . .

Meanwhile, the Dream People couldn't leave the Locomotive alone, of course. It had captured their minds. They smallwished more track and a long train of carriages to go with it. They drove it around and held parties on it. And after a while they began to find the track too confining and the Earthbound journeys too simple.

So its travels gradually became more outlandish, until, one forgotten day, it transcended the realms of the Rainbow and ventured into a dimension of the Greataway, sustained by the imagination of its passengers.

It had, in fact, become a figment of the Outer Think.

"There is a strange beauty in this monster," said Manuel, comparing the Locomotive with storms and hills and Belinda, his own yardsticks. The smell was of sulfur and hot oil and pounding metal, of smoke and steam. It touched something deep in his inherited memories and made him a little sad.

"Greetings, travelers." A tall man stood before them, pink-cheeked and ageless, wearing a dark suit and a curious hat, tall and glossy black. "You wish to ride?"

"Yes." Zozula watched the man uncertainly. Like the Locomotive, he might not be real at all; he could be a smallwish — the Composite Stationmaster. "Are there many passengers aboard?" he asked.

"More all the time." The stationmaster shook his head slowly. "I honestly don't know what the world's coming to, I really don't. Can you believe so many people are tired of life?"

"We're not staying on. We have a particular destination in mind."

He smiled sadly. "So they all say. Nobody will admit they're taking the final trip. Nobody likes to admit that after they've done it all, there really *is* nothing more to do. Mark my words, you people, nobody ever gets off the Train."

And with these portentous words he nodded to them, touched his hat and withdrew once more to his place among the pillars.

Zozula led the others forward. As he walked past the Locomotive he noticed for the first time a brass nameplate attached above the central splasher.

It read: SHENSHI

For the moment he couldn't remember why that name sounded familiar, but the sight of it was oddly comforting to him.

THE CAPTAIN WAS A SPECIALIST

Captain! Captain, burning bright,
In eternal cosmic night.
— Kiwi Lambella, 93,404–93,458

*T*he Song of Earth spans a huge slice of time, from the human viewpoint. It starts with legends dating from the year 1 Paragonic, when Starquin, the great Five-in-One, arrived on Earth. It continues through the year 250,746,523 Paragonic, supposed to be the crucial year of the Penultimate Ice Age, which became the year 1 Cyclic.

Somewhere around the 52nd millennium, Mankind developed written records and, shortly afterward, crude computers and their data banks, which were to culminate in the Rainbow. So the later legends and songs became supported by fact.

And the knowledge and the songs accumulated up to the present day.

Since it covers such a vast span, it is not possible to tell the whole story in sequence. It is necessary to digress and explain from time to time. Thousands of years ago, a few of the remaining humans held a Great Telling. They spoke for a century and a half, yet covered a mere fraction of the Song of Earth.

They sang of Manuel and the Girl, however; that much is essential. Then it became necessary to explain what happened previously, at the end of the great Age of Resurgence, which lasted 17,000 years and culminated in the discovery of the Greataway and the Outer Think and in the short life of the Invisible Spaceships.

If that had not been explained, how could the listener know how longevity came about? How could they know that the Inner Think, which preserves youth, is actually due to a small parasite living in a substance called bor . . . ?

And so the minstrels sing of Captain Spring.

*

Her story happened long ago, even before the discovery of the Greataway, at a time when Earth's powers were at their height and the solid ships were like dust across the Galaxy, and it seemed that the Age of Resurgence would never end.

The trouble broke out a million light-years from Earth, which was a long way in those days, when there was no Outer Think and travel took time. A crewman went mad and ran screaming through the corridors of the *Golden Whip*. Nobody knew what drove him mad. The Red Planet was not even heard of in those days, and the crew's quarters were designed to give every pleasure. Just maybe, he thought of home . . .

He burst into Captain Spring's quarters, found her spraying on her night wear and flung her to the floor, slavering like an animal.

Reflexively, she killed him, cuffing him as he descended on her and breaking his neck.

There was trouble. The law dictated that an inquest be held, and Captain Spring was unable to sit on the panel, due to conflict of interest. After all, she did have to justify killing a man.

"Were you at any time in any danger?" asked the examiner, who was the first lieutenant.

"No," she admitted.

"Then perhaps you'll explain to the court why you killed this man."

Her hands curled on her knees, an involuntary movement that did not escape the notice of some people. She sat in the ship's koting room, the biggest cabin on the ship and the only one big enough to accommodate the audience. She sat on a chair, dressed in candy-stripe, outwardly calm — as befitted the captain of the *Golden Whip* — inwardly raging at the indignity of it all, at the fact that she should, in effect, be on trial. And her hands curled on her bare knees, and the nails dug into the flesh. She was a big rangy woman, beautiful, with the slanting eyes of a Polysitian, although she was not of that race. Her hair was a russet mane, her movements as she stroked it back were slow, and heavy with suppressed power.

People watched her, this superb and beautiful woman, with contempt and not a little fear.

She said, "It was a reflex action."

"A reflex action. A *reflex action.*" With heavy emphasis the examiner turned from her and stared at the panel, making sure they had taken the point. "Our captain says she killed a man reflexively. That is an alarming admission."

Spring's eyes were amber and steady, betraying none of the shame and confusion she felt. She looked over the audience — people she'd been in command of until nine hours ago — and caught sight of Perry, the ship's cook. He smiled back at her with sympathy, a small tubby man dressed traditionally in white, although his job was more a combination of mechanic and agrologist. *Don't let them get to you, girl,* he thought.

Spring looked back at the examiner. "I killed him in the same way that you might, if you happened to be holding a loaded gun and somebody jumped you unexpectedly."

"But you had no weapon but your bare hands."

"Are you criticizing me for my strength?"

"Certainly not." The first lieutenant backed adroitly out of the trap. "I was merely suggesting that your analogy might not be appropriate." He smiled, a thin smile. "Even you must admit that it is unusual for a man to be killed by a slap across the face, as you claim."

"*Even* me?" Suddenly she rose to her feet, a lithe movement that took her to his side, so that she towered over him, a head taller — and he was no runt. "We are here to determine the cause of death," she said, her voice low music with just a hint of menace, "and I've told you what happened. It seems you doubt my word. Perhaps you would like me to prove it . . ." And she raised her hand, and the audience gasped. The first lieutenant flinched . . .

Later he said to the chief navigator, "We should have locked the bitch up permanently. She's inhuman — she's a danger to us all. A woman who kills without thinking is no captain for a ship."

"This *is* a cruiser. There *have* been hostile craft. She has the reflexes she needs, wouldn't you say?" The navigator's face was darkly spiteful. "Are you saying you could do a better job, First?"

"Well . . . Of course you'd support her. I mean, you're —"

"Don't say it." The navigator, a small grey person of indeterminate sex, trotted off with an odd jerky gait, head nodding.

The first officer made for the bridge. For a while he was in charge. Captain Spring was in the sickbay undergoing physical and psychiatric examination, as prescribed by the panel, this being the most the first officer could achieve without laying himself open to charges of mutiny.

Elsewhere, Perry the cook was discussing the matter with two biologists. "You can't condemn a person for fulfilling the dictates of their genetic make-up," he was protesting. "It's a matter they have no control over."

"You can say that about any murderers."

"*Any* murderers?" The cook flushed. "Your trouble is, you're scared of her. She's bigger and stronger and *better* than you, and you don't know how to handle it. You accept the other Specialists, like the navigator, because their purpose doesn't require them to be fast and clever — dear God, can't you see how *primitive* your prejudice is? It's simple physical fear, and you try to make all kinds of excuses for it. Try thinking about the hurt and the loneliness you're causing when you all avoid her. Try remembering she's as much a human being as you or I. Her only difference is that she has a little bit *extra*. Two extra chromosomes, that's all, planted there by people like you. And you'd throw her in the brig for that? You bastards. Everyone on this ship's been waiting for the chance to bring her down!"

Later he visited the sickbay.

Spring lay on a couch, chest down, one leg drawn up beneath her supple body, the weight of her torso propped on her elbows. Despite himself, Perry thought it was a jungle posture. He sat beside her. She looked up from beneath that weight of hair, looked at him with those eyes. She was crying.

He wanted to stroke her. "What did the doctor say?"

"He wants me to stay here for a few days for observation. I think everybody wants that. He says it's not because of *me*, you understand? Not because of what I am. But because of the shock to my system. I might overreact at the controls, that's what he says. The liar."

"I wish the Enemy were around. I'd like to see how the first would handle them."

"Perry . . . that's not all. I . . . For a while there, in the koting room, I was *glad* I was different. You know what I mean? I *despised* them all. What kind of a way is that, for a captain to think of her crew?"

"They were acting stupidly." He looked away from the intense blaze of those amber eyes.

"No. I despised them because I thought I was *better*. I was suddenly proud of what I am, seeing them all sitting there so small and slow and weak. I wanted to get up and walk among them and stare them in the face." She moved on the couch, an involuntary twitch, and he saw the muscles of her thigh harden. "I think I wanted to harm them, Perry. I felt murderous. Maybe I still do . . ." She shook a hank of hair out of her eyes, and he shivered with the effect of her beauty.

"What in hell is this? I said no visitors!" The psychiatrist stared down at them angrily.

"I was just going." Perry stood. "I'll drop by later." And as he turned to leave he caught sight of something glittering at Spring's ankle.

She was chained to the couch.

Outside the door, beyond range of her hearing, he said to the psychiatrist, "What are you people trying to do to her?"

"She needs therapy. She's overexcited, you know. Her kind of people . . . we don't know a lot about them. They can be unpredictable, unreliable — you know what I mean?"

"No, I don't. What I do know is that the authorities thought her reliable enough to give her command of a ship. This ship."

And the ship shook.

Grabbing for support as the alarm blared out, Perry shouted, "Release her right now! We need her at the controls!"

"I have my orders." As running crewmen began to fill the

corridor, the psychiatrist retreated to the sickbay. "I tell you this — I feel a hell of a lot safer now that the first is on the bridge, instead of that creature in there!"

*

They gave the planet the name Talk-to-Yourself, but that was much later and it never was the official name. At the time of the *Golden Whip*'s crash landing it was known as C31674/5 and the crewmen, stepping out onto the Earth-type ground, called it Salvation. It was to become the most important alien world in the history of Mankind, and its inhabitants would walk with men forevermore.

They radioed for help by fastcall and found a ship in the vicinity. It would be with them in six standard months. They had plenty of food for the hundred or so people on board, and even if they hadn't, there were plenty of edible-looking fruits hanging among the lush vegetation, which, after testing, would probably provide unlimited food.

And there was the river, deep and swift, on the bank of which they camped. Fishlike creatures leaped from time to time. There appeared to be no insects, no predators.

"Paradise," said somebody, and they settled down to await rescue in comfort.

Within a couple of days, discipline had relaxed sufficiently for Perry to visit the sickbay again. The aseptic room, tilted strangely in the absence of artificial gravity, was empty. The chains hung from the foot of the bed, the leg-irons broken. Spring was gone.

"What have you done with her?" Perry confronted the psychiatrist and the first officer. A tent had been set up in a clearing beside the river. The sun warmed the ground and people lay around talking and laughing.

The psychiatrist took Perry aside. "She went berserk. She broke her chains and ran, yesterday." The first stood by, nodding. "It's better that people shouldn't know," said the psychiatrist. "We have enough problems right now. And the first is capable of handling things."

"But she's the captain!"

"She's been relieved of command, due to mental instability."

The first's voice was sharp. "I don't want to have to give you a direct order, Cook, but I'd look on it as a favor if you kept your mouth shut for a while."

"Why? We have to get a search party organized, don't you understand? She could be lying injured out there!"

"She's in her element. She's an animal, isn't she? Any search party going out into that jungle will have to be heavily armed." The first glanced around at the crew. He knew they had no love for Spring. He smiled. "Maybe that's not a bad idea, after all."

Perry heard himself say, "Forget it." He found himself a tree and sat down against it, watching the dappled sunlight dancing over the ground while he thought of Spring, his captain. Inside him was a huge hurt because she'd run off without consulting him first. Over the months they'd had many discussions, the cook and the captain, and Perry had always thought these had been for Spring's benefit, to assist her in dealing with the full-blooded humans who formed the majority of the crew. Now he began to realize how much benefit he'd got from the talks, too.

*

The forest sang to Spring. It sang a song of light and darkness, of youth and strength and simple things. Spring awakened, yawning, and stretched. Her arms were powerful motors, her fingers steel claws. She stood, a movement of fluid grace. The jungle vegetation rustled while she listened and sniffed, but she detected no menace, nothing but the breeze.

She snapped off a stem and drank dew from a cup-shaped leaf. She stepped quietly through the lush growth and soon arrived at the riverbank, where bright flapping things, blue bats, hovered above the river and drank from its surface. Spring tensed, the muscles of her calves bunching, then flung herself out and down, cutting the water in a clean dive. Bats scattered, and the ripples widened, and the river flowed on.

Spring slid beneath the surface, parting water plants and investigating rocky little caverns in the riverbed, watching big fish retreat, watching shoals of smaller fish dividing to swim around her. None of these creatures was frightened. Spring surfaced, blowing water . . . And swallowed some.

The partnership of Macrobes and Man had begun.

Now the ship seemed a long way off and, like the indignities of the past few days, unimportant. Strength and confidence flowed through Spring like brandy. She swam rapidly to the other side of the river and clambered onto the bank. Hearing a rustling, she climbed a tree, peering down from among the foliage.

She caught herself uttering a strange, low sound. It escaped from her throat involuntarily.

Two men were pushing their way through the jungle beneath her. One was a mechanic — she couldn't remember his name. The other was the plump little cook, Perry. Her throat seemed to vibrate as she uttered the sound again. Perry paused, looked around, but not up; then the two men moved on. Spring relaxed. She bore them no ill will, but they were encroaching on her territory, the jungle . . .

That night she dreamed bizarre dreams of a land she'd never seen. She was alone in this land, and she was hungry. The hunger fed the power that surged through her body and she paced to the edge of the forest. The small creatures ran aside, sensing that she hunted. Other creatures were less perceptive. They went about their complicated business as though she weren't there — monkey-shaped creatures with complicated rituals, motley pelts and little strength: men.

She watched them from the shadows and her belly was a chasm of longing. They chattered, chanted, clashed metal objects and blew through pipes. They stripped off their pelts and rubbed them on river rocks. They rode elephants. Only their numbers made them difficult prey. They were weaker than the boar, softer than the ghavial, more cowardly than the bull and smaller than the elephant. But they were many and she was one.

Then a solitary man approached the forest.

*

"I told you. Hell, I told you she was dangerous."

The second regarded the mutilated remains, his stomach heaving. "Oh, God. You're saying *she* did this, First?"

"No doubt about it. Look at those scratches. Those were made by human fingernails."

"But . . . He's . . . He's been *emptied out.* Where are his organs and such? Hell, First, he's been disemboweled. She wouldn't do that. No human being would do that."

"But the big cats would. That's what they used to do. They'd make their kill, then they'd eat the soft parts first. The entrails. The delicacies."

"Oh, God. Don't talk like that."

"She's out there, you know. She's out there listening, sniffing, waiting. We can't treat her like a human being — she'd kill us all. She's reverted to type." The first stared at the green curtain of the jungle. "We should have hunted her down right at the start."

"You can't hunt down a woman, First." Another crew member spoke. "O.K., so she's different. But not *this* different. I can't believe she did this. Hell, we don't know what monsters are out there. Anything could have got him. This jungle is full of possibilities!"

As the day went by and another night approached, their fears grew. They lit huge fires and crouched beside them, staring into the blackness around. They huddled close and whispered horror stories to each other, and whimpered at every sound.

Meanwhile, out in the forest, Captain Spring slept alone — or not really alone, because in truth she would never be alone again. She had drunk the water that in years to come would be called "bor." Nobody else had drunk from the river yet; that would come later. The ship's instruments had detected something peculiar in there, tiny living organisms with an unusual unity of purpose. So the microbiologists took samples for analysis and for the time being everybody drank rainwater.

In the morning the first officer gathered his posse. "I'm not going through another night like that. I doubt if I slept ten minutes. We're going out there today and we're going to hunt that thing down."

"The captain?" One of the officers looked doubtful.

"We're going to hunt down whatever killed our man. Maybe it isn't the captain — I could be jumping to conclusions."

Wisely, the first was adjusting his position. "Maybe it's an indigenous carnivore. Whatever it is, it has a taste for Man now, and it'll come back for more. We have to get to it first."

*

Now she stood beside a fern-fringed lagoon, naked and glistening in the sun. Motley bats fluttered about her and other small creatures had gathered, too — a beaverlike thing with a smiling duckbill, a varied shoal of fish with big-O mouths, tiny spider monkeys that wove webs to catch drifting spores, and many others. They all gathered around Spring in unafraid curiosity. She was the only carnivore they had ever met. They examined her, twittered at her, sat on her.

Spring was changed. She watched them all with her amber eyes and she registered what she saw from three conflicting viewpoints: human, feline — and alien. Sometimes she smiled, sometimes she uttered her low growl; and when she growled the creatures moved away. They were learning fast.

Spring hadn't eaten for a day and a night. The hunger aroused a threefold tension in her mind, which was why she stood smiling and growling at the lagoon, irresolute.

She heard voices and a crashing in the bushes. The tip of a laser rifle waved like a deadly banner above a field of arrow-reed. The animals scattered, leaving Spring alone. Snarling, she turned, backing into a cave within the root system of a giant tree.

"You hear that? I heard something. Over there!"

Next, Perry's voice. "Don't shoot! For pity's sake don't shoot! Wait until you see it properly . . ."

Now Perry, clutching the rifle that he'd brought just for show, followed the others to the water's edge.

"She's around here somewhere." The first's head snapped this way and that. "I can smell her. Like a zoo."

Perry, about to say something, suddenly found himself turning around.

Later, he could never admit to himself exactly what he saw. Afterward, he described to others how he saw Spring emerging from behind a twisted tree. He told himself that, too. He saw a beautiful, naked woman with extraordinary eyes, a wealth of auburn hair and a wonderful figure, walking their way.

He did not — not even for an instant — see a Bengal tiger, eyes blazing as it paced toward them, muscles rippling and gathering, tail flicking, ready to charge. Maybe some other Perry saw that, some other fat cook on some other happentrack.

Spring said, "Hello, men. Could someone lend me a jacket? My clothes fell in the river."

The silence, the stillness. The first officer like a statue, the guns pointing carefully nowhere. The moment when it must be done, if it was going to be done at all. And Perry taking two quick steps away from the hunting party toward the quarry, getting in the line of fire. Unhesitatingly he did this, still uncertain whether that quarry was animal or human, only certain that it didn't matter. And the quarry herself, very much a lovely woman, smiling at them all and walking toward them with a swaying grace that was almost feline, but totally feminine . . .

And the first was peeling his thermocoat off, while the others grinned foolishly, unable to look away from all this beauty.

"Here," said the first. "Put this on. And then maybe you can help us, Captain. There's some kind of dangerous animal around here. We've lost a man. You have more of an empathy with this kind of country — no offense intended. Perhaps you'll join us."

"And where have you been all this time, anyway?" asked Perry.

∗

Perry was forgotten by history, but Captain Spring captured the imagination of ages. Not only because of what she did, but also because of what she was, a tiger-woman of exceptional beauty — some say the most beautiful woman who ever lived, although standards change. In recognition of what she was and what she did, humans found a place for her in the Song of Earth — just a verse or two, but enough to ensure her fame. At first reviled as a villainess as notorious as the earlier Marilyn, she later became a heroine, when bor was recognized for what it was: a great gift to Mankind. And now, who is to say whether bor is good or bad? The only certain thing is that Earth is a different place because of it.

The captain and crew of the *Golden Whip* were rescued from the planet Talk-to-Yourself six standard months later and taken back to Earth. Before the Macrobes — which were the active constituents of bor — were isolated, they had spread. Their advantages became apparent, so their carriers were outlawed by the heads of Earth . . .

Ages later, the Macrobes resurfaced in a felina named Karina, daughter of El Tigre, who passed them on to her son John.

The centuries passed, and the Macrobes reappeared in the body of a young poet named Jimbo in a village then called Puerto Este . . .

> *The Captain was a Specialist of feline-human link.*
> *She brought to Earth the captivating seeds of Inner*
> *Think.*

So runs a couplet in the Song of Earth.

THE LITTLE PASSENGER

It's what you do when you've done everything else.

There was a little man on Dream Earth who was doomed to many years of living among people much bigger and more beautiful than he and who, through his own foolishness, had lost a chance of real love. In his time he'd had many names and now, like the Girl, he had none. And like many Dream People before him, he'd given up hope. So there was nothing to be lost by taking a certain step into a world that — yet again — seemed exciting and different. A world of action and adventure, with perhaps a seasoning of *real* danger ... He could even persuade himself that it was a courageous and creditable thing to do.

So the little man, trembling, did it.

*

The Song of Earth relates his adventures in the normal dimensions of Dream Earth, as though he were a secondary character. Now, however, for a short time, he becomes a principal, with several stanzas to himself, commencing:

> *There came a little passenger who climbed aboard the Train.*

*His heart was full of sadness and his eyes were full
of pain.*

He'd been scared when he joined the Skytrain and he was
still scared. All around him people were laughing, drinking,
yelling, quarreling — the women blonde and brassy and
bouncy-beautiful, in the current vogue, and the men strong and
handsome. Strong enough to break him in half. Beside him, a
tall suntanned man told endless stories of hunting and valor, of
facing the charging rhino and of the sniveling coward who fled.
The Great White Hunter stared challengingly around often, as
though sniffing the air for cowards. It seemed to the scared
little man that the hunter sniffed him out every time.

Meanwhile, the carriage swayed and the metallic clicking of
rail joints sounded as a counterpoint to the brittle laughter. It
was dark outside, but occasionally a tiny gleam passed by.
Whether these were lighted houses or stars, the little passenger
had no way of knowing. Mostly the black windows showed
merely a reflection of the inside of the carriage and the bluff,
noisy travelers. What was he doing here? Whatever had possessed him to ride the Skytrain?

More to the point, why hadn't he at least had the sense to
wait a few years until he'd built up the psy to Bigwish himself
into some more suitable form?

A small girl cuddled near, watching him with big doe eyes.
She had pointed ears and there was a *brownness* about her, a
toylike furriness. "Isn't this wonderful?" Her voice was
childlike and squeaky. "Aren't all these people just the *nicest?*
I love a train, too. Don't you?"

"Yes." There was something artificially naive about her that
the little passenger found even more subtly frightening than
the more brazen characters around. She would go to her death
without ever finding out what the world was really like.

And who can say she isn't better off? thought the little man
wildly. He remembered the ballroom and the blue rain and his
hopeless quest, and he wished he were back in Dream Earth,
where at least he could control his own destiny. Here on the
train a smallwish had no effect, so it seemed. His psy seemed to
be drained, flowing into a common pool.

Nearby, a tall person of indeterminate sex — who had introduced himself earlier as Psycaptain Hilary Yes — leaned forward, caught his eye and began to relate the tale of the Invisible Spaceship on a foray near the dread Red Planet. He'd heard the story twice already, when the psycaptain had told it to a heavy-jowled man and then to a bejeweled blonde. The psycaptain's crew had aged forty years in ten minutes, so the story went, and their teeth had dropped out. Their bones had turned to jelly and they had collapsed to the ship's nebulous deck, quivering blobs of protoplasm. The psycaptain himself had escaped with a flesh wound. The little passenger didn't want to hear it again.

"What do men fear most?" the psycaptain asked. "Not death. Not maiming. But *age*. The gradual, horrible rotting away of mind and body. And that is the weapon of the Red Planet. They have the power to —"

"Excuse me." The little passenger stumbled to his feet and fled. He ran up the central aisle, through the connector, and found himself in a dark passage leading through the tender of the Locomotive. He paused, then pressed forward again. He would talk to the driver of this train, and ask to be let off . . .

But when he saw the scene in the cab of the Celestial Steam Locomotive, he very nearly went right back to his seat.

He heard the singing first, a solitary, rough voice raised in lusty song:

> *Broach me a bottle of Old Jamaica,*
> *Heave-ho! and down she goes!*
> *Drink with the Devil and meet your Maker,*
> *Heave-ho! and down she goes!*

The cab held two men lit by the fearsome glow of the furnace, one bent and shoveling coal into the roaring flames with a long-handled shovel, the other leaning against the spectacle plate, a bottle of dark liquid in one hand, steadying himself with the other hand, singing at the top of his voice.

"Heave-ho! and down she goes!" And on each ho! the fireman's shovel clanged against the open doors of the firebox and another load of coal scattered across the inferno. "Steady there, me old shipmate!" called the driver. "Avast there! That's enough for now!" But the fireman shoveled on, working steadily and inexorably. The driver shrugged, raised the bottle to his lips and took a deep swig, then caught sight of the little passenger lurking in the shadows. "Ahoy there, my lad!" he shouted. "And who might ye be?"

"I have no name."

"Yesself, are ye? By the Powers, I admire ye for it!" The driver put down the bottle and lurched forward, and it became apparent that he was a cripple, with a wooden leg and crutch. He swayed with the motion of the Locomotive, a big, strong figure with a large, pale face, smiling. "And what might an upstanding fellow like you be a-doin' here, among the muck and din?"

The Locomotive heeled and shuddered as it clattered over phantom crossovers with a shriek of chafing steel. The fireman shoveled on, an apparition clad in a swirling black cloak and a hood that covered his head and concealed his features — *Unsuitable dress for his work*, thought the little man.

"I've come to ask a favor . . ." He was even more nervous. The smiling features of the driver failed to reassure him. There was a *wrongness* about the hectic scene in the cab. The furnace seemed to draw him, the flames churning within the firebox like a maelstrom. Why didn't the fireman stop stoking and close the doors? There was a red mark on the pressure gauge at 250, and the needle stood slightly beyond it.

The driver suddenly observed this, and with an oath he hurled himself at the regulator and jerked it wider. The throbbing of the exhaust deepened and quickened. "Blessed safety valve's jammed tight, messmate!" he shouted back at the little man. "Only way to get the pressure down is to use more steam going faster. Lay off stoking, will ye, else ye'll blow us all to kingdom come!" he said to the fireman, who ignored him, shoveling on. He turned back to the little man. "A favor, ye say? Never let it be said that Long John Silver refused a shipmate a favor!"

"I'd like to get off the train."

Silver's face changed instantly, becoming deadly serious. He staggered close, speaking quietly. "Well, now, that ain't so easy, my lad. Y'see, you're important to the voyage. Each and every passenger has a dooty to the train and ye wouldn't be shirking yer dooty now, would ye? Ye wouldn't spoil the ship for a ha'porth o' tar, would ye?" He took a long drag at his bottle, belched and wiped his lips with the back of his hand.

"I don't understand. What difference does it make if I get off?"

"Well, shiver me timbers." Silver was laughing, tears running down his broad cheeks. "Here's a pretty state of affairs. Here's a pretty kettle o' fish. What d'ye think keeps this here Train going, eh? Has there ever been a Train like it before, eh? Can ye tell me, lad — has there ever been a Train as can fly to the stars like a comet? Has there ever been a Train as can sail through the sun and come out the other side no hotter'n she went in? Messmate, this here ain't no ordinary Train. Why, ye're free to walk the full length, a thousand cables and more — free and welcome. Ye're free to enjoy yesself more'n ye ever thought a poor man could — there's fun enough for all on the Train. But ye must stay. And above all, ye must *believe* . . ."

His voice dropped to a portentous whisper and he leaned forward, propped on his crutch, staring into the little man's eyes. "What d'ye see on my shoulder, shipmate?" he asked quietly.

"Nothing . . . Coal dust maybe. What do you mean?"

"Mebbe a parrot?" Silver's tone was menacing. "Mebbe a parrot named Cap'n Flint?"

"Well, maybe." Terror chilled the little man's spine as Silver loomed over him. The shovel rang against the firebox like a knell.

"Damn your eyes, ye lie!" Silver shouted the words into the little passenger's face. "There ain't no parrot on my shoulder, nor ever will be — leastwise, *unless ye believe it!*" Balancing unsteadily on one leg he raised his crutch as though to smash it upon the other's skull.

"There is! There is!"

And there was.

Captain Flint sat on Silver's shoulder, shuffling emerald wings. He stared at the little man with a knowing eye. "Pieces of eight!" he screeched.

"Ah-hah!" Silver backed off, tucking the crutch under his arm. "Now get this into that head o' yers, lad. If ye can believe in the parrot, ye can believe in the Train. And if ye can believe in the Train, then there ain't no way we can afford to let you off. Because y'see, shipmate, we need every bit o' belief we can muster!"

"You mean . . ." The little man passed a tongue over his lips. The furnace seemed to be sucking the moisture from his body. "You mean this is all a composite smallwish? The Locomotive, the rest of the Train — a smallwish?" Now the terror was in every bone of his body, chilling him despite the heat. "What would happen if everyone stopped believing? Where would we be?"

"Ah, now — that's a thing we'd never want to find out, would we now? Because I tell ye this, shipmate — I figger you and me would be nowhere. Just nowhere, somewhere between Jupiter and Pluto. All alone in the cold, cold Nothing, in our birthday suits, falling forever. Frozen dead like a schooner lost in the ice."

"I've got to get off!"

"Ye knew ye were coming on an adventure when ye joined. The greatest adventure of a lifetime, they call it. The biggest thrill of all, for the cost of a smallwish. False fear ye've known, a lifetime of it. Now ye know real fear. Shiver me timbers! But you're a craven dog!"

"I thought we were on . . . on Earth. This is impossible!" Lips trembling, the little passenger turned and stumbled back through the passage of the tender. He didn't believe. He didn't — couldn't — believe.

And the walls of the passage turned soft.

A roar of rage sounded behind him and he heard the irregular thumping shuffle of the one-legged man. "Back here, ye dog!"

The Locomotive hit a curve and the little man, off balance, fell full-length through the corridor connector and onto the carriage floor. People gaped at him, glasses pausing on the way to mouths. A Neanderthal woman asked, "What are you lying down for? Get up and join the fun!"

"Avast there!" thundered the voice from behind him, and the

Locomotive let out an unearthly shriek. "This dog will be the death of us all, ye may lay to it!" Silver towered above the little passenger, standing on one leg, his crutch raised in both hands. "I'll crack him like a gull's egg, and we'll hear no more of his bellyachin'. Make yer peace, Mister!" And he swung the crutch back.

"Stop!"

At that moment an odd figure appeared — a girl, or something very close to a girl. Dressed in a white robe that failed to conceal her ungainly figure, she lumbered forward and thrust herself between Silver and the fallen man. One or two passengers cheered.

"Ah-hah! Now what do we have here? A circus freak? Out of me way, girl!"

"Get up." She addressed the little passenger, ignoring the fuming Silver. "He won't harm you, I'll see to that. Come and sit over here with us." And then he found himself sitting with two new arrivals, an elderly man and a barrel-chested youth. Meanwhile the Girl — for it was she — faced Silver. "Pick on somebody your own size next time."

"Why, ye . . . ye . . . I'll . . ." Inarticulate, Silver hefted the crutch.

And the parrot reappeared on his shoulder.

He glanced down at it in surprise. Evil-eyed, it leaned sideways and pecked viciously at his cheek. He yelled with pain, dropping the crutch and clapping a hand to his face. Grabbing a stanchion for support, he watched the Girl, the fury in his expression quickly changing to a shrewd look.

"Might I suppose ye wished that bird on me, me girl?"

"You might suppose that. Next time it'll be a griffon. You're just a big bully, you know?"

Silver smiled easily, all trace of fury gone. "That's as may be, me girl, and mebbe you're right. Old Barbecue gets carried away occasional, but all in the line o' dooty . . . So ye three be new passengers, eh? Well, now. Shiver me sides!" And he laughed heartily, playing the welcoming host, picked up his crutch and swung forward, his hand extended to greet his guests.

The little passenger was still watching the Girl in awe and admiration.

He didn't recognize her, though. How could he? Neither did the Girl recognize him — which was fortunate, because the Ifalong held more important matters than the Girl's love for a little man who used to be called Burt. This love, which to her had seemed the most important thing in Dream Earth, was already beginning to fade under the influence of Reality.

In time the Girl would forget Burt altogether, which is one of the minor tragedies in the story of the Triad.

Dreams Alone Are Not Enough

"*P*leased I am to meet ye!" Silver shook hands with Zozula, Manuel and the Girl, and even nodded affably to the little man. "Welcome aboard." He glanced at the parrot, now sitting quietly on his shoulder, and shook his head in admiration and disbelief. "Never seen the likes o' that, not I. Anyways . . . Beggin' your pardon, but I must discuss matters of importance with me shipmates here."

Zozula spoke quietly to the Girl. "Be careful. You can get hurt here. This isn't Dream Earth, you know."

"I smallwished the parrot on him, didn't I?"

"True. And if he'd hit you with that crutch, I think you'd have felt it. Just as he felt the parrot's beak."

Manuel said, "This place is strange. Can we get off soon?"

"I don't think the one-legged man will let anyone off," the little man told him. The rattle of the wheels had settled down to a steady, soothing rhythm. Faintly they could hear the beat of the Locomotive's exhaust.

Silver was moving among the other passengers, chatting, bowing obsequiously, smiling a lot. Every so often he would indicate his parrot and ask somebody to try to make it speak. "Pieces of eight!" the bird would squawk in varying tones of conviction.

"He's gauging their psy." Zozula was concerned. "This train has closer links with Dream Earth than I'd realized. You can call a unicorn into existence and you can ride it across a meadow. But to sustain your belief in the creature for more than a couple of hours is nearly impossible — unless other people see it, too, and reinforce your belief. A lot of people must believe in this train, right now. I hope they can keep it up . . ."

"Smallwishes drain you," the Girl agreed.

"So Silver will welcome new passengers with fresh psy."

"Messmates! Give me yer ears!" The roaring voice of Silver broke up their deliberations. "'Tis time to discuss the voyage and the destination. And the reason for you fine folk being on the Train. Aye — we have a powerful assemblage here, to be sure. Smart as paint, ye are!" Standing at the head of the aisle, dressed in his picturesque uniform, he cut an impressive figure as he dominated the carriage. The parrot clung to his shoulder, darting quick, cold glances around, and the whole regalia was surmounted by a salt-rimed cocked hat. "Now, we all know why we're here. We're here for adventure. Adventure the likes of which ye've never clapped eyes on afore! Death we'll face, and the most terrible fear, and monsters like ye've never dreamed of in your worstest nightmares. And we'll win through, shipmates! We'll win through!"

Even as he spoke, he couldn't resist snatching a quick, nervous look over his shoulder, back toward the Locomotive where the hooded stoker toiled.

"Where are we going, Silver?" shouted the tall, weather-beaten man dressed in a bush jacket.

"And what might yer name be, sir?"

"Charles Willoughby-Amersham. Baronet."

"Where are we going, Sir Charles? I'll tell ye where we're a-going. We've set course for a planet so dreadful that no man durst say its name — so that is the name we give it. The Nameless Planet. Aye, in the Ifalong mayhap it will get a right and proper name, so I hear tell. But as for the here and now, the Nameless Planet it is!"

Silver went on to describe the perils of the Nameless Planet in full and gory detail, with obvious relish. "Dragons big as blue whales, shipmates, with mouths like volcanoes." The passengers reacted according to type.

Sir Charles Willoughby-Amersham said, "By Jove! I really must bag a brace of those!"

Telma, the Neanderthal woman, said, "Fire and shelter. Will we find shelter there, and be able to build a fire?"

Psycaptain Hilary Yes said, "I remember well our sixth encounter with the creatures of the Red Planet. Now, that's what I call a battle. If the dragons of the Nameless Planet are anything like those devils, then —"

Bambi, the little brown girl, said, "My father dreamed up dragons — they were such fun! Fat bodies and great teeth and long tails. They always died in the end, though. They rolled over on their backs and gave a final puff. Then they were gone, and the good people had won again."

Wilbur Q. Mallet, star baron, said, "In point of fact, I believe the brutes are called Bale Wolves — although for some reason the real name went out of favor thousands of years ago."

Blondie Tranter, of the most durable profession, said, "People have always been superstitious — even in the year 100,000 Cyclic they were. They don't like to say the name of the thing that scares them, because this gives them an image in their mind. And as we all know, an image in the mind is tantamount to having the monster standing right beside you, eh, smallwishers?"

And the strangest smallwisher, a robot named Bot, said, "The creatures of the Nameless Planet are Bale Wolves, and no euphemisms will change that. The people on this train regard it as fun, going forth to do battle with these creatures. It is one step more daring than the fictitious adventures on Dream Earth, where nobody gets killed. It seems there is something in the human make-up that demands danger — real danger — and Dream Earth cannot provide that. The Bale Wolves can. They can kill. They can condemn humans to Total Death. I hope that every passenger realizes this. We are soon to face Total Death."

The words rang around the carriage, metallic and relentless. "Total Death. When both mind and body are wiped out. It isn't a game any longer. We are in a dimension beyond the help of Dream Earth and its cosy heroics. Silver offered you adventure and he spoke the truth. But I'm not certain that everybody understands the implications."

"Just how dangerous can these brutes possibly be?" Sir Charles bristled. "God, man, I've faced down a charging rhino!"

"In the days of Galactic exploration, no ship passed within a light-year of the Nameless Planet and lived to tell of it," said Bot.

"What do they look like?" asked Bambi. "Do they have black fur and shiny white teeth?"

"Logically enough, no living human being knows what they look like."

"I don't like the sound of this." The little man spoke quietly. "It seems to me there's a difference between adventure and certain death. Honestly, I wish I'd never set foot on this train. I've been a fool." These remarks were addressed to Manuel, who sat beside him.

"We're going to get off, soon. Why don't you come with us?"

"I don't have the psy. I Bigwished not long ago, and then I smallwished myself onto the Train, and now I'm all psy'd out. I asked Silver to let me off, but he wouldn't listen."

Silver cocked an ear in their direction. "And rightly not, shipmate. Rightly not. I told ye afore — we'll have no lily-livered whelps deserting the ship. Belay there!" he suddenly shouted, as the discussion about the Bale Wolves dragged on. "'Tis high time to splice the mainbrace." He produced a bottle of rum from his pocket. "I'd like to propose a toast, if I might make so bold. To the finest bunch o' shipmates I ever set sail with!" He raised his bottle, smiling broadly at the passengers. They cheered. He drank, blinked and wiped his lips.

Sir Charles shouted, "And a toast to Long John Silver, the finest skipper in the Galaxy!"

When they were quietened, Silver spoke more soberly. "And here's to the Celestial Steam Locomotive, lads, and may she carry us fair and far, and may we soon see the color of our enemies' insides! To the Locomotive and the voyage!"

And with this stirring toast he drained the bottle, threw it to the floor, where it shattered into glittering fragments, and raised his hand high.

"The song, lads. The song!"

He thumped his crutch on the floor and led the passengers into the famous song that echoed down the aeons, even after the Locomotive was forgotten — but for a mention in the Song of Earth — and the Domes were deserted and dead. It is a rousing song, part solo for a strong, lusty voice, part chorus. Its rhythm echoes the rattling of the railbeats, and its tune is simple and sturdy.

> We're all aboard for the trackless night.
> (Close your eyes and believe! Believe!)
> Wheels a-clanking and the firebox bright.
> (So cross your fingers and convince your brain,
> And clutch your rabbit's-foot and drink champagne,
> Lest Reason should annihilate this phantom Train)
> As our way through the stars we weave!

Now Silver raised his crutch in the air. "Mark one! Mark two! Mark three!"

And they all yelled back: "BELIEVE! BELIEVE! BELIEVE!"

Smiling, Silver waved his crutch, swiveled on his foot and stumped back toward the Locomotive.

Manuel caught sight of his face a second later as he plunged into the corridor connector. The mask had dropped and there was a terrible fear there, and the lips were trembling...

Silver's Nemesis

"This is getting out of hand." Zozula looked around at the other passengers drinking, playing cards, making love. "It's obvious the math creature isn't among this bunch of fools. He must have got off somewhere, and it's time we got off, too. I'm almost beginning to believe all this claptrap myself. That damned song keeps running through my mind. It's meant to, I suppose."

The little passenger said, "Nobody can get off."

"We'll see about that," said Zozula irritably. He'd been in charge of events for so long that he resented this insignificant little fellow telling him what he could and couldn't do — even if he meant it kindly. The small passenger was somehow familiar. Where had he seen him before? He seemed to see the man peering, searching. No matter . . . "I'm going to have a word with Silver," he said.

"It's time," said the Girl. "We could miss our stop."

"How do you know?" Manuel was surprised at her certainty. "It's all dark out there. All I can see is stars."

She tried to explain, but gave up after a few words. How could she tell him of this rare gift she had, this occasional sense of predestination that enabled her to choose the right course whenever a decision had to be made? It was as though she had the knack of seeing a little way along the diverging happen-tracks and picking the one that counted. It was as though a little of the Oracle had splashed on her.

Zozula led them through the tender.

A deadly scene greeted them in the cab. The firebox door was still open and the flames roaring. The boiler pressure was well beyond the danger mark. Everything was washed in a flickering crimson glow.

Silver fought with the fireman.

His crutch cast aside, he lay across the fireman's back with both hands locked around the other's throat, his jaw jutting and his eyes narrowed. The fireman crouched there with bowed back, facing the flames. He still held his shovel. He made no attempt to shake Silver off.

"I'll teach ye who's skipper in this cab!" Silver's voice was a rasp of hatred. "I'll wring yer neck like a spring chicken, that I will!"

And the fireman laughed. He laughed quietly, easily, as though he had about his neck a loose collar instead of the murderous hands of Silver. It was the first sound anyone had ever heard him make, and its effect was instantaneous. Silver's jaw dropped open, his eyes widened and, as the fireman twisted around, he fell to the footplate. At first the others thought that the fireman had deliberately thrown his assailant off, but as the hooded figure swung his shovel it became apparent that he was simply continuing his stoking chores, as though the attack had never happened. He lifted a shovelful of coal, swung back and scattered it smoothly across the fire. The flames brightened and the coal dust sparkled into little stars whipped upward by the draught.

"Ye'll kill us all . . ." Silver crawled to his feet and opened a large black trunk built into the side of the cab, extracted a bottle of rum, knocked the neck off and drank deeply, watching the fireman as if hypnotized. Then a movement at the rear of the cab caught his eye. He looked up and saw the three, and his expression changed immediately. He smiled, hopping forward. "Come to visit the poop deck, eh, lads? And what can I do for ye? Yer pleasure is my command."

"It's time we got off the train," said Zozula firmly.

"Well, now, and I had ye figgered for a gentleman of fortune. Get off, ye say? Well, now, isn't that just too bad. Shipmates shirking their responsibilities, is it? Mebbe ye don't know this, but I have a saying: Dooty is dooty. *Ye'll stay.*"

"I'd rather not force matters."

"Ah-hah!" Silver's voice was quiet and menacing. "Mutiny, is it?"

"Stop the train."

"That I can't do — leastways, not unless ye want to send us all to Davy Jones. 'Tis a little matter o' steam pressure."

Now the Girl spoke. She was tired. Living in her gross body had taxed her more than she'd realized and the swaying motion was making her feel sick, too. "Listen, you phony. We can leave anytime we please. We want to make it easier for everyone, that's all. We don't want to cause any credibility problems by stepping out into High Space against your wishes, if you get my meaning."

And just for a moment the fireman paused in his relentless stoking and looked straight at them. Zozula drew in his breath, a quick hiss.

Silver didn't notice. He was laughing, slapping his thigh with the palm of his hand. "Why, shiver me timbers! And here's a wee fat girl that thinks she can outwish a thousand souls! You and me should get along well, me darling — smart as paint, ye are! Dash my buttons if the girl doesn't mean what she says!"

"So stop the train."

"See here now, girl." Silver's tone had undergone another change; it was mock-pleading now. "Here's a blessed hard thing on a trainful of honest souls. We need every bit of psy we can lay our hands to — and ye've got it aplenty, girl. Don't take a spyglass to see that."

"All right." The Girl sighed, then took the hands of Manuel and Zozula. An unearthly strength seemed to be flowing through her mind and body, washing away the fatigue. "Come with me, you two. Just let yourselves drift." There was a vision in her mind: a blue glowing thing with a number of flat surfaces, hard, but not cold. It seemed to beckon, and it seemed to be an easy thing to concentrate on. Beckon . . . her subconscious played with the word. Beckon. Beacon. The blue thing was a beacon somewhere out in the Greataway — maybe on Earth, maybe elsewhere. But it was something she could lock her psy into and draw strength from.

"Now . . ." she said.

*

It was a dusty hillside, a bluff above a river. Beyond it was another bluff, a sign of the old river level before the years had carved the soft ground and the river had sunk. The land shimmered with heat. Sagebrush dotted the hillside in clumps.

Manuel thought he caught a flash of purple nearby, a rectangular object among the brush. But the heat was creating small mirages above the ground, and he must have imagined it. Despite the heat, he shivered, remembering. "Did you see the fireman's face?"

"He looked very pale. I thought he was sick," said the Girl.

Zozula was silent for a moment. Then he said, "The firebox door was open. Everything was glowing red — the floor, the window, yourselves, Silver, even the coal. Everything was red. Except for the fireman's face . . ." And he shivered too, at the memory of that ghastly visage.

THE WHEELED DOG

There's a little green lanky iguana;
He's the basilisk men understand.
He runs over water when startled
And dwells in a tropical land.

But the Dream Basilisk is a Gorgon,
And his tail bears a venomous tooth.
For facts are the fabric of fancy,
And fiction is stranger than truth.
— Darryl Du Piking, 129,643–130,125
"Song of the Dreamers"

"Don't go that way if you want to stay alive!" It was an unusual voice. Afterward they could never agree quite on its inflection or tone. Zozula found it supercilious, whereas the Girl thought it a warm bass. Manuel suspected that the voice spoke into their minds, not their ears.

They had been walking for over an hour with no set destination, following a ridge of burned grass above the river, urged on by Zozula, who pretended to have some mysterious objective of his own. The Girl was exhausted and Manuel was helping her along. At last Zozula had agreed to descend to the river, where they could slake their thirst and rest. The ridge was disheartening. It offered only a view of other ridges, rolling into the distance like a gigantic frown on the face of the earth.

And now, the voice.

"Who said that?" asked the Girl. They were descending the slope among small bleached rocks. Nothing was big enough to conceal a person. "Did you hear that, Zozula? Was it you,

Manuel? You're not playing tricks again, are you? We can do without practical jokes, right now."

"It wasn't me," said Manuel.

"It came from over there," said Zozula positively. "Show yourself!" he commanded.

First there was silence in the air and in their minds. Then, the tiniest rattle of loose stones and a feeling of decision that communicated itself to all three of them, so that they relaxed without knowing why. Then a small high-pitched and rhythmic squeal that set their teeth on edge, and a quick pattering.

A creature appeared.

It was like no creature they'd ever seen before. It was the most familiar creature on Earth. It was a machine. It was all of these, and it moved them to pity.

"H-hello, boy," said Manuel. The others said nothing.

It was small and brown, with a questioning face, floppy ears and a white spot on its forehead. Its eyes were soft brown and it carried its head erect and alert. It watched them, tongue lolling.

It was a dog on wheels.

Perhaps at some time in the past the dog had been involved in an accident and his hind legs had been crushed and he had been valuable enough (or conceivably, wealthy enough) to undergo an amputation and to be given a harness securing a pair of light, rubber-tired wheels under his abdomen. Behind the wheels, his tail wagged. When he ran, he trotted with his front legs and the rest of him rolled behind.

"I said, you'd better not go any farther along this trail." The dog indicated the narrow, dusty track that ran beside the river.

"And who are you to tell us where we may or may not go?" Zozula's tone was lofty.

"They call me Roller. I live hereabouts. I'm not real, of course, and neither are you, but I don't want to see you get killed — even if you are a figment of someone's imagination." The dog regarded them critically. "Although anyone with an imagination abnormal enough to dream up the likes of you three, I wouldn't like to meet. Maybe it would be kindest to let you follow the trail after all."

"I know I'm ugly," said the Girl quietly. "There's no need to remind me."

"You're no great beauty yourself, Roller!" Manuel moved to the Girl's defense.

Zozula's initial pity had also turned to irritation. "Step aside, dog. Those who pretend superior knowledge are the most stupid of all. You're real and I'm real, and the only unreal thing is the monster, or whatever it is, along the trail! Now — we're looking for a thing called the math creature. Can you direct us to it?"

The dog looked cunning. "I've heard my master referred to as the math creature. He lives in a land he has created himself. Such a strange land it is."

"Will you take us there?"

"The way lies through the monster's country," said the dog in some triumph. "I've been stuck here for days because I'm frightened to go back that way."

"What does your monster do?" asked Zozula sarcastically. "Roast people with its fiery breath?"

"Strikes them dead with its stare," said the dog sulkily. "And when I say dead, I mean Totally Dead. This is no dream. The monster is the only real thing in this region. You and I, we're no more than charismas in the Land of Lost Dreams, but the Little King is flesh and blood and venom."

Zozula stiffened. "The Little King . . ." he repeated softly. "The Basilisk . . . Yes, I've heard of the creature."

"Is it bad?" The Girl sat on the riverbank, bathing her sore feet. The cool water didn't seem to help.

"I don't think so. The Basilisk never really existed. It was a mythical beast recurring from time to time in legend, a little changed in appearance each time. What it looks like now, I can't imagine."

"Like a dragon, and everybody knows what dragons look like. Something like a crocodile" — the dog seized on Zozula's admission of ignorance — "and something like a giant bird with huge bristly wings. It's ruled this region for ages, killing everything that comes near, even the grass under its feet." Briefly the dog pawed the blackened ground. "And the eagles and the pterodactyls."

"Ugh!" The Girl's cry was not intended as a tribute to the fearsome nature of the Basilisk. She had scooped up a cupped handful of water and tried to drink it, then spat it out. "This water's awful — it tastes bitter."

"The Basilisk fouls the very rivers —"

"Enough of that! Let's try to get some sense out of you." Zozula interrupted the dog. "First of all — if the beast is so fearsome, how come you're still alive?"

The dog seemed to cower, assuming a sloping posture, head down, tail between its wheels, rump high. "It's because I'm not real. I'm not worthy of the Little King's attention. And I travel at night, so that he can't see me."

"Then how do you know what he looks like?"

"I've seen him at dusk, silhouetted against the sky. I've seen him by moonlight, trying to mate with the Cactus Asp. I've heard his cries rolling across the land like storm waves. I've seen what he does — the dead things, the stink. And the worst thing of all is that I've envied him. He's real, like nothing else in this place."

"I have to see this miraculous beast," said Zozula sceptically.

They rested by the fouled river and felt the sharp pains of hunger. They hadn't eaten for hours. But where could they find food in this burned and blasted land? Evening came and the dark hills closed around them and the river ran sluggishly past them like mercury, and just as poisonous. As the light failed, a cold mist arose from the surface, damp and choking, and Roller told them stories of the fantastic inhabitants of the Land of Lost Dreams — the cat-headed elephants and soft-bodied robots and walking bushes, and all the baroque things that humans had dreamed up in millennia of sleeping and that had been cast out by the Rainbow as being inappropriate to Composite Reality.

Zozula told the dog that all these things were not real.

"If they can kill me, then they're real enough," said Roller. "Shall we go now? It's dark enough to be safe — although why you should want to take the chance is beyond me."

Zozula couldn't explain that, either. It was an urge, an itch, a giant curiosity. No doubt they could have taken a detour to the math creature, but he just had to see the Basilisk. Was his path being influenced just a little by Starquin?

The Girl complained. "I don't want to walk just yet. Let's find a cave and sleep, shall we?"

Zozula's impatience got the better of him. "Listen to me. I'm not sitting by this stinking creek all night. I'm hungry and there's no food around here, that's for sure. And we can't come to any harm in the dark because the Basilisk can't see us (just supposing Roller is telling the truth, that is). And if he is telling the truth — well, we might come across a kill and find ourselves some venison for roasting! Now come on!"

He gestured them to their feet, then set off up the trail, followed by the dog. Roller's bearings squealed and his wheels occasionally seized, sliding on the loose scree and dragging him to a temporary halt. He freed them by backing up, then scampering forward again. Zozula's impatience grew with each occasion. The Girl took advantage of the delays to sink to the ground. Manuel remained standing, lost in a reverie of his own. Night flowed around them, cold and full of unfamiliar smells.

They saw only one other living creature on their journey to the Basilisk's lair: a man, tall and muscular, striding toward them, passing them with barely a glance and disappearing into the night. Manuel, lagging behind with the Girl, caught an impression of dark hair and heavy brows, and of full lips in a half-smile, as though sharing a secret joke with the night air. He never knew why the Girl gasped and stopped dead, staring after the figure long after it had gone.

"Are you all right?"

"I . . . Yes." Her face was even paler than normal and her plump arms quivered. "I'm fine. Stop staring at me, will you? Come on — we're getting left behind. Without Roller, we'll be lost."

"We're lost already, with or without Roller. I don't think Zozula knows where he is. He's just pretending. And anyway, we could hear Roller's wheels squeaking a kilometer away." Manuel was in a contrary mood, caught up in a quest of which he wanted no part.

In a moment of mutual unhappiness they stumbled forward and blundered into Zozula and the dog, who were standing tensely in the middle of the trail.

"Quiet!" Zozula warned them.

They froze and listened. The dark cliff of a steep hillside loomed below the stars, and they heard the sound of harsh breathing. They had reached the Basilisk's lair.

The Basilisk

<hr>

"*H*a!"

It was a sharp exhalation. The Basilisk had scented them. The dog gave a yelp of fright and cowered behind Zozula. Manuel found the Girl's hand in his, and was glad. They clung together. Only Zozula stood firm, secure in his long belief that he was immortal and invincible.

"Don't be frightened," Manuel whispered shakily to the Girl.

"Me, frightened? I can always wish the brute away — can't I?"

Now they heard the Basilisk's approach, a quick, pacing run, four claw-tipped legs moving swiftly in pairs, in fast rhythm, chik-chik-chik. The beast stopped and sniffed. They were aware of its smell, pungent as the mist that had risen from the river. They could just discern its outline. It was not large, maybe about the size of a deer, but bulky, with four clawed legs set close together beneath a globular body. When the wings fluttered they sounded leathery rather than feathery, and they flapped the stink of the beast into Zozula's face.

"Stop that!" he said sharply, as though addressing an errant pet. He felt Roller trembling against his legs and said, "It's all right, boy. He can't see you. He's not going to strike you dead, if you want to believe all that stuff."

The Basilisk sounded. A harsh screech pierced the night, followed by a chattering and gobbling.

"He's saying we're in his territory," said the dog.

"You speak his language?"

"I . . . I suppose so. I can tell what he means, anyway." After the Basilisk had made some more noises, Roller continued, "He says he's king of the hills and we've offended him, and he wants to know why he shouldn't strike us dead, right now."

"Because it's dark, that's why," said Zozula.

"He can follow us until daylight and then kill us." The dog was so fearful it could hardly voice the words.

"A fine, spirited beast. Ask him how we can satisfy him."

The dog whined and trembled and probably transmitted thought-images, because after a while the Basilisk began to reply.

"He says he's roamed these hills for many years killing everything that moves, since that is his destiny. He says he's at the height of his powers." Indeed, the very ground seemed to vibrate with the dynamism of the Basilisk's presence. "He says he is the superior in combat of any creature on Earth. But this very ability has its drawbacks. Recently he has been feeling urges that any lesser being would have had no difficulty in satisfying, but in his case it isn't so easy. He desires a mate. He wishes to reproduce himself, many times over."

"Are there no females around?"

"If there were, he would inadvertently strike them dead."

"That's quite a problem for him," Zozula observed.

"He says it's our problem too, because unless we find him a suitable mate, he'll kill us. Two of us must search, the other two he will hold hostage. The hostages must stay in the dark at the back of his lair, where they'll be unharmed. While they're prisoners, they must devise a way for the Basilisk to sire offspring without killing his mate."

Amused, Zozula said, "That sounds fair."

"Who stays behind?" asked Manuel.

"You and the Girl. You lack courage, and she's physically unfit for the search. Roller will be my guide."

So Zozula and the dog set off on their quest. They traveled

for many days and little is known of the strange things they saw. The Land of Lost Dreams is not endless, because it has only existed since the creation of Dream Earth. Nevertheless, there were at that time 80,000 years' worth of rejected and homeless oddities wandering the limbo between the computer and the many happentracks of Reality. They were disorganized, anachronistic, often separated by relatively as much space as separates the particles within an atom — which is to say that you could walk a long way in the Land of Lost Dreams without meeting a living thing. Not once during the journey did it occur to Zozula that there might be no such creature as a female Basilisk. He plodded on confidently, sustained by that sense of destiny that had possessed him ever since he had reincorporated the Girl from Dream Earth. The dog trotted behind, bearings squeaking continuously.

And on the eleventh day they found a female Basilisk.

She stood on a low hill, staring proudly around. Roller uttered a yelp of fear and hid behind Zozula, who strode forward confidently. The Basilisk was plump and of arrogant stance, and in the daylight they could see that her wings were in fact leathery like bats' wings, although the ostrichlike body had a fair covering of metallic-green feathers. The four legs were stout, scaly and clawed like those of a turkey, and the tail was tipped with a villainous spike. The head was crocodilian, although it bore a scarlet comb like a rooster. She was a proud-looking creature.

She looked at Zozula. Her eye was red and fierce, but if Zozula felt any misgivings, they have not been recorded in song:

> He faced the fiery Basilisk and stared it in the eye –
> Zozula stood triumphant where a lesser man would
> die.

Set in bare green skin, that eye was a fiery little ruby that swiveled to follow him as he walked forward. The dog howled, but he didn't die, either.

"See," said Zozula, "it's all superstition. There is no conceivable way in which one creature could kill another by the power of its eye alone. I hope we hear no more of this nonsense, Roller."

"Why do you suppose the land is all charred?"

"Doesn't it occur to you that there may have been a bush fire burning through here recently?"

"Look," said Roller, "she's eating a burned-up bird. How do you suppose she got hold of that?"

Zozula said patiently, "The bird flew into the fire and was burned by it. Or it flew over the fire and was asphyxiated by the smoke and fell. So the Basilisk eats it. Clearly, the creature is nothing more than a scavenger. Its gaze is harmless."

"There is another explanation."

"I doubt it. But you may tell me."

"The bird was real, but you're not. She can't kill smallwishes."

"Ridiculous!" Deeply offended, Zozula drew his cloak about himself. "Now, tell this creature our mission, before I take a stick to you!"

So the dog began to communicate in his mysterious way, and soon the Basilisk began to pay attention and to gobble and croak back. She shuffled her claws and pranced briefly, showing intense interest. Her eyes widened and blinked rapidly and she flapped her wings, but did not leave the ground. Roller cowered as he communicated, afraid that the Basilisk's excitement might trigger the power to strike him dead.

Finally the Basilisk was still, standing tensely and sniffing the air. She pawed the ground.

"She's offering us food," said Roller.

Zozula regarded the mangled carcass and shuddered. During their quest, food had been hard to come by, but finally they'd found a stunted tree that nourished bitter fruit. A meal of these had blunted his appetite for some time. *Maybe forever*, he thought. "Not now," he said. "Later, perhaps."

"Then she wants us to lead her to her mate."

The three began their journey over the sere hills. The dog led the way, retracing their scent, while Zozula and the Basilisk walked behind. At night they rested under the crippled trees and nibbled the fruit, and by day they traveled the misty land.

Shortly after dawn on the first morning of their journey back, a flight of geese arrowed across the sky and the Basilisk stiffened with interest, glancing up.

Two geese fell smoking to the ground.

"Remarkable," said Zozula, after a moment's silence.

The dog was quiet, reasoning that Zozula could take a stick just as easily to a right dog as a wrong dog.

"The Basilisk practices some kind of smallwish," theorized Zozula. "The geese aren't real, of course," he said, stripping the blackened skin and feathers from one and biting into the hot meat hungrily, "but the flavor is excellent." He threw the remains of the carcass to the dog, while the Basilisk gnawed at the other bird.

There were several such killings during their journey and the manner of them fascinated Zozula. The Basilisk's fast, pacing gait would slow and she would cock a crimson eye at the sky. The hue of her comb would deepen and she would utter a short gobble of anticipation. The bird would approach, winging across an empty sky. The Basilisk would observe it askance, waiting until it got within range, still trotting along. Suddenly the beast would stop dead and, standing foursquare, would raise her head like a gun turret and let the bird have it with both eyes. The bird would roll over in a puff of smoke and feathers and plummet to the ground. Zozula and the dog would race the Basilisk to the body, and, if the bird appeared to be of a natural species, Zozula would appropriate a portion and leave the Basilisk and the dog to squabble over the rest.

Finally they reached the lair of the male Basilisk. It was noon and the land was silvery bright. "Tell the creature to wait here," Zozula instructed Roller, "and we'll go on into the cave. Maybe we'll have to wait until night before we can bring the Basilisks together, or maybe there's another way."

They left the female behind a rocky outcropping and made for the cave. The male Basilisk suddenly stepped forth, stared fiercely around and spotted them. The dog yelped. He'd been immune from the female's glance, but that didn't mean the male was harmless. But he survived, and so did Zozula. They entered the cave, to be greeted by Manuel and the Girl.

"Where have you *been?* We'd given up — we were going to leave tomorrow. This Basilisk, he can't kill us, you know. We found that out quickly. Birds, yes. And mice and suchlike. But we were safe — he even killed a kind of lion that came sniffing around!"

"Basilisks can't harm us." Zozula patted the creature's feathery flank. "Probably because they exist on a slightly warped happentrack. But they are king of their own dimension, all the same." He went on to describe their quest and its success. "The female is nearby, but we can't introduce them to each other yet or I'm afraid she'll die."

The male Basilisk became restless, pawing the ground. Zozula threw a restraining arm around his neck.

"He's scented the female," said Roller.

"I'm not sure I can hold him. Quick, Manuel — give me your shirt. We'll have to blindfold the creature, or our quest will have been pointless."

Manuel ripped his shirt off and Zozula wrapped it around the Basilisk's head. It did little to calm the brute. A muffled chattering and gobbling filled the cave, and the animal's claws scratched for a foothold, sending the dog rolling into a corner. Manuel and the Girl hung on while Zozula secured the mask. Even then, as they relaxed their grip, the Basilisk made his way purposefully and unerringly toward the cave entrance, swishing his barbed tail. They followed.

Zozula felt the occasion demanded a short speech. "I don't know why we're doing this thing, but I like to think it's part of something bigger, some destiny we're fulfilling. Don't you feel it too, Manuel? Haven't you had the feeling there's an ultimate importance in our actions, Girl? I can sense some great cosmic Scheme, with ourselves as its instruments. Exactly where this creature fits in, I'm not sure — but you can be sure it's going to be important somewhere, on some happentrack."

As they hurried along after the Basilisk, Manuel said angrily, "You haven't been sitting around here for days doing nothing, like us. Do you know what I think? I think you've spent so many years in charge of your Dome that you think everything you do has some special significance. You've got a bloated idea of your importance, if you don't mind me saying so. You think you hold life and death in your hands. Listen, Zozula, out here you're just another man. This isn't a real animal; it isn't from real Earth. It's just a man-made Dream thing."

"Manuel!" whispered the Girl, aghast.

But Zozula ignored him. The Basilisk had reached the open air and had stopped, sniffing the breeze, his cowled head turning blindly and questingly this way and that. He trembled with desire, the scent of the female strong in his nostrils.

And sensing him, too, she came. She emerged from behind the rocks and saw the group at the cave mouth, and her head jerked up and she uttered a roaring screech. Zozula, Manuel, the Girl and the dog backed off. The male Basilisk turned uncertainly, facing his mate but unable to see her. He took a tentative step forward.

She bounded toward him, tail high, comb glowing. Her wings rustled and flapped, her feathers were iridescent with lust. She reached him and came to a skidding halt and, as he took another step toward her, she turned crimson eyes on him in a glowing look of love.

He gave out one croak and fell dead, smoking.

Appalled, Zozula seized a gnarled stick and set about the female Basilisk, beating it furiously. He shouted incoherently with rage and desolation.

Manuel said to Roller, "You're safe now. I told you the Basilisk wasn't all-powerful."

"Another Basilisk is still here. And it's proved what it can do." The dog trembled.

The Girl said, "You can come with us. I think Zozula will want to go soon."

Later that evening they built a fire at the mouth of the cave and sat staring into the glow while the fog deepened into night, and the voice of the female Basilisk could be heard somewhere out there, calling hopelessly for her mate.

Zozula spoke at last. "What a waste of a magnificent animal. And we've wasted days searching for the female when we could have been locating the math creature. Why did it all have to happen?" The fog lifted around the upswirling smoke and suddenly the stars were there, and the Land of Lost Dreams was just like any other land, and the cries of the lovesick Basilisk might have been any animal cry — the screech of a cougar, maybe, back on Real Earth.

Manuel sighed. The night held a mysterious beauty. Feeling sorry for Zozula, he said, "Nobody can be expected to understand everything. You said yourself there were programs in the Rainbow you knew nothing about and memory banks you couldn't even get into. It's big out here, Zozula. Bigger than the sea, bigger than the sky. Even the Rainbow might have forgotten what it's dumped in this place. And perhaps there are no happentracks; perhaps Time is just a straight line, or even a circle. How can we tell?"

Zozula was silent.

The Girl's eyes were shining as she gazed into the fire. The image of the female Basilisk was vivid in her mind: dynamic, prancing, death-dealing. "I've never had anything so real happen to me before," she said. "I've learned something from all this, anyway. Do you know what I think, Zozula? I think that we're not just looking for the math creature, or True Humans, or Manuel's Belinda. I feel there's something else we're being readied for. I was once told something by the Oracle . . ." She relapsed into a sudden silence, embarrassed.

"Funny . . ." Manuel looked at her. "An old *bruja* spoke to me once. And God speaks to me occasionally, too. We might not understand everything, but I think somebody else does."

Zozula sat in silence. The sounds of the Basilisk faded and he was left alone with his futility — which was the way it was meant to be. No man should have the arrogance to presume that he has been specifically chosen by Starquin. The Almighty Five-in-One does not need individuals. He arranges the pieces according to his overall plan — some of those pieces may indeed be individual humans, just as some may be mastodons or fleas — and then he lets them jiggle about on their own, like atoms. And, like atoms, they form an observable whole, a planet, a plan. Zozula was newly from the Dome, and he needed to learn humility. Maybe, like the Basilisk, he couldn't conceive that he, too, could be killed.

He was no longer in charge of Composite Reality. He was a vulnerable human, and although he was indeed a part of Starquin's plan, he could no more affect its eventual outcome than a ballroomful of Marilyns could affect the Cuidador Ebus.

LEGEND OF THE WOLF-CAT

*L*egendary figures and mythical beasts . . . As Mankind grew older and his knowledge of the Universe around him more complete, so his craving for the inexplicable grew. There were ages about which he knew nothing and could never know anything, because these ages were before the advent of recorded history. So where he was unable to deduce the facts from fossils and ruins, he invented legends. The legends were not pure fabrication, because they were assisted by the Rainbow — often through the medium of the Oracle — so that many of these legends first emerged on Dream Earth.

Legends. They are stories about the distant past that have passed by word of mouth through countless generations of humans who, perhaps, were not satisfied with the Rainbow's explanations. They are stories of what *might* have happened, based on known facts, and told as though they *did* happen.

Such a story is the Legend of the Wolf-cat, which concerns a not quite mythical beast and two Paragons — those unusual people, born of Dedos, who cannot become Dedos because of an inability to reproduce themselves. This does not mean all Paragons are permanently sterile. Their method of reproduction had not evolved by the time of the Wolf-cat's story, when they were perfect, celibate creatures.

Starquin had a purpose for them, even though the Dedos considered them useless. Their purpose was fulfilled when Siang performed his legendary deed, but the Paragons continued to appear at intervals during human history, living among humans incognito, like the Dedos.

*

In the year 210,652,166 Paragonic, all southwestern Pangaea was ruled by two Paragons. The land they ruled was already ancient and covered tens of thousands of square kilometers — mountains, valleys, rivers and forests. Through the middle of the land ran a canyon that was without water except at the rainiest times of the year. This canyon separated the domain of Lob, who lived to the west, from the domain of Fel, who lived to the east.

It is well known that Paragons were honorable and had no mortal faults. Pride, lust, envy, covetousness, gluttony, anger and sloth were unknown to them. What is not so well known is that they were lonely. This was because they were few and because they regarded their lands as a sacred trust, rarely venturing beyond their borders, spending their time looking after their animals and plants.

Since the Paragons were honorable, however, they were capable of love. They loved one another, but most of all they loved the creatures in their care.

Lob had a pet. In his pavilion there lived a great doglike creature who shared his food and drink. Long of leg and fleet of foot, it had a shaggy coat of yellowish red, with white tips at tail and chin. It had a pointed muzzle and ears and was the fastest animal in Lob's domain — so swift that it could run down any prey. And although it possessed most of the sins that mortal animals do, Lob loved it dearly. It was called the Maned Wolf.

Fel also had a pet. Although it was bigger than the Maned Wolf, it was no faster; nevertheless, it was the swiftest animal in Fel's domain and he was very proud of it. It was long and sleek, whereas the Maned Wolf was tall and angular. It had round ears and thick legs and a long tail, and it moved with sinuous grace. Its most striking feature was its coat; close-textured and thick, golden yellow and covered with a multitude of black rosettes. Fel considered that there was no finer animal in all Pangaea. It was called the Leopard.

One day Lob and Fel met at the foot of the canyon near the Many-faceted Rock, where their domains abutted. They had their pets with them, on leashes. The pets, being mortal animals, sniffed and then snarled at each other. The hair around the neck of the Maned Wolf rose, and the lips of the Leopard curled back. Each thought the other was too close to its domain — and besides, they found each other odd-looking. They strained at their leashes and the Paragons had difficulty in holding them apart, so eventually they tied them to stunted trees. The pets were close enough to sniff and snarl, but too far away to attack.

"That's a fine-looking animal you have there, Fel," said Lob politely.

"Yours is a good-looking beast, too."

"Wolf is the swiftest in the land. I've seen him run down a guanaco in fifty paces."

"I'm sure that is so. But I tell you this: Leopard can catch a fleeing gazelle in the time it takes a leaf to fall!"

So saying, they both paused to consider their animals, each gazing with fondness at his own pet (but not with pride) and with thoughtfulness at the other's (but not with envy or covetousness). Strange and unaccustomed thoughts grew out of this scrutiny. It seemed that there was some natural outcome to all this, but because of their perfection they were unable to give voice to it.

The Maned Wolf trotted to and fro on tall legs, within the bounds of his leash, and the Leopard slunk in fluid circles. And the Paragons loved each other. So what was this unfamiliar sensation? It was growing inside them, bursting to be let out. And they couldn't contain it any longer.

"It seems to me that friendly sport is a good thing," remarked Lob casually. "Exercise for the pets, and a lesson to one of us to be magnanimous, and to the other to be humble."

"The greatest distance in the time it takes a leaf to fall?"

"I think the first home over a distance of fifty paces would be more equitable."

While the Paragons discussed the race rules, the animals looked at each other in astonishment, hostility forgotten. They had understood every word, because Paragons conversed in thought-images much of the time. And although Paragons were said to have no sin in them, it seemed to the animals that this new project was tempting fate.

But the rules were arranged and the Paragons climbed in opposite directions out of the canyon with their pets, having arranged to hold the race in five years' time — time meaning little to them. The Paragons returned to their pavilions as excited as their pets were disillusioned. Time went by, and it happened that one day the Maned Wolf met the Leopard by the Many-faceted Rock. And this time there was no snarling.

"My master makes me run every day until I'm ready to drop," the Maned Wolf said. "And he sets loose small animals for me to chase and kill. More animals than he needs for food."

"Me, too." The Leopard spoke in a sad purr. "He flies birds with clipped wings and I must leap and catch them, and if I fail he . . . he . . ."

"He beats me. It's not right." The Maned Wolf marveled at what he'd said because it didn't sound as though he was talking about a Paragon.

"We must do something about it."

"We cannot race. Whoever wins, the Paragons will lose. It has become too important to them, this silly game. I don't care who is the faster," said the Maned Wolf.

"Neither do I. In fact," said the Leopard, "I like you, Wolf. I don't want to race against you."

"Nor I against you."

Thus, even as the two Paragons were growing further apart, the two animals came together in friendship and love, and a desire to do what was best for their masters.

The years went by.

At the appointed hour on the appointed day, the Paragons met in the ravine by the Rock where their domains abutted. They embraced.

"I kept my word," said Lob, "but I have no animal. Maned Wolf left me over three years ago. I've seen him about the domain, but he won't come to me."

"Leopard went too. It's a great pity, because he was undoubtedly the swiftest animal in all Pangaea."

"I doubt it."

"That's a strange statement, Lob."

"I was merely expressing an honest difference of opinion, Fel."

The Paragons drew apart and turned their backs on each other, and as they climbed back to their own lands, three animals trotted down the canyon from the north. On one side was the Maned Wolf, older, but still swift. On the other ran the Leopard, limping a little, but agile enough. And in the middle . . .

In the middle was an animal the like of which the Paragons had never seen. It possessed some of the Leopard's features; the coat was dense and tawny and covered with small black spots. But the legs were long like the Maned Wolf's and the head small, and the claws were dull and did not retract. The Paragons regarded this strange animal with astonishment. Then the Maned Wolf ran to Lob, and the Leopard ran to Fel, scrambling up the slopes. The animals greeted their owners, then turned to regard their offspring, as if to say: *See what love can do.*

And somewhere in the Greataway, Starquin was enraged that his perfect Paragons had been shamed by the animals of Earth. The ground trembled with his anger and boulders tumbled into the canyon and the sea burst upon the land. A mighty cataract swept along the canyon, bearing down on the love-animal in a wall twenty meters high. The Paragons backed away from the edge, stared at each other in fear from opposite sides, then looked at the trapped animal in pity. The Maned Wolf yelped and the Leopard screamed.

The Wolf-cat saw the advancing wall of water, threw back its head and uttered a kind of barking howl. It looked up at the distant Maned Wolf, its father, then at the equally distant Leopard, its mother, and it didn't know which way to run.

So it ran along the bottom of the canyon, pursued by the

roaring water. The Paragons' pity changed to amazement, because the animal was the swiftest they'd ever seen — swifter even than the Maned Wolf or the Leopard. It moved like the wind itself, bounding and fluid, with all the best of both wolf and cat in perfect motion. It was the most beautiful thing the Paragons had ever seen — and in their awe there was covetousness.

Starquin sensed this, and the land shuddered and the walls of the canyon moved farther apart. Because Starquin had at last realized that perfection can only exist in isolation and that the Paragons were becoming contaminated by their very nearness to each other.

The love-animal, his great speed waning as he tired, felt the ground move, too, and saw that the water was almost upon him. So he made his decision, veered right and bounded up the canyon wall to join the Leopard, his mother, because this is the way a mortal animal's strongest bonds lie. The Maned Wolf, far away on the opposite bank, barked for joy to see his son safe, although he knew he would never see him again.

Neither would he ever see the Leopard again, because this part of Pangaea had divided into two great continents moving ever farther apart, which in the Ifalong would become known by new names — South America and Africa. The Maned Wolf would never leave South America, but the Leopard would find vast new lands, because Africa was destined to meet Asia and India.

And the Wolf-cat? Lob saw him go to Fel's side of the canyon and knew beyond doubt that Fel now possessed the swiftest animal in the world. He was overcome with envy. Thinking Fel had used the power of the mother Leopard to capture his prize, he shouted again and again, "You cheat! You cheat!" until the Earth rumbled again and the new continents moved ever faster, until they were lost from sight of each other.

As time went by, the incident became lost among new legends of the new lands, and Lob and Fel died. But the love-animal carried the stigma of Lob's taunt down all his generations into the Ifalong, and his kind became known as the Cheater.

THE MAY BEES

•••

*T*he noise of pounding water increased and Manuel guessed that he was approaching a waterfall. The trail took a sudden bend, hugging the wall of a rocky outcropping. He trod carefully because here the trail was little more than a pebbly shelf ten meters above the river, which flowed fast and foamy with swirling eddies. The nature of the rock changed, the dry redness giving way to a more mellow brown, with here and there a plant thrusting its roots into a crack. Manuel left the outcropping behind, the trail widened again and the scene changed completely.

Now the narrow river valley was filled with lush vegetation. Manuel was filled with a longing for home. The valley was similar to one he'd known not ten kilometers from Pu'este: the rushing water, the tall trees with their thick old trunks acrawl with insects, the rustling life in the undergrowth and everywhere the hanging, looping vines. Even the smell was similar, a nostalgic recipe of damp earth and rotting leaves, of aromatic herbs, animal droppings and resin. He wandered on more slowly now, stepping carefully, because there was a waiting stillness about this place. The trail descended precipitously toward a broad pool that formed a tranquil backwater to the river.

On the bank of this pool sat the Girl.

She didn't look up as Manuel approached. She sat with drooping shoulders, staring down at the slow surface. Her hands were clasped loosely in her lap and her plump legs swung idly above the water. Manuel sat beside her, easing himself quietly into her company.

"That's me down there," she said. A tear dropped from the end of her nose, and ripples widened for a moment. The reflection soon reformed, however — remorselessly.

"No, it's not," said Manuel. "It's just a package your soul's wrapped up in. There's an old priest in the village called Dad Ose. That's what he used to say when the girls from the village complained boys wouldn't mate with them because they were too ugly. He used to say the package doesn't mean a thing . . . Why am I talking as if it all happened a long time ago? Anyway, he says that there are even places where people could unwrap you and put you in a different package if you wanted — which shows the package doesn't matter."

"I lived in a place something like that. The package did matter, more than you'd ever believe."

"So why did you leave?"

"Zozula took me away. Anyway, there were other things wrong with Dream Earth."

Manuel thought for a moment. "There was something terrible about that place you lived in — I could tell by the way you spoke about it. And by that name you didn't want to be called — Marilyn. You wanted to get out."

"Look at me — see that face? These arms, and this great pudgy neck? I wish I *were* a Marilyn, you know that?"

"What can be so good about a Marilyn?"

"If I were a Marilyn, sitting here right now, you'd love me. You wouldn't be able to resist me."

"Is that really what you want, Girl?" Manuel regarded her reflection, trying to imagine a girl so beautiful that she could make him forget Belinda.

"I didn't say I wanted it," she said hastily. A mosquito landed on the pale flesh of her arm and she regarded it, felt it sting, then frowned. "Go away," she said. The mosquito remained, drinking her blood.

Manuel slapped the insect and it dissolved into a small

smear of blood. "That's how you do it. You keep forgetting, don't you."

"I hate this place! It's worse than the Train! Nothing will do what you want it to!" The Girl felt like a fool.

"That's where the fun is."

"You call this fun?"

"The fun's in fighting when you know that everything on Earth has the power to kill you if it got the chance." He was watching her wrist and he saw the smear of blood turn pale and disappear, leaving no mark, no sign of a bite. "Even this place isn't real enough," he added. "You remember that pool where the axolotls were? That's the kind of place I like. All this dream stuff scares me almost as much as the real things scare you. But it doesn't bore me. You got bored in your Dream world. It's enough to bore anybody, having everything done for you."

"Manuel . . ." She turned and looked at him. *Her eyes are quite pretty,* he thought. *Blue and wide, like sapphires in an unsuitable setting.* "How real is this place? Could we die? Really die, I mean? This pain I feel often, and I'm always tired. I never knew what tiredness and pain were, before. The ground's so rough, and it gets so cold at night. Everything keeps changing, and I can't keep up with it . . ."

"You'll be all right. This is a halfway place — the monsters are fake; but nobody spent any time on the scenery, so it's almost real. It's like an old store where a merchant is showing all sorts of beautiful and impossible rugs and drapes from far-off places, and behind them the walls and floors are dried mud because it doesn't matter. And in the back are the things he couldn't sell, in a little room where they lie all colorful and alone, too weird for anyone to buy."

This reminded her. "What happened to your mind-painting machine?"

"I left it behind at the Dome. I know where it is, and one day I'll be able to finish that picture I made in it."

"One day . . . ? You talk so strangely, Manuel. Nobody talked about the future where I came from."

"I expect they missed a lot. Look!"

A small, bright bird swooped low over the water, iridescent, looking for food. It seemed to be real, lost from some obscure happentrack. It plunged under the surface, emerged with empty beak and then perched on a stump to watch the surface with a fierce, irritated eye.

"What is it?"

"A kingfisher. A bird." He eyed her curiously. "You did have birds in your world?"

"Of course we did."

She watched the tiny creature preening itself, a fragile thing of feathers that had to fight for every minute of survival, yet found time to look after its beauty — which beauty was all the more valuable for that. She wondered what else was missing from Dream Earth, where so many creatures had been lost from the mists of memory and appeared only as freakish manifestations of somebody's whim.

After a while Manuel said, "We'd better get back to the others and tell them about this place. There's food here — see that fruit?" He dribbled some dirt into the water, shattering the mocking reflections. "They'll be wondering where we are."

"Let's go a bit farther." She took his hand. "There's a waterfall down there. I'd like to see it."

And over the trees a swarm of dots circled, picking up a scent only they could sense.

"We'll just take a quick look, then. We'll have to go that way anyhow, if we want to reach the sea."

"Why should we want to reach the sea?" The dots were closer, humming on rapid wings.

"Well . . . It seems the right way to go. Toward the sea . . . Look! What are these?" Alarmed, Manuel jumped to his feet.

The May Bees surrounded them in hundreds, huge and buzzing, golden brown furry insects.

"They'll sting us!" The Girl waved them away.

"Don't be afraid . . ."

"Who said that? You, Manuel?"

"I think it was the bees. I don't think they're dangerous. There's something soothing about them."

"That's right. We mean you no harm . . ."

"Then go away!"

"*We're here to help . . . In these parts, we come along when people are lost and don't know what to do. We can sense these things. We are the May Bees and we only live for a little while . . .*" Indeed, some of the bees were dying already, zooming suddenly out of control, smacking into the ground, buzzing for a while on their backs, spinning and then lying still. "*. . . so we know all about death, and we have compassion, and we help, and we make sure people don't do anything that might bring them into danger. You're safe with us, you humans. We'll show you the way.*"

So persuasive were they that Manuel found himself saying, "Tell us which way to go." Briefly he explained their problem: their conflicting purposes, their dependence on Zozula and the dog, the strangeness of their surroundings. "I'm sure we'd be better off heading for the coast," he said.

"*You would. You certainly would.*" A May Bee hung before him on whirring wings. "*Take the riverside trail past the waterfall, then on through the rain forest, and the sea is no more than two days' journey away.*" The bee, exhausted, fell to the ground and expired.

Another took over, bug-eyed and furry. "*And then again, you could build a raft and float down . . .*"

More voices. "*. . .but the river is swift and the waterfall not far away . . . Although, beside the trail, there is a cliff where a dragon lives . . . Maybe the desert route would be better — that way you miss the delta, and the alligators . . .*"

Now a very small and somehow feminine bee hovered before Manuel's face, speaking softly into his mind. "*My advice to you, my dear, is to fly. Build yourself a kite of leaves — you see those over there, on that tall tree? Then go to the edge of the cliff and launch yourself off and you'll catch the upcurrents — I've done it myself, oh, so many times today. Then you can glide all the way to the beach.*"

Manuel said firmly, "We'll walk, thanks. We'll take the forest trail and if we see any dragons, well, we'll just outrun them. Dragons are slow. I'm not scared of them, if they exist at all."

And now the May Bees chanted in chorus:

DON'T DO IT!!!
You might trip over a log,
You might fall into a bog.
Seven percent of the people who run get attacked by
*   a rabid dog!*

"Well . . . let's just go and find Zozula first, before we do anything hasty, shall we?" said the Girl.

"*Now that's a good idea,*" said a May Bee seriously, alighting on her shoulder. "*It's always better to seek another opinion. Consider all the options. Act with due forethought.*"

"*This Zozula sounds like a wise man,*" said another. "*The sensible thing is to consult with him — he has the experience. And besides, he seems to know the places where you can catch the Train, if you decide on that option.*"

"Come on, Manuel." The Girl's mind was made up. "He can't be far back along the trail. Let's get away from these things!"

But the May Bees chanted in unison:

DON'T DO IT!!!
Perhaps he will slap your face,
Or decapitate you with a mace.
Ninety percent of his former companions are
*   stranded in outer space!*

Now Manuel was nervous. "These things are dangerous! Can't you feel it, Girl? They're dying, themselves, and they want to take everyone else with them! Let's get back — quickly!"

"They're right, though. Zozula hasn't exactly distinguished himself as a leader, so far. Maybe we're better off without him."

"Can't you see what they're doing to us? A minute ago *you* wanted to find Zozula and *I* wanted to make for the sea. Let's try to think this out, before we do something stupid."

"*Think it out carefully. Consider all the alternatives. That's the sensible way.*"

"Girl, whether it's right or wrong, we're going back to find Zozula and Roller. I'm not even going to discuss why I think it's what we ought to do." He took her arm and dragged her away from the riverbank. The May Bees swarmed closer and their buzzing took on an angry note.

The Girl was silent, stumbling along behind him as he began the long climb up the winding trail. The May Bees surrounded them in a cloud.

"Look before you leap ... You can't judge a book by its cover ... Tread carefully ... A stitch in time saves nine ..."

"Shut up!"

And then the Girl screamed.

Manuel, turning, saw a big bee fasten itself to her plump arm, arch its body and drive home a stinger the size of a dagger.

The Girl screamed again and as the May Bees whirled higher and zoomed off into the trees, she slid to the ground unconscious.

*

Zozula, Manuel and the dog regarded the motionless figure of the Girl. She lay on her back, a mountain of inert flesh, ashy white except for her arm, which was swollen and red-purple. The dog tentatively sniffed at her.

Zozula was angry. "You're a stupid young fool, Manuel. She could be dying, you know that? All I do is let you out of my sight for a while, and this happens."

"I couldn't help it."

"You could have protected her, couldn't you? You're from the real world, aren't you? Don't you realize how vulnerable she is? Where she came from, she was able to wish danger away. Here it isn't so easy. You should know that, even if she doesn't!"

"They were all over us in no time at all." Manuel watched the Girl fearfully. She lay very still, hardly breathing.

Roller said, "I told you this place could kill you!"

Goaded, Manuel snapped back. "The Basilisk didn't kill us!"

Zozula was feeling the Girl's pulse. It seemed very weak. He stood, looked around and sighed. "We shall have to go back, of course."

"Back where?"

"Back to the Dome. The Girl may die if she doesn't get treatment. We can't do anything for her here."

Manuel looked around the rocky land. Away to the right was the path along which he'd dragged the Girl — or was it? The short grass had disappeared and he knew without looking that the tree-lined river was now a dry gulch. They should have gone on; they should have made for the coast while they still had the chance. It was too late now. Night was coming on and screeches and yells were greeting the darkness. The sky was like a shroud. "How?" he asked quietly. He didn't know his own powers, then. It was much later that he discovered what he could do.

"How what?"

"How do we get back to the Dome?"

"The same way we came, of course. On the Train."

"And where's the Train?"

Zozula looked around briskly. "Well, it shouldn't take too long to find the Train. We'll just retrace our steps . . ." He pointed. "Back down that trail, then south across the mountain ridge."

"The mountain ridge has gone, Zozula."

Meanwhile, the dog had crept close beside their legs, whimpering. Zozula said to him, "You'll show us the way, won't you, Roller."

"Show you?" There was reluctance in the dog's tone.

"The place in this land where people come and go. Where people appear and disappear, as we appeared. There's a Locomotive — a great fiery thing pulling a string of carriages a hundred kilometers long. You must have seen it."

"My master lives there."

"The math creature?" Zozula brightened. "In the morning you will take us to the nearest trees, where we can make a stretcher for the Girl. Then you will guide us to your master, and to the Train. Meanwhile . . ." He wetted the Girl's lips with a couple of drops from a glass vial. She moved her head, murmuring weakly. "She'll be all right for the night," he said. "But no longer than that."

"If I show you the way, you'll leave me here all alone, forever," said the dog.

"Of course we shall. You belong here with your master."

Manuel interrupted. "We'll take you with us, Roller."

The dog whined. "No! I'm not real! The moment I set foot in the real world, I shall cease to exist!"

Zozula said, "Let me get this straight. You won't let us leave you, and you won't come with us — is that it? You want us to stay here forever."

"I love you," said Roller.

"What kind of a reason is that?" Zozula bent down, speaking quietly into the dog's floppy ear. "I'll tell you something, my friend. Either you do as you're told, or I'm going to unstrap those wheels of yours, right now. And where will you be then? Answer me that!"

"All right. All right." All the stuffing had been knocked out of the dog. He stood shivering, tail between his wheels.

"We leave at first light." Zozula wedged himself down into a cleft of rock, dragging dried vegetation over himself.

"Don't do it . . ."

"Don't do what? Who said that? Was that you, Manuel?"

"It was the Girl. She's awake!"

They knelt beside her and Manuel saw her eyes were open and glistening. Something about her expression made him shiver; there was a terrifying blankness there. Her lips moved. Manuel had to bend close to hear what she had to say.

> *Don't do it – not that Train.*
> *You might fall under a spell*
> *Or into a bottomless well.*
> *Eighty percent of the passengers purchased a ticket*
> *   directly to Hell!*

"What did she say?" asked Zozula.

"Nothing . . . Nothing that made sense. She's rambling, Zozula. You're right. We'll have to get her back home."

It was suddenly cold, and Manuel covered the Girl with dead twigs and leaves. In the gathering darkness he could see that her eyes were still open, but he couldn't tell whether she was looking at him.

Zozula yawned, pulling his robe about him. "We don't have to do anything right now," he said. "A night's sleep will do us all good. The Girl's resting easily."

"She's watching, me, Zozula. Her eyes look different — not like her at all."

"Go to sleep, Manuel." Zozula wriggled back into his cleft, pillowing his head on his hands and blinking at the stars.

"All right." Unhappily, Manuel composed himself.

Soon they were both breathing slowly and evenly, and the dog, whimpering and twitching, was fleeing from dream enemies.

The Girl got quietly to her feet and walked away. Her eyes were open, but they were not connected to her mind.

THE FIVE FEARS

Somewhere in a swamp in mystic crocodiles' domain,
Live Loneliness, Humiliation, Loss and Death and Pain.
— Song of Earth

The Girl found she was wading through water-logged ground between trees, but after a while she felt firm ground beneath her feet. Although daylight had arrived, the canopy of leaves and thick, twisted branches was so dense that very little light filtered through. The leaves dripped a continuous rain, however. Worn out, the Girl fell to the ground.

Later she awakened with a feeling that someone was watching her. She raised her head slowly. Had Zozula and Manuel arrived to take her back? The trees stood silently around. She turned her head sharply at a slight sound to the right and caught a glimpse of a slender naked form before it slipped behind a tree. The drizzle from above made it hard to see clearly, but just for a moment she'd thought . . . Did the creature have wings? A faunlike face appeared around the trunk, but was quickly withdrawn. The creature was frightened.

"Come here!" the Girl called. "I won't harm you."

The face popped out. The eyes were wide and scared.

"Come on!"

Now a leg appeared, slim and pale, tense and ready to jerk back. Then the body. One hand still held the trunk. It was a girl, a very beautiful young girl about thirteen physical years old. She hung onto the knotted trunk as though her hands and feet had different ideas. Then at last she let go and stood poised,

slanting eyes darting anxious glances around before they regarded the Girl.

"Are you sure you won't hurt me? I couldn't stand it if you
did."

She had wings, gossamer things that looked too fragile to
bear a kitten aloft, let alone a girl.

"What . . . what are you?" asked the Girl wonderingly.

"I'm a flaiad. I live here in the Forest of Fear. It's a terrible
place — there are all kinds of things that hurt you."

"I know. Can you really fly?"

"Not very well. The trees . . . We bump into the branches
and fall to the ground and . . . and it hurts so much!"

"We? Are there more of you?"

"Five . . ." The flaiad was gaining confidence. Now she was
looking at the Girl with curiosity. "And what are you?"

"I'm a girl."

"No, you can't be. *I'm* a girl. Look at me. This is what girls
look like."

"I know," said the Girl with undisguised envy. "But I could
have looked like you, once. This isn't my real body, I'm sure it
isn't. They try to tell me it is, but I don't believe them." Oddly,
she felt a kinship to this winged girl.

"You must be almost as unhappy as we are. You *look* unhappy. You have lines between your eyes."

"Here." The Girl extended a hand. She was about to ask the
flaiad to help her to her feet, but the creature had backed away,
flinching as though expecting a blow. "What's the matter?"

The pose was studied, almost ritualistic. One forearm was
flung across the small face, the other arm was extended, palm
flat, toward the Girl. The flaiad froze like that. "Don't . . . hurt
. . . me."

"I wasn't going to." The Girl crawled to her feet, brushing
down the ragged remains of her dress and wishing she had the
courage to go naked like the flaiad. "Don't run away," she
added. The other seemed poised for flight, regarding her as
though she were an unpredictable animal.

"You're so . . . huge. You could hurt me a lot, if you had a
mind to."

"Well, I don't have a mind to." Changing the subject, which

was becoming tedious, the Girl said, "Let's go and find your friends. Where are they?"

"By the lake." The flaiad was still wary, but after a while she relaxed a little and led the Girl through the woods.

"What's your name?" asked the Girl conversationally.

"Pain."

"Pain? That's an odd name for a pretty child."

"It has its meaning. What . . . what's yours?" asked Pain shyly.

"I'm just called Girl."

"That's an odd name, too." And the flaiad actually smiled.

"I think I have another name, and one day I'll find out what it is. Until then, I'll stick with *Girl*. It means something — like your name."

Then the trees became more spaced out and dark water glistened before them, motionless under the canopy of branches.

"This is where we live," said Pain.

The Girl could not recall ever seeing a more dismal place.

*

The lake was about one hundred meters across, dark and malodorous. Litle patches of brown scum floated on the surface, which was in tiny trembling motion from the raindrops. In many places the trees actually stood in the water, their branches intermeshing overhead. Pain and the Girl stood in a small clearing at the water's edge. Here the underbrush had been cleared back and the sticks and leaves woven into a rough hut.

"These are my sisters," said Pain, introducing four more flaiads, who stood or sat in varying attitudes of dejection beside the water. "Loneliness, Humiliation, Loss and Death."

As though discouraged by the sound of their own names, the flaiads assumed attitudes that, like Pain's flinching, appeared almost formal. Loneliness sat with arms huddled about herself; Loss wept, with knuckles pressed to her eyes; and Death simply shivered. Only Humiliation struck no noticeable pose, but after a moment the Girl realized that the flaiad was blushing deeply.

"You don't seem very happy," remarked the Girl after this had continued for a few moments.

"Would you be happy living in such a dreadful place?"

"No. In fact I'd probably leave. Why don't you?"

At this the poses became intensified, and Pain backed off as though the Girl had struck her across the face. "We can't leave," said Humiliation, blushing crimson. "This is our destiny — to remain here and suffer forever."

The Girl's pity was changing slowly to irritation. "That's ridiculous. If you don't like it here, you could walk out just as easily as I walked in."

"But what about the Swamp of Submission?"

"If you mean that patch of boggy ground out there, what's wrong with getting your feet wet? It's a small price for escape."

"There are crocodiles in the swamp."

"I didn't see any."

"They are there. They let you in — but they won't let you out. Such is the way of the Swamp of Submission and its dreadful creatures."

The four other Fears postured afresh at this pronouncement from Death, and Loss's weeping became a shrill wail. Humiliation said, "You must have been looking for this place yourself, otherwise you wouldn't have arrived here."

The Girl was silent.

"Now you're here, do you like it? You say our destiny is ridiculous, but your own destiny guided your feet through the swamp."

The Girl said determinedly, "You could fly over the crocodiles. You could walk to the edge of the swamp and take off, and fly through to the end of the forest; then up and over the rest of the swamp."

"We cannot fly well enough to avoid the trees," said Loneliness. "We've lived on the ground for so long that the powers have almost left us."

The Girl almost screamed in frustration as the wailing broke out afresh. "Well, if you can't do anything else, at least change your names!"

Pain seemed to be the most controlled of the flaiads at this

point and, although flinching, she said, "I repeat — don't you
like it now you're here? Are you renouncing the attitudes that
brought you here?"

"I wasn't brought here by my attitudes," said the Girl, annoyed. "I was poisoned by the May Bees and I woke up here."

"The May Bees only attack those who invite them."

"Nonsense!"

"Then try to leave."

"No. Not now. I'll stick with it for a while." The Girl's lips
pressed together as she stared around the clearing, beginning to
realize her own stupidity, even more annoyed with herself than
with the miserable flaiads.

*

Legend does not relate how long the Girl stayed in the Forest of
Fear, eating raw fish and weed from the lake, sleeping fitfully in
the crude hut while the never-ending rain dripped through the
roof, listening to the incessant whimpering of the flaiads. Some
say she remained there for many years, although our knowledge of her character makes this difficult to believe. It is
perhaps sufficient to say that she awakened one day knowing it
was time to go.

She stirred the flaiads with her foot. "Get up!" She was
slimmer now — her simple diet had seen to that. She could
never be as beautiful as the flaiads, though; physically she was
a big baby and would remain that way for a long time yet. She
resented the flaiads' beauty, and she was not gentle when she
roused them. "Get up!" she cried, a new restlessness running
through her.

"You're hurting me!" cried Pain.

"You're going to leave us, I can tell!" wailed Loneliness.

"No — you're all coming with me. We're all leaving. Today.
Now."

"But we told you why we couldn't leave!"

"And I told you your reason was ridiculous. Now I'm going
to prove it to you."

"How?"

"We're going to the shore of the bog and we're all going to
hold hands, and we're going to walk out into the mud, out past

the trees. And" — she held up her hand as Death was about to object — "we won't be killed by the crocodiles, simply because there *are* no crocodiles — they are creatures of your own fears. I know that now. I know what this place is, and how people get here, and how they get out again."

"A lot of them don't get out. They drown in the lake, or get eaten by the crocodiles."

"If they're stupid enough to believe in the crocodiles. I'm not that stupid."

"But I am," said Humiliation quietly.

Later they stood at the edge of the Swamp of Submission, strung out in line, hand in hand. The mud had a thin coating of water and ripples showed — and what might have been dead logs, but then again might not.

"Walk!" the Girl commanded.

Loneliness cried, "Wait! Don't go! Don't leave me alone!"

"Then walk."

Humiliation said, "I'll get scared. I know I will. And I'll run back and fall down in the mud and let you all down, and you'll think I'm a coward."

"Keep holding our hands."

Pain said, "There are snags under the water — oh, my poor feet! I'm sure I'll step on a snag and it'll go right through my foot."

"Don't think about it."

Loss said, "Maybe the lake wasn't such a bad place. We had some good times there. Maybe we should stay."

"It's a disgusting, stinking place."

Death said, *"There's a crocodile."*

And a ripple moved toward them.

The Girl said, "That is not a crocodile." She let go of the hands of the flaiads and plunged forward, snatching at the water. She held up a struggling frog for them to see, then threw it away. They moved forward again.

They were nearly out from under the trees. The sky above was dark and menacing. The Girl reassured the flaiads, "Soon you'll be able to fly away. Look — there's the sky! How long is it since you've seen the sky?"

The flaiads looked up, wondering. They fluttered their

wings. The sky roared like a monster, and a flash of brilliant light stabbed toward them.

The Swamp lit up and the hard shadows of the trees wheeled around. For a moment the Girl was scared again — and suddenly there were crocodiles everywhere, their eyes blinking red on the surface as they cruised toward the flaiads. A branch crashed down before them, blazing and sizzling. The flaiads broke the chain and, turning, ploughed frantically back toward the shore.

The Girl stood there, waist-deep in filth while her moment of fear changed to quick rage. Her hair was matted with mud, her eyes were momentarily dazzled, something nameless wriggled under her foot. A sudden wind whipped sparks from the fire around her, stinging her skin. The crocodiles closed in.

The Girl turned her face to the sky.

"You up there!" she shouted at the heavens. *"Damn you all to hell!"*

And the wind dropped and the crocodiles were gone. The last branch of the blazing bough began to slide beneath the surface, the flames flickering out.

"Oh, no," said the Girl. "You don't get off so easily."

She snatched up the brand before the glow died and carried it back to the shore where the flaiads cowered. By the time she reached them the branch was burning again. She took it to a huge rotted bole and thrust it into the dry interior — and now, as though approving of what she did, the wind rose again, fanning the flames.

"Die, Forest," said the Girl . . .

She led the flaiads back to the lake and they waited all day, while behind them the flames spread. When they huddled in the hut that evening, they could see the fire as a glow on the bellies of the clouds; and by midnight it was very close, and the crashing of trees was loud. The Girl led the flaiads into the lake and they crouched in the water close under the bank while the blaze roared overhead and all around.

By morning the fire had passed on, so they emerged from the lake and stood on the blackened shore. Smoke trailed from a few broken trunks here and there, but most of the flames were out and the trees were dead, blackened and limbless.

"Look," said the Girl.

Morning came all around them, in soft light the forest had never known before. Overhead the sky was blue and clear. As the flaiads stood in wonderment, the tips of the trees changed from black to gold and within minutes the floor of the Forest of Fear was illuminated with a golden strangeness it had never known. The sun rose, the shadows shortened and soon everything was light.

"Now," said the Girl. "Fly, flaiads!"

"But the branches ... Everything up there is strange and bright ... We're scared ..."

"The branches are burned off and you can fly straight up and out of here. Go on, now! If you don't fly, the forest will begin to grow again and the branches will close over you. Is that what you really want? To live here in misery forever? This is your chance, flaiads. Take it!"

It was Humiliation who moved first. Blushing, she fluttered her wings, stifling her imagination, which told her how foolish she would look falling flat on her back. She jumped, fluttered and came down again.

Nobody laughed.

She jumped again and this time her wings bore her up between the blackened trunks, up past the sharp tips and into the golden sky.

Laughing now, the other flaiads followed.

The Girl watched them as they rose, their gossamer wings ablaze with light, their laughter becoming faint, until it sounded like the song of distant birds and their bodies were daystars against the sky. Then she turned away and walked toward the swamp, knowing the crocodiles would be gone.

The Hosts

So the Girl shook off the May Bees' poison and freed the flaiads, who had fulfilled their use and were heard of no more. They occur in earlier legends from different parts of Old Earth but at the time of the Triad they were the tools of Starquin as he shaped the Girl to his Purpose.

Starquin's Purpose . . . This did not emerge until the Hate Bombs were planted, so the one very important event that happened before the Hate Bombs — the ingestion of bor by the beautiful tiger-Captain Spring — was accidental and had nothing to do with Starquin's will. In fact the coming of the Macrobes was ultimately against the will of Starquin because it resulted in the Inner Think and human longevity, and the Regression . . . It is ironic to think that those tiny, kindly parasites were responsible at first for *shortening* human life.

The Macrobes. There are many stories of the Macrobes and the beginnings of their partnership with Man, which resulted in the creation of a new form of *homo sapiens*. Probably the simplest is contained in an ancient recording of an event on a rock in the Asteroid Belt, sometime in the 95th millennium, at which time the new humans were known simply as the Hosts . . .

*

Agonistes took a thousand-year egg from the basket and popped it. A faint miasma drifted from the crack in the shell.

A voice said, "To the descendants of me, Anatole Ecks, hello. I hope you are in good health. I have concealed a casket beneath a rock in Cavaha which I think you . . ." The voice faded out. Agonistes crumbled the shell and allowed it to fall to the sand in fragments.

"A dud."

"How much did you pay for them, you old fool?" Enchantress, equally old, asked.

"It's not the treasure that matters. I've never followed up anything I've heard from an egg. I just like to hear those voices from the past. I like to imagine what the people were like." Agonistes' voice was wistful. He was old, almost a century old, and he clung to the past like life itself.

"Did it ever occur to you that the eggs could be fakes?" This from Sudden, a pouting, proud youth.

"They have the ring of truth. The merchant told me they were part of a cache at least twenty-two centuries old, and I believe him." He cracked another, reverently.

A stink of hydrogen sulfide. The egg uttered a string of obscenities, ending with a cackle of derision.

"That tells me something about the people, too," said Agonistes.

"Yes. They were just like us."

Now Maya spoke for the first time. "They were frightened of dying — as we are — so they had to leave a bit of themselves behind. A word, a legacy, sometimes a last stab of vindictiveness. They couldn't know it would become a racket, that eggs would change hands at high prices because so many of them contained directions to hidden treasure. They couldn't know that the descendants of wealthy folk would sell them unopened to the highest bidder."

"Some folk aren't so frightened of dying, I hear," said Enchantress, with that deep portentousness of the aged.

"The Hosts? You've heard of them recently?" Sudden looked interested.

"There are rumors again."

"I've heard the same rumors every few years, all my life," said Agonistes sceptically. "Every few years there's a witch hunt: The Hosts are among us! It's nonsense. The Hosts died out two thousand years ago — or else they were killed."

Enchantress said cunningly, "Maya doesn't seem to age. Maybe we should report her to the authorities."

Maya merely smiled.

"What exactly were the Hosts, anyway, Maya?" asked Sudden. Maya was acknowledged to be the history student among them, young though she was. She seemed to have an encyclopedic knowledge of ancient events — which lent a barb to Enchantress's comment.

"The Hosts were humans like us. Or maybe a little more than human."

"Like the Specialists? Animals? No wonder they were wiped out. Maybe we should do the same favor for the Specialists."

"Enchantress," said Agonistes equably, "you don't improve with age."

"At least I still have possession of my faculties." Her tone was spiteful. Maya watched her sadly, Sudden with delighted interest. Another quarrel would brighten this dull day. "At least I wasn't thrown out of the Guild . . ."

"You were never in the Guild."

"Tell us what happened, old man. Tell us why they threw you out." Sudden joined in, goading. "Cowardice, wasn't it? You lost your ship to the Bale Wolves?"

"I heard . . ." said Maya quietly, "Rowena's alive . . ."

The old man watched her for a moment, then nodded. "I heard that too, girl. Alive, after all these years. They say the Bale Wolves held her prisoner — for seventy years . . . Imagine that. I wonder . . ."

Enchantress cackled. "You wonder if she'll come? You're dreading that, I'll bet. To be faced with the woman you lost to the enemy. To be faced with the past, with your incompetence. Think of that, old man. Any moment she might step from the Pillar . . ."

The Pillar was a tall edifice nearby, a kind of monument whose origins were lost in antiquity, but that seemed to act as a magnet upon which the lines of force of the Greataway converged. It was a couple of meters tall and pockmarked with meteorite scars.

As though on cue, a figure suddenly appeared before it.

Agonistes drew in a sharp breath.

But it was a young girl, even younger than Maya. She looked at them uncertainly, sizing them up. She wore a tiny white skirt and her body glowed and glittered with gold and jewelry. She was small and unreal, and all that wealth sat uneasily on her, like a crown on a baby. She took three halting steps toward them. She wanted to travel on, and no questions asked, which was why she had come via this remote asteroid instead of using the Guild and the authorized routes of the Greataway. Ropes of diamonds in gold settings hung coldly against her warm, bare breasts.

Sudden said, "I'm Sudden and I have the mynde. I can take you anywhere you want to go."

Enchantress said, "Anywhere is right. With this young fool you don't know where you'll end up, my dear. Let me take you."

The girl said, "I don't mind where I go. Anywhere. Where is this?"

"Valta, an asteroid stage. Abandoned now, except for us."

Agonistes was silent, having reasons of his own for not wanting a fare at this time. Sudden took the girl's hand and talked to her quietly; then the two of them disappeared as they stood.

"Well . . . At least he got the first part right." Enchantress turned to Agonistes, ready to renew the offensive.

He said quickly, "You were telling us about the Hosts, Maya."

And Maya's face seemed to go a little out of focus, the way it always did when she reached back into the long-gone past. The shacks of the shantytown beyond the Pillar looked sharp-edged by comparison. *It is as though Maya is not quite* here *on these occasions*, thought Agonistes.

"It began on a planet called Talk-to-Yourself almost two thousand years ago," said Maya, "but the Macrobes weren't isolated until later, when they'd spread among a thousand or more people. A Specialist brought the Macrobes back, unknowingly. She was a ship's captain . . ."

Agonistes shivered. Enchantress frowned.

Maya shimmered . . . In her mind something happened; in her mind and body, in space and time. An echo of a refrain came to her, a couplet from a song that wasn't written yet . . .

> *The Captain was a Specialist of feline-human link.*
> *She brought to Earth the captivating seeds of Inner*
> *Think.*

Inner what? And why did the captain, some faceless half-woman, suddenly assume in her mind the image of a heroine? What did Inner Think mean, and why did it seem to be *good?* And yet, was it good? Changes of style, changes of thought and attitude ran through her mind, dizzying her. The Macrobes were *bad.* Humans had said they were bad.

"The Macrobes possessed their host and altered his behavior," she said determinedly. "They lived in a colorless, waterlike fluid called bor, which was at first looked on as a mild euphoric, and not addictive. Bor heightened the senses and the emotions, and even seemed to increase intelligence. After a while it was found that the effect was permanent and the user didn't need bor any more — but he remained just a little more aware than he was before. Then it was discovered that if a drop of bor was added to ordinary water, the water became bor. So something within bor was multiplying — and soon the Macrobes were isolated."

"You know *so* much, dear," remarked Enchantress, her eyes like little black stones.

"However, a lot of people had been infected. There was a fear the whole ocean could turn to bor, but then they found that the Macrobes died if bor was diluted too much — apparently they reproduced sexually, and dilution of bor meant they died before they could reach one another."

"But what were they *like?*" asked Agonistes.

"They were small organisms with a very strong sense of self-preservation. They increased the host's metabolism, made him wary, alert, content, potent, happy, scared, all of those things and more — anything appropriate to the given moment that would have the effect of helping him to *keep alive,* and so keep his Macrobes alive.

"But in a way the Macrobes were self-defeating, because when they increased a host's metabolic rate they decreased his life expectancy. Possibly this didn't happen on their home planet; in any case, it was a drawback to their life on Earth. So they evolved further ... They entered the very chromosomes of their host, thus ensuring their survival for as long as humans existed. They became a gene, a hereditary trait. In effect they changed Mankind — or at least that section of Mankind through which they spread."

"Horrible ..." said Enchantress.

And Sudden was back with them, grinning smugly, a gold chain hung around his neck. He sat down, listening.

"Mankind had two choices. Bor had long since disappeared except for a single, closely guarded laboratory specimen. But the Macrobes lived on in their hosts, and these hosts were a little *better* than ordinary people. They did not, however, live as long, which could be construed as bad. So it was decided they should not be allowed to have children ..." Maya blinked, visibly returning to the present. "It was the only way," she concluded.

Sudden said, "She paid me well. Very well ... Your history is dull, Maya. I like history about people, not bugs. Real history, like why this old man got thrown out of the Guild and had to come to this place to try to earn a living in competition with crooks like us."

"Somebody's coming ..." said Maya.

Agonistes was trembling. "The Bale Wolves can jump happentracks," he said. He remembered the confusion and Rowena screaming, and his efforts to maintain concentration while the Invisible Spaceship began to dissolve around them, threatening to leave Rowena and him unprotected and the drogues exposed. The Bale Wolves were pure evil. It's hard to concentrate, close to anything so merciless; yet he *had* maintained concentration. He knew he had.

"It doesn't matter how good you are," he continued. "They'll find you out. They'll hunt back in Time a little way and sniff out all your alternative Selves. Some of them will be a little better than you are at this given instant, and some of those Selves will be a little worse . . . They'll find a weak one. They'll find some happentrack on which you were feeling a little sicker, a little weaker, a little less brave. And they'll attack *that* You. Then they'll jump back, right beside you in your mind and your body. And you'll scream and throw them out because you've been taught the way by the Guild — but just for an instant you'll have relaxed, and the shields will be down, and the wolves will appear physically, evil brutes that can't be killed, that can always outwit you."

"Excuses, old man. Your superiors knew better. They threw you out of the Guild."

"That was standard procedure. There is no formal trial. Nobody who's been attacked by the Bale Wolves can ever be trusted again. There's no blame attached to it — it's simple fact."

"So what are you doing plying for hire?"

"Short trips, that's all . . ." Agonistes' gaze shifted around. He was cornered.

"But you never take any. You just sit here by the Pillar, year after year."

"It's the Greataway . . . There's something about it. It draws you, even since the Hate Bombs have restricted it. The Guild — it was the best thing that ever happened to me, and I lost it all. The adventure — like nothing on Earth. The fellowship, the trust." His sentences had become disjointed and emotional, and Sudden began to look abashed. "And Rowena . . . I . . . I loved her. That was what made it so terrible. I loved her better than all the Greataway, and I would have died for her. I *tried* to die for her. And yet somewhere, on some other happentrack, there was another Me who didn't love her quite enough . . ."

"It wasn't your fault," said Maya vehemently.

Four people on a chunk of rock between Mars and Jupiter: an old, imperfect man and an old, embittered woman, a young pretender and Maya. Four people huddled beside a nodal point in the Greataway for an instant in history, remarkable only because their lives were of no consequence whatever. Nothing they did had any measurable effect on the Ifalong. In the overall scheme of things, it is difficult to understand the purpose of any of these people except Maya.

Days or months later another Traveler came.

Sudden saw her first.

He stood, dashing a lock of hair away from his eyes, smiling. "I'm Sudden and I have the mynde. I can take you anywhere."

This woman was tall, quietly dressed and young. Her hair fell in dark waves about her shoulders, her face was pale but not pallid and there was a luster to her skin — not that skin-deep luster that comes from the rejuvenation salons, but a deeper glow of confidence and health and real youth.

Sudden hesitated. "I . . . Maybe I . . ."

It was her eyes, dark blue, like cobalt, and searching, moving through him, weighing him briefly and finding him inadequate. It was her step, sure and strong as she walked toward them, so that Sudden, for reasons unknown, found himself backing off. It was many things in the young woman, but mostly it was an aura of supreme intelligence . . . Or not quite that. Of supreme *knowledge.* In her short life she'd seen it all.

Maya watched her, lips parted in a half-smile.

Enchantress muttered, "I don't think I . . ."

This woman would have no truck with charlatans. Why had she come? She looked as though she had the mynde to travel alone, to cast off the Hate Bombs and journey to the end of the stars and absorb the knowledge of the Universe. She stopped walking and stood before them.

She said, "Take me home now, Paul."

Aging is good and dying is good: Humans were right to suspect the Macrobes. Death was the first great mutation of life, and to deny death might be part of the ultimate evil.

So the old man stood looking at the woman who had lived with the nightmare creatures and, knowing her, he knew something of what had happened. How they took her and tortured her, so that she wished for death — but they anticipated that and they denied it to her; they even denied her the hope of aging. She stayed young while they did their worst, while they tortured her, not to obtain information or for any other reason that a human might understand, but simply because they were Bale Wolves. They didn't torture her for the fun of it, or out of hatred, but simply because of what they are.

And she beat them.

How Rowena beat the Bale Wolves is another story. Now she was here, just as Paul-called-Agonistes remembered her. And she remembered him too, seeing through the crackled flesh to the psycaptain underneath. "Take me home, Paul," she said.

Rowena is important because of what she did, but Paul is a nobody in the vastness of Time and only appears in her life because of what he can give her — because she loved him too.

So it is of little importance that, as he walked with Rowena to the Pillar, an extraordinary thing happened to him. Maya, you see, had the power to *give* — just occasionally, when the situation demanded.

As they held hands before winking out, the years melted away from the body of Paul-Agonistes until he was as young as the beautiful woman he stood beside. But her smile as she watched him didn't change and Maya wondered if she even noticed the difference. Then they were gone.

Enchantress noticed the difference. "Did you see what I . . . No, it couldn't have been. Forget it." She was still old herself, and would remain so until she died. Something ate at her inside. A fury grew. "Why should *she* ask *him* to take her, after what happened?"

"That . . . Was that . . . No, it couldn't have been the Rowena he was always talking about." Sudden spoke haltingly, still dazed.

"It was, it was." Enchantress spat the words. "And do you know why? Because she's a Host, that's why. I'm going after them." She blundered to her feet. "I'm going to turn her in to the authorities if I have to follow her to the ends of the Greataway!"

"Stay where you are, Enchantress," Maya said. "You'll never find them."

"And what do *you* know about that? You think you know so much, but I've never seen you travel. You and your words and your baby eyes." Enchantress's spite was redirected against Maya. The old woman looked at the young girl and saw everything she'd lost. "You know so much and yet you're so young. How do you do it — tell me that! Lost your tongue, have you? Right — so that old fool and his girl got away, but I'll see to it you don't. You're a Host yourself, and don't you try denying it! You're for recycling, my girl!"

Maya shrugged, smiled and walked away. "The Macrobes evolved into a recessive gene. It was their last defense during the Pogrom of the Hosts. You won't find any of them around."

"How do you know all that, eh?"

"I remember things, that's all."

And she strolled off past the Pillar with an odd vision swirling like a mist in her mind — a vision of a beach, blue sky and blue sea — things she'd never seen. She heard words too, quiet words of a thoughtful mind: *But love should be a simple thing of silence, with no need to justify.*

She wondered what they meant, and what the beach and sky and sea meant. Her mind was a curious thing, the way it conjured up these visions. And what was love? What *really* was love? And who was this mind speaking to her from a long way off — or was she simply eavesdropping on a mind talking to itself? One thing was certain — the mind spoke in the future. Whenever she'd had a vision of something unrecognizable, it was in the future; she'd proved that by experiment.

Now the vision was fading as she reached her living quarters. She was left with the afterimage of a tiny creature yawning and stretching and coming awake in the body of a young man after a thousand years' slumber. The young man was talking to the creature, of course, not to himself. He was reasoning with the benign parasites in his body and persuading them to help him to do what was best for both of them — and this did *not* mean speeding up his metabolism. He was in fact practicing the crude and undeveloped beginnings of the Inner Think. Maya didn't know this. She wondered for a while, then forgot the young man, although his quiet words stayed with her as she greeted her ancient mother and made herself ready for the night.

Sudden watched her go. He stiffened. "That's strange."

"What's strange?"

"Oh . . . just for a moment, I thought . . ."

He didn't tell Enchantress, because he didn't want to appear a fool. He could have been mistaken. Funny things happen to the mind on a tiny asteroid.

Just for a moment, he thought he'd seen Maya disappear into a kind of purple tent, but then the tent had gone. It must have been a mirage.

THE BLIND MAN

•••

*H*e was a nightmare dreamed up by the humans of Dream Earth. He was created that way, and endowed with all the trappings of evil like the model he was based upon, a fictional character from long ago. Nobody knows why he was created, unless it was to satisfy some deep human urge to be frightened — that urge that causes children to be fascinated by monsters. Or unless, again, it was to stave off the simple tedium of Dream Earth.

Many people were involved in the nightmare and each contributed horrors from the depths of his soul, dreaming together in some blazing chasm of imagined hell. They added a feature here and a characteristic there, dank clothing and a fetid odor, and then they turned the creature loose — relatively formless, but a conglomeration of evil traits. Other dreamers came upon the thing and saw it through their own eyes, and it so happened that it made a connection in their minds, and gradually an appropriate image began to solidify; and the blind man began tapping his way around the hills and valleys of Dream Earth.

He added piquancy to the existence of the Dreamers. They would taunt him and occasionally trip him, while he, face contorted with diabolical rage, would lash out blindly with his stick, hissing oaths. And his tormentors would back off, hugging themselves with fear and delight. For a while this was fun. But as time went by, the curious logic of Dream Earth began to assert itself and the blind man evolved an unusual protective instinct. A Mohor noticed it first, but without recognizing it. This bogus emperor from the Second Dark Age strode up to the blind man, intending to scorch him a little with his pistola. The blind man skipped aside.

"He can see!" said the Mohor, surprised. "The blind man's getting his sight back. Who's been fooling around here?"

"I'll soon put it right," said a Nrindella who had psy to spare. She smallwished.

Experimentally, the Mohor aimed his pistola again. By this time the blind man's rage and language were becoming unnerving.

The blind man knocked the pistola to the ground with a sweeping blow of his stick before the Mohor had time to press the button.

"So much for your psy," said the Mohor to the Nrindella. "Come on, let's get back to Ahamat. The blind man's no fun anymore."

They disappeared — but the blind man didn't know this. For several moments he stood there tense, stick held ready, face questing emptily this way and that. Because he could not see. He had never been able to see.

What he could do, was to *anticipate*. Only on Dream Earth could such a propensity have developed. In order to save himself from injury, the blind man could see into the Ifalong for just a couple of seconds. Just enough to be able to recognize imminent danger and to avert it. A small enough gift in all the wonders of Dream Earth, but one that was of great value to its possessor.

And ultimately of great value to Starquin . . .

So the blind man became a nuisance, gate-crashing parties, annoying and frightening people, making them impervious to their smallwishes because of the very strength of his image. In the end the Rainbow had to take a hand because there was some suggestion that the blind man was actually gaining the power to corrupt people and was gathering around himself a noisome coterie of castoff smallwishes: demons and witches and dwarves.

So the Rainbow banished the blind man to the Land of Lost Dreams.

Before he went he had found his identity. It happened quite unexpectedly as he awaited his exile. The Celestial Steam Locomotive rolled into its ghostly station, and the driver, leaning from the cab, called out his jovial invitation.

"All aboard, shipmates!"

Then Silver saw the blind man and his face paled, and his hand, trembling violently, reached for the rum bottle.

"By the Powers," he whispered. "It's Blind Pew!"

*

The Girl never had a chance. Bone-weary, hungry, thirsty, yet determined to get out of the Land of Lost Dreams and back to reality, she stumbled up yet another hill. She would have to rest soon, she knew, but meanwhile she would keep going, buoyed up by her new resolve: never to complain again, never to fall into the Swamp of Submission, never to listen to the May Bees.

She passed a rock face. She didn't see the cave at first, so the sudden voice, though soft-spoken, gave her a bad scare.

"Will some kind person help a poor blind man?"

Now she could make out a shadowy figure standing just inside the cave entrance. "What do you want?"

"Just a little help along the way. I'm lost, ye see — and 'tis a lonely thing to be blind and lost. Now — ye have a kindly and clever voice, and ye can set me on me way again, I'll be bound."

"I'll try."

"Just give me yer hand and point the way south, that's all I ask."

The Girl reached toward the dim figure, touching it gently.

Instantly a skinny hand shot out and fastened on her arm.

"Ah-hah! What have we here? A lass, or is it a lad? It has meat aplenty on its bones, whatever it is!"

And the vile, skeletal hand began to explore further. The Girl resisted strongly, wriggling, trying to twist away from the arm that had been thrown around her waist — in vain, because she was quickly drawn off balance into the gloom of the cave. "Let me go!" she cried, kicking. Her heel smacked into a knife-edged shin.

"Damn ye!"

She was thrown to the ground and she hit her head against the rock wall. When the tears of pain cleared from her eyes, she stared in horror and disgust.

The creature who scuttled about the cave was quite the most dreadful thing she'd ever seen. Hunched, clothed in a tattered black cloak like some monstrous vulture, it seemed barely human. It scurried crablike to and fro, scattering twigs on the foul floor of the cave, muttering to itself, occasionally pausing and cocking a sightless eye in her direction. A shapeless black hat emphasized the rolling pallor of the eyes.

Coarse stubble covered the chin and, adding somehow to the appalling grotesqueness of the creature, a green eyeshade was fastened across the forehead. The thing paused again and the head turned toward the Girl. Toothless gums bared.

"Mebbe now I'll knock some o' the spirit out of ye, lass!"

So saying, the blind man snatched up a stick from against the wall and began to thrash away in the general direction of the Girl, crabbing toward her, meanwhile uttering cries of rage as though the very act of lashing out served to increase his fury. Many of the blows clattered against rock, but quite a number struck the Girl as she tried to roll away. At last, sobbing with exertion, the man hurled down the stick and took up a coil of rope. Seizing the Girl by the leg, he threw two loops around her body before tying a rapid knot. He then secured the other end around his waist.

"Now, me beauty," he said, "I've got meself a pair of eyes!"

It had all happened too quickly for the Girl, exhausted as she was. Lying there helpless and bruised while the blind man resumed his odd occupation of scattering twigs, she felt great sobs of despair welling up inside her. Forcing herself to be brave and to remember the lesson of the swamp, she said in a voice that she couldn't quite hold steady:

"I'm not going to help you in any way at all."

Then she waited, shivering, for the next outburst.

Instead, the blind man said quite softly, and all the more threateningly for it, "I'll be the judge o' that, me lass." He squatted before her, drawing the rope until it tightened and he could place her exact whereabouts. His eyes rolled toward her. "Now, you and me, we're going to have a little talk. First off, how did ye get here, eh?"

"I . . . I walked," the Girl found herself saying. The cave stank and the blind man stank worse. She swallowed heavily.

"I know that, me beauty," purred the man. "But before that, now. How did ye arrive on this strange shore, eh?"

"We came by the Train, Zozula and Manuel and I." The Girl's eyes filled with tears as she thought about the other two. Suddenly furious with her own weakness, she added loudly, "And they're right behind me — they'll be here in just a moment. I can tell you — they'll be pretty mad when they find out what you've done to me. You'd better let me go right now!"

"The Train, eh?" said the blind man quietly, and the Girl shuddered at the suppressed venom in the words. "And who might the driver of the Locomotive have been, lass?" He took up his stick, slapping it gently against his palm.

"S-Silver."

"Silver, is it? Long John hisself, is it?" The voice was a roar of rage and the Girl flinched as the blind man leaped to his feet. His hat fell over his eyes and he pushed it back, revealing wispy yellowing hair. "Well, *that* for Long John Silver!" and he swung the stick in a murderous arc that would have split the Girl's skull if she hadn't jerked back. He crouched again, breathing heavily, muttering to himself. "Silver, still driving . . . By the Powers! This is a piece o'luck, and no bones about it! This lass here, she could be me ticket . . ." He snapped the rope taut so that the Girl fell against him. Then he took her by the shoulders, his sightless eyes a few centimeters from hers. "Did Silver speak of me, lass? Pew's the name. Did ye ever hear him speak o' Blind Pew?"

"No. Never."

"And likely he wouldn't. For what he did to me, no man ought ever to do to a shipmate. Base treachery, 'twas!" The fury took hold of him again and he shook the Girl violently. "He tricked me, he did! He took advantage of me poor infirmity, and marooned me on this blasted land! He . . ." Pew was trembling with rage now. "He took me ashore saying there was gold here — then he slipped back into that Locomotive and away before ye could take a turn around a bollard! Left me here all these thirty year, he did, with nothing but the rats for company — and some creatures stranger than rats!"

Now his voice dropped to a quiet, almost conversational tone. "But now ye're here, lass, and now I've got eyes. So now ye'll take me back to Mister John Silver, and I'll settle the score!"

COLD FIRE

••••••••••••••••••••••••••••••••••••

"*B*ut I don't know where to find the Locomotive."

It was morning, after the worst night of the Girl's life. Twice she'd slipped her bonds and crept toward the cave entrance, and twice a twig had snapped under her step. Pew had flung himself at her, cursing, and thrown her to the back of the cave. Bruised, exhausted and weak, she shrank back as the blind man thrust his face into hers.

"Cold fire, lass — cold fire. Find the cold fire, then ye'll know the Locomotive is no more'n a cable's length away." He winked, one lid closing over a sightless orb.

"Cold fire?"

"Ye'll know it, lass. Ye'll know it when ye see it."

So they set off across the Land of Lost Dreams, the Girl leading, Blind Pew behind, one skeletal hand on the rope to detect any attempt at loosening the knots. The morning sun slanted across the rocky terrain, casting harsh shadows, picking out the occasional lonely creature that watched their passing.

"Cold fire . . ." Pew muttered frequently. "Watch for the cold fire, lass."

The Girl plodded on, her mind filled with a horror of the loathsome creature at her heels. He seemed to have anticipated her every move, so far. How could she possibly escape?

Later that morning she saw her chance. The trail wound into a valley littered with boulders and slashed with crevasses. Rolling pebbles made walking difficult and several times she almost fell, although the blind man seemed as nimble as a goat. In due course, however, the Girl saw what she was looking for.

A deep crevasse ran beside the trail.

She couldn't see the bottom. The gash in the valley floor was jagged and several meters across — except in one place where the two walls almost met. And it would be possible to step across . . .

Could she kill a human being?

She walked on robotlike, thoughts chasing through her mind. Pew was not human. He was the quintessence of evil, created by human minds. If she owed any duty to Mankind, it was to destroy this monstrous thing . . . Yet she hesitated.

She reached the overhanging lip.

She arrived at a decision. She stepped across — and changed direction instantly, so that the lay of the rope led Pew to a wider gap. She kept the rope taut.

Pew shambled toward her — toward the drop — mumbling. He was two meters away, one meter. He took another step. His cloak flapped in the breeze like bats' wings.

He paused.

"Hello . . ." he said quietly. "What's this? What's this, lass? Mutiny, is it?" Under the green eyeshade, the eyes were blinking rapidly. The stick tip-tapped on the ground, rang on rock, then hovered over nothingness, stabbing at air. The tone became wheedling. "Ye'd try to harm an old man who gave the sight of his eyes in gracious defense of his native country? Shame on ye, I say. Now I asks ye, lass. Fair's fair. Is this just deserts for a loyal old sailor?"

And so saying, he gave a great tug on the rope.

The Girl staggered to the brink.

"Is this just deserts?"

"No! Stop! I'm sorry, really I am!"

"Then come over here, lass. Step lively, now!" Pew jerked the rope.

Trembling, the Girl edged along, reached the lip, stepped across. Pew drew her close to gauge the distance, then pushed her roughly away and swung the stick in a wide arc. The Girl tried to jerk back, but the rope hampered her and the blow slashed across her shoulders. Pew bellowed and swung again. This time the Girl received a glancing blow across the temple and fell to the ground half stunned. Pew swiped at empty space, swore in frustration and jabbed around to relocate his target.

The Land of Lost Dreams swam around the Girl. She only half saw the nightmare figure of Pew as he towered over her like a hunched bird of prey, eyes rolling. Consciousness was slipping away from her, the world receded, to be replaced by a vision: a rock, smooth and eerily glowing. The rock was somehow important and it stood before her like a signpost, somewhere behind the flailing, flapping figure of Pew.

She had to reach that rock . . .

"Eh? What's that ye say, lass?" Pew dropped beside her, suddenly changed, suddenly tense.

"The rock, the glowing rock . . . I must reach the rock . . ."

"By the Powers," muttered Pew. "Cold fire! Ye see it, lass? Where is it?" He seized her hand. "Take me to it!"

"I can't . . . I can't move . . ." She tried to rise, then fell back, sick. The vision was fading. She would never reach it now.

"Point it out, lass!" Pew was beside himself with urgency, plucking at her hand.

She gestured toward the ghostly glow.

Gibbering with excitement, Pew fumbled at the rope, freed himself and set off across the broken ground at a shambling run.

The Girl gathered in the loose end of the rope, hardly aware of what she was doing, hardly aware that she was free. She closed her eyes and lay there quietly. There was no urgency anymore; she couldn't see the rock now.

And out there across the valley, Pew's excitement was gradually changing to rage. He quested this way and that, tripping over rocks as his precognition failed him, hugging boulders, only to reject them, slashing with his stick. In the end he gave one roar, then in ominous silence began to tap his way back to the Girl.

She lay with eyes closed tightly, listening to the crunch of feet on gravel, the ringing of stick on rock, the steps gradually coming closer, and she didn't dare look. She felt a hardness against her back as she pressed herself against an overhanging boulder. Her thumb crept into her mouth and she made little cooing noises of absolute terror as the centuries dropped away from her, leaving her a defenseless, crying baby in the unforgiving harshness of the Land of Lost Dreams.

And Pew drew near. He was deathly quiet. No shouting, not even the pant of his breath. Just the tap-tap of his stick on rock, and those footsteps, crunching close.

He stopped. There was no sound anywhere in the land, just a giant waiting silence.

And then the tapping started again, and the footsteps crunched. But this time they were receding, going away, disappearing.

THE MATH CREATURE

"Where in hell have they gone?" grumbled Zozula after he'd searched the immediate vicinity. "They ought to have more sense than to wander off like that. And the Girl was sick, too. They'll get lost, without me to show them the way."

"I'm still here," said Roller.

"You and I are going to have to leave, dog. I must get back to the console and try to locate them. Maybe they don't know what they're doing. Perhaps the poison from the May Bees affected them both."

The dog said, "They died and became spirits."

"Nonsense!"

"They did!" The dog danced his front feet in frustration. "I saw it! They got up and walked away into the night mist, and never came back. If that isn't dying I don't know what is."

"All right. Have it your own way. Now, you'll show me the way to the Train, dog, and none of your excuses."

The dog led Zozula in a direction he judged to be north, through barren dusty valleys, beside dried-up watercourses. As they walked, the hills on either side became steeper and the ground beneath their feet more level. The curve of the sky flattened out so that they seemed to be walking in a box. It was an eerie sensation, and after a while Zozula questioned the dog.

"Are you sure this is the way?"

"Of course I'm sure," Roller replied. "Do you think I can't recognize my own master's handiwork?"

Now they were approaching a vertical slit where the valley walls converged. The dog bounded forward. His spirits had been rising steadily ever since the ground had hardened to a smooth glassiness. "My master makes it easy for me, you see!" he cried. "When I'm in his land, my wheels don't bog down and I don't have to climb hills. That's why I love him!"

The rock face was glassy smooth too, as Zozula observed when he squeezed through the crevice after the dog. Now an incredible scene opened up before him.

And sitting nearby was a familiar figure.

*

The math creature's mind was a curious thing. It had developed in a vacuum, where it had extrapolated on the barest minimum of data. The creature had been able to assimilate his own shape, although at first his spacial perception was so undeveloped that he was unable to perceive it as a shape. It was simply a succession of lines — routes over which he could run his sensory extensions.

Other shapes intruded. There was the hard Underneath, there were the occasional softnesses of beings that had a superficial linear resemblance to himself and there were Things. These were small, purposeless shapes placed within his range by other beings. Then there was Food, and the Opposite of Food, both accompanied by Sensations.

Simple mathematics had occurred to him two years after his creation. He'd constructed symbols in his mind and woven them together, and gradually discovered a satisfaction even greater than Food. Algebra followed naturally, but as he built supposition on supposition, a nagging feeling of incompleteness began to obsess him. In some way, it seemed, he ought to be able to relate this mental toy to his special situation. Initially, that might seem terribly complex, but it could be reduced into order by making a few simple assumptions. As he thought, he ran his sensory extension absently along the edge of one of his Things — and suddenly the assumption was right there.

He assumed the existence of a straight line. He assumed points and angles, circles and trapeziums. Then, with an effort, he assumed infinity — just for the purpose of the exercise. Not because it really *was*. Such assumptions were easy — to an imaginative mind already three years old that had nothing else to think about . . .

Picture, now, the creature after fifteen standard years of development, his mind an intricate structure of mathematical concepts. He sat in the middle of these concepts, juggling them as he saw fit, pushing out the boundaries of new knowledge when he felt like it, always totally in control, always obeying his rigid logic. Picture a mathematical version of the imaginings of the delta's Lazy Children.

Picture within that inhuman body the greatest mathematical genius the world has ever known or ever will know. Picture, if you can, a knowledge exceeding even that of the Rainbow — at least in this one so very logical subject.

Then picture, after a period of strange and uncomfortable physical experiences, the collapse.

His work that day has no name. It dealt with a realm of pure mathematics so exalted that no words will ever be found to describe it. Theorems were propounded, demonstrated and proved, and the creature's heart was beating fast and painfully with the excitement of it. Another Truth was within his grasp. It was coming — as it always did — that moment of revelation. It was . . .

It was an extraordinary shining Thing, moving and shapeless, which tumbled his theorems and notions like atoms into confusion. It terrified the creature with its insistence and permanence. It stood there among the ruins of his mathematics. It was possessed of qualities he'd never dreamed of, qualities he couldn't even name. It stood apart, without having to be *felt*, with an existence of its own, which made nonsense of everything.

It . . . *hated* him.

The creature writhed and grunted, his sensory extensions exploring himself and the limits of physicality around him, but he could find no explanation there, either. The shining Thing *was*, yet it *was not*. Where was it?

It was totally illogical, and — the worst part — it was bent on destroying him. He could not escape; he was trapped within his own mind.

The Thing moved!

His physical self was gone, snatched away from him!

Now he had *no* sensory appendages, *no* Food, *no* Opposite of Food, *no* Underneath, nothing.

He knew the depths of fear . . .

Time passed and nothing further happened. The Thing seemed to have gone and the creature peered out nervously from underneath himself. Nothing bad happened. Tentatively, the math creature began to impress his logic on the landscape. He glided across a plain of utter featurelessness, toward perfectly triangular mountains. He passed through them as though they were composed of mist.

The sun was a brilliant faceted ruby in a sky devoid of clouds. The horizon, where there were no mountains, was ruler-straight.

The math creature moved through a flat world that grew more geometric with each thought. Soon right-angled mountains appeared and two-dimensional extensions projected from them for use in future theorems. Meanwhile, the sky had become multi-dimensional and the ruby sun glittered from all conceivable angles, repeating itself into infinity.

And the world around him obeyed his thoughts because it was that kind of world, within the Rainbow and close to Dream Earth.

Finally, from memory, he recreated himself.

*

Zozula stood still for a long time, gazing with tears in his eyes at the creature. It looked so lost, so lonely in all this savage jaggedness, a sad little lump of soft flesh banished by the Rainbow because it was too clever.

"My master!" cried the dog in delight and trotted forward and began to lick the creature. The creature flapped at it in a gesture that obviously intended affection.

Zozula walked up to the creature, swallowed and said gently,

"Come on, Mole. I'm going to take you home."

The Mole, unhearing, patted the dog.

*

The Rainbow did not relinquish the Mole easily.

Zozula explained to the dog, and the dog spoke into the mind of the Mole. And the Mole contracted and became a small irregular crystal-thing that Zozula was able to pick up. The mountains swayed and the ground heaved.

Zozula and the Mole were blown into the Greataway like a wisp of thistledown.

Zozula screamed, but the sound never left his mouth. He kicked, but there were forces infinitely greater than his at work. His mind was assailed by a series of emotions from some source outside himself: rage, hatred, jealousy. He was snatched this way and that, as though in a maelstrom, while his joints creaked and huge blows buffeted him.

On a few happentracks he died and his body materialized at the feet of the Reasoner beside the Do-Portal.

On many happentracks he lived for millennia, his brain cells being absorbed into a tired memory bank, his flesh lending substance to Bigwishes; but he never saw the Outside again.

On just three happentracks he was ejected forcibly onto the floor of the Rainbow Room, bruised, breathless and terrified, and was violently sick at the feet of Selena, who had been trying to operate the console. In his memory was the echo of the dog's cry, *I'm real! I'm real!*, but the dog was not beside him any longer.

These last three inauspicious happentracks were the ones that, in the Ifalong, encompassed the Quest of Manuel, the Battle with the Bale Wolves, and the Release of Starquin . . .

THE BEARBACK RIDERS

*T*hey had been riding for hours. Their leader was a giant dressed in robes of fur with many tails that streamed in the wind. Dark and bearded he was, and his teeth showed whitely in a fierce grin of anticipation. His eyes were the blue of the Viking and on his head he wore a brazen helmet. His right hand clutched the handle of a flail, and his left was dug deeply into the shaggy coat of his mount.

His mount was a huge bear. Brown and bounding, larger than any bear of Early Earth, it covered the ground in great leaps, scaling rises and loose ground with a surefootedness no horse could match.

The followers were similarly mounted and clad, ten of them, and they uttered yells of excitement as they rode. They were the Bjorn-serkrs.

Now they entered a region of quiet grassland and woods, and their yelling shattered the stillness. Birds left the trees in flocks and rocketed from under the feet of their mounts. Other animals watched nervously from the cover of the woods, sensing the purpose of this mad gallop and wondering in their dim animal way who the quarry was.

The quarry was a girl.

Mounted on an eland, laid across its back and clutching its horns, she went like the wind, the grass hissing under flying hooves. She wore a pale green robe that, like those of the hunters, billowed behind her and lent her an aethereal air as she flitted among the trees. As she rode, she wept, and the wind whipped the tears from her cheeks. She wept in elementary fear, while the hunters yelled in elementary anticipation.

And that was the way they rode, mindlessly, across the grassland and through the forest.

*

Manuel was never able to work out what happened that night in the Land of Lost Dreams. All he knew was that when he awakened, the scenery was different and the Girl, the dog and Zozula were gone. After his initial fright, his natural resilience took over and he began to enjoy the adventure and to assume he was back on real Earth. It was good to be able to make his own decisions again.

He walked in a place of great beauty — a place even more beautiful than Pu'este. It was warm and the afternoon sun slanted through the leaves of the elm trees and lighted the branches of gnarled oaks. The ground was carpeted with short grass and small wildflowers, blue and violet. He sat beside a lake where bright dragonflies hovered and a small furry animal was drinking without fear.

The beautiful place seemed to be holding its breath, waiting.

A youth slipped into this picture. He strolled from behind a tree with his hands in his pockets, whistling. He was dressed in a green tunic and brown pants and wore a hat with a partridge's tailfeather in it. When he saw Manuel, his whistling stopped in mid-phrase.

"Who are you?" he called.

"Manuel. Who are you?"

"John O'Greenwood. I live here. You don't." But there was no challenge intended. He sat down, picked a stem of ryegrass to suck on and regarded Manuel inquisitively. "You're a funny-looking fellow, I must say. You have a chest like a Cornish wrestler, yet your arms are skinny. Well? Have you lost your tongue?"

Manuel said carefully, "Is it the custom of this place to trade insults?"

"Custom? No — it's just my way. I'm an outspoken fellow, don't you know? People get used to me in time. You'll get used to me, I'm sure."

"Maybe I don't want to get used to you." It had been so peaceful here before this spry fool showed up.

Now the youth unslung a lute and struck a few soft chords. Without looking at Manuel, he sang a quiet song with a strange, limping rhythm:

> When first my lover came to me she wore a dress of
> green.
> The next time she was clad in white, in Avalayn's
> demesne.

He went on for a long time, telling the tale of a search for a lost lover, while Manuel forgot his irritation under the influence of the insistent chords and the plaintive, simple lyrics. When John O'Greenwood was finished and the last words had fled across the lake and melted into the trees, Manuel asked, "What's that song?"

"It's just a song. A song of Earth. It said something to you, did it? That's the way with songs, and this song in particular. That's maybe why I'm better at singing than talking."

"The song ended without saying whether you found the girl."

"The finding doesn't matter. The searching is the thing. Some things are better not found. I know of people who have everything they could possibly want, everything they could wish for. And would you believe that everything is not enough? So they have this mythical place called Avalayna, and they search for it — because it's the perfect place where everything is as wonderful as it possibly could be. They search for this perfect place even though they know they're not going to find it — or maybe *because* they're not going to find it."

"I want to *find* somebody," said Manuel stubbornly. "The search is taking too long."

"Finding can be a lot worse than searching."

"Not in this case it won't."

"Ah!" John O'Greenwood regarded him quizzically. "Another lovesick fellow, eh? Well..." And now he stood, shrugging his shoulders into the strap of his lute. "You should be here, not me."

With this puzzling statement he disappeared among the trees.

*

Manuel stood staring into the waters of the lake, where some quirk of reflection made him appear slim, like John O'Greenwood. He was thinking of the Girl and how she'd seen her reflection for the first time in the axolotl pool, and how she'd cried. It seemed a long time ago. He wondered where she was and what she was doing.

Again, the forest seemed to be waiting.

Now, filtering through the trees from a long way off, came the sound of shouting.

Manuel heard. A queer excitement ran through him.

There was death in the shouting, and recklessness. It was the kind of shout that men give when their senses have left them. It was a shout that went right back to the early Paragonic era, when men were little more than apes and the legendary Union had not taken place, when they hunted capybara with sticks and stones and yells. The sounds were that primitive.

Now Manuel heard hooves drumming.

A flash of pale green caught his eye, a half-seen movement among the farthermost trees. The hooves drew closer and Manuel saw the thing again: a large animal, running fast with something on its back. Then the creature swerved and emerged from the trees, heading straight across the clearing toward the lake.

It was a huge antelope with a girl clutching its horns, a girl dressed in green, her robe floating like a cloud. The beast's eye showed the white of terror as it plunged toward the water and, reaching the edge, leaped.

Manuel was staring at the girl.

The eland hit the surface and spray fountained from its forelegs. The girl lost her grip and flew on, striking the water a couple of meters beyond the animal and disappearing. The eland swam on.

Manuel dived in. A paleness swirled past him and he grabbed, drew it to him and found something soft and struggling in his arms. Kicking his way to the surface, he swam to the bank, crawled ashore and dragged the girl after him. She was coughing weakly. The dress clung to her, but now it was white, and the girl was slender and dreamlike; a thrill ran through Manuel's body. She lay face down, coughing water. Her hair was fair even when wet and matted. He didn't dare turn her over.

"Are you all right?" he asked, and the words seemed dull, as words always would on an occasion such as this.

"I . . . I . . . I think so." She spoke into the grass, and Manuel's mind was racing.

She turned over and looked up at him.

Her eyes were blue and her mouth sad, and the robe stuck to her like wet seaweed, outlining her shoulders and breasts, emphasizing the slender waist and full hips. Manuel thought wildly: With those eyes and that hair she's an inappropriate sea-child . . .

"Belinda," he whispered.

"Is it really you, Manuel?"

"How . . . How did you . . . ? Where . . . ?"

She touched his lips with her fingers. "Don't ask questions."

He kissed her. Her lips were warm and wet. His arms were around her, lifting her from the ground and hugging her to him. Her body was warm despite her wet clothing, with a warmth that seemed to consume him. For a long moment of wonder they kissed — and then the mad yelling drew nearer, and shouts of discovery.

They sat up, gasping from the length of the kiss.

A group of nightmare riders milled about the clearing on padding mounts, gesticulating and pointing. The leader rode up to Manuel. The bear stopped, its muzzle a meter from Manuel's face, so close that he could smell the fishy stink of its breath. The man hauled at the bear's shaggy neck so that the brute reared up, and from this eminence he addressed Manuel.

"Who the devil are you?"

Manuel would have run long before this if Belinda hadn't been there. Now he held his ground, staring up. "Manuel," he said, as it seemed he had introduced himself many times before; but this time the name came out as if it really meant something — almost as if he had said, "Starquin." For an instant Manuel wondered at the power of his own name.

The Bjorn-serkr felt it too. He blinked.

One of his followers shouted, *"He's* not the Rescuer!"

"He'll do." The Bjorn-serkr raised his flail — a handle connected by a thong to a knobby chunk of oak — and whistled it down in the general direction of Manuel's head. "Out of my way, fool! Give me the girl!"

"No." As the oak descended for the second time, Manuel grabbed it and hung on and was lifted from the ground by the power of the rider's arm. He swung against the bear's flank, snatched at the fur and then got an arm around the man's waist.

"What are you doing?" The voice was incredulous. Laughter came from the other Bjorn-serkrs. Off balance, the rider tumbled from his mount, Manuel falling with him but making sure he landed on top. Manuel still had hold of the hardwood and the handle swung free. He crashed it down on the man's temple.

Apparently unhurt, the Bjorn-serkr said mildly, "I wish you'd go away." Then abruptly losing his temper as the laughter from the onlookers continued, he flung Manuel from him, rose and kicked him in the ribs. Manuel rolled with the kick. The man reached for Belinda, roaring. She shrank away, trying to get to Manuel. Manuel jumped up. The man's back was toward him. He swung the flail again but mistimed his blow as the other made a grab for Belinda. The thong caught the man on the side of the neck, and the handle whirled around his throat and locked against a protuberance on the oak. With his neck encircled, the man staggered away, gurgling and plucking as the flail threatened to garrote him.

Manuel went to Belinda and put an arm around her waist. He felt omnipotent. The other riders were staring at him. The leader, wrenching the flail away from his neck, charged over to his bear and mounted, muttering.

Then the Bjorn-serkrs whirled their mounts around and rode off into the forest.

"You frightened them off," said Belinda wonderingly.

"I know." Manuel didn't quite understand it either. "They're a bunch of cowards."

"They'll be back," said Belinda.

Manuel did not pursue the matter. He did not realize he was in Dream Earth, even though he was standing in it. Belinda looked at him, loving him to the depths of her insubstantial heart — because, without her knowing it, that was the way he'd wished her to be.

"Why did you leave me, before?" asked Manuel. "I thought I'd never see you again. I've been looking everywhere for you."

"I knew you would."

"I'm . . ." The elation of victory was leaving him and his natural shyness began to return. He made an effort. "I'm not going to let you get away again, you know."

"I will never leave you, my love," said the beautiful figment of Manuel's imagination. . .

He drew her to the warm grass and they made long, slow love. This love had a joy and simplicity unknown on real Earth. It never occurred to Manuel to wonder why love had suddenly become such a single-minded thing, why his thoughts at certain instants did not wander to trivia, such as whether the vicunas were hungry, and if he'd tied up his boat securely, and what had got into Dad Ose to make him so irascible recently. Such distractions do not bother lovers on Dream Earth. Sex is uncomplicatedly enjoyable — which is perhaps why it becomes dull and must be enlivened by variations such as the Bjorn-serkr hunt.

"I've never felt like this before," said Manuel afterward, wonderingly. "Not even in Pu'este. It must be this place."

It is recorded that Belinda replied: "No. It's just us, my love."

And she kissed him again, hard, as though to stop him from thinking.

Later she said, "We must go."

"Why? I like it here." Manuel had found some perfect apples lying in the grass and was eating one.

"The Bjorn-serkrs will be back. This time they won't give up so easily."

Manuel was more practical now. The fight had been fought and won, and the loving was done. There was no point in asking for trouble, and Belinda's fate was at stake, as well as his own. "All right," he said. "Where shall we go?" The eland browsed at some nearby berry bushes. The beast was huge, and Manuel felt that it was too much to expect him to carry them both.

Belinda took his hand and led him along a trail that wound among the trees before climbing slowly into more open ground. Eventually they reached the brow of a hill and the whole of the land was spread out before them.

The Return of Manuel

The ground sloped down in all directions from where they stood. Behind lay the forest, to the right an immense area shrouded in a blanket of mist through which nothing showed. (This was in fact Space — an area where no Dream People had as yet imposed their smallwishes.) To the left a peaceful river wound through meadows to a delta, the ocean gleaming beyond. Ahead . . .

Ahead was a mountain.

It rose almost sheer from the flatness of the countryside, and most of its slopes were rocky and precipitous. A few trees clustered around its base and climbed fissures. The dark green of the base paled into the grey of cliffs, rising to the white of a cloud that hung over the summit, hiding everything there. This shading of colors lent the mountain an air of mystery with overtones of hope, since the cloud glowed like a halo in the afternoon sun.

"Avalayna," said Belinda. "It must be Avalayna."

"What's on top?"

"What we've always wanted." Poor, false girl, she gazed at the mountain with tears in her eyes, seeing all manner of wonders behind that mist, all manner of fruitless dreams culled from a thousand men who had chased her through forests.

"I've got what I always wanted," said Manuel. "But if you want to go to that place, I'll go with you." A memory of John

O'Greenwood came back to him. "But isn't it better to stick with what you have, once you've found it?"

"Avalayna," the girl whispered, and no involuntary smallwish of Manuel's could change her mind, the call was so strong.

So they started down the hill, and before long they heard the howling of the hunt somewhere behind them. The trees became denser and they moved as fast as they could, pushing through brambles and gorse, which, Manuel was surprised to find, bore no thorns. He held Belinda's hand, drawing her along behind him, still fearful that she would disappear like the last time. Every so often he turned around to reassure himself that it was truly she. Although the hunt was closing on them, he'd never been happier. Soon they would find a place to hide where they could lie and make love while the Bjorn-serkrs passed them by.

So: Manuel and Belinda, pursued.

Because there is an infinity of happentracks, there is an infinity of Rainbows, an infinity of Manuels and an infinity of Belindas.

A terrible thing was going to happen to Manuel on most of these happentracks. Although all the tracks would differ in varying degrees, the result would be the same. There would be two main branches of the track, and Manuel would lose Belinda on each. On the shortest, most direct track it would happen like this:

＊

Manuel said, "Through here." He drew Belinda down a narrow animal trail that twisted among shrubs so dense that he could not see more than five meters ahead, so tall that he could not see to either side. The pursuers were very near, crashing through the undergrowth all around them. Manuel caught a glimpse of a shaggy creature charging by so close that he could almost have touched it as he pulled Belinda to the ground. The bearback riders did not need to follow the trails.

Then they had gone and the couple were running again. Belinda was keeping up well; her breathing didn't seem to be troubling her these days. The trail twisted and turned, and soon Manuel had lost all sense of direction. Small animals scuttled from under their feet, plump creatures with bright eyes in their chipmunk faces, cute smallwishes not unreal enough to be banished to the Land of Lost Dreams. Manuel glanced at one as he passed. It held a nut in its paws and it winked at him.

Belinda dragged him to a sudden halt.

"Oh!" she gasped.

A giant figure barred their way. A bear, all dank fur and slavering jaws, and on its back a Bjorn-serkr.

The man roared, a brainless sound. He was not looking at Manuel. Manuel didn't matter. For all the Bjorn-serkr knew, he was just another smallwish, and an unattractive one at that. No, the hunter was watching Belinda and his teeth were bared in a fierce grin of expected pleasure. Thus have victorious warriors looked, all through the ages.

"Move aside, you!" he said to Manuel. "You've played your part."

Manuel stayed, staring up belligerently, still holding onto Belinda.

"I said move!" shouted the man impatiently.

A short silence, then: "Better do what he says, honey," said Belinda.

Manuel whirled round. Her voice was changed. Fear hit him in the stomach. He let go of her hand as though it were a viper.

Belinda had changed.

Her hair, still fair but perhaps even fairer now, was shorter. It hardly reached her shoulders. Her eyes were bigger, the lashes improbably long, the eyebrows bold arches. Her cheeks were plumper and her breasts and belly much fuller. Even her clothing was different — a white dress now hugged her figure. Her stance was not Belinda either. She stood sideways, one leg a little in front of the other, looking over her shoulder at the Bjorn-serkr, a long look from under lowered eyelashes. She was beautiful, and Manuel stared at her with sick revulsion. The Bjorn-serkr watched her with impatient lust.

Manuel didn't recognize her for what she was, of course. He was a Wild Human, unused to the changing fashions of the Dome. Had he lived in the present day, however, he would certainly have appreciated those famous lines from the Song of Earth:

> *A villainess named Marilyn destroyed the human*
> *race.*
> *What kind of fools were people then, to venerate*
> *that face?*

To him, she had the face of a Gorgon.

She was moving past him now, going to the Bjorn-serkr with her arms outstretched. He was climbing down from his bear. Manuel toyed with the idea of killing them both. He knew he couldn't, though, so he walked away in shame.

*

And the other happentracks, were they any less painful?

Manuel said, "Through here." He drew Belinda down a narrow animal trail that twisted among tall shrubs. For the next hour they dodged the hunters in this fashion, following the winding trails while the Bjorn-serkrs crashed around in fruitless search and eventually gave up. Someone among them found a reserve of psy and created another eland and another green-robed blonde, and they all pounded away into the distance.

Manuel and Belinda reached a stream that flowed quietly through a glade and stopped to refresh themselves.

"You remember my home, Pu'este? I think it must be south of here." He spoke thoughtfully, glancing at the sun, his arm around Belinda's waist. "It's a good place, Belinda. I think you'll like it there. The people in the village . . . Old Chine, he's not a bad fellow. And the priest, Dad Ose . . . And do you remember the Quicklies that came along the beach . . . ?" He fell silent, lost in nostalgia. Now he had Belinda back and his quest was over. He could take her home.

"Avalayna . . ." said Belinda.

"Much better than Avalayna. Although we can call in at Avalayna first, if you think it's up that mountain." He was eager to please. He didn't want to lose her, didn't want her even to consider going their separate ways. That would be unthinkable.

They slept in the forest at the base of the mountain that night.
The trees were curiously unformed and straggling, although
Manuel didn't think anything of it at the time. They ate pink
mushrooms that tasted like peaches and hung from the smooth
bark of the trees like lanterns, glowing in the evening light.
There was no grass underfoot, just dusty soil. They found a
drift of leaves near a rock face and curled up in their crackling
fragrance for the night.

The morning was bright and cool, and they made quick love
once more in the bouncing couch of leaves before dusting
themselves off and washing in a spring at the foot of the rock
face. Manuel added some smooth clothlike bark to his clothing
and made Belinda do the same. She looked pretty the way she
was, but they might soon be meeting people. Then they break-
fasted and began their climb.

They reached the cloud by midmorning. Suddenly it was
cold and damp, so they went slowly, suspecting that the mist
concealed sheer drops on either side of the path. At last they
reached an opening in a rock: Some kind of entrance, because
the path ran to it with precipitous cliffs on either side. It was
dark in there and Manuel hesitated, feeling misgivings.

Belinda tugged at his hand. "Let's go back."

"Not after coming this far."

There are many kinds of doors, and Manuel didn't recognize
this one for what it was. He stepped through.

Instantly a voice spoke, startling him.

"You wish to pass?"

He stared into the darkness. Soon he could make out the
figure of a man — but was it a man? The jaw was so underhung
that it was almost a snout, and rows of sharp teeth gleamed.
The head was unbalanced by this so that the jaw — or snout —
hung down on the chest. The eyes peered up from under heavy
lids that blinked at slow, regular intervals. The man sat curled
in a seat formed from the solid rock, his hands resting passively
in his lap. The arms were very short and the hands gnarled,
with thick, sharp nails.

"Let's go back," said Belinda again.

"That would be wise," said the man. His voice was slow, and

when he spoke his whole head moved as though governed by the huge jaw.

"We're going through," said Manuel.

"You might not like what you find."

"We'll take that chance, thanks."

"Back where you've come from, there is everything you could possibly want."

But Manuel was a real live Wild Human, and his curiosity was aroused. "That's not true. I want to see what's on the other side." It had occurred to him that Pu'este might be there, or at least a quick way out of this strange land. Perhaps there was a railway station where he and Belinda could catch the Train home.

"You cannot conceive what's on the other side." The man's head bobbed with slow words. Farther down the tunnel, tiny flecks of light swam in a blue haze. It was beautiful and somehow familiar.

The whole situation was familiar. Where had it happened before?

"Let us through," said Manuel determinedly. Holding onto Belinda, he began to edge past the man.

With a quick slithering motion the man jumped down from his chair and crouched on all fours, barring their way. He looked as if he might bite.

"I say this for your own good. On the other side is pain, sorrow and death. That means nothing to you, I know. You cannot conceive the horror of these things, but believe me, you would not like them. They are not fun. They are not exciting."

"I know what they are," said Manuel.

He hadn't felt pain for hours.

"I'm a real Wild Human," said Manuel, remembering the Girl, and suddenly realizing he might still be in Dream Earth, but not realizing the significance.

The man on the ground said, "I believe you. In that case, there is nothing further I can say. Pass."

So Manuel and Belinda left the crocodilian Reasoner behind and passed through the Do-Portal.

And Manuel's hand was suddenly empty.

Re-education of the Mole

••

*T*he Cuidadors stood around in silent sympathy. Even Juni felt
sorry for the young Wild Human. Someone brought Manuel his
Simulator, as an adult brings an unhappy child his favorite toy.
Manuel switched it on and watched the storm clouds and the
girl.

"She never was real," he said. "I should have known. That
kind of thing doesn't happen to a fellow like me. I must have
imagined that whole thing from start to finish. I smallwished
her. Nobody like her could be real. It was all a dream . . ." And
dreamlike, the storm-painting swirled.

"She was real," said Selena urgently. "The first time you saw
her, she was real, Manuel!"

"How do I know that?" He was not convinced. He was a
simple tool in the hands of these gods and they were using him
as they might use a trowel to fashion their purpose. They had
the power to do whatever they liked with him — or with the
whole of his world, if it suited them. "I'd like to see the Girl,
now," he said.

Zozula hesitated, avoiding his eye. "She's still in there," he
said eventually, nodding at the Rainbow.

"What! You mean you just left her in there all alone?"

"It's been her home for a long time, Manuel."

"You abandoned her! After dragging her all over the place,

after all she's been through to help you fix your damned Rainbow, you just abandoned her. Why? Was she too much trouble for you?"

Before Zozula could answer, Helmet, the electrician, said, "I must say, Zo, it does seem a little thoughtless. And we need her here in the Rainbow Room."

There was a murmur of agreement and Zozula found himself faced by a hostile crowd. "Fetch her out of there, Zo," said Juni.

"The Girl will come to no harm," said Zozula forcibly. "Believe me. Right now, our most important task is to diagnose the fault in the Rainbow and get it corrected."

"We'll need the Girl, too," said Selena. "Eulalie gave her the knowledge."

"What about your Mole?" asked Juni. "Didn't you say he was a pillar of common sense who could talk the Rainbow's language? Didn't you go to all this trouble to get him out of there? Didn't you say he would be the saving of the whole human race? Well, wheel him out! Plug him in!"

Impatiently, Zozula said, "The Rainbow's rejected him once. It snatched his mind and hid it away in the Land of Lost Dreams without our even suspecting what had happened, leaving us with a brainless body. There's no point in sending him in again until he's good and ready. He's got to adapt. He's got to be taught about the real world so that the Rainbow will accept him like any other Dream Person, instead of seeing him as some kind of rival genius thinking in abstract concepts. And he is a genius, make no mistake about that. Eloise says she's never known a mind like his — and she's lived with some clever people. But the Rainbow has to *trust* him, can't you see that?"

"So what are you doing about it?"

"Eloise is working on him now," said Zozula.

*

The shining Thing had gone and the Mole calmed himself the best way he knew, by probing a new branch of mathematics. Things began to fall into place. Equations sprang into his mind. Problems solved themselves, clickety-click, giving rise to new theorems.

Theorems proved themselves . . .

Oh!

Another Thing! Another Thing!

It was gone.

Theorems . . .

It was back! It flickered there, as though it were scared too. Cautiously now, the inquiring mind of the Mole approached it. It must be part of the overall scheme, otherwise it couldn't *be*. Perhaps it was something external to his mind, like the discomforts he'd suffered recently.

The Thing was four-dimensional, not like the horror that had threatened him before. It meant him no harm. It possessed symmetry. It moved with an illogical freewill. It sat uselessly in his mind like a disproved proposition, but at least it was friendly.

The Mole did something of supreme genius.

He imagined his mind to have tactile extensions, like his physical limbs. He passed imaginary hands over the Thing.

The shape of the Thing matched the shape of his own body. The topographical lines coincided. It was an image of himself!

A whole new world of discovery opened to the Mole. Quickly grasping the concept of vision, he moved out into that world.

Eloise designed it for him.

He stood on a great Underneath . . . a Plain. As he *saw* the things there, their names came into his mind. He moved through soft *grass* toward the *horizon*. The *sky* was *blue*. The grass was *green*, and had a harmless life of its own. For a while the Mole wandered through a world of peace and silence, a world where nothing moved contrary to his own wishes, a world without animals, winds or water, jagged peaks or glassy plateaus.

*

Lord Shout was watching the Mole. "What's he . . . like?" he asked. "I mean, what's he really like as a person? He's my own son, and I don't have any idea what kind of a man he is."

Eloise felt pity for Lord Shout. "He's good. He's good and kind and clever — very clever, even though he doesn't know as much as you or I about the real world, yet. A big part of his

mind works like the Rainbow, calculating . . . He may not need
me much longer. He can probably build all he needs on the
things I've shown him. He'll go on and invent a world that isn't
much different from the real one."

The Mole was changed. Instead of lying limply against the
wall, he now sat, his arm appendages caressing the floor, his
foot things twitching as he walked in imagination through the
gentle world that Eloise had created for him. His puttylike
color had improved and his breathing had deepened.

"What's he doing?" asked Lord Shout.

"Exploring."

"By himself? Shouldn't you be in there with him?"

"Not all the time. He's very inventive. He must get used to
the bare outlines I've given him, first. There's plenty for him to
discover for himself. Plenty of logical extensions to the ideas
I've given him."

Lord Shout watched his son. "But . . . you say he's inventive.
Suppose he invents something that harms him."

Eloise said something he didn't understand. "The worst
thing I can imagine is that he might trip over a hypotenuse. It's
all mental, Lord Shout. Nothing in there is real."

"It's as real as the Mole is likely to get," said Lord Shout
doubtfully.

Eloise's eyes were hollow from lack of sleep, her frame pulpy
from a lifetime of inaction. "Do you think I could rest now?"
she asked. She coughed — a hoarse sound from deep in her
chest. "I'm so tired."

Looking at her, a new worry came to Lord Shout.

*

The wind blew against the Mole. It was irritating. He tried to
think it away, but it persisted because Eloise made it do so. A
tree appeared on the plain, tossing in the wind and scattering
leaves. It creaked and a leaf hit the Mole sharply. He flinched.
The tree wouldn't go away. He didn't want it in his mind, yet it
stayed.

"This is the real world, Mole," said the gentle alien whose
designation appeared to be *Eloise*.

He'd already grasped the idea of another person with freewill sitting in his mind. It interfered with his thoughts, but it was little different from another person sitting physically beside him, interfering with his body. He hadn't, however, grasped the idea of replying.

So he accepted — the way he accepted a proven hypothesis. And with that, things began to move fast. The sky darkened with heavy clouds and rain began to fall, drenching and chilly. Trees sprang up all over the plain and the wind was full of their leaves. He glided through this stinging blizzard, unable to control his environment. Soon he began to enjoy himself.

Reaching the banks of a fast river, he flung himself into the current. He was swept away. He watched the banks slide past and, choosing his moment, pulled himself ashore.

The rain had stopped and the clouds had gone. He was in a quiet glade. Creatures, Things, were cropping the grass. They had slender necks and long-lashed brown eyes, and they glanced at him shyly as they ate.

The *Eloise* told him they were guanacos.

They were — he sought for the concept — *beautiful* creatures and he *liked* them. They were gentle and meant no harm to anyone. He watched them, content to let this new world take its course and take him with it. But soon he discovered the drawback to this kind of world.

A *jaguar*, all rippling muscles and bared teeth, charged from the bush, knocked down the smallest guanaco and bit into its neck. Then, as the Mole rose from the ground in alarm, it saw him, snarled and padded away silently.

The guanacos had all fled except for one that lay twitching on the grass. The Mole approached it, unaccountable sensations building in his mind, sensations that seemed to spread to the rest of his body. In sorrow and pity, the Mole watched the guanaco. It looked back at him, but it didn't really see him. Everything else had gone; the Mole was not even sure the trees were there. There was just the dying guanaco and himself. Then the guanaco shuddered and stopped breathing, and there was just the Mole.

And now he couldn't simply accept the situation. There were tears in his soul, and he looked into the Greataway and said, "Why, for God's sake?"

THE DEATH OF ELOISE

Zozula had been searching for three days.

He'd fought the Rainbow, which persisted in scanning everything but what it was instructed to scan. His meals had been brought to him personally because the valets were not functioning. The air was becoming stale and he suspected that the conditioning plant had failed — which could mean the death of everyone in the Dome when the next Chokes came.

On the odd occasions when the Rainbow had allowed him to see Dream Earth, he'd been horrified. It was as though the computer had deliberately set itself the task of driving every neotenite mad by indulging in crazy pyrotechnic effects at the same time that it systematically transformed the Dome into a place unfit for habitation.

Why?

Only two people might know the answer: the Mole and the Girl. One had been defeated by the Rainbow already and the other was trapped in there.

Zozula rubbed his eyes, jerking awake as a herd of elephants lumbered across the Rainbow Room, trumpeting their alarm at some forgotten historical incident. A cleaning cavy nibbled at his clothing, while another disposed of a tray of spilt food at his feet. At least they were animals and not subject to the Rainbow's whims. A raccoon-nurse approached, bringing another tray. He motioned her away. He wasn't hungry. He was too tired to eat.

He stood, rubbing the circulation back into his legs and re-membering — yet again — that he hadn't practiced his Inner Think lately. It seemed he felt older every day.

The time had come to face the others and admit defeat. He would be replaced as head Cuidador, of course. Probably Selena would take his place; she deserved it and she was a good, kind woman. She'd come to visit him often during these last eternal days and nights when the history of aeons and the mathemat-ics of genius spun past his eyes, and she'd comforted him and tried to take part of the blame herself.

He erased the elephants with difficulty and took one last look at Dream Earth. For once the effects didn't look too bad. The sky was blue and the fields green, and a milkmaid was strolling down a footpath carrying empty pails to a byre. A curiously peaceful and relaxing scene, and there were very few Dream People in sight.

Some fool must be setting this up for a tactical strike, thought Zozula bitterly. *It's just the kind of violent contrast these people love.*

Annoyed, he wiped the scene out and made for the door. The nurse walked alongside, concerned over his appetite. He motioned her away again, accidentally tilting her tray. Washdogs and cavies darted in. He reached the door, which slid aside reluctantly.

Eloise stood outside.

*

She was thinner, and the flesh had dropped away from her face, so that her neotenite origins were less apparent. Her body was still incurably gross, however, and the clothing drooped from the upper part of her body, showing fatty, immature breasts.

"Is everything all right?" asked Zozula anxiously, as he led her to a couch and a washdog began to clean her.

A paroxysm of coughing doubled her up and Zozula saw she had lost most of her hair. Gathering her breath, she said, "Everything's fine, except . . ."

"Except what?"

Suddenly she burst out, "It's cruel, what everybody's doing in this Dome. Taking people into the Rainbow and leaving them there. Breeding people and killing them. Keeping thousands of people alive who would be better off dead — people like me . . . And the Mole — it would have been much kinder if I'd left him alone instead of prying into his mind. He had a good world of his own in there, but now I've had to teach him all about killing and I've turned his world upside down."

"Is he . . .?"

"Oh, he's all right. He's nearly ready to die in the Rainbow, if that's what you want." She stared at him wildly, blinked, bowed her head and mumbled, "What's the use? It's all predestined anyway. Everything's happening the way Trevis said."

"Does the Mole die in there? If so . . ."

"On some happentracks he does. Isn't that bad enough?" Now she was watching Zozula again, and for the first time she realized the extent of his exhaustion. "I'm sorry," she said. "It's not your fault. Nothing is ever anyone's fault. And you have your problems, too." She drank from a cup the nurse handed her and relaxed with a little shudder.

Zozula said simply, "I can't get the Girl out of there." Tired and weak, he buried his face in his hands.

"You mean you can't reincorporate her? Or is she just lost?"

"She's lost. I should never have left her alone there. But the Rainbow is so damned *big*. And now the special effects —"

"I don't want to hear about the special effects," said Eloise. "You've got to have a better reason for wanting her out of there. After all, she won't come to any harm." She stared at him fixedly. "Can't anyone in this Dome show a glimmering of human decency, just once?"

There was nothing to lose except his dignity, and since Eloise could read his mind, Zozula had lost that already. Carefully, wanting to get the words right, he said, "We Cuidadors do not have children, as you know. Generations ago we used to, but they were all . . . defective, and so in the end it was agreed that we would depend on the genetic program on the People Planet to supply our successors. So we've never known what it's like to have children of our own. My wife, Eulalie . . . She chose the Girl as her successor and I went along with it. At the time it didn't matter to me much who succeeded her; I couldn't think about anything beyond the fact that I'd lost Eulalie.

"Then, gradually, I began to get to know the Girl. Oh, at first I found her unattractive and demanding, but I made allowances. She'd come from a place where she could have anything she wanted just by asking for it, and she'd suddenly found the real world isn't like that. So she complained a lot. But she had a lot of good in her, and a lot of courage, and soon she began to adapt. She fought to come to terms with the real world, and she didn't give in. And soon she stopped asking to be put back where she'd come from. She actually preferred the real world, and all the hardships and pain, in spite of the fact that she could never live comfortably in it, not with a body like hers. She gave me hope for all the people in Dream Earth.

"She was a fighter. If . . ." He looked away, embarrassed, then remembered that Eloise knew anyway. "If Eulalie and I could have had a child, I couldn't have asked for a better daughter than the Girl.

"And I left her somewhere in the Rainbow. And . . . And now I'm wondering if she's decided she likes Dream Earth better after all, and intends to stay there.

"I wouldn't blame her."

After a while, Eloise said, "I'll help you find her and get her out of there, Zozula. The Mole and I will help you, that is . . ."

*

The Mole had been suffering through many days of bewilderment.

When the Alien Thinker, the *Eloise*, had withdrawn from his world, a Vision had appeared. Instead of a mind thing it was a whole creature, like the guanaco in its three-dimensional mobility, but quite different otherwise. It was smaller and it was nakedly hairless and soft, and it had an inexplicable emotional content, like the guanaco kid, and yet not like it. It was disturbing and very pleasant, and it stayed with him for a while before it disappeared, moving physically beside his own physical body.

So, alone again, he'd extrapolated on the landscape, and thought the guanacos back to their ancestors and beyond —

much farther beyond, until eventually he was able to conceive a primal form. Fascinated, he conjectured upon the fac-
tors that would influence the development of such a form, and
using an evolutionary theory more complex and accurate than
the Rainbow's latest version, he'd progressed far enough to
create mentally a creature that bore a remarkable similarity to
a gibbon — and incidentally and thought-provokingly, to the
Vision.

But he'd never been able to visualize the dawning of intelligence and the newer life-forms because, secure in his closed
world, he had not conceived of the existence of the Greataway
and Starquin, the Five-in-One.

The Vision recurred from time to time during the succeeding
days. It would come around a corner of his mind and walk
across his landscape. He was unable to subject it to any real
control; like the *Eloise,* it seemed to exist apart from him. It
walked with a grace all its own. It stirred him in a way he
couldn't explain. He tried to capture it, to extrapolate on it, to
trace it back to its origins, but he couldn't. It *was,* and it was
strangely *beautiful,* and he couldn't control it. So he let it play
with the gibbons and ride the stegosauri.

Then one day the *Eloise* was back.

*

Quickly he asked it about the Vision.

"I am *she,* Mole," said the *Eloise,* and he knew that *she* was
sad. "The Vision is myself, and I want you to think of it that
way. You see, we won't be meeting again. You're going away,
physically away, to a place where dreams will come much
more easily and you'll be able to share them with other people.
So please take my Vision with you, and look after it always."

Then she stayed with him for a long time and walked
through his world in the form of the Vision, and put things
right where they were wrong — and, to his regret, obliterated
the dinosaurs, which had been an enjoyable part of his evolutionary game. But she put so many wonderful things in their
place that it was worth it: whales and stars and orchids, and
humans with animal genes and beautiful faces.

And before she left him forever, she gave him the final gift.

A new creature appeared, and the *Eloise* merged his ego with it.

"This is the real *you*, Mole," she said.

*

They buried Eloise beside a tall ironwood tree not far from the Dome. It didn't seem right to recycle her. After they'd tamped down the dark soil and returned to the Dome, Lord Shout said, "She'd been ill for some time, Zozula. She knew she would never see the delta and her people again."

"How does the Mole feel about this?" asked Zozula.

"I have no way of knowing." The Mole had been sitting quietly on the floor when they carried Eloise out and he was still sitting there, attended by the pretty nurse, Tashi.

She looked up. "He's fine, Lord Shout. Eloise was thinking to him just before she died."

"Does he know she's dead?"

"I think so."

"Well . . ." said Zozula uncertainly, thinking of Eloise's pathetic, flabby body. "She wasn't much." In his way, he was trying to console Lord Shout.

"The Mole isn't much, either."

Zozula glanced at him and said, "According to Eloise, he's ready for the Rainbow. Let's get him to bed. Would you like to come and watch?"

Lord Shout thought of the shelves, the drips and the electrodes. "No, I don't think so." He walked across to the Mole and kissed him briefly, and when he turned back there were tears in his eyes. "Thank you, Zozula," he said. "Thank you for your hospitality and everything. It's time for us to go home now. My men are waiting outside."

"Us?" Zozula glanced at the Mole.

"I hope you don't mind," Lord Shout said evenly, as the nurse left the Mole and joined them. "Tashi is coming with me."

Zozula sighed. "I don't need to remind you —"

"No, you don't. You made that point very clear. But I have to remind you, Zozula — there are other considerations in life

besides the perpetuation of the species. After all, you and
Eulalie . . . It's a pity that Tashi and I can't have children, but
it's not a disaster. The human race is far from extinct." He held
out his hand. "Goodbye, and thank you again."

Zozula clasped it. "Thank you for the Mole," he said.

Within an hour the Mole slipped quietly into Dream Earth,
and the Rainbow hardly noticed his coming.

ELIZABETH'S RETRENCHMENT

*T*he Girl had left the Land of Lost Dreams several days previously. Elated by her success in the Forest of Fear and her defeat of Blind Pew, she had forced her way into the more normal planes of Dream Earth by sheer strength of psy. She was confident that she could return to the real world by the same method, but meanwhile she needed time to recuperate.

She intended to use this time to good purpose. Her experiences in the real world with real people had made a profound impression on her. Zozula, Lord Shout, Eloise, the Cuidadors, Manuel — particularly Manuel — had taught her that there was no substitute for genuine relationships and emotions. She was longing to get back out there — contrary to Zozula's worst fears — but meanwhile she was not unhappy. There was much to do. She had to instill a little sense into these phonies.

Eulalie would have been proud of her.

She visited the Coconut Shy, where people stood in a huge circle throwing stones at a crowd of whimpering, abandoned smallwishes, and she strode into the middle of them. Using her own psy, she galvanized the smallwishes and organized them into a quick-witted team that began to chuckle and dodge, catching the stones and throwing them back, making the Dream People look like fools, until the game was no fun anymore.

"Who is this girl?" a powerful felino asked. The 122nd millennium was in vogue at the time.

"I don't know," boomed an Us Ursa, "but she's the ugliest creature I've ever seen! Is she real, or is she a smallwish? Wish her away, someone, and let's get on with the game!"

"I have the psy," announced a slender jester, jingling his bells and advancing on the Girl.

He disappeared in a puff of smoke.

"He had nothing," said the Girl, facing the Dream People as they began to move toward her. "He was only a smallwish, bluffing. Just think about that for a moment. You people have drifted so far away from reality that you don't know a smallwish when he's right beside you!"

"So what?" someone called. "As long as it's fun!"

"All of you are phonies," shouted the Girl, as an angry murmur began to build up. "But some of you are *totally* fake! You're not even really there! You exist in other people's minds! Once they stop believing in you, you'll cease to exist, just like the Celestial Steam Locomotive!"

"Wish her away!"

"You can't!" And suddenly a podium appeared behind the Girl, and she turned her back on them and mounted the steps. Taking a microphone, she stared deliberately at the crowd. The felino was real, and that fighting *grupo* of felinas, too. And the cai-man, and the kikihuahuan digger. But that huge Us Ursa, blustering and calling on others to pool their psy and eliminate her . . .

"You!" she shouted, pointing at him. "Fade out!"

And he did. He was gone in an instant and the grass where he'd stood was not even bruised.

"Has it ever occurred to you," the Girl asked, "that many of those people you call friends, whom you share your adventures with, are not real? Did you ever think they might not have minds of their own, but were just somebody else's smallwish that battened onto you — not because they liked you, but simply because they needed your belief to maintain their existence? You're surrounded by a crowd of freeloaders, leeching away your psy! Look around and ask yourself — how many real friends do you have?"

And in the thoughtful silence, a small voice cried, "How can I tell?"

A leonid roared, "Use your common sense, of course! Shut your ears to questioners and rabble-rousers, and just believe that human beings are good — and fun — and that Earth is the most wonderful planet in the Universe! Our psy is the gift of the Rainbow and we must use it wisely and well. This girl has taught us a lesson we needed, and I for one am thankful. Now, I'm sure we all have a lot of thinking to do!"

He strode away and was cut down by a dozen sceptical smallwishers and flickered out like a snuffed candle.

Felinos stared at felinas and cai-men eyed tumpiers. A group of identical El Tigres held their breath, glancing at their legendary wives, the beautiful Serenas. A lone Saba could be seen running her hands over her own body, her wondering eyes scared. A faint sigh came from the aether where an invisible god thing had been hovering, and a small pack of African hunting dogs began to sniff one another, whimpering uncertainly. Robots watched Mohals and Solons gazed at Esmeraldas.

A Karina disappeared.

Then the panic began.

*

Elizabeth's Retrenchment, as it later became called, occupied a tiny period in the life of Dream Earth, yet later historians agreed that it was perhaps the most important event ever to occur in that imaginary world. During one subjective week the observed population fell from some 50,000 to around 15,000 persona, and the effects spread from Dome to Dome throughout Earth by way of the Rainbow's circuits. No doubt the Rainbow accelerated the process, once it had started, on the grounds that it was beneficial for the population as a whole and freed up vast areas of the computer for more useful work. The Retrenchment was followed by a period of comparative significance known as the Age of Caradoc, during which the environment of Dream Earth became more logical and increasingly subject to the natural laws found in the real world. In this way, the neotenites became prepared for their eventual release from dependency on the Dome, although it was many years before they lived Outside in any numbers. By which time, of course, they were not neotenites.

The Retrenchment did not happen easily. Thirty-five thousand people do not give up their identities without a fight — and after the initial panic even the Dream People began to resist the rate of disincorporation as their friends and creations disappeared before their eyes.

On the fifth day of the retrenchment, the opposition got itself organized. A thousand Dream People had called for a night's respite from the orgy of suspicion, and an unnatural quiet hung over Dream Earth. Ten thousand smallwishes — waitresses, mistresses, stunt men, gigolos — trembled in their beds. One smallwish bided his time, surrounded by a bodyguard of real Dream People who were expending the last flickers of their psy in reinforcing his credibility. In four days they had identified the origins of the Retrenchment, identified the Girl and learned something of her past. They and their smallwish were ready.

The Girl awakened on the sixth morning. Having seen no reason why she shouldn't sleep comfortably like anyone else, she had taken a room at the Admiral Benbow Inn. This was a pleasant place that had been operated by its smallwisher, Mrs. Hawkins, for several years. Mrs. Hawkins was an anomaly in Dream Earth: a person who liked to get through the day with a minimum of smallwishes; a person of abundant common sense who had supported the Girl through some of the more difficult phases of the Retrenchment.

"Stay in bed this morning," said Mrs. Hawkins. "I'll bring you breakfast."

"That's a good idea," said the Girl gratefully. "I'm all psy'd out. I need to hole up for a while, otherwise somebody might take advantage of me. I have plenty of enemies out there. And anyway, now I've set everything in motion, it can carry on without me."

"You've earned a rest." Mrs. Hawkins drew the curtains. Outside, it was still dark.

"Somebody's interfering with the sun," said the Girl, suddenly uneasy.

"It must be those people who call themselves the Reactionaries," said Mrs. Hawkins, scanning the eastern sky for signs of daybreak. "They sent a public broadcast through the village yesterday afternoon while you were away, asking people to stop wasting their psy searching for smallwishes. They said the whole structure of Dream Earth might break down, with so much scepticism abroad."

"That's nonsense," said the Girl. "The Rainbow handles Composite Reality."

"So you've told me, and I believe you — but it doesn't make the day any lighter. And there are a lot of people out there who are getting pretty scared. Even real people aren't sure whether they might be smallwishes themselves, and they don't want to find out."

"I'm sorry," said the Girl after a moment. "I hadn't thought of that too much. It seemed there were bigger issues."

"You did the right thing, all the same," Mrs. Hawkins reassured her, leaving the room.

Still uneasy, the Girl got up and went to the window. A few lights were on in the handful of houses that constituted the village. The single winding street was empty in the predawn greyness. The villagers, no doubt questioning the lateness of the sunrise, remained indoors, where their authenticity was less likely to be challenged. Then the Girl caught sight of a movement to the west, where the lane disappeared into mists and rolling meadowland. A lone figure was approaching the village. At least somebody was not afraid.

She would not have been human if she hadn't felt some regret for the disappearance of all those smallwishes. It was not their fault they were not real. And false or not, they felt a very real fear at the prospect of ceasing to exist. Consoling herself with the knowledge that it would all be over in a couple more days, she opened the window and leaned out to see who this lonely traveler was.

The figure was moving slowly between the high hedgerows in a curiously zigzag fashion, so that the Girl might have thought he was drunk if it had not been for the steady purposefulness of his gait. It was almost as though he were searching, the way he walked steadily from one side of the lane to the other, working his way toward the village like a sailboat against the wind. Then, as she watched, his course straightened and he walked beside the eastern hedge. And now she could see that his arm was extended and he seemed to be jabbing at the foliage as he walked, possibly with a stick, almost as though he was . . .

Blind.

As the Girl moved back from the window and the great pounding began in her heart, the figure passed a lighted window and she saw the black cloak, the pallid face. She sank into a chair, trying to smallwish herself somewhere else, knowing that she had already exhausted her psy, beginning to tremble uncontrollably . . .

Then she heard the tap-tap of the blind man's stick on the street, and a pause.

"Go away," she whispered. "Go away, please."

Then shuffling footsteps, and a long scraping as the stick was drawn along the wall of the inn.

*

She heard the door latch rattle downstairs. Then there was an insistent knocking and she heard Mrs. Hawkins call, "Wait a moment, there! I'm coming as fast as I can!"

She heard the front door creak open, and a muffled conversation. Next, footsteps on the stairs . . . Mrs. Hawkins' footsteps. They stopped outside the door.

"There's a man come to see you." Mrs. Hawkins lowered her voice. "A poor old blind man — such a sorry sight. I think he wants you to help him."

"Send him away," whispered the Girl. Then she heard the dreadful shuffling on the stairs. "Oh, no . . . no," she groaned.

"What's that? I can't hear you."

"For God's sake, get rid of —"

And the door crashed open.

She caught one glimpse of Mrs. Hawkins' startled face before the innkeeper was thrust aside and Pew sprang into the doorway, cloak whirling about him, rolling eyes staring this way and that from under the green eyeshade, stick jabbing toward her like a rapier. He scuttled forward, slammed the door behind him and threw the bolt.

"Now, me beauty . . ." he snarled.

The Girl had moved into the far corner of the room. Beside her stood a table with china ornaments on it. Striving to concentrate her thoughts, she dragged her gaze away from the terrifying figure of the blind man to a small figurine: a china shepherdess. She looked from the shepherdess to the blind man, gauged the distance and said "I wish . . ."

Too slowly, the figurine rose from the table and soared toward Pew's head.

He swung his stick contemptuously and batted it aside.

"Ye forget," he said quietly. "'Tis no simple fool ye deal with." He began to advance a slow step at a time, crouching, stick stabbing at her. "'Tis a troublemaker you are — and I'm going to make an end to all that."

"Yes, but I'm real" — the Girl's stouthearted effort was spoiled by an involuntary gulp — "and you're only a smallwish! You can't hurt me!"

"Ha!" Judging her position by her voice, he swung his stick. It crashed to the wall a fraction from her head, bringing down a shower of plaster. She stumbled aside, and Pew, casting his stick away, flung himself on her with a yell of triumph. "By the Powers, I have ye!" He ran his fingers over her, chuckling. "Now, lass, ye'll suffer."

The Girl slumped to the floor, paralyzed with fear. Her success in the Swamp of Submission was forgotten; all past events faded into the horror of the present — the stinking form of Blind Pew pressing her into the floor, his bony knees digging into her flesh, his skeletal fingers kneading and probing her body while all the time he chuckled and cursed and drooled, until his fingers, tiring of their entertainment, crept upward and began to fasten themselves on her throat.

He can't do this, she thought. *He simply can't – he's only a smallwish!*

"Now we'll see who's real," said Pew, an age-old creation reinforced by a thousand of yesterday's wishes.

There was a thundering in the Girl's head like storm waves against the base of a cliff.

*

As though from a different happentrack, she heard a voice say, "You don't know what's real and what isn't, blind man."

"Eh?" The pressure relaxed for a moment as Pew swung round in surprise. "And who might you be, me lad?"

Pushing the blind man's cloak away from her eyes, the Girl saw a vision. Standing in the middle of the room was a handsome young man wearing a crimson doublet and black pants. Beside him stood a girl of unusual beauty, fair-haired and dressed in a long silver dress studded with jewels. They made a somewhat foppish couple, but the Girl was in no position to criticize them on that count. The young man smiled. "I am Caradoc," he said.

"Never heard of you."

"I don't often bother to appear in person," said Caradoc, "but you and a few others have been making a nuisance of yourselves this last couple of days. Speaking of which . . ." Noticing the darkness outside, he drew his sword and pointed it at the window.

The sun crept over the horizon and the village lit up.

"By thunder," muttered Pew, as the sunlight warmed his face. He scrambled to his feet and edged toward the door. "Ye have strange powers, mister!"

"Wait!" The sword was at Pew's throat and Caradoc's expression held no mercy. "Give me one good reason why I shouldn't kill you here and now."

"Have pity," Pew began to whimper, pawing at the blade. "I'm only a poor wretched smallwish, the creation of other men's evil."

"A little more than that by now, I think. You've been around too long, Pew. You've taken on a kind of substance." A trickle of blood showed at the tip of the sword as Pew jerked back with a squeal of fright. "But not so much substance that I couldn't finish you off if I wished. I'm not going to, however — not right now. I've spoken with the Oracle, and she tells me there is a twisted purpose in your existence. So you must live — for a while, anyway. But I'll tell you this, Pew: Once you've fulfilled your destiny in the Ifalong, I shall dispose of you. Until then, I advise you to get back to the Land of Lost Dreams, where you can't do any harm."

He dealt the blind man a stinging blow across the shoulders with the flat of the blade. Pew gave a yelp of fright, scuttled for the door, tripped over his stick and fell heavily, snatched it up as he scrambled to his feet, slid the bolt aside and jerked open the door, and was gone. They heard his footsteps thundering down the stairs and out into the street, then the frantic tap-tap-tap as he hurried back down the lane the way he'd come.

"And now," said Caradoc, smiling, "it's time we sent you home, Girl."

DELTA'S END

*F*orty-three standard minutes later the Triad was reunited in the Rainbow Room. Manuel was the first to see the Girl as she waddled through the Do-Portal, still shaken, but smiling as she caught sight of them.

"Girl!" The room was empty now; all the images had gone. There was just the distant figure toward which Manuel ran, Zozula following with more dignity.

"Girl!" Manuel seized her hands, grinning. "How *are* you? What have you been doing? I thought we'd never see you again!"

The Girl, laughing too, said, "Manuel, you don't know the half of it."

"Well, tell me! Come and sit over here. Get her something to eat," he ordered a passing nurse in peremptory fashion.

Zozula arrived. "It's good to see you again, Girl," he said formally. Then, to Manuel's amazement, he took her hand and kissed her lightly on the forehead. "Tell us what's been happening to you," he said.

They sat on gossamer couches and the Girl luxuriated as Manuel arranged cushions under her head and feet. "It's so good to be back," she said. "So good to see you both again."

"No regrets about leaving Dream Earth this time, Girl?" asked Zozula, more anxiously than he'd intended.

"I don't belong in there anymore. Dream Earth is no substitute for the real world. The sooner we can get those people out of there, the better." She went on to describe her success in persuading the Dream People to show some common sense.

The Triad compared notes, ate and drank. And at some point Zozula had to say, "Eloise died, of course. You knew that?"

"I'd guessed as much."

"I wondered if the Mole really understood. It must have been a shock to him."

"He took it very well, " said the Girl with a small, private smile.

*

It happened later that day, and it happened without warning.

Selena and Juni had joined them, the former a little more cheerful, now that the failure of last year's breeding program was behind her and the new season had started. With the Mole now safely in the Rainbow and the Girl at the console, she was optimistic.

"Now, perhaps, we can start getting some help from the computer," she said.

And the Rainbow chose that moment to go crazy.

It had been brooding for centuries in its mild electronic way. It had observed a certain tribe of neotenites in the delta, but for a long time it had done nothing because no real threat had developed.

The Song of Earth relates that it was the death of Lergs that triggered the Rainbow, because this resulted in Trevis's joining the gestalt on the mud flats. The gestalt's potential immediately increased a hundredfold, and there was no limit to the knowledge they could amass. They began to impinge on the Greataway. Some minstrels suppose they could have turned the whole Universe into their own private Dream Earth, but that is perhaps too fanciful. Nevertheless the foreboding of Trevis was very real: *Then we will be destroyed, because someone more powerful than us will want it that way...*

The Rainbow decided the time had come.

The walls of the Rainbow Room resonated like a sounding board.

"What was that?" Zozula cried.

Manuel found the Girl in his arms and held her as she trembled. Other Cuidadors arrived at a run, followed by a train of valets, trolleys, suckers, waiters and other robots, out of control and running to the Rainbow. Chutes began to spew food and drink, while the Cuidadors gazed in awe at the show the Rainbow was putting on. The entire chamber, a kilometer long and half a kilometer high, was ablaze with color, dancing and crackling around the humans — solid color that seemed to press on the eyes in the same way that the sounds, deep and vibrant, pressed on the ears. More people arrived: engineers and astronomers and dieticians, nurses and administrators, edging into the Rainbow Room with fear in their eyes.

"Is this the end?" whispered Juni.

As the panic spread into the far reaches of the Dome, there was a sudden flash, searing the eyes of the watchers like a bolt of lightning. All the robots froze where they stood.

When Manuel was able to see again, a young man was standing tensely in the room, all alone where previously the colors had rioted. The sounds became muted. The young man looked around but didn't appear to see them; it was as though he were blind.

The Girl shouted, "Caradoc!"

The young man was trembling violently. He shouted, his voice thin in the vastness of the room. "I will try —"

Then he was gone for an instant and it had become clear that it was not fear that caused him to shake, but strain and tension. *He is fighting the Rainbow,* guessed Zozula. *Who is he?*

Caradoc was back. "If you can hear me, listen!" he shouted. "I will try to force a visual . . . please understand you must . . . no other way . . ."

He disappeared. The Rainbow Room darkened, as though a thunderstorm were coming. The people murmured with apprehension.

A monstrous image of Brutus appeared in the center of the room.

Someone screamed. Zozula heard Juni shout, "The Specialists have rebelled!"

The figure of Brutus was terrifying, squatting gigantically before them, towering over them, beady little eyes shifting this way and that as he hunched over a piece of wood. A vast knife flashed as Brutus whittled, chips flying like spears toward the Cuidadors.

"The Rainbow's trying to tell us something," Zozula said to Juni.

"It's telling us Brutus is doing something terribly wrong! And that doesn't surprise me, either. Where is he?"

"Down in his quarters, I suppose. Come on!"

They pushed through a knot of Cuidadors and, followed by Selena, Manuel and the Girl, took an express elevator, dropping through endless levels in a two-kilometer descent to the lower areas.

Brutus's quarters were empty.

"Think!" said Zozula. "The background to that image. Where was it?" The lights were flickering and there was an electrical smell in the air.

"It was dark. I couldn't tell."

"There aren't many dark places in the Dome."

"Could he have been Outside?"

"No . . . I saw machinery. Piping and conduits."

"One of the service areas." Juni thought. "The sewers! That's it!" It was the kind of place where she would expect to find Brutus. When he was on Earth, much of his time was spent in the disposal areas, operating the deprocessing units. You could smell it on him.

They took a circle speedway, changed to a radius after a few minutes, rode it to the very wall of the Dome, stepped off and ran through an ever-darkening catacomb of corridors, shouting: "Brutus!"

In the end they found him sitting in a dark corner near the outfall, whittling . . . and crying. The floor was covered with wood shavings. In the middle of the shavings lay a model boat, a very simple boat, little more than a tiny raft with low sides.

Selena had known about Brutus's hobby for a long time. Like his father before him, Brutus spent his spare time modeling ships along the lines of the ancients' vessels — a harmless enough pursuit. The little boat in the middle of the floor was a very poor example of his work.

"What's the matter, Brutus?" asked Selena.

Suddenly aware of their presence, he jumped to his feet, dusting himself off, blinking, his fierce little eyes flicking constantly to a corner of the chamber.

"There's something funny going on here," said Zozula. "What have you been up to, Brutus?"

"Nothing . . . nothing."

But Juni had found the baby. She brought it into the light. It was wrapped in a blanket, and it was quite dead. Brutus blinked at it.

Selena said, "This is one of the batch we brought back from the People Planet for deprocessing, Brutus." Her voice was uncharacteristically cold. "What were you doing with it? Why didn't you put it in the recycler with the others?" She stiffened, staring at him. She strode across the chamber and read off a bank of dials. "You didn't put *any* of them in, Brutus! Where are they? *What have you done with them?*"

"I didn't . . . I never . . ."

Now Juni stepped forward, staring at him with loathing. "What did you do with all those neotenite babies, you Specialist?"

Zozula, watching her, felt sick.

She turned to him. "Make him talk."

Zozula said slowly, "All those boats he's making — I know where they've gone. This lock — it leads Outside. It vents into the river. He's been *playing* with the babies. He's been sailing them on the river, like dolls. Oh, God."

"Haven't you anything to say, Brutus?" asked Selena. "You're the best assistant I've ever had. You knew what you were doing. Why did you do it?"

And slowly the gorilla-man's demeanor changed, and the animal receded while the human in him took over. He drew himself up, and he was taller and broader, stronger than anyone there. He tossed the knife to the floor, where it clattered among the wood shavings. He straightened his clothes.

Quietly he said, "I was giving them a chance."

"What!"

The words came calmly. "They deserve a chance, just like anyone else. We've bred them and we have a responsibility, don't you see?" His deep eyes watched them, begging for understanding. "We can't kill them just because they don't measure up to our ideals of Humanity."

"But Brutus — they're neotenites." Something of his sentiments got through to Selena and she moderated her tone. "They'll never grow up properly. You know that — we tested them all. They wouldn't stand a chance out there. By sending them Outside you prolong their suffering. They take longer to die, like this little one here." She held the dead baby out to him, but he wouldn't look.

"I didn't build enough boats this year," he said stubbornly. "And by the time I —"

"*This* year?" Zozula broke in. "How long has this been going on?"

"All my life, and the life of my father and his father — and others."

"My God — we could have populated the world with these monsters!"

"No," said Selena, "they have no sex. I only add that quality when I'm satisfied with the other results."

"Just what qualities do they have, Selena?"

"Nothing that could help them Outside. A very strong capability for visualization — that would help them in their dream lives, if ever they went into the Rainbow. They're telepathic and highly intelligent, of course. But nothing to help them survive in the wild. They're babies, Zozula. If they haven't drowned or starved, the crocodiles will have got them." She turned back to Brutus. "It's cruel, cruel, this thing you've been doing!"

"I meant no harm." His tone was resigned. He couldn't win. He could only preserve the dignity of his people and behave like a human being.

"I hope not."

"It won't happen any more."

"You can be sure of that," said Selena.

*

In years to come, the great civilization of the delta faded piece by piece as, with no children to pass their wonderings on to, the people died. The spaceships dissolved and the minarets tumbled, the paintings and statuary blew away, the underground machines fell silent and the solid rock moved back into the caverns.

The last inhabitant died young, insane, his mind teeming with the accumulated imaginings of generations, unwilling to let go, unwilling to forget the smallest wonderful detail, hoarding the images of genius until his mind exploded, and, gibbering, he wandered away and fell among Wild Humans, who treated him as a god until he died.

And a certain remote dimension of the Greataway fell silent.

The Rainbow rejoiced.

*

It was a later Cuidador who built on an ancient report of Zozula's and discovered the truth about Eloise's tribe. The Rainbow parted with the data grudgingly, bit by bit, but in the end the story of the great delta civilization became known. The Cuidadors were amazed and stunned, and ultimately overcome with guilt because the destruction of the tribe reflected adversely on their integrity as guardians of Mankind's art, science and knowledge. They tried to hush it up, and among themselves they blamed the whole affair on the organic components of the Rainbow.

But the details leaked out, of course. Legends grew from rumors, and the minstrels and the bards pieced them together. The Story of Brutus became an important part of the Song of Earth, and his name became a symbol of compassion through all of Late Earth.

ELOISE'S LEGACY

···

*T*he Triad sat in the Rainbow Room. The Girl was at the console, finishing up the work she'd begun on Dream Earth, but now from a position of some power. On stage, the Dream People went about their business in surprisingly placid fashion. A group of them seemed to be building a house with bricks and mortar and sawn lumber. And nearby, in a sunny meadow, a few Dreamers were involved in a chess tournament. No gaudy costumes were on view, and the lack of outlandish scenes caused the Girl some satisfaction. It was uncannily quiet, and she was struck by how few people there were. Scanning, she saw mountains and forests in the distance, people talking, laughing, building and creating, but no monsters and no fighting.

Zozula watched too, but in his mind's eye he saw a different scene. It was a scene he would remember all his life . . .

The buildings had soared into the stratosphere, slender and pointed, pink and blue. The ships were like birds spiraling in from the Greataway, graceful and fragile, circling the minarets and landing like leaves on floating pads from which stairways hung. The people who emerged from these ships were beautiful — young and slim, dancing lightly down the stairways, leading strange beasts from other worlds into the towers. From the tallest building another stairway twisted upward, and although Zozula had reactivated the focus, he'd been unable to discern where it led.

That was days ago, and it didn't matter now because it would all disappear. And there never were any True Humans there, anyway.

Manuel said, "I'm going home now."

Zozula looked at him in surprise. "You're very welcome to stay, Manuel. We have work to do, soon. We have to search for True Humans — they're out there somewhere. Your Belinda proved that."

"I don't think she was a True Human," said Manuel. "And anyway, you don't need me. You people can do anything. You travel to other worlds. You can ride the Skytrain, and the shuttle to the People Planet, and you can . . ." Running out of words, Manuel waved at the interior of the Rainbow Room, with its banks of instruments, all wonderful, all incomprehensible, and at the magical Dream Earth display.

Zozula said gently, "Please believe me, Manuel — we're simple fools, we Cuidadors. Only the Rainbow is clever. So clever that we have no means of fully understanding it. We can only snatch at fragments of knowledge, which we'll have forgotten by tomorrow; the Rainbow never forgets. We're only humans, like you. We aren't gods, even though we might delude ourselves sometimes. Yes, Selena travels to the People Planet on the shuttle." He touched a panel and Dream Earth disappeared. The lights of the Rainbow shifted and coalesced into a view that Manuel recognized: the night sky. Then the stars grew, billowing from the Rainbow in great clouds as though driven by the cosmic wind like sparks from some primal fire. Soon the room was full of stars, all around them and beneath their feet, too, so that they seemed to be suspended in the Greataway. Manuel gulped with vertigo.

"Manuel, look at the very bright stars," Zozula continued. "See that one? And that? Those are the nearby planets, and they all orbit our sun . . . there." The planets became more distinct against the backdrop of stars, so that even little Pluto was clear and the sun a burning orb.

"One of those planets — or perhaps a satellite of one — is the People Planet. Selena travels there often to look after the creatures there . . .

"*But we don't know which is the People Planet.* We know Mercury, Mars, Jupiter, Saturn, Uranus, Neptune, Pluto. We know the moons of each, and we know the larger asteroids. Every few days Selena and Brutus climb aboard the shuttle and press a button, and later they find themselves on the People Planet. But we don't know where they go. Oh, the data's there somewhere, in some bank of the Rainbow. But where, and how to retrieve it? Nobody knows, not even me, and I'm the programmer —

"Programmer!" Zozula uttered a bark of laughter. "I've never written a program in my life, and I wouldn't know what one looked like. The Rainbow is *old*, Manuel. Almost as old as Mankind — it started to be built somewhere around the year 53,000 Cyclic. Imagine that! It knows too much for our minds to comprehend. It records everything that happens on Earth, and it thinks, and it weighs alternatives, but it hardly ever *does* anything. It just waits for us to tell it what to do.

"And we don't know how to tell it. It's all too complicated for our minds. I'm sure it knows where we can find True Humans, but I don't know how to ask it. I'm hoping the Mole does, wherever he is.

"Don't be overawed by us, Manuel. We'd be very glad to have you stay with us and help us."

But Manuel had made his decision. He picked up the Simulator and kissed the Girl on the cheek. She frowned, pretending to concentrate on the console. "Goodbye, Girl," he said. "Come and see me if you get the chance. And . . ." He hesitated, then clasped Zozula's hand, rather to the surprise of the old man. "And you too, Zozula. You're welcome at my place any time."

"I think we'll be meeting again," said the Cuidador.

"Possibly," said Manuel, looking from him to the Girl. "Yes, I'm sure we shall." He seemed oddly cheerful. Whistling, he sauntered off down the Rainbow Room, and for a short while passed out of their lives.

Zozula looked after him. "He's a funny boy."

"He'll be back," said the Girl, "after he's searched for Belinda in his own way. He's not a follower, Zozula — hadn't you noticed that? And he has to get this quest out of his system before he can help us. You know . . ." she hesitated, "I think he knows something we don't, and he's going to check it out."

Zozula was convinced and oddly comforted by her certainty. She was often right about this kind of thing. Feeling better, he departed to let the other Cuidadors know that the Girl was back in charge of Dream Earth and that the memory banks and other parts of the Rainbow would be more accessible, now that the Mole was in there. Everything was working well again, and a little robot wheeled up and offered him a drink in answer to his slight gesture. As he rode a radius, he planned his little speech. It wouldn't be too presumptuous, he thought, to refer to this as the dawning of a new era . . .

Now the search for True Humans could really begin.

The Girl sat at the console, smiling to herself. All was well, and, in the Ifalong, all would be even better. Manuel hadn't found Belinda yet and she didn't think he ever would. His fun would be in the searching. And at the end, he would still be around — and so would the Girl. And he would need comforting.

But she was a neotenite. Her life in Dream Earth had taught her that nothing is impossible, and that people need not be trapped forever within their own bodies. One way or another there was always room for a little loving cheating, a white lie or two, an illusion . . .

Like the Vision that Eloise had planted in the Mole's mind.

The Girl summoned up images of Dream Earth. She allowed her fat fingers to pass over the console, scanning here, scanning there, finally holding the image of a young couple, the man darkly handsome, the girl fair and very beautiful.

They sat on the banks of a quiet stream, holding hands, saying nothing. The birds sang from the trees and a fawn stepped down to the far bank and began to lap at the water. Occasionally a fish would rise, sending ripples over the surface. It might have been that the lovers were watching these fish slipping through the deep water under the bank. But in fact they were watching their own reflections, which were a source of constant delight to the young man.

No, in real life they weren't much, but in the Mole's dreams they were Caradoc and Eloise, a prince and his princess.

*

And so the Triad accomplished the first part of their Purpose, and Shenshi saw this and was satisfied. They had come together, knitting happentracks into a single yarn that would stretch unbroken into the Ifalong, encompassing Manuel's search for Belinda, the battle with the Bale Wolves, the removal of the Hate Bombs and the release of Starquin from the Ten Thousand Years' Incarceration.

So —

Zozula was reassuring the Cuidadors that Dream Earth was at last under control and the Rainbow functioning as it should.

The Girl was watching Caradoc and Eloise, smiling to herself, thinking of Manuel.

And that young man strode sturdily into the Ifalong and a meeting with Wise Ana, the mystery woman of Pu'este.

If any of them had known where their present happentrack would lead them, they would have turned around and tried to retrace their steps and in some way — any way — forced the future into a different pattern. Because the perils they had faced already were nothing, compared with the nightmares awaiting them in the Ifalong.

And yet, such is the nature of Time that there were many happentracks on which the Triad ceased to exist as such at this point — on which Zozula lived uneventfully as an elderly Cuidador, never venturing from the Dome again; on which the Girl spent her days at the console, so wrapped up in her work that her body ceased to trouble her; on which Manuel sighed and gave up on his dream of Belinda and took a willing village girl into his shack on the beach and lived happily ever after.

Here ends that part of
the Song of Earth known to men as
In the Land of Lost Dreams

In time our tale will continue.